ENVOY EXTRAORDINARY

'What can such as I do?'

'You are an earl of Scotland, two earls indeed. And you are Cospatrick! You can speak for Lothian, the Merse and the East and Middle Marches, some of the most vital lands in the realm. And you could speak with others first. Carrick, Mar, Fife, Lennox. And my father, to be sure. See you, it is possible.'

'But, woman – I, I am not the man for this sort of achievement . . .'

'How do you know that? You have never tried the like. But you are your father's son. And could have been sitting on the throne, if all had been just. Try it, Patrick – try. It could greatly benefit Scotland.'

'Nigel Tranter is a first-rate historian, a good teller of tales . . . His novels are invaluable guides to the Scottish landscape, past and present.' *Historical Novels Review*

Envoy
Extraordinary

Nigel Tranter

CORONET BOOKS
Hodder & Stoughton

First published in Great Britain in 1999
by Hodder and Stoughton
A division of Hodder Headline
First published in paperback in 2000
by Hodder and Stoughton

A Coronet Paperback

10 9 8 7 6 5 4 3 2 1

A CIP catalogue record for this title is available
from the British Library.

ISBN 0 340 73924 X

Printed and bound in Great Britain by
Caledonian International Book Manufacturing Ltd, Glasgow

Hodder and Stoughton
A division of Hodder Headline
338 Euston Road
London NW1 3BH

Principal Characters in order of appearance

Patrick, 7th Earl of Dunbar and March: The Cospatrick. Great Scottish noble.

Christian Bruce: Wife of above. Daughter of Bruce, Lord of Annandale.

William de Home: Cousin of Patrick.

Pate, Master of Dunbar and March: Son and heir of Patrick.

David de Lindsay: Baron of Luffness. Another cousin.

Alexander the Third: Child King of Scots.

Neil, Earl of Carrick: Kinsman of Christian Bruce.

William, Earl of Mar: Great noble.

Robert Bruce, 6th Lord of Annandale. Father of Christian. Powerful noble.

Bishop David de Bernham: Primate of the realm.

Queen Marie de Coucy: Widow of Alexander the Second. Mother of the king.

Malcolm Macduff, Earl of Fife: Hereditary Coroner.

Alexander Comyn, Earl of Buchan: Great noble from the north.

Alexander Stewart: High Steward of Scotland.

Alan Dorward, Earl of Atholl: Hereditary Doorward and High Justiciar.

Walter Comyn, Earl of Menteith: Great noble.

Bishop de Gamelyn: A Comyn prelate.

Bishop Clement of Dunblane: Senior prelate.

Lady Margaret: Illegitimate daughter of Alexander the Second.

Dand Shaw: Shipmaster.

Hakon, King of Norway:

Henry the Third, King of England:

Queen Eleanor of Provence: Wife of Henry.

Princess Margaret Plantagenet: Daughter of Henry.

Simon de Montford, Earl of Leicester: Brother-in-law of Henry.

Archbishop Sewel of York: Chancellor of England, and Metropolitan.

Alexander Seton of that Ilk: Lothian laird.

Sir William de Ros of Wark: Prominent Northumbrian baron.

Richard de Clare, Earl of Gloucester: Great English noble.

John de Brienne, Titular King of Jerusalem: New husband of Marie de Coucy.

William Wishart, Archdeacon of St. Andrews: New Chancellor.

Sir Hugo de Gifford of Yester: Vassal of Dunbar.

Magnus, King of Norway: Successor of Hakon.

Adam Hepburn: First of the Northumbrian Hepburns to settle in Scotland.

Robert Bruce, Earl of Carrick: Son of above. Married countess in her own right. Father of King Robert the Bruce.

Edward Plantagenet, King of England: Son of Henry the Third.

Yolande de Dreux: Daughter of the Count de Dreux, and Duchess of Brittany.

Sir Thomas Learmonth of Ercildoune: Vassal of Dunbar, and seer, known as True Thomas or Thomas the Rhymer.

Eric, King of Norway: Son of Magnus.

Princess Margaret: Daughter of above, known as the Maid of Norway.

1

Patrick, who until now had been Master of Dunbar and March, eyed the assembled members of his family and near relations gathered in the great hall of Dunbar Castle with a doubtful, somewhat quizzical look, before glancing over at his wife, who stood a little apart. Her nod, brief but firm, gave him support.

"I have asked you to come here today for good reason," he said, less confidently than he would have wished. "It grieves me to tell you. I . . . I . . . my father is dead!" He swallowed. "Slain. By the infidels." A pause. "Ada, my sister, not present, knows it, knew it before I did. Before I won back from Argyll. Our father. Uncle and cousin to you others . . ."

He got no further in that halting announcement, with exclamations and cries from the dozen or so men and women grouped there, staring at him and at each other, appalled.

"It is grievous indeed, yes," he went on. "I learned of it only yesterday, when returning here from Melrose, where we buried our liege-lord Alexander. The king – he died at Kerrera, near to Oban. An isle. That my father and he should die all but together, although those thousands of miles apart, is, is scarce to be believed! But it is so. They were . . . close. He, Cospatrick, fell at Damietta, in Egypt. He had taken the cross, with King Louis of France. The Sixth Crusade. More than that, I know not. Neil, Earl of Carrick, my wife's kinsman, new home from the Holy Land, brought the word. He is dead, my father – but died in Christ's service. God rest his soul!" His voice broke a little.

1

His wife, Christian Bruce, came over to him, to press his arm.

Most there gazed at him, silent, although one or two exclaimed.

The speaker, a well-built, fair-haired man in his early thirties, not handsome but with pleasing, open features, over-open possibly for such testing occasion as this, drew himself up, and patted Christian's hand, as if in reassurance.

"A man could not die in better way and in better cause," he continued, voice stronger again. "*We* are the losers, not he. Aye, our king was less fortunate! Dying of a fever, there on an island of Argyll. And leaving only a seven-year-old son to be our monarch. Scotland has lost much. France also. For King Louis is a prisoner of the Saracens, along with many of the flower of Christendom."

"What now, then?" That was another Patrick, younger, a cousin, of Fogo. "Cospatrick dead! The king dead! The crusade lost! That Norseman, Hakon, triumphant, I take it? All disaster! What now, then, in God's name!"

"Now, Pate, we take up the gauntlet! What else? Not of the crusading, perhaps. Who knows as to that? But the nation's cause; Scotland's cause. Support young King Alexander the Third, as my father supported *his* father. Prove ourselves worthy, if we can, to follow where these led." He coughed a little, unused to making such statements, not an assertive man.

Again his wife squeezed his arm, unspeaking.

"So now *I* am Cospatrick," he went on, shaking his head. "Seventh Earl of Dunbar and March, God help me!"

"Who should be on Alexander's throne!" That was another cousin, William de Home, son of the late earl's brother.

All there eyed each other. The Cospatrick family were of the blood-royal; and, they claimed, senior to the present line. That was an old story, but one never forgotten.

The new earl waved a hand in a cutting motion, brusque

2

for that man. "That is not for our thinking, not now," he declared. "Young Alexander and the realm demand our fullest aid in this pass. We will not fail them, as my father did not. Leave that, I say."

There was some murmuring.

"There is much to be done," he added. "While my father had been absent, and I was in the Netherlands, some matters have drifted." He glanced at the company, and his look might have been construed as being somewhat critical, especially by such as might have consciences. "These two great earldoms demand much caring for, heeding. I learn that this of the quarrying, the stone hewing and shaping, has been allowed to flag – and it means much in moneys from the Low Countries, where they have little or no stone. The Lammermuir wool trade is none so bad, for the shepherds and shippers see to it themselves, as they have always done. But the salted mutton and fish stocks have gone down, the salt-pans at Aberlady Bay not being fully used. This much has been told to me already. There may well be more. So we must all see to it."

William de Home sought to change the subject, as well he might. "How does it feel to be Cospatrick, Cousin?" he asked.

"Ask me that hereafter, Will," he was told. "As yet it has scarce come to me. But it is a, a burden. That I was not readied for."

There were nods at that. To be Cospatrick was a strange and notable position indeed for whoever bore the style, more so than any title of earl or lord. There was only one Cospatrick in the land, however many lords. Although it was the name of a lofty line, only one man could bear it at one time, the head of the family, the large family, whatever others called themselves. It was not a surname: the pride of the line was that they *had* no surname, like the rival line, the Kings of Scots. Descended from one of the two older and legitimate sons of Malcolm the Third, Canmore, they had been superseded on the throne by the later sons of Margaret, St Margaret, Malcolm's second queen – three of them, Edgar, Alexander and David – and then by David's grandsons Malcolm the Maiden and William the Lion, and lastly Alexander the Second. Out of a sort of guilt, David had given the earldoms of Northumbria and Cumbria, these English counties having been ceded to Scotland by the weak King Stephen, however much this was contested by later Plantagenet monarchs in the south, to these two slighted brothers, Maldred and Waldeve. Maldred's son Patrick, Earl of Northumbria, had become known as Comes-Patrick, count or earl Patrick, pronounced as Co-spatrick. The other, Waldeve's, line had died out. And now this Cospatrick, standing there, was the ninth such, as seventh Earl of Dunbar and second of March – and scarcely prepared for its responsibilities.

He was spared further questions and a prolongation of this less than easy interview by an unlooked-for development. Into the great Hall burst a newcomer and a loud-voiced one, a five-year-old boy being pursued by a distracted nursemaid. When the latter saw all there turning to stare, she halted, gulped, and turned to flee. Not so the boy, who ran to fling himself at Cospatrick's legs, to clutch and exclaim.

"A, a puffin!" he cried. "With a big nose! I have found a puffin. Up on the walkway. It has broken its wing, I think. Come you, see it." And he reached urgently for the man's hand.

This was Patrick, now Master of Dunbar and March, who, God willing, one day would himself be Cospatrick.

His father shook his head, but not censoriously, indeed all but relievedly, and when his wife smiled, took the child's hand, and made to lead him away with gentle chidings, stopped her.

"No, Chris," he said. "Let him be. I have finished here meantime, I think. This young man has his rights also. He has not seen much of his sire these last weeks, months. We shall go and inspect his puffin. Refreshments for our kinsfolk," and he gestured towards the long table, set with flagons and goblets. Nodding to all, he let the boy tug him towards the door.

The Countess Christian spread her hands, and moved over to the table.

Son and father had three flights of twisting turnpike stairs to climb to reach the parapet-walk of that principal tower of the castle, and from the masonry's constrictions to issue out into the reverse of any enclosure. Suddenly instead of constriction it was infinity, boundless, almost breathtaking. For Dunbar Castle was unique indeed, built on isolated stacks of red rock rising out of the sea, a series of these linked by covered bridges, each having a tower built on the rock-top, and stretching out into the Norse Sea. So east, north and south the blue ocean spread to far horizons, only the white cliffs of the Isle of May showing a dozen miles to the north. To the west the Lammermuir Hills filled the view, the rounded green and heathery summits and ridges stretching far and blocking off all the prospects in that direction, the source of much of the Dunbar earldom's wealth. It was all space and light and boundless sea elsewhere.

Young Pate was much upset to find his puffin not where he had left it; but they discovered it nearby in one of the drainage spouts of the parapet-walk, an extraordinary bird, almost a foot in length, black and white, with a most curious head and wide beak, the latter almost as large as the former, with large eyes bearing a permanently surprised expression. There were not many of these haunting the cliffs around, among all the gulls, fulmars, kittiwakes and the like which roosted there and filled the air around the castle with their whistling and screaming. It was certainly not to be expected to find one on the building itself. It clearly had a broken wing.

Nothing would do but that the boy must gingerly pick it up, fearing pecks from that great beak, and declare that he was going to take it down and look after it until it recovered and could fly again, meantime feeding it. Would it eat oatcakes? His father suggested that it might be kinder, probably, just to wring the creature's neck and put it out of its misery rather than trying to keep it confined in the castle; but Pate was having none of that. He was going to call it Puff. He would show it to Johnnie. Would he understand what it was? John was his two-year-old brother.

Downstairs, Cospatrick avoided the hall and went lower down, to cross two of these covered bridges, the second of almost seventy feet in length, to the outermost tower, which he and Christian had made their own living quarters while his father dwelled in the main keep. He was not antisocial and liked much of his kin well enough, but in his present state of mind, and seeking to come to terms with his father's death and the changed life that this was bound to mean for him, he was not eager for over-much of the sort of talk and chatter that was bound to follow.

That last bridge spanned the narrow entrance to Dunbar harbour, quite large, for its fishing-fleet and other craft, and had a notable device which allowed the castellans, if desired, to drop a great gate therefrom, a kind of portcullis, which could effectively seal off the haven and keep vessels either in or out; this with its advantages in that the lord of the hold could thus demand his due share of the fishermen's catch, as rent or payment for their protection and the harbour's facilities – not that this was often done these days.

He and Chris and the two boys would continue to dwell in this furthermost tower, he thought. He had always liked it, from youth, as somehow remote and secure, his own; possibly some indication of his character, his preference for quiet retirement and being alone, or with those he loved, rather than social intercourse and consorting with others frequently. Shy, perhaps, he had been always, although his feelings could be intense enough, and he was no shrinker from required action. And now he was Cospatrick suddenly, and inevitably so much would have to change for him.

In the children's room he saw Pate and his puffin installed, and ordered a servant-girl to keep an eye on him and the sleeping Johnnie. Then he went upstairs, to the battlements, to lean over and gaze down at the surging tides far below, and to think.

He had much to consider. Quite apart from the running and management of two earldoms, he had large duties of state to fulfil, nothing more sure. His father had been High Chamberlain, Keeper of the Privy Seal and High Constable of the realm; and as one of the great earls of the kingdom it was inevitable that he would be expected to take some quite major part in the nation's affairs. He would certainly seek no high office but could not refuse to take some share in the monarch's service. The fact that that monarch was now suddenly a boy in his eighth year only added to the uncertainty of it all. Who would be acting regent in his name? Walter the High Steward had died only recently, and his son was inexperienced; David of Atholl had also died on the crusade; and Dorward, succeeding him, was an ambitious man. Neil, Earl of Carrick, related to Christian, had indeed got back from Egypt; but he, wed to one of the Steward's daughters, had never been of the pushful sort. The Comyns, however, were certainly that, and would undoubtedly be seeking highest office, the Earls of Buchan and Menteith and the Lord of Badenoch. And, for that matter, there was also Bruce, Lord of Annandale, Christian's father, who, until the young Alexander had been born, had been nominated by the Privy Council as heir-presumptive to the throne. He might well seek to have his son-in-law take some prominent part in affairs. A child monarch, with no possibility of a direct heir for many a year, was a sure recipe for upheaval and intrigue in a kingdom, especially an unruly kingdom like Scotland.

So he, Patrick — no, *Cos*patrick — could soon expect demands to be made upon him.

He had got thus far when Christian arrived at his side. "I guessed that I might find you hereabouts," she said. "You have no great love for your fellow-men, have you? Not that I blame you, my dear — so long as you are not a lover of my fellow-women, like some of those back yonder!"

He shook her shoulder, although it was more of a caress than a shake. "You are wrong, quite wrong!" he asserted. "I do not mislike my fellows. And I *can* appreciate the opposite sex! But in this pass, I am at something of a loss. I fear that I am going to have to change my whole life – ours – to some extent. And . . . I could do without that! Have you considered it all, lass?"

"I think that I have, yes. I realise that you will have to become a deal more prominent, more active in the land, not just in Lothian and the Merse. You will be on the Privy Council now. And almost certainly Justiciar of Lothian. A Warden of the Marches. And so, sadly, I will see the less of you. But that is fate, since you are your father's son, my reluctant spouse!"

He sighed. "Yes. Although I fear that I am not like my sire, in this. But so long as I have *you* to aid me, Chris . . ."

"Oh, I will do that, never fear! I am not Robert Bruce's daughter for nothing! But it may not be so ill as you think. You may come to find it even pleasing, helping to steer the ship of state." She took his arm. "But, see you, Patrick, we cannot leave our guests overlong. We will give them a meal – I have already ordered it. Then hope that they will depart before too long. Come, Cospatrick the Earl! And play the kind host!"

Fortunately, none of their visitors lived so far away that they could not reach their own homes before the August dark, in Lothian and the Berwickshire Merse. If some were expecting to be invited to stay the night, they were disappointed. Young Pate packed off to bed, the puffin in a covered basket by his side, its wing bound to its body, and Johnnie already asleep, the parents went down to their own chamber, presently, hand in hand.

These two, although six years married, were still very much in love, this rather unusual in such as themselves, and in their circumstances, wherein the heirs of great lands

8

were expected to wed heiresses, love tending to be a secondary consideration, frequently sought for, on the men's part at least, elsewhere. Not so in this case, although Christian was sufficiently high-born, to be sure. Patrick had met her at the High Steward's house of Renfrew, and had fallen in love with her almost at first sight, diffident about it all as he had been. But then she was an exceedingly attractive and good-looking young woman, lively and friendly, and appeared to find his somewhat cautious approaches to her, however evident, more appealing than those of not a few more forceful and self-confident young men. At any rate, she had not discouraged him in his attentions, and he had at least been very dedicated in his wooing however unassertive about it, and despite living so far from Annandale and Ayrshire where were the Bruce seats, managing to find excuses for visiting these areas not infrequently. If Christian perhaps grew a little impatient over his modest approaches, she did not show it; and in due course, it all came to fruition and they were wed. And thereafter she had found him no backward lover.

Now, these years later, he had lost none of his enthusiasm for her and for her person. In their own bedchamber, knowing his predilections, Christian steered him first past the canopied bed and the steaming water-tub for their ablutions to a window-seat in the thickness of the walling, there to sit and to pat the space beside her invitingly.

"Before we settle for the night," she said, "have you been thinking of how you are going to act, to choose, to vote, at the council? For nothing is more sure than that you will be summoned to one very soon. I am surprised, indeed, that you have not been sent for already. I would have expected it before this. For young Alexander must have a regent, and quickly, with all this of the Isles and King Hakon looming. To say nothing of the problems of Northumberland and Cumberland and the Plantagenet. There will be great competition for the regency, that is certain. Dorward will want it. And so will the Comyns. Others perhaps. You will require to vote . . ."

Patrick was not surprised over this concern of his wife. She had always been more interested in the affairs of the realm than he was, no doubt because of her upbringing in the family of the one-time heir-presumptive to the throne, and being a very positive young woman, however gentle could be her attentions in family matters. She was, after all, great-great-granddaughter of King David.

"I know it," he told her. "Know that I will be called upon. But this of regent, I know not. These men anxious to control the boy, the new king, and so rule the land in his name. They are themselves but names to me, the Comyns, Dorward and the rest. You, Chris, were you an earl, how would *you* vote?" He nodded, and added, "Indeed, do you see your father perhaps as regent?"

"I do not think so, no. I judge that he would not wish it. The throne itself, yes, were it to become vacant, but not the regency. Regents make enemies, always. There is ever envy and efforts to subvert. And if Alexander died and my father did win the crown, he would wish for support from the nobles, not bickering and strife. No, I think not. It will be between Dorward, Earl of Atholl and the three Comyns, the Earls of Buchan and of Menteith, and the Lord of Badenoch. Mar could seek it, but he is getting old."

"What of Neil of Carrick, your brother's wife's father?"

"He is not the sort to seek it. A quiet man, more like yourself. Religious. As he proved by the crusading."

"Then who do you suggest that I vote for? I do not much like the sound of any of those. The Comyns or Dorward."

"No-o-o. But it will be one or the other, I fear. Unless . . ."

"Unless . . . ?"

She gazed out of the window at the August dusk. "I have had a notion. I do not know if it will serve. Or be accepted. But it might be the answer. Three regents!"

"Three! How could that be? *Three*?"

"See you, Patrick, Dorward and the Comyns will rally all the support that they can in this for themselves. All in

10

the north-east, and in Moray and west to Lochaber, will vote for the Comyns. The Red Comyn is Lord of Lochaber as well as Badenoch and Speyside. And all the centre of the land, with Fife, or most of it, will vote for Dorward of Atholl, although Mar may not. MacDuff, I think, will. So it could be a close call. The council, and a parliament to follow, as necessary, to confirm it all, and divided. The south and the west divided also. So why not *both*? Both regents? They would fight each other, cancel the other's efforts. All indecision. But if there were *three* regents, another appointed also, a moderate and leal man, he could temper matters. Come down on the best side in his choices. Lead to better judgments. So, two to one. For I do not see the other two uniting."

Patrick stared at her. "Sakes, lass, here is a wonder! What a notion! You, you are a marvel! A woman of wits, indeed. Always I have known that, to be sure. But this is extraordinary! If it could be brought about. Three regents. Has there ever been such?"

"I think not. But that is not to say that it is not possible, if council and parliament decided it. And you, my dear, are in a position to help to bring it about."

"Me! None there will know me. What can such as I do?"

"You are an earl of Scotland, two earls indeed. And you are Cospatrick! You can speak for Lothian, the Merse and the East and Middle Marches, some of the most vital lands in the realm. And you could speak with others first. Carrick, Mar, Fife, Lennox. And my father, to be sure. See you, it is possible."

"But, woman – I, I am not the man for this sort of achievement . . ."

"How do you know that? You have never tried the like. But you are your father's son. And could have been sitting on the throne, if all had been just. Try it, Patrick – try. It could greatly benefit Scotland."

He shook his head, all but dazed by what she had proposed for him.

"Think on it, my dear. Sleep on it," she suggested, and

rose and quickly began to loosen her garments, knowing her husband.

As he sat there still, Christian moved over to the washing-tub, it steaming only slightly now. She began to disrobe. She was in no hurry about it, discarding her garb with what was almost a ritual, loosing down her fair hair. The man watched, and in no casual fashion, however often he had savoured this before – as well he might. For Christian Bruce had a splendid and most alluring body, long and graceful of neck, wide of shoulders, shapely and full of bosom without being over-heavy or sagging despite having suckled two sons, her belly rounded but moderately, the dark hair at her groin V-pointing down to her place of promise, superb thighs and long legs. No man could resist it all, and Patrick had never tried to. He rose, now, and went to her, to hold her arm as she stepped over into the tub of water, his hands then beginning to stroke and caress and fondle. She let him do so for a few moments, and then, scooping up a little water, flicked it into his face, and pointed imperiously down to the ladle lying on the floor. Obediently stooping to pick this up, he duly went through the required pouring of warm water over that delicious example of female excellence, but lingeringly and with a certain amount of salutation going with the anointing, her head-shaking smiles less than censorious. The tub was large enough for her to sit in, and this she did in due course, which enabled her attendant to pay particular respects to her breasts, this while kissing her hair.

The routine was that then she should rise and step out of the tub for him to dry her, for which he was nowise loth, being very scrupulous and concentrated about it. Then it was his turn to undress and be bathed, Christian perhaps less meticulous about most of it, but with her own priorities. Usually she let him dry himself, and went over to the bed to await him, seldom indeed having to wait for long. This night was no exception, and arms out, she received him, falling back with him on to the blanketing, to their mutual fulfilment.

There was little consideration as to electing regents and other matters of state thereafter, before sleep took over from physical and emotional activity. Sleep on it, she had said. Would that make up his mind for him? Men's wits could work in strange ways.

2

Two days later the summons arrived. A meeting of the Privy Council would be held at Roxburgh in three days' time, prior to the necessary parliament, to consider the appointment of a regent for their new liege-lord, Alexander the Third, King of Scots. Having duly slept on it, or otherwise, Cospatrick of Dunbar and March knew what was expected of him, and what he would attempt, however unsure of his abilities and qualifications.

Christian saw him off, wishing that she could accompany him – but that was out of the question.

It made quite a lengthy ride, fully forty-five miles, from the Norse Sea coast to the junction of Tweed and Teviot in the Middle March of the Borderland. Patrick rode, with his cousin David de Lindsay, Baron of Luffness, southwards through the Lammermuir Hills. Lindsay was not a Privy Councillor, but as a baron he would have a seat in the parliament thereafter. He was a cheerful and friendly character.

They went by the Spott Burn and the Lothian Edge into the high hills and Dunbar Common, surely the largest common-land in the kingdom, Patrick's eyes ever on the sheep-strewn slopes and valleys, this the greatest stretch of sheep country in all Scotland, some two hundred and fifty square miles of it, no less, so vital to the prosperity of the Dunbar earldom and its folk, and so important for the Low Countries' spinning, weaving and cloth trade, all necessarily one of Patrick's ongoing preoccupations. Quarrying, started by his father, had become an important venture also, the Netherlands in particular being all but devoid of stone, sand and clay their base; but the quarries tended to be on the seaward sides of these hills, more convenient for the weighty transport to the shipping.

By Beltondod and the Bothwell Water and Cranshaws, they reached the Whiteadder, and began to run out of the hills at Longformacus, to face the western reaches of the Merse, fertile cattle country this, still Patrick's land, his March earldom, past Polwarth and Greenlaw and his castle of Home on its ridge, which Cousin William held, to his border at the Eden Water, none so far from Kelshaugh, or Kelso, itself, on Tweed. There were not many lords, in the Lowlands at least, who could ride for forty miles on their own land. That thought, and the responsibility for it all, now his, did tend to weigh on Patrick's mind.

Roxburgh and its royal castle lay not far west of Kelso and its splendid abbey, where the two great rivers of Tweed and Teviot joined, forming at their junction a long and narrow rocky peninsula, on which soared the royal seat, strongly sited, the township thereof still further to the west. It was a strange situation for the rulers of a kingdom the size of Scotland, which stretched north from here for three hundred miles, this on the very edge of the border with England; Edinburgh, Dunfermline and Stirling, the former royal citadels, fifty and sixty and seventy miles away; but this had been good King David's doing. He had been something in the nature of a hostage in England for many years, by an arrangement of his brothers Kings Edgar and Alexander the First, in their efforts to avoid conflict with the southern realm; and there he had made many friends among the Norman nobility, and indeed married the greatest heiress in the land, Matilda, Countess of Huntingdon and Northampton, gaining with her enormous wealth in no fewer than eleven English counties, the monies he later used, when he inherited the crown, to build all those abbeys in thanksgiving. And when he had come back to Scotland he had brought with him a great many younger sons of the English lords. And these had married Scots heiresses all over the land, and their descendants became almost more Scottish than the Celtic

Scots themselves: Bruces, Hamiltons, Comyns, Frasers, Gordons, Chisholms, Lindsays and the like. So David, with nothing to fear from England, had established this home close to the border, for convenience, partly, in visiting his new English lands; and it had remained the favoured seat of his successors, even though relations with England and the Plantagenets had distinctly deteriorated in the interim. Now the boy-king and his mother, Marie, lived here.

If Dunbar Castle was a lengthy and narrow one, on its rock-stacks, this Roxburgh was still longer, a succession of towers within high walling, reaching right to the tip of the peninsula, high above the wide rivers which ran close on either side. The gatehouse was at the far, western end, and there the callers were challenged by guards. Lindsay announced that here was Cospatrick, Earl of Dunbar and March, come to attend the council. They were promptly admitted, and one of the guards detailed to conduct them to the main tower.

One of the first inmates they saw proved to be none other than the child-monarch himself, a lively seven-year-old, coming racing behind a large hound, and yelling lustily. David de Lindsay, it seemed, was already on quite familiar terms with the youngster. He had had occasion to recover a Celtic handling-ball which the boy had dropped, and it had rolled away, at the last parliament, and quite against all traditional parliamentary behaviour he had run out to retrieve the curious stone object and given it back to the prince, to the frowns of the Chancellor and others in charge, but the smile of the boy's father, on the thronelike chair, Alexander the Second. Thereafter he had become quite a friend of the boy who was now the monarch.

Spotted and recognised by the new king, David was hailed. "Davie! Davie de Luffsnay! Good! Good! Marg'ret said that you might come today. See, come. My dog is Honey. It is a she. Honey the Hound, you see! Come. I will make her give you a paw . . ."

Grinning, and glancing at his amused cousin and superior, Lindsay could not ignore a royal command, and went over to the boy. Patrick, smiling also, bowed to the royal back, and moved on behind the guard leading him to the quarters set aside for those lofty enough to be staying overnight in the castle, all lesser folk having to be lodged in the township half a mile off.

In the great hall of the main keep a number of prominent men were assembled, drinking wine and chatting. Only two or three of them Patrick knew by sight, including Neil, Earl of Carrick, related to Christian. Over to him, talking to an older man, he went.

"Ah, see whom we have here, Will," he was greeted. "This is Patrick – no, Cospatrick, now, become Earl of Dunbar and March. In sad circumstances. Aye, sad. This, my friend, is William, Earl of Mar."

Patrick did not exactly bow, but inclined his head respectfully. Mar, this the ninth earl, was one of the most high-born nobles of the land, descended from one of the original mormaorships of the ancient Celtic monarchy, the *ri* or sub-kings, who elected the Ard Righ, or High King. Christian had mentioned Mar as one who had every right to be regent, but elderly and far from aspiring by nature, and unlikely to claim it.

This one nodded. "Your father's death is a great loss to the realm," he said. "I admired him, and his father before him. But you, my lord, will no doubt maintain the high fame of your name and line!"

Patrick did bow this time. "I fear that will be a hard task for me, my lord of Mar," he declared. "I make no claim to be of their quality. I can but do my best."

"Ever the modest one, Patrick!" Carrick said. "And how is my beautiful Christian, kin by marriage? And her sons."

"Well, my lord, both of them." Patrick raised brows in a part-humorous fashion. "She has given me my instructions for this of the council!"

"Ha! She was ever the plotter and planner, was Christian. Even as a child. But with wits to her. You do well to heed, friend."

17

Patrick asked about Carrick's experiences in the failed crusade, and heard how he had not been with Louis at the sieges of Damietta and Al Mansurah, but at Acre, further east, in Palestine, where they had suffered no disaster but no victory either.

Patrick saw his father-in-law had entered the hall, and went over to greet him. Robert Bruce, sixth Lord of Annandale, was a big, burly man of heavy features but with shrewd eyes; it was evident where his daughter had got her wits from if not her looks.

"So – the new Cospatrick!" he said. "Your sire will be a grievous loss to Scotland, young man. You will do well to serve half as well!"

Was that meant to be an encouragement?

"I know it, sir. But – I have Christian!"

"Ah, yes. And has she been seeking to guide you, that one?"

"I value her advice. She had some, for this council."

"She would! She gave *me* my advice, in the past, the wench! What says she now?"

"It is this of the regency, my lord. She believes that you will not desire it. Is she right?"

The big man looked at his questioner, silent.

Hurriedly Patrick went on, wondering whether he had been remiss in thus broaching the subject, and so soon. "If so, she makes suggestions."

"Indeed? And we should all heed?"

"I thought she spoke wisely, sir. But who am I! New to it all. She thinks three regents, not one."

"Three!" The older man stared. "Do I hear aright?"

"Yes. She judges that the Comyns and Dorward of Atholl will vie for it, and raise all support against each other. Divide the nation. Let them both gain it – but with a third to balance all, counter them. Some sound man, possibly a churchman."

Bruce continued to stare, but those eyes were searching, not just at Patrick's face but far beyond, considering, judging. He made no comment.

"It seems good sense to me, my lord. But . . . I am new to such matters."

"Have you spoken of this to others?"

"No, not yet. I am new come . . ."

"Then leave it with me, meantime. I will . . . think on it." And without another word, he left his son-in-law and strode over to others of the company.

Patrick was unsure whether this leaving it all to Bruce was sufficient for his, or Christian's, purpose. But her father was one of the most powerful figures in the land, and if he did agree to the three-regent suggestion, it could scarcely have a better supporter. And his own situation was such that few there knew him, however much they had known and respected his father, and would not be looking for such highly unusual policies coming from the like of himself. He would let it rest, for the moment.

He saw two prelates speaking together, Bishop de Bernham of St Andrews, the Primate, and another. The Primate he did know, for he had been a frequent visitor at Dunbar Castle, a friend of his father's, the most notable founder of churches up and down the land since St Columba himself. He went over to them.

De Bernham greeted him warmly, declaring his sympathy over his dire loss, and that of the nation at large, and introducing him to his companion, who proved to be Donald, Abbot of Dunfermline, Chancellor of the realm, whom of course Patrick had heard of but never met. They spoke much of the late Cospatrick, but his successor thought best not to raise this matter of the regency meantime. Presently he noticed that Bruce was over talking with Carrick and Mar. On this especial subject? he wondered.

He was still with the prelates, for Abbot Donald was a mitred abbot, which entitled him to that style, when a woman entered the hall, the first so to do, with the young King Alexander, David de Lindsay behind, along with three others. Marie de Coucy, so recently widowed, was still a young woman, slight of build but authoritative of manner. She was said to be considering returning to her native France; but since she could scarcely take her young son, the King of Scots, away with her, there were some doubts about this. She announced now, into the sudden hush, that she welcomed all to this place, and that the High Chamberlain, Sir David de Hay of Erroll, would have her guests shown to their allotted chambers in this castle. And thereafter a suitable repast would be provided here in this hall. She spoke with a very French accent.

So there was a general exit from the hall, with servitors conducting the company out to others of the towers of that strung-out fortalice. Patrick found himself taken to the second-last one and shown into an upper chamber wherein he found a man he knew, of about his own age, already installed. This was Malcolm MacDuff, Earl of Fife, the hereditary Coroner of the kingdom, whose privilege it was to place the crown on the new monarch's head at his coronation. He was an amiable character, and in fact in distant relationship to the Dunbars, for his mother had been a Corbet of Makerstoun, in the Borderland, whose sister had married Patrick's uncle, the late William of Home. Also he had lands in Lothian, and the harbour of North Berwick was the southern terminal of his ferry, starting from Earlsferry in Fife, for access to his castle of Tantallon, none so far from Dunbar.

They got on well together, and Patrick thought that he could mention the regency matter to him. Malcolm Mac-Duff thought this of three regents an excellent plan, if it could be passed. He agreed to make no mention of the matter, however, until it was raised by others. He added that he did not like any of the Comyns, nor indeed Dorward of Atholl, and he would not vote for any of them. The Bruce he favoured, but if he did not stand, would reserve his vote. He gave Patrick an account of the recent coronation at Scone, where he had duly placed the crown on, or rather above, the head of young Alexander sitting on the Stone of Destiny, with the boy complaining that the hollow on the top of the stone was too big for his bottom, and uncomfortable. And, on his hearer's admission that he had never seen the famous stone and did not know that it had a hollow on top, was given a description of the Lia Fail, as it was anciently called, of conveniently seat-height, decoratively carved with Celtic interlacing, and with rounded volutes at either side for carrying it, thought by most to be St Columba's portable altar.

They sat together at the dinner in the hall later, and were joined there by David de Lindsay, who admittedly should not have been present, not a Privy Councillor and no great noble, but ordered to attend by the young monarch, somewhat to his embarrassment. Alexander himself, of course, sat with his mother up on the dais platform, along with the Primate, Chancellor and other high officers of state. That is until, halfway through the meal, the boy suddenly jumped up and came hurrying down the steps and along to the table where Lindsay sat – to considerable confusion in the hall, for when the monarch stood none should remain sitting, by tradition, and this had many rising and staring at each other and some sitting down again, uncertain, the queen mother seeking to wave them down.

Alexander reached his friend, calling, "Davie! Davie of Luffsany!" He did not seem to be able to get the name right. "See, here is my ball. That you picked up for me that time. At the par, par . . ." He could not get parliament pronounced, but held out a round stone a couple of inches in diameter, carved with strange devices including a crea-ture with a lappet or trunk coming in a curve from its forehead, this an ancient Celtic handling-ball, for the use of allegedly calming tempers and emotions if stroked by the handler's fingers. Lindsay took it, bowing, and handed it on to Patrick who, standing, examined it with interest and showed it to Malcolm MacDuff before returning it to their liege-lord.

"Most interesting, Sire," he said. "I have heard of these but never seen one."

"It is very old," the boy said. "It was my father's. I like it."

Hay, the High Chamberlain, came down from the dais, to take the king's hand to lead him back to his mother's side, saying that the queen had sent him to do so. The boy made a face, but went, grinning back over his shoulder. Not all looked so favourably on David de Lindsay.

The repast over and the queen and son leaving the hall, Patrick was going to do the same, for he was weary after long riding, when Bruce came down to accost him.

"Say nothing of this of the three regencies at the council tomorrow, Patrick," he ordered. "The Comyns and Dorward will be there, and this could cause much to-do. I have spoken of it to the Chancellor and others. Wait until the parliament." That was all but curt, and to the point; but it looked as though the notion was being taken seriously. Patrick passed on the warning to MacDuff of Fife.

Bedding was not delayed that night.

In the forenoon the council met, with a fair turnout of its members, officers of state, earls, prelates and the most prominent of the land. In theory the king should have been present, but a restless child would be no help in their proceedings. The difficulty was got over by Marie de Coucy coming with the boy before they started, to announce that His Grace approved of the meeting, but was otherwise occupied at this time, and appointed the Chancellor to act for him. They departed. This was suitable, for Abbot Donald would be presiding at the parliament in two days' time also, and would be able to guide the members there as to the council's recommendations, for the parliament it was which must take the final decisions.

Patrick looked round the table, sitting between Carrick and Fife. He counted twenty-six present, not all of whom he could put names to, six of them obviously prelates by their garb. He could identify, besides Bruce, Mar and Lennox, Dorward of Atholl, Hereditary Doorward to the monarchy and High Justiciar, and Walter Comyn, Earl of Buchan, but few others. Bruce sat at Abbot Donald's right and de Bernham, the Primate, at his left.

The Chancellor led off. He declared that this meeting of His Grace's Privy Council had one main objective: the recommendation to put before parliament of a regent for young King Alexander, to help govern the kingdom in his royal name until he should attain full age, this vital for the good rule and governance of the nation. The office of regent so important, it was essential to choose carefully the right nominee, as all present would appreciate. Much had to be considered, the said nominee's ability and strength of mind as well as strength in terms of land and manpower to support the young monarch. Also his experience in the management of affairs, his concern for justice and his good repute with the people. Let them all consider well in this.

He waved a hand to the gathering.

There were moments of silence, as men eyed each other. Who would be the first to speak? And for whom? The actual claimants for the office could hardly nominate themselves, however eager.

It was Bruce of Annandale who spoke. "I propose Alan Dorward, Earl of Atholl, as regent," he said flatly.

Patrick took a quick breath. Was this, then, Christian's father's assessment of her proposal?

"And I second that," a man unknown to Patrick added, MacDuff murmuring that this was Malise, Earl of Strathearn.

Another voice spoke up. "And I propose John Comyn, Lord of Badenoch and Lochaber." That, to Patrick's further surprise and disappointment, was William, Earl of Mar.

"And I second!" Alexander Comyn, Earl of Buchan declared. He was the Red Comyn's uncle, his earldom gained through marriage.

There was stir and exclamation around that table. The situation was not unexpected, save perhaps by Patrick, in the circumstances; but it did signal the commencement of all but open warfare between these two great houses. Patrick looked at MacDuff, eyes eloquent.

But when he transferred his gaze over to his father-in-

23

law, it was to be accorded a nod, brief but somehow reassuring. He wondered.

Alexander the High Steward spoke. "I would nominate Robert Bruce, Lord of Annandale."

That produced drawn breaths all round, with Lennox seconding.

Bruce quite curtly answered, "No, my lords, I do not wish to be *regent*." He rather emphasised that word.

There was quite a period of silence as men considered.

Abbot Donald asked if there were any other nominations.

None was forthcoming.

The Chancellor spoke again. "We have, then, these two proposed and seconded names. The Earl of Atholl and John, Lord of Badenoch. The former is present, the other is not. My Lord Alan, do you wish to speak on this? Do you seek the regency?"

That handsome man looked round the table all but critically, as though weighing up his opposition rather than his support.

"I do," he said strongly. "I have been High Justiciar of this realm for long, my duty to see justice done for all, high and low. I would seek further that justice should be done in all matters of state, in the name of King Alexander. I say that I have the experience and the will to do it, as regent." He all but glared at various voters.

"And who speaks for the Lord of Badenoch?"

"I, Buchan, do. He is chief of a line which controls more of this Scotland than any other, from the Norse Sea to the Sea of the Hebrides. At the nation's need, he could place five thousand men in the field. He is a man of vigour, and not elderly." A glance at Dorward, who was near to sixty years. "As to this of being Justiciar, his father was that, and his grandsire before him! Forby, his wife is a granddaughter of King Donald the Third, Donald Ban. I say John of Badenoch and Lochaber, my nephew."

"I agree. My nephew also, and chief of line, would serve the monarch and nation best."

MacDuff whispered that this was Walter Comyn, Earl of Menteith.

No one else spoke.

Abbot Donald almost sighed, glancing at Bishop de Bernham. "That, then, my lords, appears to conclude our congress. Two nominations to put before parliament, which will decide, let us hope, for the best governance of the kingdom." He scarcely sounded convinced as to that.

The Primate rose. "God's blessing on all here!" he said, raising a hand high.

So that was it all. It had not taken long, although some had come many more miles than had Patrick to attend. As he got to his feet, he found Bruce bearing down on him.

"At the parliament, Patrick," he said, with some significance, however tersely, and moved on. He was not a man for words, was Bruce of Annandale.

It was as yet not quite midday. Patrick had not planned it so, but now it occurred to him that, riding fast, he could be back at Dunbar before dark. The parliament was not for two days. Two nights and a day with Christian, much to be preferred to filling in the time here at Roxburgh. Home then, with his report, his doubts, his questions.

He sought out David de Lindsay, but found him much involved with the boy-monarch. He would stay here at the castle. Malcolm MacDuff he told he would see again in two days' time.

Then, to horse.

Back at Dunbar in good time, Christian was surprised but glad to see him. It did not take long for him to recount what had transpired at Roxburgh, and his ongoing uncertainty as to this of the three regents, the reactions of her father and Carrick and Mar and Fife.

"Your sire," he said, "he says little and looks much! I do not know what is in his mind. I thought that Mar and Neil of Carrick judged your proposal well. MacDuff of Fife certainly did. Yet your father himself proposed Dorward

25

as regent at the council, and Mar proposed Comyn. I could scarcely believe it!''

She searched his face with those eyes so much more lovely than her sire's but no less keen. "They did not seem against it? Any of them? The three regents possibility?"

"No-o-o. They showed interest, I think. And then . . . that!"

"And no word to you afterwards? Despite their nominations?"

"Only, only four words from your father, at the end. He said, 'At the parliament, Patrick.' No more."

"So! He did? I think, then, that you may be over-fearful, my innocent husband! If indeed they were interested, then I think that I can see his policy, my father's, knowing him. He mislikes both Dorward and the Comyns. But recognises that they will gain the votes, either or both. So, to seem to support them. Mar also. They will go to the parliament, unsuspecting. But if *three* regents had been suggested there at the council, the others would have been warned, prepared, and could almost certainly take steps to counter it, while both fighting the other but neither wanting a third nominee. A surprise, therefore. To spring on them. You see it?"

"You mean . . . ?"

"I mean that you are dealing with wily men, my dear. If they cannot beat their foes, they can possibly counter them thus. If one of these is to be regent for the king, they will not want him to be an enemy. So seem to support. And then this. Elect both – then a third. As I suggested. But do it my father's way."

He shook his head. "Into what family have I married?" he wondered.

"You are something late in asking that, my heart! Have I grieved you with my devious ways?"

He drew her to him, to answer that. They changed the subject.

That night Patrick was glad indeed that he had returned to Dunbar. And the next, also.

*　　*　　*

He had an early start that second day, for the parliament was due to start at noon, and even his fine horse could not average over ten miles in the hour for long, especially through hills and fording rivers. But he was back at Roxburgh in time, and took his place on the earls' benches in the great hall for the first time, this between Carrick and Fife.

There was a big turnout for this so important occasion, more than one hundred and fifty present according to MacDuff, the hall, large as it was, packed to overflowing, many having to stand. They all had to stand when the king came in, for the boy's presence was necessary here, the king-in-parliament being the correct designation. Without the monarch's presence it would only be a convention, and conventions were limited in what they could effect.

The Chancellor came in, to stand at his table on the dais beside his clerks, waiting. Then, to a flourish of trumpets, officers of state came in procession with the regalia, the crown on its cushion, the sword of state held high, the sceptre and the orb. Their bearers went to stand behind the great chair which was to serve as the throne.

The Primate, de Bernham, entered, to stand in front of the chair.

The High Seneschal, with a herald on either side of him, appeared, to another trumpet-blast. He raised his hands in a lifting movement, the signal for all to stand.

Then in the dais doorway appeared the small figure of Alexander, his shoulder held by an obviously female hand and arm, clearly not that of the queen mother. A push, and the boy came forward, at something like a run, to make for the throne.

The Seneschal led the acclaim. "God save the King! God save the King's Grace!"

All there took up the chant, while the monarch scowled. Fairly obviously he had not wanted to be there.

Bishop de Bernham, in front of him, bowed, then, turning, raised hand high and the cheering died away. A prayer was intoned for God's blessing on the monarch and his kingdom, and on the parliament's deliberations and decisions.

Those who could sit, sat.

The Chancellor took over, to preside. He announced that in this, the first parliament of the new reign, there were matters of great importance to be decided upon. First and foremost there was their young liege-lord's need for due and responsible help and guidance in the affairs of his realm. It was the duty and right of parliament to select and appoint such guidance in the form of a regent, until such time as His Grace was of age to bear the rule on his own royal shoulders. The choosing and naming of this regent was vital, as all present knew, for the well-being of the nation, and it behoved all present to consider well and decide wisely. He now, therefore, opened the debate, and asked for nominations for His Grace's regent.

There was no delay thereafter. Bruce of Annandale rose. "I propose the Lord Alan Dorward, Earl of Atholl and hereditary Doorward and High Justiciar, as regent for His Grace."

"And I do so second," Strathearn announced.

There were shouts of acclaim and otherwise from all over the hall.

"We have a proposal to consider," the Chancellor said. "Is there any other nomination?"

"There is," Mar declared, rising. "I nominate John Comyn, Lord of Badenoch and Lochaber, as regent."

"And I second," the Earl of Buchan cried. "He will best serve king and realm."

More and perhaps even louder shouting, for and against, which went on and on.

Abbot Donald banged his chancellor's gavel on his table. "Silence, my lords and commissioners!" he ordered. "Is there other nomination?"

There was silence of a sort, mutterings and murmurs.

The Chancellor went on, "I remind all, as there are two nominations, of the vital importance of making the right choice, since so much depends upon it, for the weal of the realm. Does any have observation to make on this, before we come to vote on it?"

Buchan jumped up. "My lords and all present, my nephew the Lord of Badenoch and Lochaber, chief of the Comyn line, cannot be rivalled for the extent of the lands he controls, from sea to sea. And for the numbers of men he can raise for the service of our lord king. He is a man of judgment, able and of strong character. I say that none could better him as regent."

"And I say the same," Menteith, the brother, added. "Comyn support for the throne is necessary, all must recognise." That was significantly said.

"No more necessary than that of my lord of Atholl," Bruce declared. "And the Comyns can and should support the throne without one of them being regent! As High Justiciar for long, Atholl has had great experience in judging right from wrong, wisdom from folly, keeping the king's peace and putting down rebels. Vote for him, I say."

More cries resounded.

A new voice spoke up, from the back of the hall and not from among the great lords, no doubt to the surprise of many, particularly of Patrick; for this was none other than his own cousin William, there as holding the barony of Home.

"My lord Chancellor, my lords and commissioners," he said, "may I speak for some who are not earls and the like? Had my uncle, the late Cospatrick, Earl of Dunbar and March, former High Constable and Chamberlain, not died on the crusade, I would have sought that *he* should be regent. But he is gone to still higher things! And, lacking him, I would speak in favour of the Earl of Atholl."

Patrick was astonished. What, or who, had put Will up to this? He had never taken any part in affairs of state. He had not expected him even to be present. And to back Dorward, and therefore Bruce. Could this be more of Christian's work?

There was quite a deal of applause from his like at the rear.

"Chancellor." That was Alexander, the High Steward. "The regency means the rule. And the rule in this land was always, from the earliest times, vested in the High King and the lesser kings, the mormaors or earls. These appointed the High King and aided him to rule. So, surely, the ruler appointed now for His Grace should be one of the earls. My lord of Badenoch, however puissant, is not that. I feel it my duty, as Steward, to say so. I therefore would vote for the Earl of Atholl."

This time the Dorward support rang still louder. The shouting seemed to excite the boy on the throne, who added his cries.

A voice came from the churchmen's benches. "Chancellor, the Steward may be right as to earls in the days of old." This was Bishop de Gamelyn, despite his name an illegitimate Comyn. "These ancient mormaors, earls, held the power because they could field the greater numbers of armed men. Strength in men and lands is as necessary as ever today for the king's support. My lord of Badenoch may not have won an earldom by marriage, but he heads the most powerful family in this nation, and can field some forty knights of his own name, all with their tails of armed men. Can my lord of Atholl do as much?" That was not a normal churchman's speech. But it gained much applause.

The Chancellor tapped his gavel again. "All have heard the nominations and commendations. A vote on them is required. First, then, the Earl of Atholl. Stand, my lord Alan, that all may see you. Vote. Who votes for Atholl?"

Many jumped up, hands raised. Some fists were shaken also. Patrick, for one, did not vote.

Abbot Donald had his clerks counting hands.

"Sixty-one," it was announced.

"And now, my lord of Badenoch. Stand, my lord. Now – vote."

More noise, cries and thumping of fists on benches, as the clerks counted.

"Sixty-two!" the Chancellor declared, head ashake.

Uproar in the hall. One vote of difference, only one.

It was some time before Abbot Donald could gain quiet. At the throne, not on it, young Alexander was jumping up and down, affected by the excitement, however little he understood what was behind it. Bishop de Bernham came forward to speak in the Chancellor's ear.

The abbot nodded, and when he could be heard, raised voice. "It is pointed out that some here have not voted. Fifteen, I am told. This is . . . unsuitable. All should vote. I call again — vote! All. Those in favour of my lord of Atholl?"

More stir. The clerks counted sixty-six. So he had gained five, including Patrick's reluctant one, and Mac-Duff's. Carrick also had voted for the earl.

"Now, my lord of Badenoch?"

Sixty-six hands were held up.

It was chaos now. An even vote. Had there ever been a parliament like this one?

Abbot Donald, again consulting the Primate, eventually gained quiet. "Here is difficulty," he said. "Equality of votes. But some have still not voted. Fifteen before, six now. *I* have a vote, as Chancellor — casting vote. But I hesitate to use it, in this. Better if these six made their choice." A pause. "Shall I call another vote?"

Out from the prelates' benches stepped a bishop, Clement of Dunblane. "My lord Chancellor," he said, "in this pass the parliament has a duty to His Grace and the nation to make wise provision. I have not yet voted. I now make a proposal. *Both* these lords to be regents. Together. But, so right decision could be established if there was serious disagreement between them, in a matter of state, another to judge and decide. A third regent. Three! A council of regency."

There followed not pandemonium but utter silence, as men gazed at each other. Never had they heard the like. Patrick all but choked with emotion as MacDuff punched his arm.

Two men rose simultaneously, Bruce and Mar, exchanging glances.

"This, I judge, would be wise, yes," the former said carefully.

"I agree." Mar nodded. "It is right, proper."

With these agreeing, the initiators of the two names, men had to heed. Neil of Carrick rose. "I say that this is the answer, the only answer," he asserted. "Parliament has the right so to decide and appoint. The king-in-parliament." He looked round him. "And I judge that the third regent should be of Holy Church. For fair decision. And for that position, who could be better than he who put the proposal forward – Bishop Clement of Dunblane? I so propose and nominate."

There were murmurs of approval from the clerical benches, needless to say.

The Primate spoke. "I also have a vote, and have not used it as yet, not wishing to prejudice decisions. But now I do, for the realm's weal. I second Bishop Clement's appointment."

That clinched the matter. With Bruce, Mar, Carrick, the Primate and certainly most of the bishops, if not Gamelyn, all in favour, few would seek to raise voice against it – and Dorward and Comyn in no position to object, in their mutual enmity. Probably they both favoured it indeed, in the circumstances.

The thing was accomplished, however deviously.

There was other less important business for the parliament to decide upon, but not a few of the members promptly departed, King Alexander clearly wishing to do the same. So the remaining issues were got through in short time, mainly formal endorsements of recommendations already made. One last item was unexpected however, and not to be ignored since it was made by the monarch himself. Alexander had been getting more and more agitated, and now he jumped off his chair to go and tug at the robe of the person standing nearest, who was Bishop de Bernham.

"I want Davie!" he cried. "Davie de Lindsay of Luffs-nay. To be my carrier. My cup-carrier. Davie de Lind-say."

Men rising all over the hall, the Primate looked down at the boy and patted his head. "If it is your royal wish, Sire, it must be so," he said, smiling. "Cup-*Bearer* is, I think, the word for it. And, if I mistake not, it is only for yourself to decide it. Is that not so, my lord Chancellor?"

Abbot Donald, also smiling, nodded. "Such position belongs as part of the royal household. For the king, not parliament, to decide. His Grace can appoint his own Cup-Bearer."

The boy looked pleased, and, turning, seemed about to make for the door, not his throne. And since such abrupt exit would indicate the adjournment of the parliament, the Seneschal hastily raised voice.

"His Grace departs!" he shouted. "God save the King's Grace."

The cry was amusedly taken up by all present, as Patrick saw the youngster being met at the dais door by a young woman, this time clearly visible, the Lady Margaret, an illegitimate daughter of the late monarch, and so Alexander's half-sister and attendant.

The Chancellor belatedly declared the session over.

Thereafter, although there was talk of a repast available for all who might desire it, there was much departing by those who had no great distances to travel. Patrick decided that he was one of these, having had a sufficiency of statecraft and politics for one day. His urge was to inform Christian. But he did look for William of Home, to question him, but could not find him. He saw David de Lindsay and congratulated him on his court appointment, and said farewell to MacDuff. He did not speak with Bruce nor Mar nor Carrick.

Thereafter, his long-suffering horse had to make a long day of it.

The summer dusk settling, Christian was surprised to see him back so soon. "Did the parliament not sit?" she asked. "Was it postponed?"

"Not so, my clever wife!" he said. "It sat, it decided, and

33

it ended. And *your* device was passed. By strange strata-
gems, but passed. The three regents, it is, after much
duplicity. Am I to be proud of the woman I married?"

She bit her lip, eyeing him and sensing criticism.

"My cunning Christian!" he added.

"Not cunning, Patrick," reaching out to grasp his arm.
"Not *cunning*! I pray you, not that. Do not see me so. It is
for the best, for the good of many. Do not think ill of me,
my dear, over this."

"Not thinking ill, no; but wondering. Questioning. Is
what went on there how a realm is governed? In such
would you have me playing a part?"

"The cause was good," she repeated. "Was the winning
of it so ill?"

"It was gained by sleight of hand. Or of voice. Deceit, I
would call it. That is why I said cunning, lass. I am sorry if
I hurt you by that word. But I found it all . . . not to my
taste."

"Then I too am sorry, my dearest. For I would have you
to think well of me. Always. How was it done? Tell me."

"Need I? What of William of Home?"

"Will? I urged him to help in gaining this, yes. That is
all."

"He did. He, perhaps, would make a better, or more
effective, Cospatrick than will I! More after the concerns of
your father. And Mar. And Carrick."

"Was it so ill? Tell me, Patrick."

He recounted the events of that day, the manoeuvring,
the guile, the seeming trickery to gain the desired ends,
Christian listening intently. When he had finished, she
shook her fair head.

"I can see my Patrick misliking the means to the end
which my father used," she admitted. "But how else was it
to be achieved successfully? We would have had the
Comyns or Atholl ruling us otherwise. And the realm
possibly at war. It is not as I would have had it won.
But perhaps the only way possible. I fear that you will
learn, my dear, that there will be much that you will have

to have a hand in, as an earl of Scotland, that will test your conscience somewhat, my so honest one!"

"Would you have me other than I am, lass?"

She threw her arms around him. "No! No! Not that. You are my love and my heart's darling! You will remain so. I will seek not to lead you astray! Do not think me cunning, Patrick. Nor devious – never that. Only . . . venturesome of mind, perhaps?"

They kissed, and then she spoke again, in a different tone. "Venturesome . . . and, I think, pregnant again! For a while I have been wondering. Now I am fairly sure of it."

"Lass! Lass! I . . . I . . . Bless you!"

"This does not displease you?"

"Never! Will it be another boy? Or a girl, this time?"

"Only time will tell that . . ."

3

It did not take long for repercussions to the regency situation to develop, and the fears of such as Christian to be fulfilled. And for Patrick to become in some sense involved, however reluctantly.

David de Lindsay was the source of information, he now all too aware of what went on in the corridors of power – and these corridors, strangely, becoming not those of Roxburgh Castle. For the new regents at least had this in common, that they found its location at the very southern edge of the country inconvenient, so far from their own lands, and promptly moved themselves northwards, leaving the young monarch to reside there with his mother and a much reduced court.

But even before they went, the animosity between the Comyns and Dorward flared openly, to the extent that they could scarcely bear each other's company; and Bishop Clement had to approach them separately to win any sort of agreement on measures necessary for the ruling of the realm, a situation as difficult as it was extraordinary. Bruce, however, had more or less domiciled himself at Roxburgh, and was in effect all but acting as a fourth regent, able to influence the cleric, for Clement consulted him frequently and could accept his advice on matters on which he had had no previous experience, and could put before the other two with some confidence. Bruce had been heir-presumptive to the throne before young Alexander was born, and for that matter still was, presumably, since no other had been appointed; now he was helping to rule.

Then Lindsay, who now seldom left the young king's

side, even taking him to Luffness Castle to shoot wild geese, brought word that the Red Comyn, as he was being called, had left Roxburgh to establish himself in Edinburgh Castle, one of the two greatest fortresses in the land, this seen by most as an ominous move. Quickly Dorward followed suit, he going thirty-five miles further north, to occupy the other fortress, Stirling. Was this all but undeclared war? Bishop Clement, faced with this situation, felt that he had to be reasonably near both of the regents if the regency was going to be able to function at all; and since his see of Dunblane was too near Stirling, to the north, chose Linlithgow, in the west of Lothian, halfway between, this not a fortress but a royal palace used as a dower-house for queens. So the rule of Scotland, or such rule as it was, became divided between four establishments, Roxburgh, Edinburgh, Linlithgow and Stirling, scarcely a recipe for good government.

It was to Roxburgh that Patrick was presently summoned, in theory by the bishop-regent but in fact by Bruce. And since the boys were old enough to be left in the care of trusted attendants for brief intervals, Christian elected to go with her husband, he thankful for it. What did his father-in-law want of him?

They soon found out. The regency was, in fact, only a name, no more. And Bishop Clement, however sound and reliable, little versed in matters of state and rule. What was required was a group of powerful nobles to act in concert, to guide and support Clement and form a counter-force to the other two, who were more concerned with obstructing each other than with the needs of the kingdom. Bruce had already won the agreement of Mar, Carrick, Lennox, Strathearn, the High Steward and Baliol who was now ruling Galloway in the name of his wife Devorgilla; and had hopes of winning over Farquhar of Ross and MacDuff of Fife. As Earl of Dunbar and March, Patrick was, needless to say, expected to join this association, and, known to be friendly with MacDuff, was asked to go to see him and seek to have him in the group.

Distinctly relieved that this was all that was required of him, at least meantime, and Christian seeing no harm in it, the mission was agreed.

Patrick, in fact, had what none other of these nobles possessed: shipping. His grandsire and father had built up quite a fleet of sea-going vessels, as distinct from fishing-craft, for trading from the ports of Berwick, Eyemouth and Dunbar itself with the Low Countries, in wool, salted mutton and fish, and latterly stone; and these vessels could be useful also in times of national need. In the present call on him, one of his craft would provide a much simpler and quicker way of reaching Fife than by going, horsed, all the way round by Edinburgh and Queen Margaret's Ferry to get across the Forth estuary.

So it was back to Dunbar, to leave Christian there, and embark in one of the ships in the harbour, smelling of sheep's fleeces as it did, for the thirty-mile sail over to the Earl's Ferry, on Fife's coast near the easterly end.

With a south-westerly breeze, it did not take more than two hours to cross the mouth of the Forth, or the Scot-water as it had been anciently called, passing Tantallon, MacDuff's Lothian castle on its cliff-top, then the tower-ing majesty of the Craig of Bass with its unending halo of circling gannets, or solan geese, and on to the mile-long rock-ribbed Isle of May, site of a beacon kept burning of a night to warn shipping of one of the most dangerous waters around the east coast of Scotland, where there had been wrecks innumerable down the centuries, even from Pictish times; indeed the first beacon had been established by St Ethernan, one of Columba's disciples, out of great effort and dedication, for no wood grew on the May, and timber for the fires had to be brought by barges from the nearest Fife haven of Pittenweem.

Landing a little to the west of the last, Patrick hired a horse at Earlsferry to take him the dozen or so miles northwards to MacDuff's principal seat of the Earl's Hall of Leuchars, this by Kilconquhar's Loch, over the flank of Kellie Law and so to the mouth of the large River

Eden, west of de Bernham's ecclesiastical capital of St Andrews.

At Leuchars, the Earl's Hall proved to be not so much a castle but, as its name suggested, a great hallhouse, fortified after a fashion by protective curtain walling for a courtyard, but itself a long, two-storeyed and attic house with gables and steep slated roof. It had many rooms on either side of a great central hall, this reaching right to the roof, with a minstrels' gallery, all a much more commodious and comfortable establishment than were most castles. Here Patrick found the countess, mother of the unmarried Malcolm, formerly Alicia de Corbet, a sister of William de Home's mother. She welcomed her far-out relative by marriage warmly, but declared that her son was presently out some way up Stratheden superintending the felling of trees in his forested lands around Logie, about four miles off. He might well be gone until evening. Wondering at this rather strange occupation for someone of MacDuff's rank, Patrick said that he would go and seek him out, and was given due directions.

Logie lay due westwards among low hills, with much woodland. He found little difficulty in locating the timber-fellers, with smoking fires and much work going on, sawing and chopping and crashing trees, horse-drawn sleds dragging the felled and trimmed trunks, and the fires burning the unwanted boughs. This was clearly a quite major operation.

He discovered Malcolm with his head forester, choosing and marking trees to be felled, on a gentle hillside. The earl was astonished to see him there, but was obviously pleased to greet him.

Patrick explained the reason for his visit, and the need felt for an association of the kingdom's lords to aid Bishop Clement, and seek to counter the activities and follies of the other two regents. MacDuff at once agreed to join, and use his manpower to assist, if necessary, a swift and satisfactory outcome of the mission. Then Patrick asked why all this great cutting down of trees.

"It is for the new trade," he was told. "Timber for the Baltic states, and the Hanseatic merchants there. They have great need for wood, it seems. Just why, I know not. But they, the buyers, will pay good moneys for it. And I can use the siller! A trader and shipper up-Forth at Burghstone-ness, Duncan by name, has joined up with the Hanseatic League to send them the timber. Hearing of it, I offered to supply him with much, for I have great woodlands here, as you can see. So, I turn my trees into money, trimming the forest, and gain no little profit."

"Ha! Here is a notable enterprise, my friend. The Baltic lands? Do they lack trees?"

"It would seem so. Perhaps they have been cutting them down for overlong. I know not."

"*I* have much woodland. In the Lammermuir foothills and in the Merse."

"I know it. You could profit also in this, Patrick."

"It is worth considering, yes. I do much trading with the Low Countries, in wool and stone and salted meat. I have not thought on the Baltic lands. This Duncan, of Burghstone, how does he deal with it?"

"He has three ships. He sends one, the smallest, to Edenmouth, near here, towing a string of barges. There my slypes drag the cut trunks. Then, back at his own haven, he loads them up on his larger ships and sends them to the Baltic Sea."

"I see. I have ships also . . ." Patrick's wits were working.

They went back to the hallhouse, and spent a pleasant evening, MacDuff saying that he might well persuade his friend the Thane of Glamis, across the Tay, to join the league of lords supporting Bishop Clement.

This mention of the style of thane, and there were not many of these left in Scotland, had Patrick enquiring about the MacDuffs' own thaneship. Was Malcolm still a thane, as well as an earl, for that had been the title once?

"I suppose that I am," the other said, shrugging. "We MacDuffs were thanes, until Malcolm Canmore made my ancestor an earl. This for slaying MacBeth, at Malcolm's behest, his rival and on the throne." He made a grimace. "I am not greatly proud of that deed, for MacBeth was an able monarch, to whom the slayer had sworn allegiance. I know only one other thane, Arbuthnott, also in Strathmore. But this Glamis is powerful, with broad lands and many men."

"Then his adherence will be welcome, I have no doubt."

The next day, as he rode back to Earlsferry and his ship, Patrick debated with himself over this matter of exporting timber to the Baltic, the notion of which exercised him much more than any activities concerning the regency, although perhaps it should not. The well-being and prosperity of his two earldoms and his folk seemed to him much more important than any battling with the Comyns and Dorward, risking lives. It had never occurred to him, nor presumably to his father and grandsire, that the great woodlands on their estates could be the source of profit.

He wondered whether he should not sail directly back to Dunbar but just head up Forth to the haven of Burghstone, to enquire of the shipper, Duncan, as to which ports of the Baltic Sea he traded with. But, on consideration, he decided not. It might seem unsuitable, as though he were aiming to compete with the man in his commerce, and, more so, with Malcolm MacDuff, to work his way into *their* enterprise. No, he would seek perhaps to make his own way in this. After all, the Hanseatic League was the largest trading concern in all Christendom, branches in many nations. He could find out where timber was most needed, and try to form his own trade, which would not damage that of MacDuff or this Duncan. He might even find trade in timber with the Low Countries. When he had visited there, more than once, on his father's behalf, he had not seen any great woodlands in all those sandy levels.

Back at Dunbar, Christian was interested to hear of this possible venture and what might come of it, declaring that there were more ways than one of helping the realm. There might be more in this than just for Dunbar and the Merse. Her father's Annandale and Lochmaben had much of forest, used only for the hunting. He should speak of it when he went to report on the matter of Fife.

So it was off again, for Roxburgh, in due course, where Patrick told Bruce of MacDuff's adherence to their cause, and the possibility of the Thane of Glamis also joining them. And, who knew, others perhaps over Tay. He also mentioned the timber trade idea, and it was far from dismissed as insignificant.

But he found the lords much preoccupied over a development affecting the kingdom at large. King Hakon of Norway was making threatening noises over the situation regarding Man, the Hebrides, and the West Highland coast. King Harold of Man had been drowned, and his brother, Magnus, had ascended that throne, and was claiming that the Inner Hebrides were his also. This was strongly contested by John of the Isles, descendant of the great Somerled, and he had assembled a fleet of birlinns and longships to assail Magnus. A storm had much damaged this fleet, but John was claiming that Man should be part of the Hebridean kingdom. Magnus had appealed to Norway for help, and Hakon declared that *he* was overlord of both Man and the Hebrides, and would demonstrate his rights thereto. This gravely affected Scotland, since the Islesmen also claimed the West Highland seaboard, with all its sea lochs and peninsulas, and Hakon was known to covet it, claiming it as part of the Inner Hebrides, this including the great Kintyre peninsula which his predecessor King Magnus of Norway had declared was his because the weak Edgar, King of Scots, had admitted that anything that the Norseman could sail his galley round should be his; and this Magnus had had his vessel, with him at the helm, dragged over the mile-long stretch of land between West and East Loch Tarbert, so that he could claim the seventy-mile-long Kintyre peninsula as his own, an ancient saga, now presenting danger again. If Hakon did come in force to this seaboard, then there could be trouble indeed.

In all this involved situation, the lords felt that if Hakon could be persuaded not to aid Magnus of Man, and support John of the Isles instead, then Scotland could agree that the Inner Hebrides could be part of his territories, excluding the mainland areas, and accept that Hakon was overlord thereof, a bargain struck, thus preventing war with Norway.

This difficult conception was the subject of debate when Patrick arrived at Roxburgh, and listening, a thought occurred to him. King Hakon was known to be in perpetual debt to the Hanseatic League. If he could be freed from that difficulty, or some of it, he might well be more disposed to co-operate with the Scots in this Hebridean matter, instead of making threatening noises. This of the timber trade, then? Might not that be a key to the lock? Either to use Danish ports to get the wood to the Hansa merchants; or even to sell the timber to the Norsemen themselves, for them to pass on to the final buyers at their own price?

Voicing these thoughts, he was eyed thoughtfully by Bruce, Mar, Carrick and the Steward. All these had woodlands on their great properties, so there could be gain in it for more than the state, all perceived.

They did not require much convincing that such attempt should be made. And who better to make it than Cospatrick, Earl of Dunbar and March, the only one among them who already had large trading interests and shipping? They would approach the Regent Clement and gain his agreement for Patrick to go as envoy to King Hakon on this dual mission.

Patrick could scarcely refuse, although he was a little doubtful as to his qualifications, at least for the Hebridean alliance part of it. But he did suggest that MacDuff of Fife should be asked to go with him, two envoys better than one. This was accepted.

So be it, then. Once Clement's agreement was received, from Linlithgow, then the sooner the attempt was made the better. Patrick would approach Fife. They would be given full authority, signed by the regent and with the royal seal attached.

Somewhat bemused, Patrick returned to Dunbar. What would his wife say to her husband becoming an envoy of the crown, no less?

Christian, in fact, was well pleased, but urged him not to be away for overlong; and to beware of those Viking women, who were alleged to be as great predators, in their own way, as were their menfolk, for conquest.

4

They sailed, from Eyemouth in the *Skateraw Meg*, skippered by a Dunbar veteran, Dand Shaw. He had been to Norway more than once, and declared that King Hakon was usually based either at his Norse seat of Bergen, or at the Danish castle of Elsinore. He suggested that they should try Bergen first, as it was the nearer, and if there, would save them having to go down the wild waters of the Skagerrak and the Kattegat. These names meant nothing to Patrick and MacDuff, but Shaw knew best. Nearer this Bergen might be, but it was said to be almost four hundred and fifty miles distant, east by north, and would probably take them four days to reach, with a south-west breeze.

They settled in, to put up with a lengthy spell of idleness.

Patrick's voyaging in the Norse Sea had been restricted hitherto to sailing down the English coast and across to the Netherlands haven of Veere, or to another Bergen, Op Zoom; and Malcolm of Fife had never had cause to do any travel out of sight of land. So this was a new experience for them, and interesting only at first, in watching the seamen at work with the sails and gear, noting the seabirds which floated above their vessel on all but motionless wings, and in searching the horizon for other craft. But all that soon palled, and they slept a lot. Fortunately the weather was kind, and the seas not smooth but with long swells rather than great waves.

They talked with Skipper Dand, and learned much from him. The Norway west coast, he told them, was cut into by innumerable inlets, some of them many miles long, which they called fjords, very like the West Highland coast of

Scotland, and similarly dotted with scores of islands. The Bergen area was similar, and perhaps one-third of the way up from the Skagerrak channel which separated Norway from Denmark. He said that he had visited other Norse ports also, Kristiansund, Stavanger and Haugesund. As to the Baltic ports, behind Denmark, which might interest them, where the Hansa traders operated, there were Aarhus and Copenhagen and Sonderborg; Flensburg and Kiel in Schleswig; Lübeck on the Holstein coast; and Rostock, Swinemunde and Gdansk further east. Also the large and prosperous island of Bornholm, the size of Man. The Baltic, he said, was a very shallow sea, and this resulted in rough and steep waves, especially where the Kattegat brought the waters of the Norse Sea to join it, notorious for the danger to shipping.

When, eventually, they sighted land again, it had indeed a very similar aspect to their own West Highland coast, with islands everywhere, reefs and skerries, these fjord inlets opening, steep rocky shores and mountains rising abruptly. Small wonder that the Vikings felt at home in the Hebrides and Orkney and Shetland. But Patrick noted, unlike Scotland, very few trees were to be seen, and most of the land looked barren.

They drew in behind a long, narrow island which Dand called Sotra, which had Patrick wondering whether this could have the same derivation as his own Soutra, in the Lammermuir Hills, where Malcolm the Maiden had established his great hospital. This island sheltered the mouth of the fjord on which Bergen was placed.

Approaching that town, they saw that it climbed a fairly steep hill, stone houses close-packed, and above all a towering fortress where banners flew. If this had been at home, those flags would mean that the lord thereof was in residence; but it might not be the same here. At least it gave them cause for hope.

When the *Skateraw Meg* drew in to one of the quays, among a host of longships, they found a heavily armed group of warriors awaiting them, looking anything but welcoming. Skipper Dand called that they were from Scotland, come to see King Hakon. Two earls to speak with His Majesty.

That produced unintelligible shouts.

This matter of speech had been concerning Patrick, for he knew nothing of the Norse tongue, and no doubt these folk were equally ignorant of his own. On his visits to the Low Countries he had gained some knowledge of the Dutch language spoken there. That might possibly serve here in some measure.

Landing, with MacDuff, he tried the Dutchmen's speech on these suspicious-seeming Vikings, announcing his and his friend's identities and saying that they came from the King of Scots. At least one there fairly clearly understood him, and spoke with the others. Nodding then, they turned, and led the way up through the town's steep and rock-based streets to the citadel.

It took some time before they were admitted into the presence of King Hakon. He proved to be an enormous man, of late middle years, who eyed the visitors with seeming interest, no doubt wondering what could have brought such as themselves there. As they bowed, he said something incomprehensible.

"We have come, Sire, at the behest of the regents of the young King of Scots, Alexander, to make proposals to Your Majesty," Patrick declared. And at the monarch's evident ignorance of what he had said, endeavoured to put that into as fair Dutch as he could muster.

Some enlightenment dawned on the florid royal features. Hakon waved to attendants to serve the newcomers with drink from flagons on the great table, in presumed acceptance of their mission, although still eyeing them doubtfully.

Accepting the liquor, which proved to be fiery indeed, Patrick recognised well that this was going to be a difficult interview to negotiate with any degree of success. MacDuff was of no help, however anxious to be so, for he knew no other language than his own and the Gaelic, with a little

French. But picking his Low Countries' words with care, Patrick began, only to be interrupted by the king, who laughed uproariously and waved him to silence. He despatched another of his attendants off with shouted instructions, clearly a man of vehement behaviour. He went to the table, to pour and drink hugely.

The visitors eyed each other, uncertain as to how to proceed. But Hakon was now talking to one of his own Norsemen in that hall, and they could not interrupt.

Then a priest entered, and was hailed by the king, and was barked orders by his liege-lord in no uncertain fashion. Turning to the Scots, he spoke in heavily accented but fairly understandable English, saying that he was to convey their messages to the king's majesty, if he was able to do so.

Sighing with relief, Patrick announced who they were and why they had come. This was duly translated to Hakon, whether accurately or not they could not tell. But at least the monarch now seemed to be interested. He offered the visitors more of the liquor.

Supping only warily at these heady spirits, Patrick slowly and carefully started to explain their mission. Deliberately, in these circumstances, he commenced with the matter of the timber trade from Scotland, and the possibility of the king relating this to the Hansa merchants with whom he was thought to have dealings.

This produced prompt and obvious reactions, and of a favourable sort, with questions shouted. The monarch seemed to believe that when there were language difficulties the solution was to shout.

Their interpreter said that His Majesty required timber, yes.

Patrick pointed out that their mission was not so much to send timber to Norway but to have it passed on to the Hansa traders, this in a large, on-going way. It was wondered whether King Hakon could help in this?

That, it was to be hoped, would appeal to this king, who, by adding his own enhanced price to the imported wood,

48

would see his notorious debt to the merchant league reduced, or even wiped out. The visitors did not actually declare that, but the possibilities were apparent, and had Hakon sufficiently concerned as to put down his tankard on the table and search their faces.

Patrick went on to the effect that there were great forests in Scotland, and the trade could be large. And he had ships, as had others, to bring the wood over. If the Norwegians – he did not say the king – could buy it from them, pass it on, at some additional price, to the Hansa people who were known to be anxious to purchase wood?

There was no doubt as to the reception of that. Hakon all but beamed on them.

Saying that this could be arranged, then, Patrick went on to speak of the matter of the Isle of Man and the Hebrides, suggesting that His Majesty might see advantage in coming to an agreement with Scotland over this issue, and with the trade, to suit both realms. If the Inner Hebrides were ceded by statute to John of the Isles, on condition that he accepted the overlordship of King Hakon, and His Majesty agreed not to seek dominion over the mainland coasts of Scotland, then there could be peace and amity between the two greater nations, with excellent consequences for both, with profitable trading following. He especially emphasised the word trading.

Hakon tugged at his greying beard, reached again for his tankard, and announced that he would consider the matter. He would inform the Scots later.

Bowing, and thanking the priest, they backed out of the royal presence, hoping that they had achieved something, in difficult circumstances.

They did not see the king again that day, and not being invited otherwise, returned to their ship for the night.

In the morning, quite early, they were summoned back by the priest, Sven, to the royal presence. Here they were informed, to more major drinking, that it was agreed meantime that the king would be content to accept that the Scots mainland was outwith his control, but that the

Inner Hebrides should be held by John of the Isles under his, Hakon's, overlordship. As to the timber trading, it would be right and proper for all the Scots wood to be brought here and unloaded at Bergen, to be despatched onwards to the various markets of the Hansa merchants, as was required, and at the best prices offered. When the wood was received and examined here, the price would be decided. This was the royal decision, and he would see to onward delivery to the Baltic ports.

This was good, so far as it went, although the terms meantime in the agreement over the Highland situation could mean only a temporary truce, as it were. The timber matter had Hakon obviously seeking a monopoly, and determined to do the distributing. This might well be fair enough, from the Scots point of view, and save much ship-work and bargaining elsewhere. But the price gained? It was difficult to see how to bargain with a monarch; but the moneys must be right, or it would not be worth starting the trade. They could, of course, always send one shipload, to test the price offered, and compare it with that being gained by the man Duncan of Burghstone-ness. All they could say here was that they hoped that they could agree on the rates to be paid.

They were told that this would depend on the quality and kinds of the wood, and the demand for it. But a fair price was promised. With that they had to be content.

Thereafter there was no suggestion that the visitors should linger at the Bergen court, if such it could be termed. Sent on their way with more of the fiery spirits, they took their leave.

It had all been a very brief and strange mission, but they judged reasonably successful considering that they were, after all, dealing with a potentially enemy ruler. This of the timber had been the telling factor, that was clear.

So it was back to the *Skateraw Meg* and the return voyage, Dand Shaw declaring that it might take all of five days to reach home, with the wind still south-westerly and therefore in their faces, with much tacking required.

Such was Patrick's first experience as an envoy, and it nothing like what he had anticipated. That liquor: if the Norsemen always drank great quantities of it, as seemed to be the case, no wonder that they were a wild lot.

Since their mission had taken less time than they had expected, and MacDuff had to be returned to Leuchars anyway, they decided to sail on up Forth while they were at it, to confer with the shipper Duncan at Burghstone to learn what they could as to the trade, varieties of wood in demand, prices to be charged, and the like.

This they did, and found the trader to be a small wizened man, quite elderly, and much impressed by having two earls to call upon him, but nowise off-put as to shrewdness thereby. Most evidently he was prosperous, living in a large house near the quayside of what, they discovered, the local folk called Bo'ness with a large family, his sons serving as shipmasters for his vessels. It seemed that he was concerned with other trading as well as timber, salted fish and beef, tanned hides and leather, even desks and furnishing made by local carpenters, a man of initiative. Patrick took due note of it all.

As to the timber, Duncan was interested to hear of Hakon's reactions, declaring that that one would double the price he had paid for it all, for other markets. He himself preferred to find his own buyers, avoiding the Norwegians as potential foes, and concentrating on the Hansa ports in the Baltic itself, despite the difficult seas. But he admitted that, for the earls, it could be quicker and simpler, if less profitable, to deal through the Vikings, at least while they were not at war.

The woods in demand were oak, elm, birch and pine, beech being seldom asked for. Price depended on the size and girth of the trees, their age, and for how long felled, for sap-dried fetched better money than new-cut. So it was wise to fell and stack well in advance, as oak and elm could take a full year to dry out, birch faster. But fungi and insects had to be watched for, as these could spoil the trunks. Prices could vary according to demand, and could change at different destinations, but this need not concern them if the Norsemen were going to do the onward selling. Sometimes the buyers offered goods, not money, in exchange. But again, this would probably not affect the Norse trading.

Duncan advised using mature timber only, up to one hundred years old for the broad-leaved trees, although birch could be much younger, this used for flooring and furniture, poles and masts and oars; also the bark could be used for tanning leather. Oak was required for shipbuilding, and fetched the best price.

All this much interested the would-be traders.

After Eden-mouth, and taking leave of MacDuff, back home at Dunbar Patrick found Christian, glad to see him back earlier than expected, also interested in all this of trees and wood, and the useful effects of trading on national affairs, other then just the moneys and prosperity to be gained. She announced that she much admired her husband's foresight and enterprise in this, which *she* had never thought of, and declared that others of the lords and leaders of the kingdom would likewise approve and thank him.

This proved to be the case when he rode over to Roxburgh to report, and he discovered his credit to have risen considerably over it all. Without becoming in any way vain, it did help his self-esteem, which he recognised to be needed. Perhaps he would, in time, make none so inadequate a Cospatrick after all?

5

There followed months in which Patrick was able to get on with the business of running two earldoms without over-much involvement in the nation's affairs, no invasion ensuing in the Highlands and Isles. This of the timber, of course, occupied him greatly, prospecting his lands for the best forested areas, always remembering the problems of transporting heavy tree-trunks to ports for shipment, and so concentrating on territories reasonably near the coast, or near large rivers such as Tyne and Tweed and Whiteadder, where rafts could be made of the wood to tow seawards. Not that this of the shipping was of immediate concern, for the man Duncan had emphasised that a year's drying out was necessary for hardwoods like oak and elm and ash, although birch required less. So stacks of felled timber had to be built for the drying purpose. Patrick decided that he would try out King Hakon's behaviour in the matter in the spring, by sending over a cargo of birch logs, this not only to test the profitability of it all but to demonstrate that peace with Scotland was worth main-taining.

As well as this of the trees, there were the established trading ventures of wool and stone and meat and fish, salted, for the Low Countries, all to be superintended, as well as the duties of a lord of great lands in keeping the peace among his folk, acting justiciar, settling disputes between tenants, farmers, millers and the like, and seeking to improve the fertility of the soil in places by treating with dung and seaweed, draining, heather-burning and dyke-building. So there was no lack of activity for a great landowner, if so he was inclined. Satisfaction in it all, also, this enhanced by the joys of Christian's loving association and involvement, and the bringing up of the boys. Simple things were often the most fulfilling.

Then, word came, actually from Bruce although in the name of the regency, calling a council meeting at Linlithgow, the need unspecified. Less than enthusiastically he felt bound to comply.

On this occasion he found Dorward come from Stirling, none so far off, to co-operate with Bishop Clement, but not the Comyn. It seemed that never all three came together, ridiculous as was this situation. But there was a good turnout of the senior nobility. Patrick was congratulated on his visit to King Hakon by the bishop, but not by Dorward, who quite ignored him.

The business was a request by Henry the Third of England for a meeting with the regents, to discuss his proposal, all but a demand, that young Alexander should marry his eleven-year-old daughter Margaret, this to cement peace between the kingdoms. There were few objections to this, indeed almost all present saw it as a worthy development, however young the couple were to be betrothed, so long as it did not lead to unsuitable further demands from the Plantagenet, these English monarchs ever having to be watched for their aspirations to dominate Scotland. Henry's suggestion was that the meeting should be at York, as approximately halfway for both sides to travel, and for it to take place in the auspicious Christmas season. This was accepted, although weather conditions might well make that travel difficult. A good representation of the realm's nobility and churchmen was advisable, and as many earls as possible.

So Patrick would have to pass his Yuletide apart from his family, which did not please him. In three weeks, then, they would be off southwards.

Bruce mentioned the success of the embassage to Hakon, at least for the time being, although Patrick had to explain and emphasise that monarch's use of the term "meantime". He indicated that trading matters had aided the envoys, but forbore to go into details as to timber, not wishing over-many rivals in this new venture at this early stage.

The only other business was Dorward's complaint about the Red Comyn's hostility and absence, although both Buchan and Menteith were present and asserting that their kinsman was fully informed on all that went on in the kingdom, and well capable of playing his part as regent without having to attend meetings such as this. That was greeted by Atholl's sneers, and the silence of the others.

Back at Dunbar therafter, Christian made a face over the Yuletide situation, but agreed that her husband had to be present at the York meeting. They would make up for it otherwise, and hopefully celebrate Twelfth Night together.

The travel down to York was a major event, a large contingent of the nation's great ones, in Church and state, accompanying the young monarch on the one-hundred-and-fifty-mile journey, all clad in their finest under their travelling cloaks. Alexander was much excited and, good on a horse, was impatient at the modest pace imposed on all by some of the ladies and elderly prelates. What he thought of this talk of betrothal and marriage was anybody's guess. His Cup-Bearer, David, said that the boy shrugged it off as though of no consequence, not even wondering aloud about what this Margaret Plantagenet looked like. Because of his kinship and friendliness with Lindsay, Patrick was apt to ride close to the youthful monarch, and got on well with him. Comyn, Lord of Badenach, did not join his fellow-regents in this expedition, no reasons given. The weather was grey and chilly, but not such as to incommode them greatly.

They went by Jedburgh and over Carter Bar into England, and had barely crossed the borderline when they met a smaller party coming in the other direction, and this none other than the Chancellor's, Abbot Donald. He had been on a mission to Rome, and was returning with interesting, indeed significant news. Pope Innocent had apparently been sufficiently impressed by him to make him a papal chaplain, something new for a Scots abbot. But as well as that, he brought word that Henry Plantagenet had approached the Vatican with a petition to declare that the Kings of Scots could not, in future, be crowned and anointed without the consent of the King of England. This had been refused by the pontiff. As well as that, Henry had demanded that he should receive one-tenth of the Scots ecclesiastical revenues, this on the pretext that there was no archbishop north of York, and therefore the Scottish Church came under the jurisdiction of the English metropolitan. This also had been refused, on Abbot Donald's protests.

These tidings made a major impact on the royal company, needless to say, warning them that they could be in for a difficult and demanding time at York, their present destination. Indeed, there were those among the group who thought that they ought to turn back, there and then, and not meet Henry at all. But the overriding need for peace between the two kingdoms, especially with the rivalry prevailing between the two regents and what that could result in, was paramount, and any turning back, which would amount to a rejection of the proposed royal marriage, could well so greatly offend the Plantagenet that actual war could result. But, warned, they would go warily indeed, despite Henry's former good relations with the young monarch's father.

There was another item of news from the Vatican, however, more heartening. Innocent had agreed to the canonisation of the former Queen Margaret, second wife of Malcolm Canmore, Alexander's great-great-great-grandmother, on the grounds that she had brought to and established the Roman Catholic faith in Scotland, replacing, all but single-handed, the ancient Celtic Church of St Columba, which had been the worship and profession of the northern kingdom for five hundred years. For this it seemed that she should become St Margaret hereafter, this seen as a notable uplift for Scotland, unrivalled in recent times in Christendom. So here was something to tell Henry; although it was possible that it could make him only the more assertive. Obviously Abbot Donald had made a major impression at the Vatican. In the circumstances, the Chancellor and his small party turned round, to accompany the royal entourage southwards.

Unable to cover more than forty miles in a day, they reached only as far as Bellingham that first night, where there was a monastery to provide limited hospitality, for at least the loftier members of the company.

Still in hilly country, they made for Walsingham for the following night, where there was known to be a priory for accommodation and a village to house the lesser folk. What would travellers do without Holy Church, with its hospices, monasteries, priories and abbeys? They were halfway to York here, and ought to reach Northallerton, in Swaledale, for the third night, and the last. Young Alexander was much interested, indeed excited, by all that he saw, and declared that England was not so very different from Scotland, although the hills were smaller.

York impressed more than the monarch, a fine city with its towering minster, archepiscopal palace, other handsome buildings, ecclesiastical and otherwise, providing a sufficiency of worthy lodging for all. There Alexander and those close to him were installed in Archbishop Sewel's splendid house where, although King Henry had not yet arrived, they found Queen Marie de Coucy already in residence. She had gone to France the previous year, but had returned for her son's betrothal and marriage. Alexander was pleased to see her, although mother and boy had never been very close. She had never really settled contentedly in Scotland.

Alexander, that night, shared a room with David de Lindsay, as usual, not with the queen.

At noon next day the English royal party arrived in state, quite a host, taxing even York's hospitality. Despite all his efforts for domination and overlordship, Henry proved to be quite affable, and presented his daughter to her future spouse in elaborate fashion. Eleanor of Provence, his queen, the bride's mother, a detached, calm woman, seemed scarcely concerned over it all, and was more interested in meeting again Marie de Coucy than in the forthcoming wedding.

Eleven-year-old Margaret Plantagenet proved to be a shy and plain-faced stocky girl, and an unlikely seeming bride, very different from her brother, Edward, who was also present, a forceful, self-confident youth of little more than a year older but seeming more, who appeared to look down on Alexander, his junior, all but scornfully.

In the to-do and excitement of the meeting it was all but forgotten by most of the travellers that this was in fact Christmas Day. Religious observances were, in consequence, fairly brief.

It was not long before Henry showed his teeth, as it were. He declared, coming out of the crowded minster, that his son-in-law-to-be should be knighted before his marriage. It was normal for monarchs to be knighted only by other monarchs, although this was not always possible. Alexander, at only eight years, was on the young side to receive the accolade, and not all there were pleased that the Plantagenet should be proposing to do it. But it was difficult for the boy's advisers to reject such royal decision, especially when the youngster himself became quite eager, demanding whether, when it was done, he would become King *Sir* Alexander, or Sir *King* Alexander? Ignoring that, Henry said that he would perform the ceremony in the great hall of the palace within the hour.

So presently, the two kings, leaving the dais, confronted one another. The Plantagenet turned to the Earl Marshal of England. "Your sword, my lord," he said, to the only man who could carry such weapon in the presence of the monarch. And taking the blade, waved to Alexander. "This is a great occasion, and worthy to be celebrated thus. Knighthood is a notable distinction and dignity. I am King of England, Alexander, so we name you King of

Scotland. Knighthood does not depend on age. Whomsoever I elect to knight becomes a knight, even an infant. It is an honour which I can bestow on you. Suitable, before your marriage. To be celebrated thus and remembered by all. Come then, Alexander, King of Scots, and kneel before me, and I will dub you knight."

"Kneel?" Alexander stiffened and looked quickly at Lindsay and Patrick nearby, who had well warned him about never allowing himself to be put in a position of seeming inferiority to the English monarch, who was seeking to call himself Lord Paramount of Scotland. But David nodded, indicating that on this occasion he *should* kneel, that being always done when knighthood was conferred, whomsoever by. But the boy took the nod to mean otherwise, that he should speak the required statement taught him, to avoid making gestures of submission.

"I, a king, kneel only to my God!" he jerked, in something of a rush.

There was silence in that hall for moments, until Simon de Montford, Earl of Leicester, Henry's brother-in-law, came to the rescue.

"Bravely spoken, Sire!" he said. "Here is a young monarch indeed."

The Plantagenet looked doubtful, then shrugged. "Very well," he said. "Come, Alexander. Kneel."

As doubtfully, the youngster knelt, set-faced.

Raising the sword high, the Plantagenet intoned the formula. "I, Henry, knight, as is my right, do hereby before all dub and create you knight, Alexander." He brought down the sword to tap the boy with the blade, first on one shoulder then on the other. "So, and so! Arise, Sir Alexander. And be thou good knight until thy life's end."

The boy stood, looking around at all, almost warily, waiting, in the hush

De Montford maintained his helpfulness. He stepped forward to touch Alexander's arm. "That is all, Sire," he told him. "You are knight now."

The boy looked at him, and back at Henry. "All? Only . . . that!"

"Only that, yes. Much done in brief moments. You are truly knight now. And you can create your own knights – and only a knight can do so."

"I can . . . ?"

Edward Plantagenet came forward to be knighted also, and Alexander went to his mother, to tell her that she must now address him as sir, grinning hugely. Then he went over to David de Lindsay, and tugged his sleeve. "That man said that now that I am a knight I can make my own knights too, David. Is that right?" He was not very good at lowering his voice, that one.

"So I understand, Sire," David answered. "Any knight could knight another, it is said. But it is customary for only kings, great lords and commanders in the field to do so."

"Then I *could*." And darting back to Henry, who was handing the sword over to the Earl Marshal, he held out his hands. "Will you give that sword," he said.

Glancing at Henry, the marshal hesitated, but it was a royal command, and he could hardly refuse. He handed over the weapon doubtfully.

It was heavy, but Alexander was strong for his age. He gripped it with both hands, at haft and blade, and bore it back to Lindsay in triumph. "See!" he exclaimed. "I can do it. Davie, *you* kneel!"

Lindsay gulped. "Alex! Sire! No! Not, not . . ."

"Yes. You must. I want it. I, I command it. Kneel."

Looking around him helplessly at all the gazing throng, wagging his head, Lindsay knelt on one knee.

The boy, holding the sword unhandily, raised it, to bump it down on one of his friend's shoulders. There it rested. "Davie Lindsay. I, Alexander, *Sir* Alexander, do, do make you a knight," he got out. "So, get up!" Then he remembered. "And be a good knight until, until . . ." Clearly he could not recollect the final phrase. "Up, Davie; up, *Sir* Davie!"

Into the ensuing silence, as Lindsay rose, a strong voice spoke. "Bravo! Bravo!" That was Simon, Earl of Leicester.

Thereafter the new knights acted rather differently, Alexander strutting proudly, Edward Plantagenet accepting congratulations in offhand fashion, and Sir David looking distinctly embarrassed at being thus included.

Archbishop Sewel provided a magnificent banquet for the many visitors. There was little room up at the dais table for other than royalty and the prelate himself. Alexander wanted his Cup-Bearer up beside him, but his mother persuaded him otherwise. But he did come down to Lindsay's comparatively lowly table during the meal, causing a certain amount of upset in the hall, with a monarch on his feet, which meant that lesser men should not remain sitting. Moreover, he brought with him a handsome silver goblet, to the astonishment of all. This he presented to Lindsay.

"Look what that man has given me!" he exclaimed, loudly enough for all around to hear. "I like it. I asked him for it. For *you*. You are my Cup-Bearer. But you have never had a cup to bear! Now you have, Sir Davie!"

David, on his feet, drew a deep breath and, taking the goblet, bowed. "Sire, my, my thanks! It is . . . very fine." He glanced up towards the dais, where amusement was evident. Then, lowering his voice, he said, "See you, Alex, go back to your seat. Men stand. It is causing . . . uncertainty. But I thank you, Sire."

Laughing, the boy all but ran back to the dais.

The royal children, and such women as were present, retired early from the hall, but for many the drinking would go on far into the night. Lindsay felt that he had to go to Alexander, and Patrick took the opportunity to depart with him. MacDuff stayed on, to wake his friend, with whom he was sharing the room a couple of hours later.

The wedding ceremony was celebrated next day in the minster, the archbishop officiating. It made a somewhat bizarre occasion, with neither bride nor groom really knowing what it was all about, Margaret bewildered and doing what she was told in vague fashion; and Alexander much more concerned about now being a knight than in becoming a husband, restless and looking round and behind him from the altar steps even at the most significant moments, all but ignoring the girl at his side, the celebrant having to repeat himself more than once, and himself looking very uneasy about it all. The prelate was clearly thankful when he could eventually pronounce them man and wife. In the circumstances, nuptial mass was dispensed with. The musicians and choristers provided the most effective part of the ceremony.

Thereafter the bridegroom headed for the great western doorway, arm-in-arm at first, at his mother's direction, but quickly finding that not to his taste, leaving his new wife, to stride ahead. If this was a marriage of convenience, the convenience was not evident on the groom's side, at least.

At the bridal feast which presently followed, there was another small ceremony, too small in the opinion of many of the Scots present. This was the handing over by Henry of his daughter's dowery. Normally this was apt to consist of lands and estates which would provide the bride with a personal income; but on this occasion it was a promise to pay the sum of five thousand silver merks, to be collected later, a comparatively modest sum for the new Queen of Scotland. Alexander, however, cared nothing for this, whatever eyebrows were raised among his supporters.

Entertainments followed, the married couple very evidently partaking of these apart and separately.

When it was evening, and more feasting on a minor scale, the new Sir David wondered as to the bed-going, as did Patrick, and no doubt others – although not their liege-lord. Were the youngsters expected to share a room for the wedding night? Surely this was scarcely suitable. Alexander himself obviously assumed that he would use the same chamber with his Cup-Bearer as on the night before, certainly not having to put up with a girl also. Patrick thought that the mothers would probably advise.

They did. The two queens came over to them, and Eleanor announced that, if King Alexander did not object, it would please her if she and her daughter might spend their last night together, Marie saying that she considered this right and proper. Her son had nothing to say to that, obviously considering where Margaret slept as nothing to do with him.

Relieved, the men concerned agreed heartily, and in due course the new Queen of Scotland retired with the Queen of England and her son.

Once the women were gone, there was a change in the proceedings. The archbishop it was who initiated it, changing his hats as it were and becoming the Lord Chancellor of England. Raising his hand for silence, after a glance at the Plantagenet, he came to the point promptly.

"Your Majesties and my lords," he began. "It is, on this auspicious occasion, appropriate that the two realms, now happily in unity through the marriage of Alexander of Scotland and Margaret of England, should celebrate more than just the wedding. The harmony of this day's union should be reflected in harmony between the two kingdoms, and all cause for dispute and enmity put away. Now is most assuredly the time for such necessary and desirable improvement, all will agree."

He paused for the required applause, which was hearty on the English side, rather less so among the northern visitors.

"Disagreements frequently arise in matters of state over borderline issues," he went on. "They should be resolved, for all time coming, for the benefit of both realms. King Knud, or Canute, King of England and Emperor of the Anglo-Saxons and the Danes, obtained the submission and fealty of King Malcolm the Second of Scotland in the year of our Lord 1031. Ever since then the Kings of England have been entitled to use the style of Lords Paramount of Scotland. This continues . . ."

The rest was drowned in outcries of protest and anger from the Scots, to the offence of the others. There was an unseemly disturbance in that hall, in the presence of the two monarchs, Alexander biting his lip and looking to his lords for help, and Henry and his Earl Marshal banging on the table for silence.

Frowning, the archbishop-chancellor proceeded. "I say that this of the royal paramountcy is a fact, a historic fact, which cannot be denied. The said Malcolm bowed the head and bent the knee to the said King Knud or Canute, accepting him as overlord. That fealty has never been abrogated by deed or statute. And now is the time, all should agree, for it to be acknowledged and accepted in amity and goodwill, on the occasion of this illustrious marriage."

"No! No!" came the shouts from practically all the Scots. But they were in a difficult position nevertheless to express themselves more fully on the issue, with their monarch present, and none able to speak before he did; except perhaps the regents, Clement and Dorward. The latter chose to remain silent, but the bishop turned to Alexander.

"My lord King?" he invited.

Alexander, darting glances right and left, was scowling. "No!" he declared. "It is not so."

"You cannot deny the facts of history, Highness," the archbishop said sternly. "It happened. The Scottish king paid fealty to the English king for his kingdom. Admitted him as superior. Which superiority has been asserted and retained ever since, in state and Church."

Alexander looked unhappy. Old history was not his particular study. He turned to seek Lindsay's aid, who in that lofty company was standing well back.

It was another Walter, however, and a Comyn at that, who came to his aid, the Earl of Buchan. "Sire, may I speak? That of King Malcolm, as I understand it, was not homage for Scotland, his kingdom, but only for Lothian and the Merse, which Knud Svenson had overrun. It was but a device to get the Dane out of the lands south of Forth which he was occupying. These were not themselves part

64

of Alba, ancient Scotland. So to get rid of the invaders, Malcolm did homage for them, at Stirling. Them only. And only to the Dane."

"Moreover," Mar broke in, "the English King Stephen, no Danish invader of his own kingdom, grandson of the Conqueror, abandoned any such claims to Scots territory, indeed ceded English-held lands *to* Scotland, Cumbria and Tynedale. As my lord of Dunbar and March will agree, since his ancestor got these lands."

"That is truth," Patrick declared. "So my lord Archbishop's claims are in error. False."

The prelate glared. "You all greatly err," he declared. "King Stephen was a weakling and usurper. His failures do not prejudice the right of the Kings of England."

"You cannot hold your sword both ways, my lord Archbishop," Bishop de Bernham put in. "If your Stephen was a weakling and his deeds can be ignored, so can Malcolm of Scotland's! This harking back is folly. We live today, not two centuries ago and more."

Simon de Montford of Leicester was speaking quietly to Henry Plantagenet, who inclined his head.

"This is unseemly," the latter said. "This dispute in our royal presence. On this day of all days. Let us have an end to it. My position and style of Lord Paramount is *beyond* dispute. Let it be acknowledged by my new good-son, and be done with it. A simple word is all that is required."

Lindsay had moved nearer to Alexander, in answer to the mute appeal, for the boy was looking agitated.

The Cup-Bearer's position was awkward. Among all these great ones, his was a very minor role, however much Alexander relied on him. He could by no means raise voice in that company. But he could shake his head, and did.

Patrick aided him. "His Grace should not," he said.

"No!" Alexander said promptly to his new father-in-law.

As Henry frowned and tapped a foot on the floor, the Earl Simon did his share of advising. "His Majesty of Scotland could pay homage for his *English* lands," he suggested. "That is required, is it not? For any lands held in another realm."

The Scots eyed each other. That was correct, the law. And as well as the feudal territories in Cumberland and Tynedale, Alexander had inherited estates in the earldom of Huntingdon, held by King David and his successors.

Dorward found his voice at last. "That is so," he said. "If King Henry owned lands in Scotland, he would make homage for them to King Alexander." Which was a safe enough observation, since the situation did not arise.

Mar and Patrick had to nod now.

At Lindsay's whisper, Alexander reluctantly moved forward to face Henry, tight-lipped. He did not kneel, although this was normal.

Henry held out his hand, and the boy took it between both his own, muttered something vague, head lowered, and then dropped the hand and backed away. It could have been the briefest oath of homage ever.

The Plantagenet looked displeased, but Simon de Montford smiled and made an easy gesture, a wise man.

And that was the end of it. Henry had had enough for one day, it seemed. He turned and quickly left the hall, to hasty bowing, his queen and family hastening to follow him, the archbishop also.

Back in their own apartments, Queen Marie, after some discussion of the day's events with her Scots party, gave praise for her son's stance. When Dorward had returned to his own chamber, Chancellor Donald dropped *his* bombshell.

"The Archbishop Sewel has informed me," he declared, "that Earl Dorward of Atholl has petitioned the Pope, and with great gifts, to legitimise his wife, the Lady Margery, who, as all know, was a bastard daughter of the late King Alexander, His Grace's father. And sought His Holiness's decree that she was next heir to the Scottish throne!"

There were gasps from his hearers.

"All will perceive what that implies," the abbot added.

Men gazed at each other, and outcry arose. Dorward – he had designs on the throne!

Bruce of Annandale, who was the heir-presumptive until young Alexander produced offspring, raised a clenched fist high. For a space there was all but pandemonium in the lesser hall. Queen Marie, tense-featured, took her son's hand and led him off.

Bishops Clement and de Bernham, conferring, the regent took charge. "My lords," he said, when he could gain silence. "Here are dire tidings, which have to be considered calmly and carefully. My lord of Atholl is a regent. And he is present in this palace. If this report is true, then it behoves us all to recognise what may be behind it. And take due steps. Not now, not while he, Atholl, is with us in England."

"I know what steps *I* would take!" the Comyn, Menteith, cried. "I . . . we all know that it was folly, and worse, to make him a regent. Now, it is proved beyond all doubt. He should be . . . put down. This could be treason, high treason!"

More exclamations.

"Let us not be over-hasty," de Bernham advised. "Here in England, and at Henry's court. No place to display our divisions, our weaknesses, to play into the Plantagenet's hands. When we win home, *then* we can come to our decisions on this."

Mar and Carrick backed him up, Patrick likewise, Even Bruce nodded.

"Say naught of it, then, meantime," Bishop Clement urged. "It *may* not be truth. Archbishop Sewel, who said that he had it from John de Brienne, King of Jerusalem, at the Vatican, could be but seeking to sow seeds of division among us, to divide and weaken us – although I cannot think that he would stoop so low. Say nothing to the Regent Atholl. We will all be off northwards in the morning. Time for the truth and decisions thereafter. I will have word with the Queen Marie and our young liege-lord."

This was accepted. But men went to their various rooms set-faced, Patrick and MacDuff as set as any.

In the morning, then, it was all partings and farewells, tears from young Margaret Plantagenet as she realised that she was to be left by all that she knew save one or two attendants, and to go off with strangers. Patrick was sorry for the child. Who would be a princess?

The leave-taking of her father was restrained, on all sides, he announcing that he had appointed two suitable representatives to attend the Scottish court in order to keep in touch with his daughter and to advise on her conduct and well-being, these to be the Lord de Ros of Wark, near to her at Roxburgh, and the Lord John Baliol, now in Scotland at Galloway. He was also giving her the Lady Matilda de Cantalupe as her lady-in-waiting.

Archbishop Sewel was still more reserved, and the Scots lords wondered. Simon of Leicester was the only affable one, a man to consider well. Dorward kept a low profile.

Then it was off northwards, with Northallerton Priory their target for the night. But without delay the Regent Atholl announced that their nation had been left in Comyn hands overlong as it was, and he was for heading back at swiftest pace, not dallying at the speed of children and womenfolk. None there sought to detain him.

At least for the first three nights there would be no problems of room-sharing for the royal couple, for in monasteries and the like the women were always allotted separate quarters from the men. But once back at Roxburgh, what then?

It had been a dramatic and significant interlude, from every aspect, and none underestimated the consequences that could arise.

6

Patrick's home-coming, with all this news, had a very pregnant Christian much concerned, especially this of Dorward's petition to the Pope. He had been married for many years, with grown daughters. Why apply for legitimation for his wife now? Unless he had designs on the throne? At ten, it would be years before Alexander and Margaret could produce an heir. So! Their young monarch might well be in danger. Dorward, ambitious, with his wife occupying the throne, could be king-consort and rule all, his daughters in line to succeed. Patrick agreed that it was an ominous development. The Pope might not grant it, of course. Meantime Alexander must be guarded well.

As for the paramountcy issue, that was an old story, and could not be enforced without war, when their French allies might help. Henry was unlikely to risk that. Admittedly he could make trouble otherwise. Christian said that she often thought that the Kings of Scots should sell off their great Huntingdon lands in England, despite the source of wealth, so that they did not have to pay homage for them to the Plantagenets.

They celebrated their Yuletide, belated as it was, in satisfactory fashion, with Christian expecting her delivery in only a matter of weeks. Actually, the birth came early, or births indeed, for Christian produced two little daughters, to the delight of all, both well and their mother likewise. Joy at Dunbar.

Patrick realised that he would be summoned to Roxburgh, or perhaps Linlithgow, soon, for a council meeting, when large matters would be discussed and decided upon. But meantime he had his own affairs to attend to, as well as daughters to cherish and admire. This of the timber trade was much on his mind. He would have large numbers of birch trees felled, give them months to dry out, and then send the trunks over to Bergen. It would be interesting to see how they were received by Hakon and his merchants, and what moneys they would fetch. Whether indeed the Norwegian connection was his best course at this stage. He would have other trees cut down also, of course, oak and elm and ash, these logs taking longer to mature; but the birch for a start. He had many areas bearing birch, but he knew of a large wood of them down on the seaward slopes of the Lammermuirs, near Oldhamstocks, none so far from Eyemouth, reasonably convenient for the transport. That would serve. They would require to make many slypes, or sleds, which, horse- or ox-drawn, would carry the timber to the ships. And he must have many men trained to become expert in tree-felling. There was much to be done. But this was the sort of activity he could enjoy, rather than taking part in the realm's affairs. Why had he been born to be an earl, two earls?

Christian said that it was a pity that there were not more earls like him, and Scotland would be a more prosperous and happier nation – this from the Bruce's politically shrewd daughter.

So it was prospecting woodlands, having men trained, felling no simple task when falling trees could damage others nearby, as well as the fellers themselves, and care to be taken that the woods should not be clear-felled, which would provide no shelter for new growth. The construction of the slypes was no difficult task, simple as to design, but taking the carpenters much time, for large numbers of these would be necessary.

And, of course, this of timber was only one of Patrick's concerns. The trade with the Low Countries in wool, salted meats and stone had to be monitored constantly, at both ends of the commerce, to ensure best returns and the merchants of Veere and Bergen-op-Zoom kept co-operative. He had formerly gone there himself, at least once each year, as representing his father; but now he was using his cousin, William de Home, for this duty. On his next visit, he would tell him to question the traders there as to whether there might be a market for timber in their lands also, as had been suggested.

The expected call to the council meeting arrived within the month, this for Bishop Clement's Linlithgow. Patrick was glad of Christian's good advice as to attitudes that he might usefully take thereat. Decisions were bound to be very important and probably difficult.

He rode the forty-odd miles westwards, avoiding Edinburgh to the south, to find a goodly company assembled in the palace beside the loch, including Dorward, come from Stirling. But not the Red Comyn, although his two cousins Buchan and Menteith were there. There was inevitable tension in the air.

Dorward's presence, of course, contributed to the discomfort. But he was a regent, and he had his supporters, even though the great majority there were otherwise. It was an uneasy assembly which took seats at the great table, the two regents sitting one at each end. Patrick and MacDuff sat near Bruce, Carrick and Mar.

Which was the senior of the regents was hard to say. However, at a council, as at parliament, the Chancellor acted as chairman, so there was no debate as to that.

Abbot Donald was probably wise to choose to discuss the subject of the renewed English assertion of paramountcy first. There was, to be sure, no divergence of opinion as to the falsity of this claim. But what could be done to counter it? It was decided, at Clement's suggestion, and all but without argument, that a statement from the council, signed and sealed by the regents, should be drawn up, declaring Scotland's age-old and complete independence, and pointing out that the Scots monarchy had been established many centuries before there was an England as a nation. This to be sent to King Henry, with the request that he formally drop all pretensions to overlordship, for himself and for his successors. He would ignore it, of course, but the affirmation would have been made. What else could they do? No other proposal forthcoming, it was left to Patrick to suggest, somewhat diffidently, Christian's notion that the English lands held by Alexander should be sold off, so that there was no cause for any sort of fealty and homage to be offered to the English king for them, this as unfortunately required at present. There was some support expressed for this proposition; but it was negated by both regents. They said that, acting as the monarch's representatives, they could not acquiesce to such intrusion and limitation of his royal property rights and revenues. Once Alexander came of age, it would be possible for him so to decide, but not before that.

This dealt with, men eyeing each other, it was the Comyn Earl of Buchan who raised the subject on all their minds.

"We are reliably informed, my lord Chancellor, that one of His Grace's regents, Alan, Earl of Atholl, has besought the Pope in Rome to lift the obstacle and handicap of bastardy on his wife, the Lady Margery, daughter of the late King Alexander of fair memory, and legitimise her, thus making her in direct succession to her half-brother our present liege-lord, heir to the throne until he should produce a child of his own, which will be a matter of years. This is a matter of great moment, which could greatly affect the realm."

All round the table voices were raised in agreement, in assertions and questions.

Dorward stared straight ahead of him, eyes narrowed, silent.

Bruce spoke up. "I can see only one reason for this petition to the Pope," he said. "My lord of Atholl seeks the throne for his bastard wife. And for himself, through her. *I* am heir-presumptive, until Alexander and Margaret have a child. I say that this is beyond all bearing!"

More angry shouts.

Dorward slammed the table-top. "It is false!" he cried. "This of the throne, the crown. My wife, the Countess

Margery, has ever taken ill out of being named bastard, she a king's daughter. *Our* daughters also. My plea to Pope Innocent is to end such burden on her. Would any say that she should suffer it always?"

"You have taken your time to seek to change it!" Mar put in.

"Our daughters have also grown to mislike it."

"And this of the Pope to declare them in line for the throne?" Menteith demanded. "Which means yourself, likewise!"

"Lies! All lies."

Uproar.

Bishop Clement made himself heard, but only just. "Hear me! I have already sent word to His Holiness not to grant legitimation, this with the Primate's approval."

De Bernham nodded. "I judge that this is right. And that the Pope will heed our call."

Dorward rose abruptly from his bench and stormed out of the hall, two or three of his supporters after him.

The council could scarcely continue with any order or calm. Seeking Clement's and de Bernham's approval, the Chancellor adjourned the meeting meantime.

There was great discussion and conjecture at a personal level. What now? How would Dorward react? He was still a regent. Could he be unseated as such? Parliament could do so, almost certainly. And might not – for Atholl was powerful, and could make his displeasure felt. Which side would the Pope favour? And the Comyns? Two of them present. They and their cousin would not be apt to let this be without seeking to use it all to their own advantage. Fears of civil war began to be expressed again. Some declared that it would serve the realm well enough if these two rival houses did rise and slaughter each other. But could such conflict be confined to them, and not come to involve all?

Dorward had departed from Linlithgow for his Stirling Castle without further communication with any.

That evening a resumption of the council was convened,

to decide on sundry less challenging but important matters of government. It was agreed that until word came from the Vatican as to the legitimation situation, further steps could not be taken. Probably no especial guard need to be mounted to protect young Alexander at Roxburgh. They must wait to see how the scales balanced; wait, but ready to act.

In the morning, after Bishop Clement had read out to them all a letter he and de Bernham had compounded for King Henry over the paramountcy claim, it was dispersal, with all prepared to be summoned back again at short notice.

At least Patrick, like others, got home sooner than expected.

7

There followed an extraordinary interval, scarcely of in-action but of manoeuvring and covert transactions and waiting, on the national front, when most had been expecting major upheavals if not open warfare. Indeed months passed without any demand on at least Patrick's time, for which he was as grateful as he was surprised. This allowed him to get on with his earldoms' business, particularly the timber project, not only birch, but other trees also, much prospecting of woodlands, making of slypes and the like. William de Home came back from the Netherlands, with the word that timber there would be welcomed, and no serious problems over the other trade.

And Christian was pregnant once more. Their love-making was productive indeed. Her husband prayed not to be called away on the realm's affairs.

As it transpired, it was word of Church affairs that came to disturb him, if not actually to involve him, rather than the nation's, although these did have their effect on the state. Bishop David de Bernham of St. Andrews died suddenly, a dire loss to Scotland, one of the most able Primates the land had known for long. And his unexpected passing produced major trouble among the prelates. Two successors were nominated for papal approval, amid unseemly competition, Bishop Clement proposing the Arch-deacon Abel, de Bernham's right-hand man, who was also clerk of the council; and other senior churchmen claiming that since he was the illegitimate son of a priest, he was unacceptable, and nominating Bishop Robert of Dunkeld. Both parties sent representatives to the Vatican, and these discovered Pope Innocent to be gravely ill, and in no state to make enquiries and decisions. If this was not enough, the other northern metropolitan than York, Archbishop Sigurd, of Trondheim in Norway, also died; and although a Norse successor named Bishop Sorli was selected, after much debate, his consecration likewise could not be accepted and performed in these circumstances, so that there was a gap in the metropolitan situation meantime. Archbishop Sewel of York promptly took the opportunity to announce, as the only holder of that great office north of Canterbury, that the Scottish Church indubitably came under his jurisdiction, and he would nominate his own candidate for the primacy, as well as make other appointments.

Chaos reigned in Holy Church.

Fortunately all this did not demand Patrick's services, and next mid-summer he was able to be with Christian when she was safely delivered of a second son, to great thanksgiving. They named him another Alexander; and at the christening, his father celebrated by donating lands to the monks of Dryburgh, on the edge of the Merse. So religious matters at a local level were none so chaotic.

Another shipload of birch was sent off from Eyemouth to Bergen, in the *Skateraw Meg*, with hopeful messages for King Hakon.

Then Earl Simon of Leicester, King Henry's brother-in-law, arrived in Scotland. He had come on a strange mission: to urge the Scots not to seek to fulfil their traditional part in the Auld Alliance arrangement with France, whereby if one or other of the realms was threatened in arms by England, they would help each other by a gesture of invasion of the aggressor north or south. It seemed that Henry had sailed with a large army for southwest France, to reclaim the duchy of Gascony and Poitou, which had been taken over by insurgent French nobles while King Louis was away crusading again, Gascony being a Plantagenet holding, and de Montford himself a Gascon. No doubt these powers ruling France in Louis's absence would call on Scotland to make good the Alliance commitment. Earl Simon came to urge otherwise, for he said that the expedition of Henry's was not against France itself but only to reclaim his duchy of Gascony, which, had Louis not been absent, would never have been taken over by these upstarts.

Bishop Clement, with no desire for military endeavours anyway, approached his two fellow-regents, who agreed not to favour any attacks on England.

As it happened, one of those regents did more than agree. Dorward, very well aware of his present unpopularity in Scotland over the legitimacy episode, with fears of his aiming for the throne through his wife, took a totally unexpected decision. He mustered much of his manpower from his great Atholl estates, and those of his associated vassals, and suddenly set sail for Gascony, from Perth and Dundee, to aid English King Henry. Just what was behind this remarkable venture was uncertain; but clearly, in his circumstances, it would do him no harm to earn the Plantagenet's friendship, possibly to aid him against the Comyns.

So meantime Scotland could be spared not only any gestures against England but possible warfare between those two regents. Relief was general.

Cousin William came back from Norway with encouraging information, and more than that, moneys and goods. Hakon had seen much advantage for himself in the buying and selling of wood to the Baltic states, and had paid for the birch cargo there and then, on the understanding that much greater supplies of the harder timber would be forthcoming; and that the trade would continue to be done through him, or at least his representatives. Patrick was much cheered by this, and increased his activities over the felling, drying and transportation.

Pope Innocent died, and Cardinal Rinaldo of Segni was consecrated pontiff in his stead, as Alexander the Fourth. He promptly tackled the long waiting-list of proposed nominations, appointing Sorli the new Archbishop of Trondheim and metropolitan, no doubt to the annoyance of Sewel of York; and Abel the archdeacon, Bishop of St Andrews and Primate of Scotland. The chaos in Church affairs seemed to be over.

That relief in Scotland did not last for long, in matters of state at least. With Dorward and his manpower out of the country, the Comyns acted, and drastically. Red John, Lord of Badenoch, had scarcely been active as regent, at least as far as his kinsmen judged, for they persuaded him to declare that, because of ill health, he intended to step down from the regency; and since Dorward had left the country and behaved disgracefully, *his* regency was also at an end. In these circumstances he would have two new regents to replace them, and nominated Walter Comyn, Earl of Menteith, his cousin, and William, Earl of Mar, married to his sister, for those positions; and called for a parliament to confirm it. And, without waiting for any parliament, these two descended upon Roxburgh Castle, and took the boy Alexander and his young Queen Margaret, with their attendants, back to Edinburgh Castle, declaring that this was necessary for their liege-lord's safety and the weal of the realm, Bishop Clement not so much as consulted on this.

The said realm was in turmoil again.

Bishop Clement had not been happy about it all, needless to say, although it was possible that these two earls, Menteith and Mar, might make better co-regents than had Red John. But they certainly would consolidate the Comyn power in the land. Red John had not yet actually resigned, only said that he would, so he was still a regent, and his call for a parliament acceptable. But so was Clement, and he decided to call a council meeting. Patrick had to attend, at Linlithgow.

The meeting was notable for its absentees, as well as for the decisions it was called upon to make. No Comyns were present, neither Menteith or Buchan, nor William of Mar. Did they consider that the meeting was unauthorised, as called only by Clement, and that in fact the regency was now defunct? Mar had always been fairly reliable in the past, co-operating with Bruce and Carrick. So there was much confusion and indecision. The new Primate, Abel of St Andrews, de Bernham's successor, made his first appearance as other than clerk of the council.

Bishop Clement did not greatly help the difficult situation by starting off with the declaration that, since the regency was now in obvious disarray, and he not eager to work with the Comyns, he might as well resign from the regency himself, and allow council and parliament to appoint new regents.

Bruce of Annandale was the first strongly to urge not. "You must remain in your office, my lord Bishop," he asserted. "You must be there, as regent, for the nation to rally to. Otherwise the Comyns will rule all. Remain regent. Most of the earls, lords and churchmen are loyal, and will combine to keep the Comyns under some sort of control if they have you as leader. *I* will muster all the strength and support that I can. But I am not even an earl, although heir-presumptive through my birth. You, as regent, can do what others cannot. We must unite the nation to keep the Comyns in check."

From all round the table Bruce was loudly backed.

"While the Comyns hold the king, what can we do?" Carrick asked. "What can even parliament do? We should get the boy out of their grip. But Edinburgh Castle is impregnable. No way can we take it."

"It could be starved into submission," MacDuff of Fife said.

"Think you that the Comyns will not have considered that? They will have stocked the citadel with a sufficiency of provision to last for months."

"Such talk is unprofitable," Clement said. "Siege, war, is not to be considered. We must face the situation. Agree to the parliament, and try to use it to keep the Comyns from dominating all, using the king's authority."

"I agree," Bruce said. "William of Mar is none so ill. We have worked well enough with him in the past. Getting rid of Red John of Badenoch is to the good. Menteith and Buchan may be ambitious, but they are reasonable men. This may work out none so ill. So long as you, my lord Bishop, remain as a regent, and parliament shows its strength."

With that they had to be scarcely content but affirmative.

Christian was very concerned over the taking and holding of young Alexander and Margaret, largely for their own sakes but also for the nation's. To be captives, held in a rock-top fortress, was a sore fate for children, royal or otherwise, especially for a lively and energetic boy like the king. And, with these unscrupulous Comyns, he could be maltreated, forced to act against his will, to put his name and seal to statutes and directions to the Comyns' advantage although not his own or the realm's. Somehow the pair had to be got out of their clutches. Even Dorward, whatever his eventual designs on the throne, had never attempted the like.

Patrick agreed with her. But how was it to be achieved?

David de Lindsay? she suggested. Was he still with Alexander? If so, he too would be all but a prisoner in Edinburgh Castle. But at least *he* would be on the inside, as it were. Perhaps able to help in some rescue attempt. They would have to think well on this.

Patrick went next morning along to Luffness Castle on Aberlady Bay, to discover that Cousin David was not there, and his mother very anxious. She had heard of the capture of the king and, since her son had not come home nor communicated with her, she could only presume that he was also a captive of the Comyns. What could be done about it? Surely the lords of the council, such as Patrick's self, could contrive his freedom. And of course the royal children's.

One matter regarding her son the Lady Elizabeth did reveal. He was much in love with, and actually wooing, Alexander's half-sister, who had been another of the late monarch's bastard daughters, Margaret by name, and had been acting as governess to the boy when he was younger, and still remained his close attendant. She was, therefore, also half-sister to the Countess of Atholl, but considerably younger. She, presumably, was also with them in Edinburgh Castle.

Not that this was of any help to Patrick, however interesting.

Christian, as usual, had been using her agile wits in the interval. Since any sort of assault on the fortress, or siege, was probably out of the question, they must try to gain their ends by stealth.

"The citadel itself must have daily supplies taken up to it," she said. "Even though they may have gathered much food and drink in case of siege, they will not wish to use it all otherwise. So fresh meats and other provision will be brought in, milk, wood for the fires. There must be comings and goings of men from the town. Surely you could get someone inside with these to reach David? Seeing one of the carriers with a message: to have the youngsters ready."

"Aye, but ready for what, lass? They will be well guarded."

"If you could get the leaders out of the citadel for a space. For some especial meeting perhaps. Some negotiation between Bishop Clement and themselves? And while this was going on David to win out, with the king and queen. See you, Patrick, if carts carried up wood for the fires, as they must do, in sacks or the like, then these will have to come out empty. If the youngsters, and David, were to lie in them, under the empty sacks, hidden, could they not be won out thus?"

He stared at her. "Sakes, here's a ploy! Here's a notion indeed! Steal them out, concealed in a cart. The King of Scots! Woman, you are a marvel! If it were possible . . ."

"It is our own supplies, coming here into Dunbar Castle, which came to me. Our food and goods and wood. It must be the same in all strongholds."

"Yes, yes – I see it. I would have to go to Edinburgh.

81

Discover how and when the supplies are taken up. Somehow gain the help of the carters. Wood would be best. Largest, most bulk for covering.''

"Wood, indeed. Timber. You are much concerned with timber these days! Here would be a new trade for you!'' She smiled.

"But how to get the Comyns out first? To lure them away. A meeting, yes. But for what?''

"The bishop. As regent he could call another council meeting, asking the Comyns to attend: John of Badenoch, Menteith and Buchan. And Mar. *He* is the best of them. Offer them some hope of working together. These earls all members of the council. An especial meeting, somewhere nearby. Not too near, to give time for the carting . . .''

He nodded. "It is possible. Just possible. I will have to go and see the bishop. If he will agree . . .''

"Getting Alexander out of the Comyns' hands is the great matter. He will not fail to see that. He is a sound and able man, cleric as he is. He will see the worth of it.''

"I have some tasks ahead of me, then! Again, thanks to you, lass – if it is thanks that are due! We can try it, at least . . .''

8

It was Linlithgow for Patrick again, then. But first a call at Edinburgh to learn what he could of the necessary procedure. And for that he must not seem to be the Earl of Dunbar and March, but very much one of the commonality; probably a timber merchant would be best, which would enable him to make enquiries about wood supplies for the fortress.

So he rode for Edinburgh alone, dressed in his oldest clothing, and hoped that his fine horse would not arouse suspicions.

Putting up at a hostelry in the Grassmarket directly below the towering castle rock, he set about his task, his horse stabled. He asked the innkeeper, saying that his name was Pate Stenton, and he was a wood merchant from that area near Dunbar, anxious to sell timber. There must be a good trade in fuel for the town's houses, the smoke of fires from hundreds of chimneys proving it.

He gained the names of two or three wood-sellers, and only as a seeming afterthought mentioned that the lordly ones up at the castle would need wood also, and actually learned the whereabouts, in the Cowgait nearby, of the father and sons who supplied the castle. Thither he repaired, and finding the Brodie family at work in their yard stacking timber, mentioned that he was in the business himself and could possibly supply them with sawn-up logs of a size suitable, birch in especial, at a price that they might find acceptable. He said that there was much wood-cutting going on in the Dunbar area, for export to foreign parts; but only the trunks were going, so the boughs were available for such as himself. Were they interested?

Brodie senior obviously was, and asked about prices. Patrick was careful not to seem too eager. He pointed out that he would have to transport the logs a long way, by ox-cart; and it would have to be worth his while. This was accepted, and after some bargaining, pretended on his part, an appropriate figure was agreed, depending on quality. It occurred to Patrick that here, in fact, was a hitherto untapped market for trade for some of his Dunbar people.

Thereafter he managed to steer the talk to the castle which dominated all the scene, and gained the information he required, namely that the Brodies delivered wood to the garrison every third day, and that they would be doing so on the morrow, early in the morning. Not wishing to seem over-interested at this stage, he said that he would have a sample cartload of logs sent to them shortly, and took his leave.

Then he went on up to the castle approaches to spy out the land, as it were. A street, wide by Edinburgh standards, called the Lawnmarket, this lined with the booths of cloth- and clothing-sellers, led up to the tourney-ground which fronted the fortress, a wide space topping the sloping area below the actual craggy rock summit. At the head of this was a broad moat and ditch, with gate-house behind, this having a drawbridge. All here was bare and open, and not for unauthorised lingering; but at the head of the Lawnmarket itself there were narrow closes and entrances to tenement stairs, where a man could hide readily enough of an early morning.

Satisfied, he returned to his Grassmarket inn, and an early bed-going.

In the morning he was up betimes, and climbed, before breakfast, to the Lawnmarket head, where he established himself in a close mouth, to wait and watch.

Actually he had quite a lengthy wait, to the surprised glance of a woman who came down from one of the houses, carrying baskets. The wood-sellers were not quite so early in their deliveries as they had suggested.

But at last a clanking and clopping sound heralded the appearance of horse and cart, laden with cut logs. Patrick was glad to see that there was a piece of sailcloth folded near the two drivers, the Brodie sons, not actually covering the wood but no doubt there to keep it dry in rainy weather. He hid himself as this passed, and then watched it trundle up to the gatehouse. The drawbridge was already down, and horse and cart disappeared under the arch and within, without any hold-up or delay, this obviously a routine performance.

He waited for a while longer until the empty cart emerged again and went whence it had come. Satisfied, he returned to the lower ground to collect his horse and ride the eighteen miles to Linlithgow.

There he had little difficulty in persuading Bishop Clement that his Christian's proposed strategy was a good one. The regent was enthusiastic as to the possibilities, so much better than any attempt at an armed assault or siege. An extra council meeting would be in order, inviting the Comyns to attend, as was their right, this to try to work out some co-operation between the two sides for the kingdom's benefit – as indeed was necessary. Where could they hold it? Not here at Linlithgow. Somewhere nearer to Edinburgh, but not too near, so that the Comyns would have to stay overnight before returning, or the early morning venture would not be effective.

Patrick suggested Seton Castle, not far beyond Mussel-burgh. Alexander Seton of that Ilk was one of his own vassals, and a friend of David de Lindsay. That was only some ten miles from the city, and he could put up the councillors in some comfort.

When? It would take time to organise this and gain the Comyns' agreement. Ten days? Patrick pointed out that the fuel supply to the citadel was every third day. So, twelve days from this present? Or eleven, for the meeting. And not have Seton providing breakfast too early on the twelfth!

There was one concern which was on Patrick's mind,

however. That was persuading the Brodie family to act the rescuers. They could be ordered to, in the name of the regency, of course, but that might arouse reluctance, hostility, even reports to the Comyns. After all, this wood supply was part of their living, and they would not want to offend the fortress authorities. Concern for the young king's need? The realm's weal? Duty? Would such tell with these? Or money? Payment? It was difficult. So much must depend on their co-operation.

The bishop thought that promise of quite rich rewards would be the answer. They might lose the trade with the citadel, but that would make up for it. Patrick was doubtful. But meantime they left it at that.

Back at Dunbar, when he had put the matter to his wife, the ever resourceful Christian had her own suggestion – but it would mean Patrick taking actual part in the venture in person. Let him reveal his identity to these Brodies, offering them substantial reward, yes, but also declaring that, to cover them from blame by the Comyns afterwards, he and a companion would, when the wood had been unloaded, threaten the carriers with cold steel, daggers, if they did not do as they were told. Tell them this beforehand, so that there would be no delay or upset at the actual taking aboard of the king and queen and Lindsay, with the cart to be covered with that sailcloth. Then, later, if need be, they could tell the castle keepers that they had only done it in fear of their lives; although whether the Comyns would bother to accuse such as these was questionable.

That seemed to be a practical solution. Trust Christian!

There was one last problem: David de Lindsay. How was he to be informed and involved? Patrick had been thinking about this on his way home. Bishop Clement would have to send messengers to the fortress to inform the Comyns of the council meeting and urge their attendance. It ought to be possible for one of these to seek out Lindsay while there, a priest perhaps, and inform him. After all, it might well take the envoys some time to see and convince the Comyn lords. There ought to be opportunity to see Lindsay. And it was unlikely that he would not be eager to play his part.

Husband and wife thought that they had considered everything, so far as possible, in advance.

Patrick ordered a cartload of logs to be sent off to the Brodies.

The great day dawned, with so much at stake. Three days before, word had reached Dunbar from Linlithgow that the Comyn lords had accepted the invitation to the special council meeting, and that the bishop's messenger had indeed reached Sir David in the citadel, and instructed him to be ready, he greatly favouring the attempt. Patrick had then gone, in old clothes again, to Edinburgh, and spoken with the Brodies. Astonished at his revelation that he was in fact the Cospatrick Earl of Dunbar and March, and over the object of his visits to them, they were less reluctant than he had anticipated to take their important part in the venture. All the city knew, of course, of the boy-king and his queen being held all but prisoners in the castle, and judged this a shameful situation for their monarch; so the Brodies were in favour of ending it if possible. They were, to be sure, somewhat alarmed at first at the part they were to play in the rescue attempt: but Patrick's assurances of not only his own support but that of the Regent Clement and all the other anti-Comyn lords helped to lessen their fears, especially when they were told that if any action was taken against them afterwards by the castle keepers, they would be protected, and they could come to Dunbar, if they chose, and be accepted there as part of the timber-trading project, where their experience with wood products could be quite valuable. So the timing was agreed, the young men becoming quite excited at the prospect.

On the eleventh evening then after that interview with Clement, Patrick and Cousin William, clad at their humblest, went to Edinburgh, bypassing Seton Castle where the council meeting would be taking place, to call again at the Brodies' house and yard to check on details for the morrow, and then to instal themselves in the Grassmarket inn, intent on an early rising. William de Home saw it all as a notable adventure, even if Patrick himself was well aware that matters could go awry.

They were up with the dawn, whatever the innkeeper thought of them, and found all ready at the Cowgait, indeed having to wait there so as not to get up to the castle gatehouse before the portcullis was raised for them and the drawbridge down. The supply of logs had been carefully arranged so that there was space for Patrick and his cousin to lie in a hollow therein, with the canvas screen hiding them.

It made a bumpy and uncomfortable journey in that position, up the West Bow and into the Lawnmarket, over the cobblestones. They could guess where they were when the bumping ceased and the cart wheels ran over the comparatively smooth tourney-ground. Then they heard the drumming of the drawbridge timbers beneath the wheels, and all but held their breaths. They heard shouts, but there was no halting of the cart, so these were presumably customary greetings, and with a surge of elation Patrick knew that they were inside the fortress walls.

The horse slowed now, as it had to toil to drag its load up the fairly steep ascent thereafter, climbing over the naked rock to the cluster of buildings and towers which formed the living quarters and nucleus of the great establishment with its outhouses and stabling, all leading up to the highest point of all where rose Queen Margaret's Chapel. Patrick had been in Edinburgh Castle many times in the past, and could guess approximately where they were.

At length the cart halted, and they heard the Brodie brothers talking with someone. Then the sailcloth cover was thrown back and, blinking in the sudden light, there they saw Cousin David standing nearby, gazing. Struggling up out of their log-heap, the pair had to restrain themselves from crying out greetings, in case there were others about or they could be overheard by guards. But David hailed them openly, grinning widely, and came to help them down from the cart, with exclamations of joy and congratulation. But also of wonder. How had this been achieved? And what was it intended to achieve further? Their coming to the castle thus? To spy out the land? For an attack? An armed assault?

When Patrick told him that it was to effect a rescue of Alexander and Margaret, also himself to be sure, Lindsay stared, bit his lips and then shook his head.

"Patrick! This is, this is . . . not possible, I fear," he declared. "The shame of it, after this effort! But it cannot be, see you. Alexander and the girl are guarded all the time. Close guarded, day and night. They are in two chambers, in a tower. Not permitted to go out without guard, even within this fortress. The lady Matilda and myself, we can go in and out to them, but always the guards are there. No way could I bring them down here. No way."

Appalled, the other two cousins eyed each other.

"Then, then this is all to none effect!" Patrick exclaimed. "All but wasted effort! Is there no way? Nothing that we could do, or *you* do, to get them here? Some excuse?"

"I see none. The guards are strict. No way past them. Even if I managed to get the youngsters out of their tower, the guards would come also. I fear, Patrick, that your notable attempt is to no effect."

The Brodies were busy unloading the logs, but no doubt heeding.

Patrick was cudgelling his wits. What to do now? All this for nothing!

He sighed. "So be it, David. But, look you, what of yourself? *You* could come out with us in this cart, hidden. Then, in our further efforts to free the king, you could help us, advise us, knowing the situation here. You would come?"

"Leave Alexander?"

"Are you doing him any great service here? When outside you could help, with your knowledge of this place and what goes on. Help to win him freedom.''

The other looked uncertain. ''Think you that would be best? For him. And, and there is my . . . wife!''

''Wife?''

''Yes. Margaret. Alexander's half-sister. We, we have become . . . close. We had a priest in this hold to wed us secretly. I would not leave her here.''

Perhaps Patrick should have congratulated his cousin, rather than wagging his head at this complication, as they watched the log-piling. ''Well, you both could come out, no?''

''If, if you believe it wise. I would have to tell Alexander first.''

''Can you get to him? Watched as he is by guards? Then come back. With your Lady Margaret?''

''Oh, yes. The guards are in a different room. And I can come and go freely enough. Margaret also. But not *out* of the castle.''

''Then do so. But quickly. We cannot wait here without arousing suspicion. But you must tell Alexander, and *his* Margaret, and her attendant, this Cantalupe woman, not to speak of it, when others might hear. And warn your wife. Get her here.''

''Yes. I see that. See it all . . .'' Nodding, his cousin left them.

The wood's unloading and stacking did take time, and the Brodie brothers did not rush it. They were undisturbed, their activities of no interest to the garrison. Agitated, Patrick and William waited.

At length David and the king's half-sister reappeared, this Margaret looking less troubled and upset than they had feared, an assured and attractive young woman. She even managed a smile towards them.

''Alexander was much concerned,'' Lindsay said. ''But I persuaded him. And Matilda. She will see to him. I said that we would rescue them soon.''

There was no delay now. Patrick had decided that there

was no point in the dagger-threatening gesture towards the Brodies now. When Lindsay's absence, and this Margaret's, was noted, it was unlikely to be suspected that they had got into the log-cart. They could have managed to slip out at the gatehouse, in the dark, perhaps, or got away in the various comings and goings which were bound to go on in a fortress not being besieged.

So the four of them climbed into the empty cart, the young woman making no fuss over it, hitching up her skirts. They were covered over with the canvas, and a move was made.

Breaths were held as they rumbled past the gatehouse guards and over the drawbridge. But apart from a shout or two there was no reaction. On they went down across the tourney-ground.

It all made an odd and unexpected end to the great venture, their plans ending in only freeing a doubtful Cousin David and his new wife. Christian might well be somewhat mortified. Ought they to have foreseen this situation, of king and queen being so closely watched and guarded? Even the most carefully planned and ingenious schemes could go amiss. What next, then?

Back at Dunbar, having dropped the Lady Margaret at Luffness meantime, it was to find the former castle in a great and totally unexpected stir, crowded with visitors. And highly important visitors at that, come from Roxburgh with Christian's father Bruce. They included the Earls of Carrick and Strathearn, Alexander the High Steward, the Lord Walter of Moray, and others of Clement's supporters. That was not so astonishing, in the circumstances, as were their companions; one none other than Dorward of Atholl himself, come with the English Earl of Gloucester as representing King Henry, and a senior cleric, John Maunsel, Provost of Beverley, a representative of the Archbishop of York. All but overwhelmed by this invasion, Patrick sought to play the less than bewildered host, staring at his father-in-law. His wife seemed able to take it in her stride.

When he could have a word with Patrick alone, Bruce explained. King Henry, back from Gascony with Dorward, was appalled at the capture and imprisonment of his daughter in Edinburgh Castle, young Alexander also, to be sure. But it was Margaret's incarceration that had moved him to urgent action. He had sent Gloucester and Maunsel to Scotland, with Dorward, to demand the royal pair's immediate release, or he would himself invade with a great army which he was preparing to assemble at York. Bruce was equally anxious to see Alexander and the girl released, but was however almost more concerned over the possibility of an English armed invasion of Scotland. This must not happen, for it could well be only a first step in an overlordship campaign, with the army, in the present disunited state of the kingdom, remaining on in occupation, with the Scots in no effective state to repel it. So, somehow, the royal youngsters had to be got out of Edinburgh Castle, and speedily, before Henry made that move. This Dunbar was the nearest and greatest loyally held fortalice to Edinburgh, and on the coast, which could be used as an assembly-point for a Scots military force, and this could be supported by troops in ships up Forth to Leith, the Edinburgh port.

Patrick, wits in a whirl, disclosed the situation now prevailing, and Christian's plan for rescuing the king by stealth rather than force, her father doubtful indeed. His daughter, joining them, was not long in voicing her views on the matter, playing down her disappointment over the outcome of this first attempt. They must try further. The time factor was vital, she emphasised. To assemble the necessary armed force, and the shipping, could take many days. Meanwhile, Bishop Clement's special meeting had taken place, with the suggestion of co-operation with the Comyns. If, then, Edinburgh's citadel was to be besieged, it could all run into weeks, months, and Henry's army probably coming north to end it all. This was to be avoided at all costs, surely. So why not go ahead with another attempt at getting the royal pair out secretly? And then, when the Comyns found their so important hostages lost to them, they might well be less ambitious to rule the land, and prepared to act in co-operation.

Patrick strongly backed her in that.

Bruce, seeing sense in it, said that he would consult Carrick, the Steward, and the others.

Patrick and Christian, alone, debated. This of King Henry's initiative, and Dorward's involvement, certainly changed matters. And it could create civil war with the Comyns as well as English invasion. Their own plans, if successful, could avoid anything such. If these new arrivals would wait for a few days, and let it be attempted . . .

Patrick felt that David de Lindsay's position in the Edinburgh fortress was probably the key to success.

A conference was held that evening at which, as hostess there, Christian chose to sit in, whatever some of the visitors may have thought of it. Forces should be assembled, and word sent back to the Plantagenet at York telling him that intervention was unlikely to be required. If the Comyns were still proving hostile, and determined to hold on to the king and queen, then another attempt to smuggle them out of the citadel could be attempted, however sceptical, even scornful, some of the magnates seemed to consider it. But Dorward was for it, eager to associate himself with Bruce and his friends now, possibly in an effort to regain his regency position. Patrick, for one, did not particularly approve of working with this character, especially linked as he now was with King Henry; but in present conditions it might be useful.

He had only the one observation to make at that conference, discussed with Christian beforehand. This was that Sir David de Lindsay should somehow be got back into Edinburgh Castle, probably by log-cart again, to try to get the royal pair out by the same means. Even if this did not succeed, his presence in the fortress could be of value, in various respects.

This was accepted, with some shrugs and raised eyebrows.

Patrick and Christian, in bed together that night, talked long before sleeping.

In the morning, with Bruce and Carrick and Lindsay, Patrick rode westwards for Seton Castle, to see if Bishop Clement was still there, and if not to follow him to Linlithgow or wherever he had gone. The Earl of Gloucester rode south to inform the Plantagenet, at York, of the situation. The others would go back to Roxburgh meantime.

Calling in at Luffness to acquaint Lady Elizabeth that all was well with her son, they went on to Seton, where they found the bishop preparing to leave for Linlithgow. Surprised to see them, he told them that the meeting had gone reasonably well, with the Comyns prepared to deal with him at least in some respects, but as from a position of strength, in that they would continue to hold the king. The Lord of Badenoch had reiterated his decision to resign his regency, but only on condition that Menteith and Mar were appointed in his place. The cleric, Gamelyn, had taken a prominent part in the discussion, clearly a shrewd and able individual, who might well be the best brain behind the Comyns. He had hinted that the two proposed regents might consider taking Alexander and his wife north to their Highland fastnesses in order to protect the royal pair from any attempt by Dorward, with English help, to grasp them.

This would be a highly significant development, the visitors recognised. It made it all the more urgent that their plans to rescue the youngsters were carried out, and successful.

One last item of news affected them likewise. They learned that the Comyns were preparing to go in strength to Stirling, to take over that important stronghold, which had been Dorward's base, in case he came back and sought to resume possession. It was as strong as Edinburgh Castle, which it greatly resembled, and they wanted it in their hands. If they were going to lead an armed force there, then this might well alter conditions in Edinburgh in the meantime, and possibly to the advantage of a rescue attempt.

A discussion, and it was decided that Patrick and David, with young Seton, should go on the ten miles to Edinburgh, to try to discover the situation there now, and to return and tell Bruce and Carrick, who were anxious to get back to their own territories to raise the manpower agreed upon at Dunbar with Dorward and the others, this to assemble at Roxburgh.

The trio went on to the city. There they learned that that very day a large Comyn force had left the citadel, presumably for Stirling. Making further enquiries at the Brodies' timberyard, they were told that included in the Comyn array had been de Soulis, the governor of the castle, and many of its garrison. This was valuable information, for it meant that comparatively few would be left in the fortress, and that the deputy governor, the elderly Sir Alan Dalry, was left in charge; and he was not a very strong character. This might greatly help in their efforts regarding the king and queen, David asserted. He knew Dalry, and thought that he could possibly be dealt with.

Timing again could be of the essence. For if Stirling yielded to the Comyns quickly, they and de Soulis could be back here within a day or two. So – next morning? That would not fit in with the three-day interval of the wood supply. Would it be possible to have an extra load up on the morrow? Would that look odd, suspicious? The Brodies thought not. They could say that they had to go to replenish their stocks of timber over the next two days, and so were replenishing the castle's stocks thus early. They thought that would be accepted without question.

The attempt the next day, then.

On their way back to Seton they sought to plan it. David thought that the three of them, once inside the citadel, could make their way to the deputy keeper's lodging, which was some distance from the royal tower, and there grasp him. Use the dagger tactics which they had contemplated in the previous attempt. He might well not be out of his bed at that early hour. Then, using him as threatened hostage, get him to order the king's guards to come to him for special instructions. These could not refuse such command, and while Patrick and Seton held Dalry at knife-point, David himself would hasten to get Alexander and Margaret out and down to the wood cellar and into the cart. Patrick and Seton must then somehow win their way down there also, if necessary bringing Dalry with them as hostage, and there tie him up and enter the cart and away. It would take careful timing, but ought to be possible at that time in the morning and with the garrison much reduced.

Somewhat doubtful as to the last part of the plan, Patrick agreed to the attempt, Seton not objecting.

Bruce and Carrick were still more sceptical when they heard of it all, but said that they would go on with the forces mustering, which they reckoned would be necessary in the end.

Next morning the cart, with its three hidden passengers, had to wait at the gatehouse for the castle's drawbridge to be lowered, amid explanatory shouts from the Brodies. But that was all, no other hold-up occasioned.

At the cellar, the trio, Lindsay dressed as usual but Patrick and Seton at their poorest, told the brothers that they might be a little longer about it today than on the previous attempt. Then, quite openly, they went out and climbed the steep ascents of that rock-top, between the various towers and buildings, passing the royal quarters on the way. There was a notable lack of men to be seen. It was early, to be sure, but the garrison was obviously much reduced. The only two men they passed, these drawing up water from a well, ignored them. David was a familiar figure about the castle, of course, and his brief absence, if known, of no concern to such.

At one of the topmost towers, where was the governor's lodging, they entered. At a kitchen on the ground floor a woman was working. David told her that he had to see Sir Alan, and she replied that she doubted whether he was yet arisen, for he had not sought his breakfast. Shrugging, he led the way upstairs, and was not challenged for doing so. It all seemed almost too easy.

Lindsay reckoned that the bedroom above the small dining-chamber would be Governor de Soulis's, the one higher Dalry's. They mounted to this, and listened at its closed door. They thought that they could hear a faint snoring. Nodding, David opened, and they went in quietly, closing the door behind them.

There was only the one bed therein, and a man lay on it amid an untidy scatter of clothing. As they neared him, the sleeper did not waken.

At a gesture, Patrick and Seton drew dirks from their belts, and went one on either side of the bed. Then David stooped to shake the sleeper's shoulder.

The man who opened his eyes, and peered up frowning, was greying of beard and lined of features. Blinking, he stared.

"Sir Alan," Lindsay said. "We disturb you. But in a good cause! Do as you are bid, and you will suffer nothing. But . . . !" And he gestured towards the other two, their daggers very evident.

The older man opened his mouth in astonished protest, and then, as the dirks were prodded towards him, thought better of it. He eyed them all in unspoken alarm.

"Have no fear, Dalry," David told him. "We come on the king's business, on his regent's orders. So long as you do as you are told, you will come to no harm. Indeed, you may well gain suitable reward. But if you make any wrong move, these will not spare you. And their steel is sharp!"

The man remained silent.

"Rise, and dress yourself, Sir Alan," he was directed. "Do not delay. We will take you to Their Graces. The guards there you will order as I direct. But I will do the speaking. These two men will be close at your back. One false step and you will pay for it! You understand?"

Dalry, fully awake now, and aware, inclined his grey head.

"Very well. Get clad, sir."

Their naked victim rose and began to collect his scattered clothing, making something of a botch of doing it in his agitation. Patrick almost felt sorry for him, handing him his doublet.

"Hurry," David said. "We are in haste."

When he was dressed, however untidily, Dalry was told to walk at Lindsay's side, with Patrick and Seton immediately behind, daggers still in hands but hidden from view. They went to the door and out, to descend the stairs slowly, and all close together.

As they passed the kitchen door they saw a man with the woman there now, but they did not pause to speak and were not addressed.

Down to the royal tower they walked, the deputy governor still silent. Was he a naturally silent man, or was he too alarmed for words? Or just reserving his comments? The two men at the well had gone.

"Now past the guards," David said. "And no speech with them. Yet. Just wave them away, if necessary."

So it was up more steps to the first floor, where they entered a chamber where two men were eating their breakfast. These stared, rising. Dalry did not actually wave them away, but David did. They remained standing.

Beyond another door they could hear a young voice raised. Going to open it, they went through and closed it behind them.

Three sat at table, eating, the king and queen and the Lady Matilda de Cantalupe. At sight of Lindsay, Alexander leaped up.

"Davie! Davie!" he cried. "You, you have been away. You left me! You left me, Davie!" That was a mixture of welcome and reproach.

"I had to, Alex," he was told. "For your good. And yours, Margaret. Lady Matilda, heed me. We are taking the king and queen away. Not yourself – not yet. You will be freed later. Sir Alan Dalry, here, will be told to free you. He is . . . aiding us!"

Alexander, much excited, was staring at Patrick now. "Why are you dressed like that?" he demanded. "You are the Earl Patrick! Come with my Davie?"

"Not now, Alex," David said. "You must do exactly as you are told, and all will be well. We all go down to the wood cellar. Not Lady Matilda. You are to say nothing. Nor you, Margaret. I will hold your hands. Leave all the talking to me. And leave that breakfast. Sir Alan, here, will see you past the guards."

"But, Davie . . .!"

"Quiet, Alex!" That was no way to speak to a monarch, but it was necessary.

The woman spoke. "I, I would come with you, Sir David," she said.

"That is not possible, lady," she was told. "You remain here meantime. Come, Margaret." He held out his hand to the girl. "And you, Alex."

The boy began to see adventure in this, whatever his young wife saw. He came to take Lindsay's other hand.

"You, Dalry, you will be very heedful. For your own good! My friends will not hesitate to act. I will do the talking. You but sign," David declared.

They made for the door. This would be the test.

In the anteroom, the two guards were back at their breakfasting. They rose again, eyeing the six of them questioningly.

"Sir Alan takes the young king and queen to show them something that I have brought them," Lindsay said.

A nudge on the back by Patrick had Dalry nodding, tight-lipped.

"The Lady Matilda yonder may require help," David added, and jerked head backwards.

One of the guards looked enquiringly, and then went to the chamber they had just left. The other merely stood where he was.

"Come," Lindsay said, and led the way out.

Scarcely believing that it could all be so simple, so easy, Patrick and Seton walked out behind the unfortunate, set-faced, deputy governor.

Downstairs they went and out into the yard, to walk downhill to the area which housed the wood cellar and other outbuildings, Alexander grinning, exclaiming, questioning.

In the vaulted cellar, by the cart, the Brodies waited. Patrick acted now, passing his dagger to Lindsay. He had the cords and cloth ready in his pocket for use. With Seton twisting Dalry's arms behind his back, his wrists were quickly bound and tied. Then the cloth was used to encircle head and mouth, and gag the man. Finally, Patrick stooped to bind the ankles, and Seton pushed their victim to sit on the pile of stacked logs, Patrick actually muttering apologies.

Meanwhile, despite the boy's chatter and demands, David was aiding him up on to the cart, telling him to lie down. Then Margaret who, bewildered, was ordered to climb and lie beside him. Then Lindsay himself joined them, sitting up meantime until Patrick and Seton were finished with their attentions to Dalry. Then they too clambered up into the cart and all lay down close together, huddled on the bare boards, while the Brodies spread the sailcloth over them, David urging their giggling liege-lord to be quiet.

So, leaving the castle's deputy governor bound and gagged there, the horse was led out and the cellar door shut, and the cart rumbled and bumped its way over the cobblestones towards the gatehouse, a king, a queen, an earl and two knights huddled under a canvas cover. Had the like ever been seen before?

Once they heard the drawbridge timbering creaking beneath the wheels, the passengers knew that they were safely out of the fortress, objective at last achieved. Sighs of relief and congratulation.

There was no delay at the woodyard. Alexander and Margaret had to be got out of the city as quickly as possible, and inconspicuously. So the Brodies found some rough clothing to put over their fine garb, and disguised thus, they were mounted to ride pillion behind David and Patrick. Sincere thanks, and promises of reward, were given to the Brodies, and the five of them set off for the eastern gate at the foot of the Cowgait, near to the Abbey of the Holy Rude, and so out without challenge, to head for Seton Castle. Regrets were expressed at having had to leave Lady Matilda Cantalupe behind, but she was unlikely to suffer over it all, and would be released probably.

At Seton the youngsters were provided with horses, and a small escort, and all set off forthwith for the Borderland.

Margaret Plantagenet was scarcely a notable horse-woman, however good and eager her husband; but they ought to get as far as the great monkish hospice of Soutra for the night, and be at Roxburgh by noon the next day.

9

As a result of that royal rescue and the excitement and closeness generated by the hiding and huddling beneath the cart's canvas, Alexander had developed a marked regard for Patrick, and demonstrated it with his usual enthusiasm, so much so that he and David and Seton were commanded to share a room with their monarch at Soutra that night, the monks there having to provide bedding for the floor for their distinguished guests, to their astonishment, while Margaret had her chamber in the women's quarters all to herself.

At Roxburgh next day they found a large gathering to welcome them, including Dorward and the cleric Maunsel. Much satisfaction was expressed at the safe arrival of the king and queen, all but surprise, and due praise accorded to the rescuers, even by the less than affable Dorward, who was now assuming himself to be regent again, although whether he was in fact still that was doubtful; indeed the entire regency situation was uncertain, only Bishop Clement, not present, undoubtedly still in office.

It was good, for Alexander at least, to be back in his own home.

That same afternoon de Ros of Wark arrived, with news. King Henry was now as near as Chillingham, on the Till, less than a score of miles away, and greatly anxious about his daughter. He was to come up to Wark itself the next day, and Dorward, and such Scots lords as he had rallied to the royal cause, were to come and meet him there, this a command rather than a request.

However reluctant many of his hearers, including

Patrick, were to obey such order, with Dorward assumed by the Plantagenet to be leading the loyal Scots, they could hardly refuse; and at least they had Margaret to present to her father, and the King of Scots' authority to demonstrate. And the English monarch had an army mustered none so far away, it seemed.

So next morning a notable party set off eastwards, along Tweed the dozen miles to Wark, this on 5th September.

At the ford of the great borderline river, opposite de Ros's castle, where always by long tradition, in peacetime at any rate, Scots travellers waited for due permission to enter England to come from the castle, they halted, even with de Ros himself with them, the lion rampant standard much in evidence. They had not long to wait before three horsemen appeared, and those in the know were glad to see that Simon, Earl of Leicester, Henry's brother-in-law, was one of them, always a man to be relied upon to be as helpful as possible The Scots' satisfaction was reflected in de Montford's own when, as they splashed across Tweed to him, he saw the young king and queen among the visitors. There were relieved greetings all round.

Henry was up at the castle awaiting them, they were informed, arrived the day previously, but unfortunately Queen Eleanor, who had come north with him out of concern for her daughter, had fallen ill. Lady de Ros was caring for her, the husband much concerned.

This unexpected state of affairs produced sympathetic noises; but it occurred to Patrick that it might in fact prove to be an advantage to the Scots cause. Surely the English monarch was less likely to involve himself in vengeful hostilities over his daughter's treatment in Scotland when his wife was there sick?

Henry proved to be so glad to see Margaret there, safe and well, that he was quite amiable, especially to her rescuers. He all but ignored young Alexander himself, but took the girl off almost at once to show her to her mother, here confined to bed, leaving Earl Simon to deal with the Scots party.

Thereafter the situation that developed was a strange one, something of an anticlimax indeed. For what had brought the Plantagenet north in wrath no longer applied. And with his new friend Dorward there and acting as though *he* would now rule Scotland in Alexander's name, and the Comyns seemingly thwarted, all need for armed intervention receded. De Montford, as ever, was a helpful influence, and clearly Henry heeded him considerably. It was all not exactly harmony, but there was little in the way of threat and challenge.

Alexander found the proceedings tedious, and made a few faces at David and Patrick.

In the end, with Henry declaring that Margaret should remain with him and her mother meantime, the boy by no means objecting – for wife as she might be, Margaret meant little to him as yet – it was departure for the Scots, better relations and peace of a sort established. For how long Henry would detain his daughter and Scotland's queen remained to be seen, but, in the circumstances, that was hardly a vital matter.

Wishing Queen Eleanor a speedy recovery, the return was made to Roxburgh.

There, Alexander, much elated not only by winning his freedom but by his new association with King Henry, felt himself to be more of a monarch than he had been able to be hitherto, and was determined to demonstrate it. To the three who had rescued him he now displayed his appreciation. He declared that Davie Lindsay was to be his High Chamberlain, that office having been vacant for some time, although Patrick's father had once held it for Alexander the Second, this position demanding closeness to the sovereign at all times, and much more prestigious than Cup-Bearer. Patrick himself should be a new regent.

Patrick, needless to say, was distinctly doubtful, all but concerned, over this of regency. He had no desire to be anything such. And, anyway, was it in Alexander's power to appoint him, or anyone? The very fact that he required regents, because he was under age, indicated that he was in no position so to do. It had to be the Privy Council that did so. He, Patrick, therefore did not see the nomination as in any way valid, but could scarcely say so to the youngster, especially as his father-in-law, Bruce, and to be sure Dorward by no means took it seriously.

Nevertheless, there were rejoicings at Roxburgh Castle that night, and the day following. The entire situation was so vastly improved, not only the royal pair being freed, the Comyn power obviously much reduced, and the English threat removed, at least for the time being. All had reason to be well pleased with developments.

Patrick was no exception. But his principal preoccupation now was to get home to Dunbar and Christian as soon as possible. There was the life he wished to live, not at court nor at the seat of power. He would seek the royal leave to depart.

But the day following, de Ros arrived again from Wark. The Plantagenet, his wife seemingly considerably better, would bring back their daughter to Roxburgh the next day, to her husband; and would seek a conference with King Alexander and his councillors, with a view to drawing up a definitive treaty of peace and harmony between the two realms, to ensure his son-in-law's benefit and well-being.

All at Roxburgh were curious as to the meaning of this last. When last had a King of England set foot in Scotland, save in warfare? This of a treaty: was it good news, or otherwise? What was Henry's true objective? Dorward was obviously well pleased. But the others had their doubts.

Patrick recognised that he could hardly depart for Dunbar just yet, in the circumstances.

The Plantagenet duly arrived the next day, with a great company, bringing Margaret but not Queen Eleanor. Included were the Earl Simon, Richard de Clare, Earl of Gloucester and the cleric Maunsel, these last two, it seemed, to be left as Henry's representatives at the Scots court.

There had been discussions before the English party arrived as to how best to deal with such an exceptional, indeed unique, occasion, to give it all the flourish and seeming dignity that it probably deserved, and suitably to impress the visitors. It had been decided that to go in procession from Roxburgh Castle the miles to the fine abbey of Kelso would be an appropriate procedure, and therein to hold the conference which Henry was proposing; better that than having it in the castle itself.

So this was organised, Henry shrugging, and preceded by the High Sennachie and the Abbot of Kelso with a choir of singing boys, the two monarchs rode side by side, followed by their trains of nobles, prelates and magnates, to the rhythmic clash of cymbals, all save the royal pair on foot, a lengthy and proud procession. Past the joining of Tweed and Teviot they marched, and through the abbey-town to the handsome minster. Whether the Plantagenet realised that it had been built by King David of blessed memory a century before out of the great wealth gained by his marriage to the rich English Countess of Huntingdon was uncertain, but this was not mentioned.

Within, the Bishops of Dunkeld and Glasgow conducted a brief service of praise, whereafter the principals were conducted to the abbey's barrel-vaulted chapter-house for their conference, the others to find their way back to the castle.

Henry, flanked by his two earls, very much took charge of the proceedings from the first. He declared that this was a most significant occasion, as representing the coming together of the two realms, for the benefit of both, but especially of Scotland, which kingdom had been torn by division and strife in this minority of King Alexander, and the shameful imprisonment of the said monarch and his queen. Now that grievous and treasonable wrong was righted, the foundations must be laid for the due and uncontested governance of the northern realm until King Alexander came of age to govern in person.

That had to be accepted by all, although why it should have to be stated by the King of England was not obvious.

The Plantagenet went on to state that the Comyn faction, having proved themselves unworthy of any say in the rule of the land, should be deprived of any authority; which meant that the triple regency at present constituted was no longer in being, and a new regime required to be established. Then he gestured towards Dorward.

Almost certainly Patrick was not alone in wondering whether this was all, on Henry's part, something of a move to further his claims to overlordship of Scotland.

Dorward, undoubtedly aware of his unpopularity with his fellow-Scots, glanced over at some of them, Bruce, the heir-presumptive, in especial, and spoke carefully.

"Sire, we all, I swear, much value your Majesty's concern for our realm and its young lord, His Grace Alexander. And, to be sure, your daughter, the Queen Margaret. None, I judge, will disagree that a new ruling authority must be set up, in His Grace's name, effectively to govern the land and to prevent any further wickedness and grasping at power such as we have recently seen." And he glanced round the company again.

None could, of course, gainsay that; but Bruce spoke up.

"Bishop Clement of Dunblane is still regent of the kingdom," he pointed out. "A worthy appointment." And he looked all but accusingly at Dorward.

Was that man, Patrick wondered, seeking to have himself made regent again, with Henry's backing? Surely he would not go that far?

"It is unfortunate that Bishop Clement is not here," Neil of Carrick put in. "He is at Linlithgow. Can we make decision without his presence?"

"Unfortunate, yes," Dorward declared. "But the regency was set up by the council of state, a *triple* regency. Now that the Lord of Badenoch has resigned, and my own position is . . . questioned, that regency is no longer in being." He looked at Henry. "I say that the council should meet to appoint a new regency. And it would be my proposal that it should be a council of regency. That is, not one nor three, but a group of the councillors ourselves. Many of whom are here present. With, to be sure, Bishop Clement."

That word "ourselves" was significant, to Patrick at least.

The Plantagenet nodded. Undoubtedly this had been decided between them beforehand.

The Scots all eyed each other. A council? Had this ever been known before Was it possible? Would such be able to function? *Many* members!

Henry spoke. "I judge this sound policy, Alexander," he said, turning to the other monarch, who had remained silent throughout, although frequently eyeing Lindsay and Patrick. "If your council can meet, and so decide, then I can return to Windsor with a more easy mind, knowing that your realm will be better governed. Is it your royal will?"

Alexander blinked, looked around the lords whom he knew best, and, at their nods, cleared his throat and said, "Yes."

"Your council, Sire, is not all present here," Bruce pointed out. "Not only Bishop Clement, the regent, but others. On it are the Earls of Menteith and Buchan, Comyns. And Bishop Gamelyn. And the Earl of Mar. If decisions are made in their absence, as by the council, they will declare them unlawful, void. It should be the full council of state which makes the decisions." Although he seemed to be addressing Alexander, it was at Henry that he looked.

"Then summon them all. If they will come!" the Plantagenet said shortly.

"If they fail to attend, after being summoned in their liege-lord's name, then surely they cannot question the council's decisions?" That was Simon de Montford.

"That may be so," Bruce acceded. "But summoned they should be. And that will take time. For they are, we understand, north of Forth."

Henry frowned. "I cannot linger here, nor at Wark," he jerked. "And I would see to King Alexander's good cause, and his kingdom's weal, before I return southwards. I have much to see to. *How* long?"

The Scots lords eyed each other. Did their council have to time its meeting on the Plantagenet's pleasure and convenience? And yet, so much depended on it.

Patrick, after whispering to Malcolm MacDuff at his side, ventured an answer. "Four days? Five? That should be sufficient to bring them here, Sire. If they will come. Bishop Clement will, I believe. Possibly the Earl of Mar. The others . . .?" He shrugged.

Bruce nodded. "If His Grace Alexander will give us five days, then I say that we can have a council meeting here which cannot be disputed. Valid."

"Very well. I shall go back to Chillingham. From where I can reach my people, who wait for my instructions." Henry paused for that to sink in. "Then I shall return to Wark. In, say, seven days. Eight. And trust that all will then be . . . in order!"

There was silence round that table.

The Plantagenet rose, so all must rise also, except Alexander. The conference was over.

Henry did not delay his departure. Of course he had to be escorted back to English soil by the King of Scots. So most there had to ride down Tweed again to opposite Wark, after her father had said goodbye to Margaret, Earl Simon and Dorward riding beside the two monarchs.

At the parting, Patrick announced that, since they had five days before the so important council meeting, he was for Dunbar, with His Grace's permission. Malcolm MacDuff also was for home, as no doubt were others, but these two, well down Tweed, were some ten miles on their way. David de Lindsay, as Chamberlain, would remain with Alexander meantime.

That monarch told Patrick to come back soon.

* * *

At Dunbar, Christian was much interested in all that she was told about the situation and developments at Roxburgh. She approved of the council of regency project, even if it was Henry's and Dorward's idea, since it would in effect mean that the loyalist lords and prelates would be ruling Scotland, and the Comyns pushed northwards, and in a distinct minority. Would any of them attend this council meeting? Mar probably would, but the others? At any rate, there would be little doubt as to how the voting would go. Bishop Clement would probably be grateful to be relieved of his all but sole responsibility.

Patrick was concerned about his own responsibilities in all this. Alexander's declaration that he should be a regent could be sidestepped, but this of the council of regency would almost certainly be expected to include himself, and further state commitments were not his desire; and for years ahead, until the youngster came of age. Christian urged him to see it differently. It would be none so ill, she declared. He need not take any very prominent part, unless he so wished. She did not want him gone from her side overmuch, to be sure. But on vital occasions his vote could count in helping the ship of state to steer aright. If she knew her father, he would play a leading role in the regency, especially in keeping Dorward in order and the English influence lessened. Patrick's support could be valuable in this, like her kinsman Neil of Carrick's and MacDuff of Fife's. It would probably demand but little of his time, and he would still be able to get on with his preferred labours here in his earldoms, and be at her side sufficiently for them both.

Hoping that she was right, Patrick heeded her advice, as always; and he spent three days superintending his trading ventures, in especial the felling and preparing and stacking, to dry, of the hard woods of oak and elm and beech, arranging for the shipload of these to be sent off to Norway before the winter storms made the Norse Sea voyaging hazardous. Cousin Will would go again with it to Bergen, and hope that King Hakon would remain co-operative.

Then it was back to Roxburgh.

At that castle Patrick found an air of tension prevailing, for not only William of Mar had arrived but Menteith, Buchan and Bishop Gamelyn, with some of their supporters, Dorward very obviously avoiding their company. Clearly this council meeting was going to be no easy and harmonious affair. There was a good attendance of the anti-Comyn side, to be sure, and Bishop Clement was there, but a clash would be unavoidable.

Patrick and his father-in-law had more than one quiet talk with Mar, with whom they had always got on well enough. Would that man serve to act as some sort of bridge between the two factions? After all, he was not a Comyn, only married to one, and uncle of Menteith. Moreover he was the direct descendant of one of the oldest noble lines in Scotland, stemming from the Mormaors of Mar, while the Comyns were but comparative newcomers, of Norman extraction.

In due course, Bishop Clement called the council to convene. Alexander was led in, attended by Lindsay, to sit, not at the great table itself but nearby, where he could watch and listen without actually taking part in the debating, this his privilege. It was to be hoped that his presence would have a suitably calming effect on the deliberations. He grinned and waved to Patrick.

It was as well that this was not a parliament, for at such the Chancellor presided – and now there were two contenders for that important office, for the Red Comyn, before he resigned, had named Gamelyn for it, and Clement put forward the Bishop of Dunkeld, lords spiritual being considered to make the best chancellors, as apt to be more temperate, at least in public behaviour, than many of the lords temporal. So Bishop Clement was able to preside, and after prayer for their worthy decisions, and His Grace's cause, opened the meeting.

He announced first that this was his final appearance as regent. With the Lord of Badenoch retired and the Earl of Atholl's position in doubt, since he had left the country for months, the triple regency could no longer be said to be maintained. So he now tended his resignation to the council. However, His Grace still required a regency to act in his name until he was of an age to rule as well as reign. This council therefore must so decide and appoint.

All round the table eyed, in especial, three men, Dorward, Menteith and Mar, all of whom could make claims. But it was Bruce who spoke up first.

"My lords, the regency of three has not proved satisfactory, as all here know. And *one* regent can be to the ill of the nation. Now a different form of rule has been proposed: a council of regency. Not all the Privy Council, but a number of its members, with responsibility for decisions in His Grace's name. This is judged as wise and right by many here. It is advised that we discuss and decide on it. Or . . . other."

There were exclamations of approval.

"How many?" Menteith asked. "Gaining agreement from not a few could well be difficult on some issues. Ending in chaos. If three can disagree, how much more could many!"

"A majority of the regency council would make decision," Dorward said. "After due debate."

"And who to choose the members?"

"This council."

"All members equal? Or one leading?" That was Buchan.

"Equal," Bruce declared.

"How many?" Menteith repeated. "Four? Six? More? This, I say, could be unwieldy. A sure prescription for dispute, for delay and indecision."

"No more so than with three. And better than one, who could misjudge."

"My lord of Badenoch, regent, named myself and my

lord of Mar as regents, with my lord of Atholl absent, before he retired," Menteith asserted.

"It is this council, not a regent, who names other regents," Bruce pointed out. "So – how say all? A council of regents? Or no?"

The affirmative vote did not require to be counted, so obvious was the preponderance. Indeed no actual voice was raised against, only one or two headshakes.

"It is agreed, then." Bruce was taking the lead. As still heir-presumptive to the throne, he probably had the right to do so. "Now, how many?"

There were various suggestions, from five up to a dozen, men eyeing one another.

Bishop Clement spoke up. "It is *who* we have rather than how many, I judge. Names that can be relied upon to serve the realm well and justly."

"I agree," Bruce said. "And I would name you, my lord Bishop, who have proved yourself an excellent regent."

There was applause at that, and no contrary voice.

"If so it is wished . . ."

"And I propose also William, Earl of Mar," Bruce added.

That produced some indrawn breaths, not least Menteith's and Buchan's.

"And I second it," Patrick put in.

There were murmurings before Mar himself spoke. "I thank my lords of Annandale and of Dunbar and March. But I would prefer not. As yet. Later, it may be . . ."

The councillors digested that before other nominations were made.

"I say that my lord of Annandale should certainly be on the regency," Clement declared. "None more entitled to be. And also my lord Cospatrick of Dunbar himself, of the ancient royal line."

Patrick was about to disclaim any such appointment when a hand-clapping forestalled it. For it was a very special clapping, from Alexander's chair, and as such all but a royal command. Patrick could only bow his head.

Then other names were put forward: Neil of Carrick, Malcolm of Fife, the High Steward, the Bishops of Dunkeld and Aberdeen. Then there was a pause, and all but reluctantly Bruce suggested Dorward, Earl of Atholl.

More breaths were drawn at that, but no actual negative was announced.

"That is eight," Bruce pointed out. "A sufficiency, I would say. The council could add to it or change it later." He glanced over at Mar. It was noteworthy that no one had nominated Menteith, Buchan or Bishop Gamelyn, and the significance of that was not lost on the three Comyns. Set-faced, they remained silent.

"That, then, concludes our business, my lords," Bruce said. He was obviously going to be the prime mover in this new regency. "Hereafter, the regency council will forgather, I suggest, to decide on details and procedure. With His Grace's permission, we adjourn."

"Why not Davie?" That was Alexander, as Bruce rose. "Davie Lindsay."

There was silence, save for a scraping of chairs. How to explain to the boy that this was not suitable, that Lindsay was not a member of the Privy Council, nor of sufficiently lofty rank to be included in a regency. Even Bruce was temporarily at a loss.

Patrick came to his father-in-law's rescue. "Sire, my good cousin, Sir David, is already your High Chamberlain and Cup-Bearer. I cannot think that he would wish to be saddled with being a regent also! Spare him that, I beg of you!"

The king made one of his faces, but let it be.

The meeting broke up.

Patrick did not get home until the next evening, for there was another meeting, and a long one, this of the new regents to decide upon responsibilities, commitments and priorities. Fortunately this was not productive of any especial duties for himself, Bruce accepted as leader, with Bishop Clement. Dorward's position was peculiar in that he was all but suspect by the others, yet he had the very important links with King Henry, so must be tolerated. Oddly enough, David Lindsay became all but an unofficial member of the regency, his close association with Alexander proving very useful.

A reluctant regent returned to Dunbar.

At bed-going that first evening, after bidding goodnight to
their three small sons, Christian was not long in giving her
husband her views on his regency duties and responsibilities, not assertively but persuasively and shrewdly; which,
she perhaps ought to have recognised, being the able and
far-seeing woman that she was, was not the best time to be
doing so. For, despite child-bearing and raising, she remained a notably attractive female, her figure only a very
little fuller than when Patrick had wed her, and firmly
rounded, her carriage proud, her shoulders finely
moulded, her breasts provocative, her legs long and shapely. The sight of her undressing seldom failed to have the
man aroused, and this night was no exception; so her
observations and excellent advice tended to fall on fairly
deaf ears. She could hardly fail to become aware of this, by
his reactions, of a physical rather than a mindful nature,
and she yielded with a fair grace to his attentions, even co-
operating, however head-shakingly – but not before she
had told him that the Comyns would not take their
removal from power lying down, Gamelyn in especial,
and he was a clever man and in touch with Pope Alexander;
that there could be civil war still; that Dorward would have
to be carefully watched, ambition for dominance part of
the man, and could well use his influence with the Plantagenet to promote his own position, regency council or
none; and that Queen Margaret, however inoffensive a girl,
could be a danger to the realm, in that her well-being gave
King Henry unending opportunity and excuse for inter-
ference in Scottish affairs, in alleged concern for her
position and treatment. All this she warned Patrick of,

especially of incurring papal enmity through Gamelyn, this before he closed her mouth with kisses, hands busy elsewhere.

Thereafter, although it was traditional good advice, with problems, to sleep on them, it is to be feared that the new regent failed deplorably so to do.

In the days that followed, busy as he was with his own affairs, Patrick did consider these matters, and more, especially when the word reached Dunbar, by travelling friars, of an extraordinary event. King Henry, long eager to subdue Wales to English rule, had invaded that Celtic land from Chester, and had been soundly repulsed by Llewellyn, Prince of Wales. This news was not only surprising but of import for Scotland, for the Plantagenet could hardly just shrug it off and forget it; and if he now concentrated on large-scale war against the Welsh, he was unlikely to involve himself in Scots affairs for some time. And that would limit Dorward's influence.

Despite this optimistic calculation, it was this Welsh matter which had Patrick summoned to his first real regency meeting. He arrived at Roxburgh to discover that Henry had sent Gloucester to Alexander, via Dorward, to request Scottish aid in subduing the rebellious Welsh, and this on the pretext that they were negotiating with the Irish to form a Celtic alliance against England, which might well affect the Isle of Man and the Hebrides, and so threaten the Scottish realm also. These Celts must be kept in their place.

The regency met, with Dorward of course strongly upholding the Plantagenet's appeal, but none of the other members agreeing with him. Even though many of the Lowland Scots nobility were largely of Norman stock, most had Celtic blood also; and since there was the traditional native background, through the Picts and the Dalriadic Scots from Ireland, they had pro-Welsh rather than pro-English sympathies. So Gloucester was sent back to London with the reply that unfortunately, with the ever-present Comyn threat looming in the north, no force could be spared to help assail the Welsh, and the regents advised that an approach should be made to Llewellyn to settle differences round a conference table, to which the Scots could send delegates to help with a satisfactory solution for all parties. Whether Dorward sent a different message privately was a matter for conjecture. Patrick, very much of the pure and ancient Celtic royal stock, was strong on this.

That was not all the business. The Primate, Bishop Abel of St Andrews, had suddenly died, and the Lord of Badenoch had nominated Gamelyn as his successor. This, needless to say, was contested by Bishop Clement, and for that matter, Dorward, and they nominated the Dean of Dunkeld. Now Gamelyn had gone to the Vatican, and Pope Alexander, never friendly towards Scotland, had confirmed him as Primate. What was to be done about this?

All there agreed that this appointment was to be disputed, rejected, as far as was possible. To have a Comyn in charge of the Church in Scotland would, in the circumstances, be grievous indeed. The Bishop of Aberdeen, one of the regents, should go to the pontiff and declare that this appointment was contested by both the regency and the College of Bishops. Elderly, and beginning to fail in health, Clement, who the others would have preferred to see as Primate, declined. So William Wishart, Archdeacon of St Andrews, and effective leader of that diocese, was nominated, with the backing of all.

Christian had warned about Gamelyn's ambitions and influence with the Pope. She was proved to be right, as usual. Patrick felt that it was a pity that women could not be considered for the regency, for he judged that his wife would outplay them all. He told her so on his return, to her amusement. Just as well not, she said, or soon there would be no men on the council and it would be all talk and chatter and no action, if she knew her kind!

Cousin Will came back from Bergen well pleased with this latest timber trading. He had received the requisite payment, although he had been told by one of the Norse shipmasters at the port that King Hakon was practically doubling the price for the wood's onward sale to the Baltic buyers. Ought they not to be considering sending their cargoes on thither themselves? Clearly there were great profits to be made there. Patrick decided not. They were doing very well with it all as it was; and they did not know these markets. It would involve much more ship-work, and it would get them wrong with Hakon. Let it be the way it was.

Actually that late summer and autumn they were all thankful for the wood trade, like that of the wool and salt meats, for the weather produced the worst harvest on record, storms and flooding devastating the hay and grain, leaving the barns empty and the millers unemployed. Most fields and rigs were still uncut and flattened in November, and much of the crop would never be saved, lying under water and mud.

It was in these distressful conditions that Patrick received his next call to Roxburgh, there to face a very different dire situation. They were all excommunicated.

Scarcely able to believe this, the regents were informed that Pope Alexander, clearly a man of no half-measures and headlong in his decisions, had condemned them all for not accepting his appointment of Gamelyn as Primate. King, regency, lords, churchmen and people were all now under the curse of excommunication until they recognised the papal authority and Gamelyn as Bishop of St Andrews. Peter of Aberdeen had brought back this pronouncement from Rome.

Appalled, the regents gazed at each other. Excommunication meant in theory the cessation and invalidation of all Church functions and services. Not only could there be no communion, but no Christian baptisms, no weddings, no interments, no consecrations, no religious observances of any kind. To condemn an entire nation to excommunication was beyond all belief. That one man, St Peter's successor as he might be, could so decree was scarcely conceivable. What was to be done about it, in God's name?

Clement said that there was no way round the edict. They could advise and urge the churchmen in Scotland to ignore it, and continue to act in normal fashion, but this was unlikely to be heeded. The entire Church authority was built upon the Holy Father's supreme prerogative, and even though the College of Bishops was to condemn this decree and to proclaim defiance, which was unlikely, the priesthood in general throughout the land would never accept that. He feared that there was nothing for it but to recognise Gamelyn as Primate and have the excommunication lifted. The other two bishops agreed with him.

It would be triumph for the Comyns.

And this was not all that that troublesome line was devising. They were told that Buchan and Menteith were mustering their substantial manpower to form an armed force to go to the aid of King Henry against the Welsh, this to counter his accord with Dorward and the present regency, a cunning move. There did not seem to be anything that the regency could do about this, save be prepared for further Comyn ventures.

Just in case the nation was not sufficiently informed of the papal curse laid upon all, at Stirling, held by Buchan and Menteith, a great ceremony was staged, with the bells of Cambuskenneth Abbey ringing all day and night, candles lighted and paraded, and the decree of excommunication read out repeatedly, the names of monarch, regents and prelates announced, a demonstration never before seen in Scotland.

At Dunbar, Patrick asked Christian whether he was lacking in due religious zeal in that he did not feel in the least different from before in becoming an excommunicate? She assured him that since God the Father was love personified, and he alone to be worshipped, so long as his people sought to do that, the pronouncements of men, lacking love, whether in Rome or elsewhere, ought not to be taken to heart. She and their children were also presumably excommunicate, and she was not going to let it affect their life, their worship, or their peace of mind.

How many others thought as she did was not to be known, although certain of the more superstitious declared that the ongoing storms and bad weather and failed harvest were all part of the curse. One who did take the situation seriously, although perhaps not on purely religious grounds, was Dorward of Atholl. Whether he could not bear the thought of Gamelyn back in Scotland, and in ecclesiastical authority, or otherwise, he suddenly departed for England and Henry's court, leaving no indication as to when he would return to regency duties. His fellow-regents did not weep over that.

11

Gamelyn's return to his native land, to major Comyn rejoicing, produced a very strange situation. He announced that, so long as all recognised him as lawful Primate and Bishop of St Andrews, he would petition the Pope to lift the sentence of excommunication; and since the said edict had created dire upset and concern all over the kingdom, and the regents were not in a position to ignore him nor refute his appointment, they had to accept the position, and make the best of it.

So, with Dorward gone, there were two powers in control in the land: the regency, with the king, at Roxburgh and Edinburgh; and the Comyns at Stirling, St Andrews and the north, with the Church under the sway of Gamelyn. Both sides played it quietly meantime, but all recognised that it was a situation that could not go on indefinitely.

The excommunication was lifted, but undoubtedly would be reimposed if Gamelyn did not gain his way.

There were two factors in the situation which were advantageous, however, from the regency point of view. One, that Gamelyn, however ambitious and unscrupulous, was an able and clever man, and could be expected to act with some discretion at this stage, concerned not to rouse Church and people against him. And second, Bruce kept in quiet touch with William, Earl of Mar, who was in a position to influence his Comyn kinsfolk in some measure, towards moderation.

So Yuletide came and went, in a sort of uneasy truce, and Christmas festivities could be celebrated, if less joyously than usual because of the near-famine resulting from the wretched harvest. Would this be a better year for Scotland? King Alexander was now of fourteen years.

In January, there was a circumstance which suited the regency, however deplorable it was from a general point of view. On the way home from allegedly aiding King Henry's assault on Wales, the Comyn force misbehaved itself in northern England, ravaging and raping and burning, presumably having been doing the like on the Welsh Marches. This much angered the Plantagenet, needless to say, and Fergus, brother of Buchan, in command, had much damaged the credit of the Comyn faction.

It was a couple of months later that Dorward returned from England, and brought with him interesting companions, none other than Alexander's mother, Marie de Coucy, and her husband John de Brienne, titular King of Jerusalem. Her son scarcely knew her, so little had he ever seen of her, and the reason for this visit was unclear. They did not linger long at Roxburgh, but headed off northwards, for Dorward's castle of Kinross, despite this being on the edge of Menteith's territory and between that and Gamelyn's St Andrews, a peculiar move. De Brienne, of course, was ever in close touch with the Pope, because of his crusading concerns, and the suspicion was that this visit was Vatican-inspired, and probably to aid Gamelyn towards the rule of Scotland, which made it the more odd that this royal couple had come north with Dorward.

Patrick, it was to be feared, did not greatly concern himself with all this, he and his fellow-regents being more worried about Bishop Clement. That prelate had been failing in health for some time, and now he was a very sick man. His loss to the regency would be serious indeed.

The said regency council was, in fact, in no very effective state. With Dorward ever less than reliable, and apt to be outwith the country frequently, his negotiations with Henry questionable, and Gamelyn ever more powerful in the realm as well as the Church, indeed now the leading force in the Comyn faction, the regency's authority was much reduced. Bruce, its self-appointed leader, shook his head over the situation, but kept in touch with Mar, as a precaution. Clement died. Meantime no other appointment was made to replace him.

Patrick, never anxious to be a regent in the first place, contributed little to the situation, not seeing much that he could usefully do, and having a sufficiency of responsibilities at Dunbar and the Merse. At least he had the satisfaction of seeing his two earldoms prospering and his folk co-operating. Christian was not critical in this, agreeing that meantime they could only await events; but be prepared for action, possibly at short notice.

That short notice eventuated in the late spring, and in highly dramatic fashion. Neil, Earl of Carrick, died suddenly and quite unexpectedly, of no great age, his loss greatly felt. Bruce had gone to Ayrshire for his kinsman's funeral, along with the High Steward, his brother-in-law. And while they were gone from Roxburgh, Dorward had taken Alexander and Margaret, under strong guard, up to his castle of Kinross, allegedly at the request of Queen Marie de Coucy.

Consternation reigned when Bruce and the Steward got back from the funeral. The young monarch out of their hands! And why? What was Dorward's objective? Would he bring the royal pair back to Roxburgh after the meeting with the youth's mother? Or was this some plot to seek to take over supreme power personally by holding the monarch?

A meeting of the now reduced council of regency was hurriedly summoned.

It was unanimously decided that they should go at once up to Kinross, all or most of them – there were only the five regents now, to be sure – and bring back Alexander and Margaret to Roxburgh, whatever Dorward's reason for taking them, and Queen Marie's concern in the matter.

Patrick, with the most readily available manpower near at hand, was to provide a strong escort.

So three days later a large party set off for the north. They crossed Forth at Queen Margaret's Ferry, and proceeded by Dunfermline and then up through the Cleish Hills to Loch Leven, at the head of which lay Kinross. How would they be welcomed there? Just what was behind this move of Dorward's, and presumably Queen Marie's, they could not be sure, but it was ill done, quite apart from the unauthorised removal of the monarch from his home, and choosing to do it while Bruce and the Steward were away at that funeral.

However, if the visitors had envisaged possible opposition, nothing such materialised. Indeed the castle, soaring above the lochside, seemed quiet, not exactly deserted but not thronged with armed men, and giving no impression of being on especial guard. When, before the gatehouse, the guard was hailed, to ask for the Earl Alan, it was to be told that he was not present, but had gone north to his great properties of Atholl. When Bruce, in the name of the regency, demanded more information, they were invited within, where the keeper would tell them what he knew.

And there they learned the grim truth. The king and Margaret Plantagenet were prisoners in Stirling Castle. The Comyns had come for them in force, the score of miles, allegedly to join Queen Marie and the King of Jerusalem, brought there three days previously. On their approach, given due warning, Dorward had fled to his Highland fastnesses.

Stirling Castle! Consternation! That was the most impregnable fortress in all Scotland. They had lost young Alexander, and therefore all claim to the rule of his realm, their regency no more now than an empty name. The Comyns had won. Or, rather, Gamelyn had, for almost certainly this was all of his contriving. Queen Marie and John de Brienne were the key to it, at the Pope's behest. They had been sent to Scotland to get Alexander into

Gamelyn's hands, and it had been this way. Dorward? *He* had brought them to this Kinross. Could he be in the plot, he, the inveterate foe of the Comyns? It seemed unlikely. And yet, why had he co-operated with Marie and John? And personally escaped, off to the safety of Atholl? Had he decided to work with, or at least not against, Gamelyn? Share the rule, possibly and eventually, with him?

What now, then, for themselves, so very much the losers? Just retire to Roxburgh and lick their wounds? Quite possibly the nation at large was still favourable towards them. But their power was gone, save as individual lords in their own lands and dioceses.

They turned southwards, men betrayed, angered and bemused.

What would the Countess of Dunbar and March have to say to this?

Christian proved to have few doubts in that practical head of hers. Faced with this dire situation they, the regents, or *former* regents it might be, could just accept, shrug and retire to their own broad lands, and leave all to the Comyns and Gamelyn. But would not that be to betray the realm and young Alexander? Better, surely, to seek to improve matters, if possible? To all intents, Gamelyn had now become ruler of Scotland, that devious and clever man. Seek to work on that, then. He almost certainly would not wish to have a powerful section of the nobility, with much public support, ever seeking to counter him. So, face realities, and be prepared to work *with* him, not against him. For the good of the realm, since, with the Vatican's strong backing and probably King Henry's also, Queen Marie and her husband had come to Scotland through England, not by sea, it must have been under Henry's safe-conduct. Alexander could not be rescued while he was immured in Stirling Castle, that was certain. Accept realities, therefore, and seek to do what they could on his and the nation's behalf. Approach Gamelyn.

Patrick did not fail to ponder that.

And what of David Lindsay, in all this? Christian wondered. Where was he? Did he remain with the king? If so, he might be able to act as link in some fashion.

Before the inevitable meeting at Roxburgh, Patrick went along to Luffness to learn, if he could, of Cousin David's position. He found that he had not returned home, nor had sent any message to his mother, which he almost certainly would have done had he been able so to do. Therefore he probably was with the king in Stirling Castle, a prisoner also. Which would almost certainly be his own wish in these circumstances, and to Alexander's considerable comfort.

At Roxburgh, a week later, it was proved that heredity could work in the mind as well as in the body. For Bruce came up with very similar reactions to the circumstances as those of his daughter, however doubtful were the others. They must approach Gamelyn and offer to work with him, not resigning their regency but, as it were, offering to adopt him into it. He might well scoff at that, as almost certainly would Buchan and Menteith; but Gamelyn was made of different stuff, and would not fail to see that it would be better to have much of southern Scotland and the Borderland working with him than against him. And William of Mar would almost assuredly favour such a move.

How was this to be achieved, then? Bruce said that two of them should go up to Gamelyn, not himself, for that would look like capitulation. The word was that he was not at Stirling with the others but at the ecclesiastical capital of Scotland, St Andrews in Fife. Neither of their two bishops was prepared to go to see this up-jumped new Primate, who had had them excommunicated; so Patrick should be the envoy, with MacDuff of Fife, as was suitable. There was no one else, after all.

Patrick had guessed that it might come to this, little as he would look forward to the occasion. As two of the most senior earls of the land, they would at least be listened to, it was considered. He wished that he could take Christian with him, needless to say, but that was out of the question; but she would at least advise him as to procedure.

So it was back to Dunbar, where Christian had most evidently expected this decision. She said to treat Gamelyn with respect, without being in any way humble, frankly recognising the facts prevailing and expressing desire for harmony in the kingdom, and no disharmony with the Vatican. Emphasise this last, declaring that the College of Bishops was of a like mind. This should still tell with that man, far-seeing as he was. And disassociate themselves entirely with Dorward.

All this they were glad to accept. They would sail for St Andrews in a day or two.

No escort required on this venture, they went in a smaller vessel than the *Skateraw Meg*, the voyage of some thirty-five miles, with a south-westerly breeze, taking them only four hours.

St Andrews was quite a busy port, the more so since MacDuff had started his timber trading. The ground rose fairly steeply behind the harbour, and soaring high above the roofs of the lesser buildings, warehouses and sheds, were the great castle of the primacy and the cathedral-church of St Regulus; also the towers and steeples of a veritable host of priories, monasteries and churches. None could mistake this for other than the ecclesiastical metropolis of Scotland.

The two earls climbed the ascent between the flanking storehouses, yards, tenements and booths. Where would they find Gamelyn among all this plethora of church-like buildings? In the castle presumably. They would try there first.

They had no difficulty in entering this, at least, unlike so many strictly guarded gatehouses. A group of clerics were coming out as they approached. No guards challenged them. In the wide courtyard, busy with folk coming and going, mainly monks and lay brothers, they asked where they might find the Primate, and were stared at as though they were seeking the whereabouts of God Himself. One merely shook his tonsured head, but another pointed to the main tower of the castle. Thither they went.

Again there was no problem of access, unlike the usual reception at a lord's stronghold. Ignored by a servitor, they approached a richly robed individual and announced that they were the Earls of Fife and Dunbar, and sought the Primate, Bishop Gamelyn. Looked at strangely, they were told that the archdeacon-depute would be informed, and were ushered into a small chamber, and there left to wait.

It was some time before they received attention. Evidently earls represented little of import here. Eventually an elderly, stooping cleric appeared, to ask their business, and when they said it was to speak with the Primate, he eyed them assessingly and asked if they had an appointment with his lordship. When they admitted that they had not, there was head-shaking and chin-stroking, which had Patrick announcing that they were two of the regents of the kingdom come on His Grace's affairs, and that the matter was important. MacDuff added that they were not used to being kept waiting like this. That gained them only frowns, and they were left alone again.

Another lengthy wait.

Then the archdeacon-depute reappeared and beckoned them to follow him, this without a word.

They climbed wide stairs, the walling hung with fine tapestries, to a second-floor landing where they were ushered into a richly furnished chamber, the many large pictures of the Virgin and Child, the Last Supper, the Crucifixion and the Ascension into Heaven holding the eye, and they were left to admire and wonder. Another proud cleric came presently to say that the Lord Primate was occupied at this moment, but would seek to spare them a brief interview presently.

Gamelyn appeared fairly promptly thereafter. He was a slender, lean-featured man of early middle years, thin-lipped and keen of eye. He inclined his head but did not speak.

The visitors did likewise, waiting. They had done a deal of waiting.

"Well, my lords," the other said then. "To what circumstances am I favoured by this visit from such as yourselves?"

"We come from the other members of the regency council, my lord Bishop," Patrick said. "On the realm's affairs. To discuss with yourself the present situation, this being . . . delicate!"

"The regency council which *was*, my lords! But now is not. And, delicate for whom?"

"For all His Grace's realm, Sir Primate. The regency was appointed by the Privy Council and confirmed by parliament. Until these decide otherwise, it stands. But we recognise changed circumstances, deaths and departures. And King Alexander's present . . . residence! Also your own new role in Church and state. And wish to see the nation no longer grievously divided."

"Ha! So that is it! You and your friends do not wish to be left powerless? You would seek your betterment?"

"Scarcely powerless, sir. The Lord of Annandale, heir-presumptive, the new Earl of Carrick, the High Steward, the Lord of Douglasdale, my lord of Fife here, and my own two earldoms can control most of southern Scotland. If the kingdom is to be effectively governed, then these great areas must be at one with the rest, no? Not divided from the north. Thus we see it. As, we believe, must you!"

Gamelyn plucked his thin lower lip. "You would act, then, with myself? And the others? With, not against?"

"Yes. Where, in good conscience, we could. For the weal of all."

"You speak for the Bruce? And the others, also?"

"We do."

"And the Earl of Atholl?"

Patrick shrugged. "We know naught of him. He acts . . .

for himself. We understand that he has gone north. That is all.''

''Here, then, is change. On your part.''

''Conditions change, my lord Bishop. So must we all. And, and the Pope's concern means much.''

''Ah, yes. But it has taken you some time to heed the supreme pontiff!''

''To hear and consider and act, with others, requires time,'' MacDuff said

''M'mm.'' Gamelyn took a pace or two away and back. ''And now, what?''

''We would suggest a meeting. Of both parties. A conference of sorts to seek all possible agreement.''

''And soon.'' That was MacDuff again.

''You are something . . . eager!'' Gamelyn looked from one to the other. ''See you, my lords, I will consider this. Consider well. And inform you.'' He waved. ''The archdeacon will see to your comfort meantime.'' He bowed briefly and turning, left them.

Gamelyn proved to be a man who could make up his mind without undue delay, for the visitors had been led to an anteroom and there were beginning to sample a generous provision laid out before them, when the prelate reappeared. He came to announce that he was willing to consider their proposals for a working together of the two sides in the disputed rule of the kingdom, and would recommend his colleagues to that effect. A conference at Stirling Castle, in the royal presence, would be called to settle all details, at a date to be decided upon. They would be informed at Roxburgh, or whatever or wherever. Meanwhile all hospitality was available for them here at St Andrews.

He left them again. It was very clear who the Bruce party were going to have to deal with at Stirling, and indeed who was probably going to rule Scotland.

Patrick had no desire to linger at St Andrews, and MacDuff wanted to return to his Earlshall of Leuchars, comparatively nearby. So they went back to their ship, to sail the six or seven miles northwards to the Eden mouth, where Malcolm could be dropped off at a small fishing-haven little more than a mile from his house. They would see each other again at Stirling in due course, no doubt. Whether that would be an occasion to look forward to or otherwise remained to be seen, but almost certainly it would be a memorable one.

12

It was three weeks later that the southern lords converged on the great fortress, which possibly might be judged the most significant in all Scotland, midway between the two seas, midway between Lowlands and Highlands, at the first and only place where the Forth could be crossed by bridge, with the impassable Flanders Moss stretching for over a score of miles westwards, dominating all from its mighty rock, impregnable, proud, threatening, holding the gaze from major distances all around and in every direction. A host of banners and standards flew from its towers, all topped by the lion rampant red on gold – however much of a prison this was for the youth whose presence that signified.

Even Robert Bruce was silent as they rode up through the narrow town streets and wynds to the lofty citadel.

Their reception was not the usual one, of having to announce their presence before guarded gatehouse, up-raised drawbridge and barred portcullis, but a welcome of a sort consisting of rank upon rank of armed men under flags and pennants, drawn up in silent array on the tourney-ground, hundreds and hundreds; for of course the newcomers' approach had been observed for an hour and more. No greetings were offered to them from among all those lines of bannermen, spearmen, swordsmen, bowmen and macer-bearers, only silence and straight-ahead staring, all distinctly unnerving.

Past it all they rode, and even at the gatehouse the guards gazed past them, through them, as though the visitors did not exist. Whose notion was this? Who had given these orders? Gamelyn? And what did it imply?

Within the walls, and up at the palace wing they halted, uncertain – as undoubtedly they were meant to be. No grooms came forward to take their horses when they dismounted.

Bruce, eyeing his companions, threw back his shoulders and strode over to the steps which led up to the main entrance, leaving their mounts. And there, within the doorway, at least their presence was acknowledged. A herald in tabard of red and gold awaited them, and asked who they were and what was their business.

"The Lord of Annandale and his fellow-regents to visit the King's Grace," he was told. "Announce it."

"Wait you, my lords," the other said, and left them standing.

"This is beyond all bearing!" Bruce declared. "Folly!"

"Play-acting, rather," Patrick suggested. "They would . . . impress! We should laugh at it, I say."

None actually laughed however. The two bishops in particular were looking unhappy.

When the herald returned he had another with him, this William, Earl of Mar who, after all this strange display of ignoring and distancing, greeted them, or at least Bruce, Patrick and MacDuff, in reasonably friendly fashion, indeed looking all but amused. Without commenting on the situation, he led them upstairs to a lesser hall, and there left them to help themselves to wines and spirits.

It all made a very strange interlude, and had them wondering what would come next.

In fact it was David Lindsay who came next, alone, looking rueful and head-shaking, but obviously glad to see friendly faces.

"At last!" he exclaimed. "Save us, here is something to be thankful for! How long! Patrick! My lords. At last!"

"David!" Patrick went to grip his cousin's arm. "It is good to see you. We have heard naught of you. We judged you to be with the king, but were not sure. All but prisoners?"

"Prisoners, aye! I have not been furth of these walls for

weeks. Months it may be. I know not. Alexander beside himself. He will not speak with his mother. It is all crazy-mad! But, now! Now we may all see sanity prevail!"

"The Queen Marie? She is here?" Bruce asked.

"Yes. With her husband, de Brienne. In league with these Comyns. As from the Pope. I say that Rome is ruling Scotland now. With that Gamelyn. It is insufferable . . ."

The herald arrived back, with Alexander, Earl of Buchan, High Justiciar. With a flick of his hand, the Comyn dismissed Lindsay. "My lords, follow me!" he ordered.

Bruce reached out hands to hold them back. "We are come to confer, Buchan," he said. "Not to act out Comyn behests! And for His Grace's service and the well-being of his kingdom. Only that. How say you?"

"I say come you, my lords. We will confer, yes. It is for this that I take you." And he gestured.

They were led along a corridor to another, larger hall, with benches set round two tables, one large, one smaller. Here they were invited to sit.

They waited.

The herald reappeared, to thump with his staff. "My lords, His Grace's regents," he announced. The regents already there remained sitting, as in filed the Earls of Buchan, Menteith, Strathearn and Mar, followed after a slight interval by Gamelyn. These, eyeing their southern counterparts, went to take seats at the other side of the larger table. No greetings were exchanged.

Another herald come in. "Her Grace the Queen Mother, and King John of Jerusalem," he intoned, and all rose, as Marie de Coucy and her husband entered, a good-looking pair of early middle years. They went over to the small table. All could sit again, save for Gamelyn, who turned to bow to the royal couple and then rapped on the table-top.

"I, Primate of Holy Church and acting Chancellor of this realm, declare this conference in session," he announced, and sat.

King Alexander, clearly, was not to be present.

Equally clear was that Gamelyn was taking the lead.

"Your Graces, my lords from Roxburgh have come to us with proposals for what they claim will be the better government of our young liege-lord's realm," he began. "Needless to say, all here are concerned with such good cause. If, indeed, our efforts may be improved!"

"The kingdom is being well administered," Walter of Menteith added promptly. "In what is betterment desired?"

They all looked at Bruce.

"We see the nation divided, all but between north and south," that man declared. "And King Alexander and his young Queen Margaret held here all but as captives. This is clearly wrongful and of danger to the realm. We, members of the regency council, would see this righted, and are prepared to work with all who are truly loyal to the crown."

"His Grace is no captive," Buchan jerked. "He is well cared for. And sees his kingdom in good hands. And with the blessing of Holy Church and in the care of His Holiness in Rome. As witnessed by the presence here of His Grace's royal mother and the King of Jerusalem."

"Has His Grace been permitted to leave the harsh walls of this fortress since he was taken by force at Kinross?"

"In whose hands was he being held at Kinross? That rogue, Dorward of Atholl's!"

"And is Dorward not still minded to grasp the king, if he can?" That was Menteith. "We keep him safe here."

Gamelyn intervened. "My lords, you came here with proposals? You say for the better governance of the realm. May we ask what these may be?"

"Yes, my lord Primate. We feel that the division in the kingdom should be healed. His Grace is now in his sixteenth year, and before long will be of an age to take over some of the rule. As his royal mother will approve?" Bruce glanced over at the other table. "It is the duty of all his regents and councillors to see that he is handed over a secure, well-maintained and united country. We, my colleagues, are prepared to work to that end with all likeminded."

"Such as Dorward of Atholl?"

"We have no dealings with my lord of Atholl. Nor know what he intends."

"That, at least, is well." Gamelyn looked at the other Comyns. "We can only welcome our friends from Roxburgh and their expressed goodwill. So long as it is for what we judge is the weal of the kingdom. They have brought proposals, I said. May we hear what these are?"

Bruce eyed his companions, who nodded, however tensely. "Until His Grace produces offspring to heir his throne, *I* am heir-presumptive. Therefore I speak for these others, his regents. We are glad of the Pope's care for Scotland, and for the presence here of Queen Marie and King John. But we are aware of dangers. In especial from England. We have been visited, at Roxburgh, by de Ros, Lord of Wark, who tells us that King Henry is much concerned for the well-being of his daughter, the young Queen Margaret, whom he sees as being a prisoner here, with her husband. This he will not tolerate. Earl Simon of Leicester has been ordered to make all necessary moves to right this situation. And none may underestimate his ability!" He paused for a moment. "Also the Plantagenet is angered that an armed force went, at your lordships' behest, to aid the Prince Llewellyn of Wales against English assault, this endangering peace between the English and Scottish realms."

"They went but as a gesture," Buchan put in. "To ensure that the Welsh maintain a threatening position towards the Isle of Man, the young king of which has placed himself under Henry's care, indeed has been knighted by him. This in order that Man does not actively side with the Islesmen and Norsemen who threaten our western Highland coasts."

"Be that as it may, my lord, it was ill done when your people harried and assailed the English of the north-west on their way home. So there is grave danger from King Henry. And war with England is a grievous possibility, which must be avoided at all costs. Therefore a united Scots nation is of the essence."

None could contradict that.

"Henry has other matters on his mind," Gamelyn said. "In France. Gascony. He will think twice before assailing Scotland." He glanced over at Queen Marie and her husband. "The Vatican frowns on the Plantagenet at this time."

The silent pair there nodded.

"Nevertheless, Simon de Montford is concerned in it," Bruce asserted. "De Ros says that Henry has told him to see that his daughter is . . . rescued. And King Alexander. Brought back to where he can reach her. At Roxburgh."

There, it was out, the challenge, the price of their co-operation with the Comyns. The southern lords must have the monarch and his wife back at Roxburgh.

Patrick spoke up into the silence. This was the crux of the matter. Its refusal could lose them their cause. "Roxburgh Castle has been the seat of the monarchs since King David's time. It is His present Grace's home. And sufficiently near to the borderline for convenient visits to and from England. You, my lords, here at Stirling, or at St Andrews, would not find it so inconvenient either. Any more than do I, from Dunbar, Malcolm from Fife, and my lord of Annandale from Ayr and Dumfries."

There it was, the offer, Comyns at Roxburgh. Joint care of the king, of rule.

It was Mar who spoke, after moments of silence. "A presence at Roxburgh? For all lords of regency? Equal as to numbers? The King's Grace in joint caring!"

"*Joint*, my lord?" Bruce said. "We are all lords of regency. One council, acting together. Is it not right? Wise? And time for it! No longer two sides. The kingdom united."

"Numbers?" That was Menteith, all but in a bark.

"There are five of us now, at Roxburgh. How many of you here?"

The Comyns eyed each other. There were six of them:

Menteith, Buchan, Mar, John, Younger of Badenoch, Bishop William of Glasgow, and Gamelyn.

"What of Dorward?" Buchan demanded.

"He is alone! Acts on his own. Leaves the land when he wills. Makes his own terms with the Plantagenet," Bruce said. "I would no longer name him a regent."

"Nor would any of us!" Mar declared. "So, there it is. Without Dorward, we make a quorum. Eleven. On any vexed issue there could be a majority vote."

The Roxburgh group did not want to emphasise that they were in a minority, when they had been seeking to establish a united council, not the two factions. But the discrepancy was there, a source of possible trouble. Bruce looked at Patrick.

They had discussed this possibility on the way here, and that man thought on Christian's suggestion, made more than once.

"I propose that our regency would be strengthened by the appointment of one other," he said, picking his words carefully. "One close to the king, to act as our voice with His Grace. He, the king, is growing fast now, and with opinions of his own. We must guide him for what is best for the realm. It would be to our advantage to have one close to him, whom he knows well and trusts. I would propose Sir David de Lindsay, High Chamberlain, my own cousin, as another regent." That was a long speech for the Cospatrick.

Men considered. All could see advantage in this of the relationship with the young monarch. But it would make their numbers equal again, a dozen on the regency council. It was back to the vote situation.

Gamelyn it was who used the opportunity to advantage. "I would agree to such nomination as useful," he said. "Helping us in our dealings with His Grace. Let us accept it. But I would also propose another addition to the council. The further north of the land is not sufficiently represented on the regency. A worthy representation from those parts would be advisable. I suggest to all here the name of William, Earl of Ross, a sound lord."

None there failed to recognise this suggestion for what it was, a strengthening of Gamelyn's own hand, for Ross was married to a Comyn, daughter to the Prelate's sire. However, it also indicated to all that Gamelyn was accepting the basic concept of a united regency based on Roxburgh.

No voice was raised against.

The Primate went on. "In effect, this all means a new regency council. And that will require the assent of a parliament. Normally, the calling of a parliament demands forty days' notice, to ensure adequate attendance. But in the circumstances prevailing, no such delay, of weeks, is to be considered. The firm rule of the land cannot be postponed, with this of the English threat. I propose that we call a parliament here at Stirling all but immediately. Let us say in four days' time, five. Sufficient for a fair attendance. I judge that we should have little difficulty in gaining parliament's approval for our decisions. Is it agreed?"

None could gainsay that. As men stirred on their benches, Gamelyn turned to look over to the smaller table where Queen Marie and her husband had sat silent throughout. He bowed.

The royal pair rose, to leave the hall. All others stood.

There was much conferring in little groups thereafter, but not much in the way of togetherness between the two former factions, save only William of Mar speaking affably with Bruce, and declaring that it had been a good day's work.

For his part, Patrick went off to see if he could find David Lindsay, to inform him that he was to be a regent of the kingdom. What would his cousin have to say to that?

Five days before a parliament allowed Patrick to get home to Dunbar and to acquaint Christian with all that had transpired, to her general approval. She emphasised, however, that they must watch Gamelyn. That one was going to rule the land, and any who stood in his way had better beware. But she declared that he was an able man, whatever else, and as such might serve the realm, as well as himself, none so ill.

She was pleased over the appointment of David Lindsay to the council, needless to say, and his closeness to Alexander would grow ever more important as the months passed and the king grew towards full manhood. Although the youngest of the regents, he might well prove the most effective.

Back at Stirling, the parliament, reasonably well attended, produced no great surprises and no major debates. The king, his throne backed by a formidable cluster of regents, showed much interest in all that went on, and more than once half rose in his concern over items being discussed, this affecting the others behind him, for the monarch standing would have disrupted the proceedings. Lindsay was able to prove his usefulness by discreetly touching the royal arm on occasion, and thus indicating the form of quiet dignity to be maintained.

Gamelyn, as acting Chancellor, presided and did so efficiently, announcing the new regency council's members for parliament's approval, only one of whom was not present there, the Earl of Ross, who had not had time to come from his far northern fastnesses. His nomination was accepted, for those in the know present were aware that his father, Farquhar, had been a good and loyal supporter of the late monarch. Gamelyn did have one rather surprising announcement to make, however, at least for Patrick and his colleagues, in that he nominated Queen Marie and her husband, de Brienne, as additional regents for parliament to endorse. Although the king's mother and stepfather, these, as well as being non-Scots, had until very recently shown little or no interest in Scottish affairs. But they were, of course, known as being close to Pope Alexander, and no doubt it was as such that Gamelyn put their names forward, thus strengthening his own position.

The nominations were not contested, but they did have

the effect of turning the king round on his throne, to stare with no great affection on the pair behind.

The Primate went on to underline the importance and value of the Vatican's especial interest and goodwill towards Scotland, particularly with the present English animosity showing itself over the Scots support for the Welsh, as a counter to the Manx and Hebridean threats, backed by Hakon of Norway. Indeed the major preoccupation of the parliament became taken up with this situation, and fears that John of the Isles, the great Somerled's present successor, was making very real preparations for war, to form a sort of island empire, with Norse backing, of the Inner and Outer Hebrides, the entire West Highland coastal area, the Orkney and Shetland Isles and the Viking-dominated north of Ireland. This threat could not be ignored. Somerled had called himself King of the Isles, and this John appeared to be intent on making it more than any mere style and title. The situation had to be watched carefully and preparations made to deal with it, especially in view of the present English attitudes, and the Plantagenet's hostility towards the Vatican.

Young Alexander demonstrated obvious interest and concern over this matter. After all, his father had died on an expedition against the turbulent Islesmen. David Lindsay's hand had to be extended again.

One or two appointments to offices of state had to be made, including that of High Constable, for Buchan, who was already High Justiciar. No doubt this was Gamelyn's way of ensuring that, in his all but complete takeover of power, he retained senior Comyn support. His new elevation of the Bishop of Glasgow to be Chancellor, also ensured further faithful backing.

The parliament was adjourned, and Alexander could rise, at last, and depart.

Patrick wondered whether he and his friends had done the right, the wise, thing in thus, in effect, enabling Gamelyn to govern the nation. Would it have happened anyway, without them? Christian's approval, but with her warning to watch that man, was all very well. But watching implied readiness to act, if need be. Act? In what way? And to what effect?

13

As Christian had prophesied, at Roxburgh thereafter David Lindsay did prove himself to be the most effective of the regents, although the youngest, this because he was always there, with the king, while the others were not, save for Queen Marie and her husband. All were great lords, with their own wide lands or dioceses to oversee, and Gamelyn necessarily based on St Andrews. So David's influence with their fast-developing liege-lord was very significant. How fast that advancement was growing Patrick learned when his cousin informed him that Alexander was now sleeping with his young wife regularly, and clearly enjoying the exercise, Margaret for that matter seeming nowise reluctant. Robert Bruce might not be remaining heir-presumptive for much longer.

Alexander was greatly cheered over his return to Roxburgh, revelling in the freedom of it all there after the narrow confines of Stirling Castle. Indeed almost every day he was for riding abroad, often taking Margaret with him, ranging the dales of Tweed and Teviot and Lauder, the valleys of Jed and Kale and Gala, of the Blackadder and the Whiteadder, even getting as far as Dunbar on two occasions, but irritated by having to be saddled with an escort other than Lindsay. It was seldom that any of the other regents joined in these excursions, the queen mother being no horsewoman, she and her husband occupying one of the succession of individual towers which made up Roxburgh Castle on its peninsula between the two great rivers, and roosting therein and keeping very much to themselves. Just what their reason was for staying in

Scotland was not clear, save that presumably it was on the Pope's orders.

Patrick had his own preoccupation after that parliament. The talk of a warlike campaign by John of the Isles, with Norse backing, concerned him in more than the military aspect. If Hakon involved himself in that warfare, what of the timber trade which had become so important for his earldoms? The loss of that would be a serious blow to his people, not only in the revenues. Would it have to cease if the Norsemen aided the Islesmen? After all, the trade was advantageous to Hakon also, the onward sale of the wood to the Baltic states. Must such commerce end because of conflict in faraway lands and seas? Christian said that she did not see that it must, when it was to mutual benefit, and would have no real effect on any hostilities.

Patrick decided that he would make a personal visit to Bergen, rather than sending Cousin William, to have word with King Hakon, not so much as a regent of Scotland but as the merchant Earl of Dunbar and March. It was now May, and the sailing season begun.

But just before he was due to set off, he learned that the said sailing conditions had also commended themselves to others. John of the Isles had led a large fleet of longships and birlinns westwards round to Donegal, where the English were fairly firmly established and could threaten the inclusion of all Ulster in his ambition for the Celtic-Norse confederation or empire. And while further south, at Connemara, he had been assailed by another fleet, under the English governor thereof, one Sir Jordan de Exeter, in which battle John had gained a notable victory, returning to his Hebrides in triumph. Was this ominous or otherwise for Scotland? It would encourage the Islesmen and their Viking allies; but could also worry the Plantagenet, and make him the less likely to indulge in ventures elsewhere. Christian suggested that it made her husband's visit to Norway the more useful, necessary, not only over the timber but, as a regent, he could urge Hakon's non-participation in the Islesmen's cause.

Before he left, the word came that Dorward had left his Atholl territories for England. Good news this, or otherwise?

Skateraw Meg took Patrick across the Norse Sea in good time, the winds favourable. It was four years since he had been in Bergen, and the trading had developed notably. That ought to help with Hakon.

Unfortunately it transpired that the Norse monarch was not at Bergen meantime, having gone to visit young King Erik of Denmark at the castle of Kronberg near Elsinore. The Danish situation was a strange and sad one. The nation's nobles and prelates, under Archbishop Erlandsen, had risen in revolt against King Christopher three years before, and that monarch slain, leaving twelve-year-old Erik as heir. Now this boy was in the care of the archbishop, all but a prisoner. Hakon, who had always tended to dominate both Denmark and Sweden, the last also under a youthful king, was very much concerned over the situation, and was keeping an eye on the ruling prelate and the boy.

So, to reach Hakon, it meant for Patrick a quite lengthy diversion southwards, some two hundred miles down to the Skagerrak, that quite notorious passage between the two kingdoms, where the Norse Sea tides were constricted to meet those of the Baltic, at the Kattegat, as warned about by Dand Shaw on the previous visit as dangerous, the joining of these waters at times creating a riot of waves and winds, which shipmen had learned to beware of. However, as Patrick pointed out, all the Scots timber from Bergen had to be ferried down through these passages to the Baltic ports which were its destination, so the conditions could not be so very bad. Dand explained that the logs were towed, in the form of great rafts, behind longships rowed by very skilled oarsmen who knew the safest routes and every mile of the way.

Turning eastwards round the southernmost tip of Norway, which it seemed was known as the Naze, with its great cliffs and inlets, they entered the Skagerrak, and soon were seeing Denmark, low-lying, far to their right. At first there was little alarming about this waterway; after all it was seventy miles across, wider than the mouth of the Firth of Forth. They had almost one hundred miles of this to sail, wind behind them, before they would reach the difficult waters, it was announced. So the rest of that day was passed without the looked-for hazards.

It was early evening, with the Skagerrak beginning to bend southwards, and narrowing as it did so, before Patrick recognised that Dand Shaw had not been scare-mongering. They were entering the Kattegat here, the width of this narrowing from being seventy miles across to less than twenty, and at the same time suddenly and notably shallowing. Their vessel's movements reflected these abruptly changed conditions, not only heaving and rolling but plunging and swinging this way and that with the crosswinds, apparently caused by the Norway heights on the one side and the Danish lowlands on the other. Sail had to be reduced to keep the vessel under control, the two steersmen busy. And it would get worse before it bettered, Dand said. But with night approaching, he was not going to risk onward passage, and would draw in, on the right, to shelter behind the long narrow peninsula which was the extreme northern tip of Denmark, known as Skagen or the Skaw. Daylight was demanded for their ongoing progress. They were opposite and in sight of the Swedish coast, and apparently the city and port of Gothenberg not far off – where the notorious Goths had come from. Presumably their descendants, the mariners here, must be a bold and hardy race.

Swinging westwards, and in consequence rolling peri-lously, they made for the shelter of the Skaw. They were thankful, presently, to settle for the night in the lee of this thrusting horn of low land, which formed a blessed break-water.

Patrick knew now why the Vikings were such able seamen.

In the morning light they were on their uneasy way

again, tacking to and fro down the Kattegat, which was widening, but producing the additional hazard of having islands and reefs in its shallows, to be avoided. Dand said that in some respects this resembled the Sea of the Hebrides, save that there were no down-draughts to complicate matters, this because of the lack of mountains, but a sufficiency of tidal overfalls caused by the uneven and shallow bed of it all.

There was another hundred miles of this, it seemed, before they would reach their destination, where the great island of Zealand all but closed this Kattegat, save for a narrow sound on either side, where the tides ran the more riotously. They headed for the one on the east, the Oresond, where only four miles separated Denmark from Sweden. And here, at its narrowest, they found the low cape of Elsinore, where thankfully they could put into a port of sorts. Kronberg Slot, or castle, lay just to the north, on a crag of the headland.

Their arrival created no stir at this haven, none so far from Copenhagen, the Danish capital, a mere thirty-odd miles.

On his previous visit, Patrick had not found Hakon difficult to approach, adopting little of the pomp and ritual required by some monarchs. On this occasion, although in a different nation, it was the same. Arriving at the slot, alone and on foot, with no trappings of rank or style, the caller was accepted without fuss or question by fierce-looking but casual guards, these even less suspicious than the Bergen ones, and thereafter conducted across a wide, square courtyard to a long two-storeyed range of buildings. These Scandinavian castles were very different from the Scots ones, not nearly so defensively built, basically just four steeple-like towers linked by these ranges of lower-set apartments, very commodious but scarcely intended to withstand siege, more palaces than strongholds. Yet their atmosphere was anything but palatial, all very casual and informal.

The caller was brought into Hakon's presence without

ceremony. Whether the Archbishop Erlandsen was here, or the boy King Erik was not clear, but if so these were not with Hakon. Patrick found that great bull of a man drinking with a group of companions, laughing loudly while fondling the person of a maidservant who was there refilling tankards of schnapps from a large flagon, her clothing much disarrayed but herself appearing to be nowise upset by the proceedings, no doubt quite used to it. The monarch scarcely noticed Patrick's entry at first, and when he did, obviously failed to recognise him.

The visitor had to speak loudly above the chatter and laughter, in his limited Dutch, to introduce himself as the Jarl Patrick of Dunbar in Schottland. Then Hakon did remember him, and banged a fist on the table, but far from unwelcoming, shouting something and continuing to laugh. He gestured to the giggling female to offer the visitor spirits from her flagon.

Patrick wondered whether there was anyone here who could speak English, like the priest at Bergen, his Dutch no better than Hakon's. He tried a greeting in his own tongue, and had it returned in some fashion by two of the company, to more hoots of laughter. Were these Danes better linguists than the Norwegians? he wondered.

Sipping his schnapps warily, recalling its potency, he announced that he had come to see King Hakon, from Scotland, on the subject of his trade in timber, as he had come before, and that he was pleased that it prospered between them. He hoped that this would continue.

This was translated, how accurately he knew not, but it did have Hakon banging on the table again, and nodding. Encouraged, he went on to declare that he came because there was talk of war arising between John, Lord of the Isles, and King Alexander of Scots, in which it was feared that King Hakon might possibly become involved. He hoped not, however. If this warfare did come about, then he hoped the more that such hostilities would not interfere with nor endanger the said trade in timber between himself and the king.

That declaration took a deal of rendering, with some debate between the two translators and others as to detail. But presumably the gist of it got through to Hakon, who nodded and waved his tankard and said something which, by his entirely genial expression, Patrick took to be the desired assurance.

He went on to assert that he had every intention of continuing to send timber, as in the past, and trusted that it would be paid for as always. There ought to be no difficulty as regards shipping, with any warfare and battle confined to the Sea of the Hebrides and the Irish and Manx waters, not the Norse Sea. This produced more nods, but also an announcement from Hakon which, as turned into halting English, revealed that more oakwood was desired, and less elm and birch. This was reinforced by the inducement of a still better price to be paid for the said oak, provided that it was mature wood.

Acknowledging that approvingly, Patrick took the opportunity to declare that he hoped in fact that King Hakon would *not* join in the Lord of the Isles' threatened warfare. He said that King Alexander had conceded the Inner and Outer Hebrides, as far as Islay and Gigha to the south, to the Islesmen, and this under Norse overlordship, thus there was no need for any actual battle. He said that he spoke thus as one of the regents of Scotland, and besought Hakon so to advise and urge John of the Isles. A conference, if so desired, could be held to settle claims and differences. No need for hostilities.

Hakon did not nod now, but wagged his head and launched into vehement speech. And in this the word Kintyre was more than once discernible, the monarch reinforcing the point by bangings of his tankard.

Patrick did not actually need to have this tirade translated. That word Kintyre was sufficient for him. It of course referred to the notorious claim by Hakon's predecessor, King Magnus Barelegs, of a century and a half before, that the Norse throne was entitled to every isle of the Scottish west coast which the monarch could sail his longship round, and this was accepted by the weak King Edgar of Scots, this exploited by Magnus's famous feat of having his vessel, himself at the helm, dragged on rollers of round logs over the mile of ground separating West and East Loch Tarbert at the head of Kintyre. An old story but still to be contested, it seemed.

Patrick was not in a position, there and then, to enter into refutation of this old claim, which he knew would never be conceded by Scotland. All he could say was that this matter was not worth going to war over, and that peace, friendship and trade between the nations were much more valuable.

Hakon scowled, shrugged, muttered something and pointed a finger at Patrick, to what effect it was impossible to tell. At any rate, since he could do no more than this, and certainly did not want to get into any dispute, he decided to take it as a sign of dismissal. He bowed to Hakon, nodded to his helpful translators, laid down his still half-full tankard, and backed out of the royal presence. He had done what he had mainly come for, ensured that the timber trade could go on, war or none. No indication was given that he should linger.

Seeing no sign of young King Erik nor the Archbishop Erlandsen, he made his way back to his ship. It was only early afternoon. Would they get as far up this Kattegat as the shelter of the Skaw before darkness? Then home, with the wind against them now, in five days? Or six?

He was glad that he had not drunk more of that schnapps, a fiery liquor. What was it made from? Their own whisky was strong enough. But this!

14

Patrick returned to Dunbar, to extraordinary news. The regency was missing two members. The new Chancellor, William, Bishop of Glasgow, had died, of natural causes apparently; but Walter Comyn, Earl of Menteith, also was dead, and of all things allegedly poisoned by his own wife – she who had brought him the earldom, heiress in her own right. This scarcely believable allegation was, to some extent, substantiated, for the lady had promptly departed for England thereafter with an English knight, one Sir John Russell.

The repercussions to this remarkable deed were, needless to say, almost as dramatic, the like never before heard of. For not only had Menteith to be replaced as a regent, but his widow, proclaimed guilty of murder, was forthwith to be excommunicated, due to be executed if she returned to Scotland, and therefore unfit to have possession of an earldom. The couple had no legitimate offspring, but an illegitimate daughter was married to Walter's grand-nephew, a William Comyn. So the younger brother of the High Steward, Walter, who had married the countess's younger sister, claimed the title and lands, this despite Comyn protests. So not only was the regency, but much of the nation itself, in a state of upset and division. Gamelyn was faced with a variety of problems, and on no small scale.

Patrick found himself involved in some degree, reluctant as he was to be so. For the regency became divided again over it all, with the Roxburgh faction supporting this Walter Stewart, brother of one of themselves, while Buchan and the Badenoch Comyns sought the earldom for the illegitimate daughter and her husband. And however much Gamelyn would have preferred to throw his weight behind these, the fact was that the succession to an earldom came under the authority of the monarch himself, by long tradition, earls the successors of the ancient *ri*, or lesser kings of the Albannach monarchy, and nominated by the Ard Righ or High King. And young Alexander, needless to say, supported his High Steward's brother. So although Gamelyn was in effect ruling Scotland, he suddenly had the monarch and half the regency against him in this, and could not deny the royal authority. He did what he could by nominating a new regent, in the person of Robert Menzies, or de Meyners, who had Comyn connections and Highland estates. Meanwhile, the English knight, Russell, was claiming the earldom in the right of his new-wed wife.

It was into this chaotic situation that it became known that young Queen Margaret was pregnant. More uncertainty. What would King Henry's reaction be? It looked as though the end was in sight of Bruce of Annandale's heirship-presumptive to the throne. Which would much lessen his influence, and therefore that of his Roxburgh colleagues.

As well as all this, Gamelyn had another problem to face: the appointment of a new Bishop of Glasgow; also finding a new Chancellor of the realm. For the bishopric, he nominated one Nicholas, Archdeacon of Teviotdale, linked with the abbacy of Kelso, just why was uncertain, for he was a little-known cleric, and jealousy was aroused. But he was sent off to Rome to be consecrated by the Pope, and was not long in returning, but *un*consecrated. It appeared that the pontiff had demanded from him a substantial percentage of the revenues of this, one of the richest sees in Scotland, which the archdeacon had been bold enough to refuse – some suggested because Gamelyn himself had bargained for them in exchange for his nomination. So Glasgow remained without a bishop; that is, until Pope Alexander announced that he had appointed an English cleric, one John of Cheam, to the position, who was presumably prepared to part with a proportion of the diocesan wealth. Holy Church in Scotland seethed, as no doubt did the Primate himself. But Gamelyn could not afford to fall out with the Vatican, the real source of his power. He had to accept this John of Cheam.

Patrick had indeed come back to a disturbed and all but bewildered land that summer and autumn. It would be a year long to be remembered. But at least John of the Isles refrained from taking any armed steps towards the formation of his Celtic-Norse confederation meantime, whether on King Hakon's advice or otherwise.

Also, fear of angry English reaction over the Comyn Welsh foray and the returning force's behaviour in Cumbria receded, for there was serious trouble south of the border. Henry Plantagenet was behaving unwisely, at least from his nobility's point of view; his brother-in-law's also, it seemed. Not only was he demanding large forces of men for his efforts to regain Gascony, but he was paying the seemingly avaricious Pope Alexander, who had been hostile towards him for long, the enormous sum of 135,000 silver marks to improve relations with the Vatican, and indeed to make his second son, Edmund, King of Sicily, and offering a crusading army into the bargain. Simon de Montford, and Gloucester also, much disapproved of all this, siding with the other English earls and lords, but were being ignored. So there was unlikely to be any trouble for Scotland from that direction for some time.

When the Plantagenet did turn his thoughts towards Scotland that winter, it was in an altogether different context: concern for his daughter, Queen Margaret, now far advanced in her pregnancy. Strangely, he all but insisted that Alexander brought her down to London for her delivery, where he averred that he had much better physicians and midwives to ease the birth pangs than were likely to be available in Scotland. Presumably he looked upon the northern kingdom as a semi-barbarous land, incapable of providing the like services. As it happened, Alexander and his advisers were quite happy to fall in with this proposal, since it could mark an end to disharmony with England; although whether the long ride southwards was the best regimen for a young mother-to-be was questionable. So it was agreed that the visit should be paid, and sooner rather than later, in the circumstances. If Henry was determined that his daughter should remain in London for the birth, Alexander might well come home before that, for he could not be away from his kingdom for overlong, he recognised, at his regents' urging. Still not yet twenty years he was not greatly interested in the giving-birth process.

So a suitably illustrious entourage was arranged to accompany the monarch southwards, with Patrick and of course David Lindsay included, with David's wife to act lady-in-waiting and attendant for the younger Margaret. Patrick rejoiced that his Christian suggested that she might also go along on this occasion. It had been long since she had done anything of the sort; but now their children were old enough to be left on their own.

Meanwhile Gamelyn made a new appointment to the vacant chancellorship, one William Wishart, Archdeacon of St Andrews, a choice which all agreed was a wise one for that prestigious and important position, for Wishart was a sound and able cleric, proven so at St. Andrews, the headquarters of the Church.

Expert and dashing a horseman as Alexander was, he and his like had to restrain their impatience sternly on that lengthy journey to London, with an heir to the throne as precious member of the company, although not yet born, Queen Margaret very uncertain as to just when delivery was due. At least she had a sufficiency of feminine companions to aid and advise her, with Christian, Lindsay's Margaret and Matilda Cantalupe. Estimates as to how long their slow progress would take varied, for not only the pace of it all was involved, but the matter of suitable nightly stops, for they made a great company, well over one hundred, beside the required escort, and only very large establishments, great abbeys, priories and major castles

155

would be able to cater for them all. They could rely on hospitality, however, since they travelled at the King of England's invitation. So, much planning had to be done, de Ros of Wark being a great help in this, familiar with routes and premises, and moreover the Plantagenet's official representative. He calculated that they might be able to average thirty miles per day, more or less, depending on the available stopping-places; so twelve days ought to be about the sum of it, provided that the weather was reasonably kind. The winter days would be short anyway. Inevitably it would be a somewhat zigzagging journey, no direct route being possible on account of finding the necessary large establishments. Outriders would be sent ahead to warn their involuntary hosts as to who and what they might expect. Etal, then, for the first night, where there was a priory, and Brinkburn for the next, all being well.

There was a notable lack of Comyns in the company, the Welsh and Cumbrian matter inhibiting association with King Henry; and the so-called Roxburgh group were well content with that.

Queen Margaret was cheerful and uncomplaining, and laughingly made no secret of the reason for her necessarily frequent stops by the wayside, however unqueenly these might seem. Suitable sailcloth screens were taken along for this purpose. Alexander rode well ahead of the female contingent, and was apt to dash off on brief side excursions to view this and that, as curbs for impatience. Patrick remained with the ladies, happy so to do. Cousin David would have done the like, but royal commands said otherwise.

They crossed Tweed at Wark ford, a strung-out cavalcade. Would they be home by Yuletide, minus the queen?

At St. Mary's Priory at Etal, almost exactly thirty miles, they were well received. It was a nunnery, but a large one, and near enough to the Scots border always to be tactfully welcoming. The women of the party were installed well apart from the men, not even eating together, this occasioning some raillery. The next day they covered a roughly similar distance to Brinkburn Priory, of the Black Canons, near Rothbury, where at least they could dine in company, although they had to sleep apart. Patrick complained to Christian that, if it had not been for Malcolm Canmore's Queen Margaret Atheling, who got the Celtic Church put down in favour of the Roman Catholic one, this separation at nights would never have been imposed, for the worshipping community founded by St. Columba had not been concerned with celibacy, and its sway had extended down through this Northumberland and on to the Roman Hadrian's Wall. His wife told him that probably such abstinence on occasion was good for him, so long as it did not endure all the way to London, which even she might find overmuch. Did they have to put up at religious establishments *every* night? He pointed out that few castles and manors, even of great lords, were commodious enough to entertain their present numbers.

They had to swing somewhat westwards the day following, to reach Hexham on the upper Tyne, almost forty miles this time, but the queen not complaining. Hexham was one of the largest and most important religious communities in the north of England, and linked with Scotland in that the great priory, larger than many abbeys, was dedicated to St. Andrew, Scotland's patron saint, indeed one of its relics of Peter's brother having been brought to St. Andrews town by St. Regulas. Here men and women did not have to separate overnight, for the whole township was an appendage of the priory, and those who so desired could choose to lodge in non-sacred quarters. Patrick and Christian shared a commodious house with David and his Margaret.

And so it went on, ever southwards, although with frequent slantings east and west to reach suitable overnight resting-places. It proved that their calculations of a thirty-mile-a-day progress were an underestimate, and forty, and even more, became accepted, especially once they got down into the level lands beyond Yorkshire and conditions were easier for horses, and there were fewer rivers to find fords across. So in fact they reduced their travelling time by two days, this without causing any worries or especial discomforts for the mother-to-be.

At the mighty Tower of London their reception was superficially welcome, but an underlying atmosphere of tension was not to be disguised. Henry's troubles with his lords were not to be hidden, and although Simon of Leicester and de Clare of Gloucester were present and helpful towards the visitors, the latter could not but be aware of enmity and disapproval prevailing.

Alexander and his advisers, of course, could not seem to take sides in this divergence, but neither could they pretend not to notice it all, an uncomfortable situation. Henry's pretence that all was well with his plans and negotiations was obviously false, and his problems underlined noticeably by the fact that his elder son, Edward, was clearly critical of his father, while his brother Edmund, he who was hopefully to be made King of Sicily, took the opposite view – and Edward was of an aggressive nature. The Scots had come a long way to become involved in the like.

The Earl Simon told Bruce privately that he feared that there would be outright hostilities between the Plantagenet and his barons. They were just not going to pay the enormous dues demanded to procure the Pope's favour, any more than they were going to provide large numbers of men to form a crusading army in present circumstances. De Montford was trying to persuade his brother-in-law of the folly of it all, and the dangers, but with little success. Henry was obdurate.

In it all, Queen Margaret's condition tended to be, as it were, pushed into the background, although this was the real object of the visit. She was interviewed and examined by the royal physicians, who seemed satisfied that all was well so far, and that there were no signs of premature labour. Indeed the opinion seemed to be that the birth would not take place until the end of January or beginning of February, much later than had been anticipated, and that was six or eight weeks ahead yet.

Alexander was certainly not going to hang around that uneasy court for anything like that time. In fact he was eager to get home for Christmas and Yule, which he was apt to make much of, the more especially when he realised that he was not yet going to get Margaret's dowery-moneys, still unpaid, and one of his main reasons for agreeing to come south thus. With Henry desperate to raise the necessary large sum for the Vatican, he could nowise afford to produce this long-delayed subscription. Alexander decided that it was all a wasted journey, although it did relieve his and his regents' minds of any fear that there might be English trouble for Scotland over the Welsh affair, preoccupations here being otherwise directed. What Margaret Plantagenet's feelings were over being left thus was not voiced by her. Henry agreed that if, by any sad chance, Alexander was to die, the newborn child would be accepted as monarch of Scotland, and would be sent there, with the mother, in the care of an illustrious escort. His son-in-law did not think, however, that he was likely to die on the way home. So it was for Scotland, and at speed, leaving Matilda Cantalupe with the queen.

15

It was almost three months before Queen Margaret arrived home, although they heard of the birth of a daughter before that. Alexander was somewhat disappointed that it should be a girl to become heir to his throne, but there would always be other opportunities to gain a son. They would call the child after her mother.

The party of English bishops and lords who escorted mother and daughter northwards also brought grievous news. The dispute between Henry and his barons had reached a dire stage, sufficiently so for Earl Simon to organise something like a confrontation, at Oxford, between monarch and his principal subjects, in an attempt to reach some agreement. This had been less than successful, the Plantagenet not yielding an inch in his demands, and the nobility the more resentful. These thereupon drew up what amounted to a declaration of revolt; and in this pass de Montford and de Clare came down on the side of the lords, not the monarch. Henry, in fury, departed for Windsor, and England was in a state of potential civil war.

By contrast, Scotland had not been so comparatively peaceful for long. The Comyns, lacking Menteith, and Buchan less than well in health, lay fairly low, as they might, with their Gamelyn proving to be an effective ruler of the land as well as the Church, and the new Chancellor, Wishart, ably supporting him, but being careful not to arouse the hostility of the king and the other regents. So the realm could enjoy a period of unusual quiet, and men could go about their daily affairs and pursuits without demands by the crown, even when these pursuits were not always of a worthy and creditable nature, oddly making the justiciars busier than usual.

Patrick was able to do what he best liked, remain at home with Christian and their children, and superintend his various trading ventures. His father-in-law found occasion to declare that he clearly had been born to be a merchant-prince rather than the Cospatrick.

And then, in May, there was an event that could herald change, not only for Scotland but for all Christendom. Pope Alexander suddenly died, his controversial rule over.

The effect was as profound as it was widespread. He was succeeded by a very different pontiff, a Frenchman named Jacques Pantaléon, known as the Patriarch of Jerusalem, who took the style of Urban the Fourth, and much more pacific, as his chosen name implied. Despite his late patriarchate, he was much less concerned with crusading efforts, probably being wiser as to the difficulties; also less inclined to interfere in the governance of nations, and so less demanding of moneys. Scotland found itself no longer under the papal frown; and Henry Plantagenet was unsure about the nominal kingdom of Sicily for his second son, although fairly quickly he learned that a son of the Emperor Frederick had been appointed to that honour, to his mortification. Marie de Coucy and her husband promptly departed from Roxburgh for France, as no longer representing the Vatican in Scotland, no sorrow engendered by their going. Gamelyn was now too firmly established to be unseated, but undoubtedly he would tread the more warily until he saw how the new regime at Rome reacted. The Comyns' power could be said to be lessened, and in consequence Alexander's authority strengthened. Indeed David Lindsay told Patrick that the young monarch was talking about assuming full royal power and rule on his nineteenth birthday.

There were sighs of relief, not only in Scotland, although King Henry must be having to reconsider his position.

There was one shadow on the Scots horizon, however.

John of the Isles, who had been fairly inactive since his naval victory off Connemara, was beginning to make threatening noises again, and claiming that King Hakon was offering him fullest support. This worried more than Patrick, especially as word reached Scotland that Hakon had recommended to the new Pope that his personal chaplain, one Gilbert, should be made Bishop of the Hebrides, a somewhat ominous appointment. Patrick and Lindsay persuaded Alexander to send an envoy to Bergen to declare that while he had no objection to this new prelate becoming Bishop of Shetland and Orkney, already under Norse control, to name him of the Hebrides was erroneous and unacceptable.

In the spring, now 1262, the Earl of Ross was sent with a Highland force to make an armed progress through the large Isle of Skye, this to warn John of the Isles to keep the peace. It was to be hoped that these gestures would have the desired effect of discouraging any attempt against the West Highland mainland.

Margaret's baby throve, to her father's satisfaction as well as her mother's, for Alexander got over his disappointment at not gaining a son, and became very affectionate towards his small progeny, displaying her to all with pride. Christian, for one, was amused that her father should be dispossessed of his long-held position as heir-presumptive to the throne by this tiny scrap of female humanity.

Dorward was said to be biding his time in England, and keeping fairly close to King Henry.

On 4th September the great day dawned, Alexander's birthday. Six weeks previously a parliament had been called, for Edinburgh Castle, with the required forty days' notice, Roxburgh considered to be less central for so much of the country. It was to be a declaration and a dedication rather than a celebration. All was carefully planned, to represent a new stage in the nation's history.

There was a great attendance for this special session, the

great hall of the fortress packed, Sir Alexander Seton, High Sennachie, now to be styled Lord Lyon King of Arms, and his assistant heralds concerned that all must go without a hitch in a ceremonial new to all present, the loftiest in the land given their instructions in no uncertain terms, at the monarch's command.

When the earls who were not otherwise involved, like the bishops and mitred abbots, had taken their seats, two prelates entered and climbed on to the dais, side by side, to a trumpet-blast, Gamelyn the Primate and Bishop William Wishart, the Chancellor. These two went to stand before the throne, but facing the hall.

Then, to another flourish, in paced the regents, or the seven of them whose continued status was not in doubt: Bruce, Mar, Fife, Buchan, the Steward, Lindsay and Patrick. These went to stand behind the throne-like chair. More trumpeting, and after a pause Queen Margaret appeared, with her child in her arms, all present now standing. This was an unusual event, queens-consort not normally present at a parliament, save up in the minstrels' gallery. She went and sat on a lesser chair near the throne, little Princess Margaret, wide-eyed, showing a lively interest in all that went on, particularly the colourful robes and trappings of the prelates. All others remained on their feet.

Finally, to a long blaring of the trumpets, the King of Arms led in Alexander himself, wearing his crown, to loud cheering. He went over to the throne, but there still stood, so all must do the same, even the queen rising.

Alexander raised a hand, and spoke. "My lords spiritual and temporal, officers of state, all commissioners to this parliament and representatives of the royal burghs, I come before you on this my birthday, commencing my twenty-second year. On this day it is my royal decision to declare my minority at an end, and to assume full age, maturity and manhood. And with it, as is my right, the supreme rule of my kingdom. From this day forth I require no regents; councillors, advisers, guides and assistants yes, but no regents." He turned, and inclined his head to the seven behind the throne. "To these, who have served me and my realm so very well over the years, I give my thanks and praise. I shall continue to value their guidance and help. But from today responsibility for rule and governance passes to myself. I pray God that I will discharge it all worthily, to the benefit of all my subjects and the nation's weal. I require this parliament to note and accept my royal will." He turned again. "My lords, I salute and thank you all. You may go."

All seven bowed and, led by Bruce, filed out from behind the throne and went down from the dais to their respective benches in the hall.

Chancellor Wishart banged on the table before him with his gavel. "God save the King's Grace!" he intoned. And everywhere the cry was taken up: "God save the King's Grace!" On and on it went.

Alexander settled the crown more firmly on his brow, and sat down on the throne. When the noise subsided, Wishart turned to the queen.

"Your Grace and Princess Margaret," he said, and gestured aloft. It was the signal for Margaret and child to go up to the gallery, where Christian, Margaret Lindsay and other ladies were already seated, to watch all.

Gamelyn now raised a hand. "Sire, my lords and friends all," he said, "I rejoice, on this most especial occasion, to approach an even greater power than His Grace Alexander, our loving and almighty Father in heaven, for his blessing on this new rule as well as reign, to cherish and strengthen this kingdom, to guide and lead this parliament, and to bless us all. This in the name of Jesus Christ his son, and of his Holy Spirit. Amen."

He turned to bow to the monarch, and went down to his place among the prelates.

The Chancellor banged his gavel again. "I declare this session of the king-in-parliament open," he announced. "Let us attend well to its business."

There was, in fact, not a great deal of business to be

transacted. Sundry speeches of loyal respect and congratulation were made by representatives of different groups and associations; the Earl of Ross reported that he had found no enthusiasm for John of the Isles' ambitions in Skye; and one or two deputy justiciars had to be replaced. That was all. But the king was not finished yet. He declared that he was going to lead a great celebratory procession down into the city, and through its streets the mile to the Abbey of the Holy Rood, established by his great-great-grandsire, David, of blessed memory, where they would make another act of worship and prayer for the realm, somewhat longer than that here pronounced, the Lord Bishop of St Andrews leading them again. This was said with just a hint of irony. The Lord Lyon King of Arms would assemble the procession. He stood, and strode out.

So, with much to-do, and inevitably some delay, the great cavalcade was marshalled, in due order of precedence; and with trumpeting and the clash of cymbals, Alexander in the lead, the entire parliament marched down to the city, something never before seen, to the astonishment of the citizenry. The ladies would remain at the castle, where a banquet would follow, for all, in due course.

Alexander the Third had come of age, and was determined to evidence it.

No longer a regent, and thankful therefor, Patrick could look forward to the sort of life that he preferred.

16

Although it was northwards that trouble might be looked for in the months that followed, it was in the south that major upset took place. Henry Plantagenet, despite those Provisions of Oxford, was still all but at war with a large proportion of his barons, Simon de Montford trying to win his brother-in-law over to wiser policies. But the son, Prince Edward, having become very assertive, came back from being his father's governor of Gascony, and urged him to put down the barons by force of arms. An army was raised, in effect led by Edward, and met the mustered rebellious lords at Lewes, in the Sussex Downs. There the royal army was defeated, amid great slaughter, and Henry and son both captured, to become, in effect, prisoners of de Montford, who sought to quieten the land in the name of the monarch.

This news, although it did concern the Scots and Alexander, more particularly Queen Margaret of course, did not worry them unduly, for de Montford had proved himself an able and wise influence in the past, and probably England would be better governed by him than heretofore.

Then, at Hereford, Edward effected his escape, and promptly set about raising another royalist army to challenge the victorious barons and put down Earl Simon, bringing over troops from Gascony. The nation was sorely divided.

But all this took months, and meanwhile the feared trouble in the north began to develop, or at least, at this stage, in the east. For one of Patrick's timber-ships returning from Bergen brought the news that King Hakon was assembling a great fleet, the largest heard of for long, as many as one hundred and fifty ships, it was reported, with the declared intention of coming over to the Sea of the Hebrides to assist John of the Isles in his efforts to establish a Celtic-Norse confederation. Not only this, but that he had ordered young Magnus, King of Man, to meet him with another, although lesser, fleet and to join him at the Orkney and Shetland isles, for a descent upon the Scottish West Highland coast.

So Patrick's pleas had been in vain.

Alexander and his advisers, including Patrick, who was accepted as the Norse expert, were warned, and in something of a quandary. This of great fleets was a problem for them, for Scotland just did not possess the like to seek to engage in sea battles. Merchant-ships yes, many, but not galleys, longships and birlinns, necessary to counter the Norsemen and their allies. Hakon would know that, as would John of the Isles. What was to be done anent this threat?

They came to recognise that there was, in fact, nothing, so far as sea warfare was concerned. They could only seek to concentrate on their land-based armed strength. They could marshal many men, horsed and foot. After all, Hakon and John, however supreme on the water, would have to land to effect and consolidate any attempt at conquest. They must then be met, and shown whose the land was. This would be difficult, admittedly, since they could descend anywhere along hundreds of miles of coastline, and it could not all be guarded, far from it. But if the invaders sought to hold the areas where they landed, and settle there, then the Scots forces would demonstrate their superior strength. That West Highland seaboard, mountainous and cut into by innumerable sea lochs, was not the easiest to fight over, all recognised; but that would apply to the enemy also.

So what was needed was a large army, ready to muster and march at short notice; and also a smaller but very mobile force, to patrol and watch over that lengthy and awkward coastline, this to discourage landings, and if and when they took place, swiftly to inform the king, and he would seek to bring his large army up to the invaded locations. Also, at the same time, to gather such shipping as they could, to distract the enemy fleets and try to prevent aid being sent to their assailed comrades on land. The Campbells of Argyll and the Earl of Ross, with sundry loyal Highland clans, ought to be able to provide this help; it was in their own interests anyway.

That was as far as king and councillors could decide, at this stage, while they waited to see if and when Hakon acted.

They did not have long to wait. Reports from the Earl of Ross, whose lands extended right up to the Pentland Firth, across from Orkney, informed that a host of ships without number had arrived at these northern isles. Promptly the decided course of action was ordered, the mustering of men by the lords, and the Highland force set to its patrolling. Alexander was very much in charge, seeming almost to enjoy the challenge. He would show his father-in-law Henry how monarchs should behave.

In all this, Gamelyn was very much superseded. This was not his scene, although he did promise Church moneys to help pay for it all.

Patrick found himself in the position of being able to provide one of the largest contingents of men, with his two earldoms, little as he relished the thought of leading them into battle. He reckoned that, given the time, he could raise at least one thousand men from each of the two fiefs, perhaps even more from the wide and fertile lands of the Merse.

No word came from the Highland west as to any preliminary actions by John of the Isles or his Irish and Manx partisans.

The situation in England rather faded from general concern north of the border.

It was in early September that they got their first definite information, from Campbell of Lochawe, that

Hakon had entered Scottish waters. He had crossed the Pentland Firth to Cape Wrath, with no fewer than two hundred ships it was said, sailed on southwards round Skye, and through the narrows of Loch Alsh, to reach the Sound of Mull, where he met Dougal of Garmoran, one of Somerled's descendants, as representing John of the Isles. He waited for John at Kerrera, off the Oban coast. That name rang an ominous note in Alexander's ears, for it was on the Isle of Kerrera that his father had died when himself trying to cope with the Islesmen. Thereafter Hakon had sailed as far south as Arran, anchoring his fleet in Lamlash Bay, and sending Dougal of Garmoran to take over the smaller Isle of Bute. That was as far as the Campbell's information took them.

It was far enough, or rather *near* enough. Alexander was incensed. For Hakon to have come as far south as this was totally unexpected, extraordinary. The assumption must be that he would seek to grasp *all* the western coastline. Islay and Gigha they had expected, then Kintyre. But Arran was in the mouth of the Firth of Clyde, none so far from Glasgow.

The Scots army had been assembling there at Stirling, with the expectation of heading north-westwards up into Cowal and Argyll. But now it seemed that the confrontation was likely to be much further south, not in the Highlands at all. Arran was opposite the Ayrshire coast. That was where their army should be. It looked as though Hakon was aiming at more than West Highland hegemony. Could he possibly be thinking of conquering Scotland itself?

This situation was what Patrick discovered when he arrived at Stirling with two thousand three hundred men, and all mounted, quite the largest horsed contingent of the assembled army, thankfully and enthusiastically received by the excited young monarch. It had to be south-westwards for them all, the entire force to head for Ayrshire, Ayr town some seventy miles, back indeed to Bruce's country, and Carrick's, these and other southern lords cursing that they had had to march all the way up to Stirling and now to march back again.

This of marching was very much to the point, for most of the Scots army consisted of footmen, unlike Patrick's contribution. All the lords and knights had their horsed parties, especially those from the West March, with their mosstroopers, but few were as well supplied with horses as were Lothian and the Merse. And footmen, however hardy and keen, could not cover more than twenty miles in a day, at the very most. So, four days to reach Ayr, while the cavalry could do it in less than half the time.

The move was made, to the thankfulness of the Stirling folk. Armies were seldom popular where they assembled.

As it transpired, it took longer than any two or four days for the host, mounted and foot, to reach Ayr, the weather ensuring that. For storms blew up and continued, unseasonable for September, fierce gales and lashing rain day after day, which not only delayed the march grievously but made a misery for all concerned, far from enhancing the military spirit called for, the only consolation being that it all would not be helping Hakon's ship-borne host either; indeed conditions at sea must be appalling.

So it was a full week later before the whole army was able to reassemble at Ayr, with the winds dropping somewhat but still blowing, a wet and battered legion demanding the townsfolk's distinctly reluctant hospitality. But there they did learn that as many as ten Norse and Manx longships had been driven ashore none so far north of them, in the Ardrossan and Irvine area, and who knew how many more around Arran and Bute. So perhaps God was on the Scots side after all?

They settled in at Ayr, sending out scouts for information, and awaited further tidings.

Strangely, tidings did arrive in the form of two prelates, come under a white flag, and by boat into Ayr harbour, these the Bishop of Hamar in Norway, and Bishop Henry of Orkney, come as envoys from Hakon, from Lamlash in Arran, despite the difficult sailing. The Norse king, weather or none, must be well informed, since he knew that the King of Scots was at Ayr. These two came proposing a conference between the monarchs.

What did this mean? It was somewhat late in the day for any conference, with the invading fleet on their doorsteps. What was there to confer about? Did it signify trouble for Hakon? Perhaps that storm had hit him and his sorely, making him prepared to talk?

Alexander sent the bishops back with the word that he was willing to speak with Hakon, but only on condition that all claim to Norse hegemony over mainland Scotland was abandoned, and this included everything south of Islay and Gigha, most certainly the isles of Arran and Bute and the Cumbraes.

They waited, to see the reaction to that. None was forthcoming.

What did become evident, with the winds abating and the seas calming somewhat, was the presence of enemy shipping sailing up and down the Ayrshire coast, presumably surveying the seaboard, for they frequently came quite close inshore. Did this mean that they were looking for possible landing-places for Hakon's host? Many different landings would be sound tactics for a seaborne force, causing the defensive army to split up to cope with them. And it was a lengthy seaboard indeed, almost one hundred miles of it, for Ayrshire alone. So there might be enemy assaults anywhere along it, although the probability was that these would not be scattered too widely apart, or they would lose their effectiveness. It would be a pity to break up the great Scots force, numbering now some twenty thousand men; but such landings could not be left unopposed.

Alexander, conferring, took Bruce's advice that the many castles which dotted this long coast, some of them his own, should be manned by sections of their host, but these should all keep in regular touch with each other, and be prepared to gather together swiftly if a major landing was learned of, with any possible enemy scatter merely a diversion. The king should base himself at Turnberry Castle, the main seat of the Carrick earldom, opposite the southern tip of Arran and the Mull of Kintyre, with parties of his army as far south as the Galloway border, and as far north as Largs, facing the Cumbrae isles and even Skelmorlie. This was agreed, with fast-riding units to seek to keep all in touch and informed.

Patrick found himself allotted Portencross Castle, fairly far north, although his manpower was largely divided up elsewhere under his son Pate, now in his twentieth year, William of Home and Hugo de Gifford, one of his most powerful vassal barons. About one-third of the Scots total force would remain at Ayr town.

It was dispersal, then, with readiness to go to the aid of others at short notice, or to reassemble in a united array if such was called for. It all made a difficult strategy, as no doubt Hakon intended.

At Portencross, a Steward house, Patrick learned that a Norse galley and a Manx longship had been wrecked nearby in the storm and the crews slain. These casualties in shipping must be having a fairly severe impact on the enemy strategy.

In fact, he had barely taken over at Portencross when a couple of his own Mersemen, acting as couriers, arrived to say that he, and all others within a reasonable distance, were to muster further north in the Largs area, where the High Steward was in charge, and where he was reporting large numbers of the enemy fleet off the Isles of Cumbrae, with scouting vessels probing shorewards nearby. It looked as though Hakon was concentrating his strength on that area for a major landing. Alexander was ordering a swift reassembly, or as swift as might be with their far-flung host. The Ayr-based contingent, mainly footmen, was on the march northwards.

At Largs Castle it was to learn that the invaders had already begun landing, coming from Great Cumbrae just three miles out in the firth, which had provided some shelter in the wild weather with the winds westerly. Largs Bay was not large, but with sandy shallows stretching to the south for some miles towards Fairlie and the great sands of Southanna and Hunterston, ideal for the landing of longships and birlinns.

The large force from Ayr had not yet arrived on the scene, nor Alexander himself, with Bruce, from Turnberry. Patrick, with his cavalry, or some of them, under Hugo de Gifford, found himself in command of the left wing of the immediately available manpower, with the Steward leading the right, mainly foot. They must seek to strike at and disorganise, as far as possible, the enemy landings, and prevent regrouping, until the various Scots reinforcements arrived.

With some seven hundred mounted men then, Patrick rode southwards, a little way inland. The Noddsdale Hills backed the Largs area fairly closely, and there was only a narrow coastal plain flanking those sands where the landings were taking place along well over one mile of the shallow beaches. The tactics were for the cavalry to hasten inland some way among the hillfoots where they could be hidden from the shore, to get back to the landing area unseen, while the Steward made his assault from the north openly. This ought to concentrate the landing Norsemen's attention in that direction, so that Patrick's horsemen could make an unexpected attack on the enemy rear, or part of it, creating much confusion and, it was to be hoped, havoc, even possibly inhibiting further landings. This could well put the invading process in disarray, making a better target for the other Scots forces as they arrived.

So, at Haylee, a wooded spur of Rigging Hill over a mile south of Largs, Patrick, leading his people, realised that there was no more shelter ahead of them for some distance. It was shorewards, then, to the enemy. Emerging from the cover of the open woodland, knowes and hillocks, they saw the great array of ships busy at their landing, all but a mile of them. How many men were already ashore and how many still to come they could not tell, but the process was clearly ongoing, with the Norsemen on land turning to face the Steward's approach.

There was no question as to tactics now, the cavalry to ride down on the enemy rear, assail this and prevent further landings if possible. Detaching Gifford with about one-third of their men, to make a flanking attack some way northwards, Patrick drew and raised high his sword, to bring it down pointing shorewards, and spurred forward, his horsemen in approximately V-shaped formation at his back.

They had perhaps four hundred yards to cover before they reached the first of the enemy, and the thunder of hooves could not fail to warn the north-facing foemen. But Gifford's group, half forward, and become evident, pre-occupied them also, apart from the Steward's more distant advance. So confusion inevitably reigned among the strung-out landed Norsemen, whatever would be the effect on those still in the ships.

The impact of charging, lance-thrusting and sword-wielding horsemen on men on foot, and not organised in any defensive formation, was dire, needless to say, however expert the Norsemen might be with their battle-axes. Ridden down, trampled, speared and slashed, they fell without being able to strike back in any effective degree. Some sought to form small defensive groups, but most fled right and left, and less than successfully, the horses the faster-moving. It was not really battle at all, more massacre, and a continuing massacre. Admittedly the charging had to slow down, but the onward progress was maintained, however erratically.

Patrick, despite his drawn sword, was doing none of the killing. His commander's concern was otherwise, to over-see, observe and direct. He saw that some landings were still going on, that Gifford's flank-attack was further distracting the enemy ahead, and that possibly half a mile ahead the Steward's array was engaged. The Norsemen were in an almost hopeless position.

But there were still innumerable ships close inshore.

How many of them had discharged their men? How many more would land? How far should he lead his people northwards before turning back, leaving this affray to the Steward, and engaging those behind, and the newly landed foe? Commanding in action was for making wise and right decisions, not acting the dashing warrior. He was wondering also how Pate, his son, was faring.

Time, in this situation, was not to be measured amid the bloodshed, the screaming and the shouting. How long it took them to join up with Gifford's men Patrick did not know. He realised that his own horsemen were much dispersed behind him in their assaults and hunting down the fleeing foe, all formation lost. He must reassemble and reassert his direction and command into some sort of order.

Gifford's company was equally busy but also dispersed now. Spurring forward, he managed to reach that man. He shouted his instructions. They must pull together again, the two sections, get into order. Turn back. Leave this part of it all to the Steward, whose force was now none so far ahead. There were more of the foe behind, and new landings continuing.

It took a deal of effecting, these orders, with his men in all the turmoil and excitement of fighting and slaying. But eventually, with horn-blowing and gesturing, they achieved a muster and formation of sorts, and turned to face southwards.

It did not take long, even in all the disorder, to recognise that there were almost as many of the enemy on the beaches to the south as in the other direction, a grim situation, with more landing all the time. For possibly half a mile there were masses of men. Patrick did not think that he had lost many of his people so far, although he did see a few riderless horses, some cantering along with the rest of them. Could his hundred tackle these thousands, with any hope of success? They had no option but to try.

So it was back to smiting and thrusting, all complicated now by the many bodies of dead and wounded of their first victims, the horses misliking these and apt to shy and swerve. Quickly, inevitably, the attackers lost any formation, and drove on as best they could. Was warfare always like this, Patrick wondered, chaos and lack of any overall command, and men often so little able to implement such commands as were given?

This time the assault was much more difficult, or seemed so, the foe here having had some warning, and the more prepared to defend themselves. Battle-axes were being thrown at the horsemen, and with some effect, the mounts more often hit than the riders. There was much rearing and plunging, sidling out of control, so that the onward charging desired was impossible to maintain as a whole, however hard Patrick tried to revive it among as many of his men as he could keep near him.

He knew frustration, his own failure to lead effectively, unreasoning anger, and at times all but panic. Was this all going to end in disaster? These hurled battle-axes . . . !

Then strangely, at some stage in it all, preoccupied as he was with every move and every moment, he came to realise something unlooked for. The Norsemen they were assailing were frequently facing the other way, backs to them. It took a little time for this fact to sink in. When it did, it caused him to raise his gaze, momentarily at least, from the immediate front, from the challenge and danger and threat. And there, beyond all the Norsemen, he saw what had turned their heads. A great host was bearing down on them from the south, horse and foot, under scores of banners and pennons foremost, and high among which flew the red lion rampant on gold of the King of Scots. Alexander had arrived, with the array from Ayr.

Suddenly, then, all was changed. Instead of a few hundred there were thousands of attackers, most fresh to the fray and under experienced leadership, the enemy now assailed front and rear, already disorganised as they were. The end could not be in doubt.

That end was as evident to the Norsemen as to Patrick. His men, enheartened, drove on, aware of the beginnings of change in the concern of their foemen, from defending themselves and throwing battle-axes to making their escape. The general move was becoming seawards, down to the tide's edge, to the ships, this almost before the king's army made actual contact.

It was probable that those behind, facing the Steward, would perceive, and make the same decision.

On the enemy part it became a confused rush, men racing for and into the water to reach the ranks of longships and galleys lined up in the shallows. There was no stopping them in this, of course. Many dead and wounded were left behind, but the vast majority of the invaders undoubtedly managed to gain the safety of their vessels, this along the mile of coast.

Patrick's people joined up with the royal host, to great welcome and acclaim, Alexander himself loud in his appreciation, Bruce declaring his modified praise and asking how the Steward fared.

Their gaze now tended to be seaward, where they could see ships loaded with men beginning to head out into the firth towards the Cumbraes. Further north they could see another fleet, seemingly inactive, unsure as to tactics apparently in this situation, which was all to the good.

So, it was over, at least for the time being, the Battle of Largs won and lost, if battle it could be called, with the king's force but little engaged. In triumph, all rode northwards to meet the Steward, who was now likewise done with fighting, and surveying the scene, well pleased.

It was salutations and congratulations all round.

The leaders all went to Largs Castle, sending troops back to look after the wounded and to deal with the dead. Patrick assessed that he might be missing perhaps only a score of men. He sent Gifford to seek them out, slain, only unhorsed or injured, and bring them to the town.

The question was, what would Hakon do now? He had suffered a grievous blow, on top of the damage to his ships by the storm; but he and his allies still had great strength.

Would he attempt another landing hereafter? Or settle down to occupy Arran and Bute and Kintyre?

From the castle they could see the enemy vessels congregating in the lee of Great Cumbrae. Decisions would be in the making. And these would be . . . ?

It was not long before the Scots learned the answer. The great Norse fleet hoisted sail and dipped oars, and set in motion. And there was no question as to the direction taken. It was west by south, away from the Ayrshire coast and heading for Arran or the further-away Mull of Kintyre. Hakon had had enough, for one day at least, possibly for more.

Alexander and his army settled in at Largs for the night, in good spirits.

In the morning, there was not an enemy ship in sight, save for storm-wrecked ones. It was decided to send out two or three of the large fishing-boats to see if they could discover the Norsemen's movements beyond the Cumbraes. After a few hours these returned, to inform that they had been as far as the south of Bute and the north of Arran, and the word was that the invaders had gone, sailed off westwards for the Mull of Kintyre. If Hakon had intended further assaults he would not have done that, surely? It looked as though he had had a sufficiency of the Scots and their weather.

Alexander declared that it was victory. But not all to go home yet. Wait at their various dispersal points for two or three days, by which time they should know how the situation was going to develop.

Patrick and his people returned to Portencross, leaving seven wounded men at Largs to recover. They had lost about a dozen slain, sad as this was; in the circumstances it was a very minor price to pay, out of seven hundred fighters. He, Patrick, would seek to make it up, so far as he could, to the bereaved families.

Two days later the news reached Portencross. The Norsemen had departed, sailing on northwards for the Hebrides and Orkney, presumably the Manxmen returning to their Man. If Hakon was heading for home, then the Scots could do likewise. Alexander was going to tell Gamelyn to order thanks to be said, and bells rung in every church in Scotland, to Almighty God.

17

Patrick, thereafter, found himself treated as something of a hero, the assumption being that his cavalry force had been largely responsible for making the victory at Largs possible. He declared this far from the truth, the Steward's attack to the north and the arrival of the king's force to the south at a propitious moment being the key to it all. But plaudits continued. Christian, even though she disclaimed the credit, declared that she was proud of him; and young Pate basked in the reflected fame, although he had not been present.

It took some time before they heard the news which changed so much on the national and the international scene. Hakon was dead. Apparently he had been failing in health for some months, and at Kirkwall, in Orkney, depressed by the failure of his invasion, and declaring that it was not the Scots who had defeated him but God Himself, in sending the storm, he had given up the ghost.

So now Norway had a new monarch, the son Magnus, reputedly a very different character, moderate and peaceable. Patrick hoped that he would at least resemble his father in maintaining the timber trade.

Possibly as a result of all this, John of the Isles and Angus of Islay promptly made peace with Alexander, declaring that they would lay claim to nothing south of Islay and Gigha, and any concern for Kintyre. No word came from the Isle of Man.

Patrick sent Dand Shaw with a cargo of wood, before the worst of the winter weather developed; and this was accepted at Bergen as before. So that was satisfactory.

Peace of a sort reigned in Scotland that winter.

In the spring, no word having come from the King of Man, another Magnus, Alexander decided that a gesture in that direction was called for, to ensure that the Hebridean-Norse confederation was not revived, with Dougal of Garmoran still maintaining his hostility, unlike his kinsmen John and Angus. An army was ordered to assemble in Galloway, Devorgilla and her husband Baliol co-operating, the Steward, Bruce and Mar again in command, Patrick thankfully being able to opt out. They made sure that Magnus of Man heard of this – after all, only a score of sea miles separated the two coasts – and there were acceptable results. Envoys from Man arrived before a single ship left the Galloway shore, to announce that Magnus was renouncing all allegiance to his namesake in Norway, and had no intention of pursuing any course inimical to Scotland.

So the scene looked almost tranquil, with England and the Plantagenet in no state to threaten the northern kingdom, Henry still more or less a captive of his barons. The great clash came in August, with the major Battle of Evesham, where, with de Montford slain, Edward rescued his less than effective sire, and more or less proclaimed *himself* ruler of England instead.

The southern kingdom was in turmoil now indeed, and had lost one of its most useful and valued subjects.

It was in this so satisfactory state of affairs that a new interest developed for Patrick and his people. Hugo de Gifford, a strange man, with allegedly some unusual abilities, not exactly a seer like Sir Thomas Learmonth of Ersildoune, deep in the Merse, but said to be able to relate to long-past events in an odd way, decided to extend his comparatively small castle at Ystrad, or Yester, near Gifford village, none so far south of Haddington, and with ambitious plans. He was a little older than Patrick and seemingly of some wealth, said to have married a rich wife. His plans for his house were ambitious enough for him to go over to France to study some of the French chateaux, which he believed to be superior to the Scots ones in various aspects. He came back with not only ideas but with a French master-builder named de Gobelin, who was to design the new extension to Yester Castle. And he offered Patrick the use of the said de Gobelin's talents, if he so wished, to make improvements at Dunbar. Patrick did not commit himself, but declared his interest.

And not only in that, for the Frenchman was interested in obtaining Scottish sandstone, which apparently had better qualities for special working, moulding into rounded corbelling and heraldic designs for panels and dormer-windows, than the available French varieties. Gifford suggested that there might be opportunities here for a new trade, which might be of advantage to them all.

This suggestion, needless to say, was received with interest and approval, as a possible addition to the Low Countries commerce.

Gifford in due course brought de Gobelin to Dunbar. He was a small, bird-like man with a darting glance, and was much impressed by Dunbar Castle, he never having seen a stronghold built on rock-stacks out into the sea. He was full of suggestions as to possible improvements and alterations – there was no room for extensions here – and Patrick took due note. And he learned that, of all things, Gifford and de Gobelin were planning to extend Yester Castle *downwards*, this by enlarging a cave in the cliff on which the castle stood, and fashioning it into a great underground hall, the like of which had never been seen in Scotland, this with sundry other strange features and novelties. Patrick could scarcely credit it all, but the Frenchman assured him that it was possible; apparently he had worked on a similar scheme in France. Gifford, chuckling, observed that the stone excavated from his cliff above the Hopes Water could profitably go to France in one of his lord's ships, for a start to the new trade. He would be obliged by the loan of some of Cospatrick's quarrymen meantime.

Christian shook her head over it all, but not censoriously.

*　　*　　*

A treaty of peace was finally made with Magnus of Norway, and, with the agreement made with the other Magnus, of Man, the Isles situation appeared to be settled for the foreseeable future, Dougal of Garmoran lying low, and Angus of Islay prevailed upon to send his young son, Angus Og, as a kind of hostage for good behaviour. The boy was handed over to the Countess of Carrick, at Ayr Castle, as some kind of guest.

There was a great stir in the land when Queen Margaret, pregnant again, gave birth to a son, a male heir to the throne. Amid rejoicings he was named after his father and grandfather, Alexander. The royal succession was now assured, it seemed. Bruce could forget any hopes of the crown.

Patrick, meantime, although he had no intention of carrying out any of de Gobelin's improvements at Dunbar, was much interested in the proceedings at Yester, the excavations and enlarging of the cave under the castle, and the necessary access thereto by a stairway cut in the solid rock. An extraordinary amount of sandstone was thus produced, which would all help to pay for it, with Patrick keen to initiate this new trade to France. He had been intending to visit the Low Countries personally one of these days, to seek to further his long-standing commercial links with the Netherlands and Flanders, and it occurred to him that it might be worth his while to go on to France while he was across the Channel, to prospect trading possibilities. It looked as though his military capabilities, such as they were, whatever ill-deserved fame he had gained at Largs, were not likely to be required by his liege-lord for some time to come. The only faint cloud on the horizon was over England. Henry was still all but a captive of his lords, and in no position to cause trouble for Alexander. But his elder son, Edward, who had tended to side with the barons, was free, and now to all intents ruling the land for his sire, with baronial support; and he was an assertive character, not to say arrogant, but effective also. So far he had not shown any interest in the Scottish situation, but if he did . . . ! He had announced his wish to lead a crusade to the Holy Land, and with the Gascony position still not fully resolved, he probably had enough on his plate, it was hoped.

Christian, after a visit to Luffness and David's wife Margaret Lindsay, came back with an amusing story. It seemed that the local folk at Yester, Gifford village and as far as Haddington, had heard about de Gifford's underground labours, and, allied to his reputation as a strange character, and the name of his French master-mason, had built up a whispered allegation which was circulating in the area, that the laird was in league with the powers of darkness and this strange subterranean vault was being built by evil spirits, goblins. They were beginning to call it Goblin Hall, the Frenchman's name lending itself to this nonsense. Christian, like Margaret, had been much amused; but Patrick wondered whether this myth might possibly have problems, in producing reluctance for men to work on the stone-hewing, even on his quarrying operations in general?

That summer, King Alexander decided that, the gesture aimed at Man having been successful, he should make similar flourishes northwards, to emphasise his new mastery of the entire realm, large forces, not intent on warfare but demonstrations of strength. Patrick was unable to avoid involvement in this, for great numbers of men were needed for three distinct parades, for that is what they were to be. One to go north-east as far as distant Caithness, under the Earls of Ross and Buchan, the people there having shown some support for Hakon based on nearby Orkney; one to go through the central Highlands up to Inverness, which the monarch himself would lead; and the third, necessarily largely ship-borne, to the West Highland and inner isles area, this under William, Earl of Mar. Patrick chose to accompany the king, not out of any pride in the royal favour, but because it would probably be the shortest, and least likely to be involved in troubles. Also Cousin David would be there with Alexander, as ever.

So, with Pate and a retinue of some two hundred men, which he considered to be sufficient, he set off to join the monarch at Stirling, which was becoming ever more in favour for the king to use as base, being more central and more dominant than Roxburgh.

In the event, it all turned out to be a pleasant excursion. Alexander made a leisurely progress up past Dunblane into Strathallan and Strathearn, to reach Perth, where they spent the night in the Blackfriars monastery. Next day, they called at Scone, where he had been crowned on the Stone of Destiny, then up Tay to Dunkeld and so into Atholl. Where was Dorward now? they wondered. There were rumours that he was back in Scotland, lying low; and certainly his great earldom of Atholl, with all its mountains and glens, forests and lochs, would provide ample cover for its lord to hide in. At any rate, there were no signs of him at Blair, his main seat, on the River Garry.

So up and over the lofty Pass of Drumochter they rode, in excellent weather conditions and superb scenery, all in holiday atmosphere, with the heather just beginning to turn purple, admiring the great, ancient pine trees, so spreading and gnarled, different from their Lowland variety, wondering at the great herds of deer which drifted like clouds over the mountainsides, and the vast flooded water-meadows of the lengthy Spey valley, alive with wildfowl. Some present had been here before, but none ever ridden in this easy fashion, and appreciation was general. Why was it that when covering the land they always seemed to be on urgent and usually armed business bent, and in consequence failed to take in the beauty and excellence of it all, Patrick not the only one to remark on this.

Leaving Strathspey they had to climb over other passes, none so high as Drumochter, and then much high moorland, clan country this, of Macintoshes, Cattanachs, Shaws, MacPhails, Farquharsons and the like, before they could drop down to the Great Glen of Scotland, with its succession of long lochs, Ness, Oich and Laggan, sixty miles of it, with their destination, Inverness, at the eastern end. This was the Moray earldom, one of the original mormaordoms of ancient Alba, its present ownership in dispute, the River Ness emptying into the Moray Firth.

It was, in fact, Alexander's first visit to what might be called his northern capital, and he was suitably impressed by it all, a much larger community than he had realised, and its folk, Gaelic-speaking as they were, courteous and friendly. He settled in at the castle on its ridge in the centre of the town, and from there summoned all the chiefs of the clans of a large area to meet him, from Beauly and Dingwall and the Black Isle of Cromarty, from Alness and Tain and Dornoch, from Strathconon and Strathpeffer, Strathglass and Strathfarrer, Mackenzies, Rosses, the Clan Chattan federation, Brodies, MacBains, Urquharts and the rest. They made a great and colourful assembly eventually, all giving the impression of dignity and assurance and pride, but not aggressively so, and treating Alexander more like another, if senior, chieftain than a monarch. He got on well with them, however, once he adjusted to their style. He told them that he relied on them all to support the crown when called upon, and to keep the peace of the realm in their various areas, under his Justiciar of the North, the Earl of Ross, who was presently dispensing justice in Caithness. Dorward's name was not mentioned.

Three days of this, and the king was satisfied with his visit, and was for the south again, with a boar-hunt on the way, at the invitation of the Macintosh, at Moy, a lively experience, with the tuskers larger than Patrick was used to in his Lammermuirs and the Merse. Then home, the latter, for one, thankful that he had elected to join this venture rather than one of the other two. He wondered how these might be faring.

It was on the way south that David Lindsay revealed to his cousin a major decision that he had taken. He was going on crusade. This, it seemed, had been on his mind for long, in the first instance at his mother's suggestion. Her brother, and Patrick's father, had been slain in his efforts to drive out the infidels from the Holy Land, and he ought to be avenged, and his pious example followed. Moreover he, David, had long felt impelled to do this eventually. For years he had had so good a life, because of his closeness to Alexander, he a mere laird, no great lord, given so much, high station and privileges on account of the fondness of the young monarch, raised to become High Chamberlain, even a regent, all out of no virtue of his own. Now Alexander needed no regents, a grown man and married with two children. If he was going to make this pilgrimage, for that is what it should be, now was the time to do it, with Pope Urban calling for Jerusalem to be cleansed of the Muslim invaders.

Patrick eyed him wonderingly. "It is a great step, David," he said. "Need you do it? Go so far? Now?"

"If Prince Edward of England can do it! And John de Brienne. Even John Comyn of Badenoch is going. Also Thomas of Galloway's son, Alan. Ewan of Lorn. And John de Vescy. Now that peace prevails here at home. So why not me?"

"And your Margaret? What does she say to this? If you have told her?"

"She is . . . resigned to it. And it need not be for so very long. Only a couple of months, perhaps. Something that I can do, and should. The Vatican is urging it on all faithful men. It is different for you. You have two great earldoms to oversee, thousands of folk dependent on you. Myself, I have nothing of that. And now is a good time, with this peace."

"The king? Does he know your mind?"

"Yes. He says go, with his blessing. As his representative. *He* cannot go himself, as he says that he would. But I can."

"You make me feel guilty!"

"No, no. Your position is quite different, Patrick."

They left it at that.

18

It was soon after this that the sudden death of King Magnus of Man, without heir, offered Alexander the opportunity to strengthen Scotland's position, not only there but over the Isles situation in general, and, to quite an extent, with Norway. This lack of a legitimate heir – although Magnus had an illegitimate son, one Godfrey – caused much upheaval in Man, dispute over authority, the Tynwald, or governing body, divided, even bloodshed resulting. Alexander stepped in, with fears of the Islesmen from the north taking over power, possibly Norsemen also. So he swiftly, even Gamelyn advising it, made an offer, backed by armed might in Galloway again. He would take over protection of the Isle of Man from all would-be challengers if the Manxmen accepted his overlordship. He would appoint his young son nominal King of Man, to maintain the status of the island kingdom, pay four thousand silver merks to the Tynwald, this over a period of four years, and send a representative as governor for his infant son. In return Man was to be prepared to provide ten longships, fully manned and armed, at call of the King of Scots. The Tynwald, in the fears and confusion that reigned, accepted these terms favourably. And to ensure that Norway did not challenge this new dispensation, King Magnus there was to be assured of Alexander's favour, and to emphasise it, to be offered a similar sum of four thousand silver merks, with one hundred more paid annually, in token of continued goodwill. The envoy to make this offer to Magnus was to be the Earl of Dunbar and March, the obvious choice, with his trading links with Norway.

So once again Patrick had to set off in Dand Shaw's *Skateraw Meg* for Bergen, with a cargo of oak and elm aboard, hoping that this time they would not have to face the navigational problems of the Skagerrak and the Kattegat. He might be able to effect further commercial dealings with the Norsemen while he was at it. Wool? Could they do with supplies of the Lammermuir wool over there?

He said God-speed to Cousin David before he left.

Fortunately Magnus Hakonssen was at Bergen. He proved to be a friendly young man, easy to deal with and seemingly less dependent on strong liquor than had been his sire. Moreover, his Chancellor, a cleric named Asketin, was good at languages, a great help in negotiations. Indeed negotiations proved to be hardly the word to use, for it became clear that Magnus had little real interest in Man, certainly no plans to take it over, and was surprised and delighted to receive four thousand silver merks, with a further one hundred a year thereafter, as price for refraining from doing something that he had not intended to do anyway. So it was agreement almost forthwith, with satisfaction expressed. Hakon had been in debt to the Hanseatic League, so this silver was welcome indeed. It was arranged that he, Magnus, would send over his representatives to Scotland, before the winter storms, to confirm all in a formal treaty, this one of Alexander's terms. As to wool, he did not know; but why not send over a shipload of it as sample, and they could consider the matter. The wood trade must continue.

Well pleased, Patrick returned home, with the *Skateraw Meg* laden with iron ore, which it seemed came from Sweden and would be highly acceptable in Scotland as much easier to turn into usable metal than the long and expensive process of smashing up local ironstone from the cliffs of Lothian and elsewhere, and heating the rubble over furnaces to provide for all the many uses that the produce would yield.

Altogether a most worthwhile visit.

Patrick was even beginning to worry a little that matters were going almost too well these days, both for the realm and for his own interests. Could this last?

Christian told him not to be foolish. He had earned his good fortune, had he not? As to the realm, peace was surely overdue.

Alexander was gratified with the success of this embassage, and urged Patrick to attend the council more frequently. He was missing Lindsay.

Magnus did not delay in seeking to collect the four thousand merks of silver. He sent over his Chancellor, Asketin, and one of his lords named Nicholas Sigurdssen, to receive it, and to sign a treaty for continuing peace and amity with Scotland, renouncing all claims to Man and the West Highland coast. Alexander decided that this important event should take place, not in any warlike castle or fortress but in a peaceful location. At Gamelyn's suggestion, it should be at Scone, the royal crowning-place, not at his St Andrews as might have been expected of him. This was agreed.

In due course, the Norse visitors were taken to see this hallowed spot, and the famous Stone of Destiny. The abbey itself was small although ancient, and without accommodation for all the great ones assembled to mark the occasion. So they adjourned to the nearby town of St John at Perth, where there were monasteries and friaries in plenty. And there the celebrated Treaty of Perth was duly signed, which put an end to the ages-old warfare between Scotland and Norway, a major jewel in Alexander's crown. Patrick's signature and seal was the first attached, as witness, after the king's own and the Primate's.

The silver was duly handed over, Holy Church supplying most of it, Gamelyn these days seeking to co-operate with the monarch. Even the Comyn Buchan was one of the signatories.

So the infant Prince Alexander was King of Man. Quiet settled over the Hebrides. The Earl of Orkney, on instructions from Bergen, promised no more raiding over into

Caithness and Wester Ross. And with Edward Plantagenet off on crusade, and his father subject to his barons' dictates, peace reigned over the northern nations, not only Scotland.

But back at Dunbar Castle there arose some concern, on Patrick's part. Pate had accompanied his father to Perth; but, not involved in the prestigious treaty-signing, he had gone off on his own during the two days of the celebrations. And during these he had met and been attracted, indeed smitten, by another not involved in it all, the daughter of Alexander, Earl of Buchan, Margery Comyn. He now announced the fact, said that she favoured him, and that he wanted to marry her.

Here was a thought indeed: the next Cospatrick desiring to wed a Comyn! It was something so improbable that his father never would have considered the possibility. But Pate was of full age, and entitled to make his own choice in such a matter. Patrick had seen the young woman at the two banquets, and admitted that she was good-looking. But – a Comyn!

Christian declared that this was not the end of the world. The Comyns had their virtues, or at least their uses. And were they not all but reformed these days? And Buchan probably the best of them, Badenoch even going on crusade. This Margery might be none so ill an addition to their family. Pate was no fool. He must be fairly sure in his mind to have so decided.

As ever, Christian spoke good sense, and to be heeded. Perhaps, of course, this brief-term infatuation would not last, on one side or both. And what would Buchan say? They would await developments.

Meanwhile there was further good news from Bergen. Dand Shaw came back with the information that the Norwegian merchants had been much impressed with the quality of the wool that he had taken over. The Scandinavian nations were not really sheep country, goats being bred in large numbers, these producing milk as well as the skin outerwear so much favoured by their warriors. But sheep, no. And Lammermuir wool was strong of fibre but soft enough to turn into comfortable clothing, blankets and the like. So there was a market for it there, and for onward trading to Sweden probably. It occurred to Patrick that there might well be a return trade in the tanned goatskin, welcome in Scotland. He would make enquiries.

Less good news was that Pope Urban had died. He was succeeded by one calling himself Clement the Fourth, an unknown quantity. Urban had been a friend to Scotland.

A council meeting was called shortly thereafter, not unconnected with this event, this to be at Stirling, with a personal call from Alexander for Patrick to attend. Less than eagerly, he complied.

An unfortunate situation had developed, ecclesiastical rather than national, although the realm's status came into it also, Gamelyn much concerned. It seemed that the new Pope had sent a papal legate to England, named Othobon Fiesci, and he had announced that he would come to Scotland, the object of his visit unspecified. He asked for a safe-conduct. Gamelyn was suspicious that this probably symbolised another attempt by the Archbishop of York to claim, as northern metropolitan, authority over the Scottish Church. He advised Alexander to refuse this permit of entry, since the legate was accredited only to England, and no word had come from the new pontiff of any mission in Scotland. The king was glad to agree to this.

But this Othobon had promptly changed his request to envoys being sent to meet him over the border into England, even stating the required composition of the delegation, two bishops and two abbots. Gamelyn was still doubtful, but felt that refusal to meet in England could not be justified. The council meeting was to consider this; and Alexander's special summons to Patrick was to the effect that if such meeting was to take place with this legate it had better be in Northumberland, where the Cospatrick influence was still strong and the landed men friendly towards the line of their former earls.

The council took Gamelyn's advice, for his shrewdness was now accepted by all. It was decided to send the Chancellor, Bishop Wishart of Glasgow, and the Bishop of Dunblane, with the Abbots of Kelso and Cambuskenneth, Patrick and a party of his men escorting them. A courier was despatched to this Othobon, presently at Durham, and, at Patrick's suggestion, the meeting-place should be at Hexham-on-Tyne. This, he maintained, was important. The Bishops of Hexham were traditionally at cross-purposes with the Archbishops of York, claiming that St Wilfred, who had been bishop there as far back as 709, had gained independence from the metropolitan; indeed the entire Hexham area of Tynedale had been created its own shire, under the prelate's jurisdiction. Durham and its prince-bishop were very much within the sphere of York, but Hexham was not. Oddly, the abbey there was dedicated to St Andrew, the patron saint of Scotland; and it had long been the common usage to hold that Hexham's bishop and its abbot looked to Scotland rather than to York or Canterbury, in favour. This was the obvious place for the meeting with the legate.

Four days later, then, the Scots delegation set off from Roxburgh south-eastwards for the border, crossing Tweed at Wark, and collecting de Ros there as a useful go-between. Patrick got on well with him, also with William Wishart, fairly young to be a senior bishop and Chancellor. He had not met the other three clerics previously. Fortunately they were all able horsemen, so, halting overnight at the monastery at Yeavering, they ought to be able to reach Hexham by the following midday.

This was achieved, and they were welcomed by the abbot, the bishop being absent. He declared that he would co-operate with the Scots, gladly, to the best of his ability.

Othobon and the Bishop of Durham arrived towards evening, the legate a tall, gaunt and severe man. He lost no time in coming to the point of this interview. He wanted one-twentieth of the revenues of the Scottish Church, as had been called for from the Church of England, this to further Pope Clement's crusading campaign. It was as simple as that.

Bishop Wishart declared that they had had no prior word from the Vatican as to this, nor any indication that a papal representative was coming to Scotland. Their Primate, Bishop Gamelyn, knew nothing of it all. They would report to him and the College of Bishops. He made it very clear that he thought the situation unfortunate, and the demand exorbitant, although he did not say so in actual words. But he did ask whether the Church in England had agreed to this imposition? To that he got no answer. The other three Scots clerics looked disapproving also; and de Ros asked the prince-bishop whether York was responding favourably. One-twentieth was a great sum of money. Patrick had no authority to speak on this ecclesiastical matter, merely sitting in on the exchange.

There was, in fact, no ongoing discussion, the legate there only to announce his requirements, not to debate, seeing the Scots merely as messengers, the Durham bishop careful in his support. It was apparent that he too was not happy about handing over so large a portion of his see's income.

Othobon did not linger at the abbey, departing almost abruptly for the episcopal palace nearby, while the Scots remained at the abbot's house.

They admired the abbey-church itself, proudly displayed as almost certainly the finest place of worship in the north of England, as well as one of the oldest, enlarged, they were told, by St Wilfred himself, extending and improving that erected by his predecessor, St Acca; this before Wilfred became Archbishop of York and was in a position to grant Hexham, his favoured place, all its privileges. It was large enough to be a cathedral. The abbot claimed it to be the greatest abbey north of the Alps. The columns and pillars, the arches and aisles, the clerestorys, the groined vaulting and the lancet windows, all were greatly admired. And beneath was excavated the most renowned Saxon crypt in all England, oddly showing Roman carved stonework with inscriptions to heathen gods.

Bishop Wishart, appreciative, did point out that in the seventh and eighth centuries the Church in Scotland was of the ancient Columban and Celtic form of worship, while England was Roman Catholic. It was monastic and non-hierarchial, and not concerned with building great cathedral-like edifices. He did not say that this was to be more admired.

They spent a comfortable night as the abbot's guests; and in the morning saw no more of Othobon before returning northwards.

Back at Roxburgh, Gamelyn advised the council that the papal imposition should be refused, on the grounds that Scotland had already contributed adequately to the crusading ventures, in men and moneys proportionate to the realm's resources, Alexander agreeing heartily. This was accepted by all. There was some wondering as to what the English reaction would be, with the Bishop of Durham's reluctance obvious, and with Prince Edward already leading a crusading army, his father Henry all but powerless, and the barons unlikely to look favourably on further papal demands. The probability was of refusal there also. This new Pope had certainly overreached himself, for other nations would be certain to be included in his demands, and would be likely to reject them also. He could scarcely excommunicate most of Christendom for disobeying him.

Alexander, Earl of Buchan had in the meantime arrived from the north for the council meeting. He it was who raised the subject, privately, of his daughter Margery's desire to wed the Master of Dunbar and March, he showing no disapproval. Patrick, who had considered the matter in the interim, expressed his agreement in moderate fashion. He was told that the young woman would receive a substantial dowery. The wedding date was left undecided. This linking of the Cospatrick and Comyn lines aroused considerable interest and speculation, needless to say. But it would all help in the unification of Scotland's troubled nobility.

19

The wedding was not long delayed, Pate eager and presumably Margery also. So a lengthy journey was involved for the Cospatrick family. The Comyn's main seat was at Boddam, just south of Buchan Ness, thirty miles north of Aberdeen, this making it some one hundred and forty miles from Dunbar, by sea. By land it would be double that, with the Firths of Forth and Tay to get round or across. Dand Shaw was given a break from his Norwegian voyaging to take the party of seven, with attendants, northwards, amid much ado, with prayers for good weather and calm seas.

It proved to be a pleasant sail, the vessel never far from the shoreline save when crossing the estuaries, and many landmarks to point out to the young people, none of whom had ever come this way before. St Andrews with its skyline of towers and steeples and belfries, the mighty red cliffs of the Red Point of Ethie, the vast bay of Lunan, the extraordinary Montrose Basin, as it was called, something like a circular sea loch behind the town, the great islanded castle of Dunnottar just south of Stonehaven, Aberdeen itself, the city between the two river mouths of Dee and Don, and the savage, cavernous, cliff-bound coast to the north right to Buchan Ness. With a south-westerly breeze they covered the distance in exactly twelve hours, so that after an early start they were able to reach Boddam Castle on its minor promontory in time for the evening meal, to a suitably genial welcome.

Even Patrick had never before met the Countess of Buchan, an Englishwoman named Elizabeth de Quincy, daughter of the Earl of Winchester, with Galloway connections, who had held office in Scotland under King David. She was a quiet, retiring woman, plain-featured but pleasant of manner, rather unlikely mother of her lively daughters and an eight-year-old son. Margery was the most striking-looking of the girls, as well as eldest. Buchan himself was now friendly, letting bygones be forgotten. The bride and groom, so obviously in love and joyful, kept all in good spirits. Marriages of the nobility were not always like this, so usually arranged matches.

Buchan announced that the property of Crichie, some two miles to the north, was to be his daughter's dowery, and Patrick added that the lands of Colbrandspath, near the coast on the Lothian–March border, were to be her portion also.

In the morning, a major cavalcade set off westwards along the South Ugie Water for Deer, at the abbey of which the nuptials were to be celebrated, some ten miles away. There had actually been a small Celtic abbey there, founded by Columba himself and named after St Drostan, one of his missionary assistants; but this had been put down when the Roman Catholic Church took over in Scotland, and the present earl's father had built a new Cistercian one nearby, dedicated to St Mary. After St Andrew's Abbey of Hexham, it proved to be a comparatively modest edifice, of red sandstone, but adequate, pleasingly situated, with a dozen monks and an elderly abbot.

The company all but filled the nave of the cruciform church, to monkish chanting. The abbot conducted the service with grave but kindly care, the happy couple seeming oblivious of all but each other's proximity, Margery looking radiant indeed, two simpering sisters in attendance.

Patrick, not for the first time, wondered at the brief ceremony, and one man's pronouncements being able to affect so greatly the entire life of two people, with the declaration that whom God had joined together let no man put asunder. But it had worked with Christian and himself, had it not?

Man and wife thereafter, to more singing, accepted the congratulations and blessings of all, this in a state of euphoria, babbling incoherences, to the excited chatter of the sisters on both sides.

They all returned to Boddam Castle by a different and less direct route, southwards out of the vale of the Ugie Water, this to view Crichie, a small hallhouse and hamlet among low grassy hills and scattered woodland, good cattle country. This was now the property of the newly-weds, although it was to be doubted if Pate took it all in.

At Boddam there was great feasting and high spirits, with so many young folk, Margery's sisters flirting with Pate's brothers. The three Cospatrick girls were nowise backward in it all, and the evening passed with music and dancing and story-telling. In due course the blissful couple were escorted to their bedroom door by the four other young women amid much giggling. Thankfully there was no suggestion of a bedding ceremony, such as sometimes was considered suitable.

Their elders continued with the entertainment for considerably longer. The Countess Elizabeth made an admirable hostess, however quietly.

Although urged to stay longer, the Cospatrick party did not long delay departure next day, partly for the sake of the married pair, who deserved to have a period off on their own, which they would not get here or on the ship; and partly in that the winds would now be against them, their voyaging to the south bound to take double the time at least, with much tacking to and fro inevitable. So it was a midday farewell and well-wishing.

Unfortunately there was not sufficient space on the *Skateraw Meg* for Pate and Margery to have a cabin to themselves, so the bride had to share accommodation. Christian thought it wisest to have her in a cabin with herself rather than with the new sisters-in-law, telling the rejected Patrick that she might be in a position to offer the

girl some womanly and helpful advice in matters relating
to marriage. So her husband had to bed down with his
sons.

At Dunbar, eventually, Patrick suggested that Pate
should take his wife for a spell to the principal seat of
the March earldom, which he himself seldom used. It was
in the care of a keeper, presently Sir Thomas Learmonth of
Ercildoune, the poet-seer, Patrick's own esquire and a
friend of the family. This lay in lower Lauderdale, near
to the joining of that river and Tweed, and was known as
the Earlstoun of Ercildoune. There they would be able to
be sufficiently alone, yet carefully looked after. And on the
way, they could inspect Colbrandspath and its small tower,
Margery's portion-land. This was gladly agreed to.

They departed next morning, joyfully.

The very next day a messenger arrived to tell Patrick to
attend another council meeting, at Stirling, reason not
given. These were getting too frequent for that man.
But he consoled himself with the thought that for Buchan,
so far to the north, it would all be still more inconvenient.

It proved to be more trouble over Vatican demands,
Gamelyn much concerned. That twentieth of the Church's
revenues was still being required; but in addition, a further
one-tenth of the like was being demanded, this to help pay
for Prince Edward of England's and Louis of France's
crusading; and also to help pay off the debts of Queen
Eleanor of England. Was this pontiff so ill-informed? Or
wandering in his mind? they asked each other. *Edward's*
crusade! And the English queen's debts, presumably over
Provence! He seemed to consider Scotland to be no more
than another part of England, or a subsidiary thereto.

At least it did not take long for the council to decide on
this matter; indeed it seemed scarcely necessary to have
called the meeting at all. A complete refusal was the only
answer, whatever papal penalties might be forthcoming in
consequence, all declaring it. For it was not only ecclesiastical moneys that were concerned. The Church, in fact,

very largely supported state finances, and always had done, the monks in especial producing the prosperity and making the money with their industriousness. Few of the lords, magnates and lesser landowners were much interested in trade and commerce, unlike Cospatrick. So any drainage of Church wealth to Rome could have its effect on the realm's treasury.

There were other routine matters to attend to. But what made that meeting one that Patrick, for one, would never forget, was Alexander's announcement, his voice breaking, that Sir David de Lindsay was dead. Details were not yet available, only that he had died at Acre, on crusade.

The king was devastated.

Patrick rode home a saddened man. He had lost his father on crusade, and now his cousin and friend. Was all this preoccupation with driving the infidels from the Holy Land worth the cost? Was it, in fact, so essential? Christ's birthplace was precious, yes; but the Saracens could not destroy the fact of his birth, and the deliverance it brought for mankind. His message to humanity had been given. Was the spot where he had achieved it so important that so many should die over who now occupied it? Was not the Christian faith what mattered, not that far away piece of land?

On the way back to Dunbar Patrick had the sorrowful duty of informing David's mother, his Margaret, and his brother, of their grievous loss, at Luffness, one of the most unhappy moments of his life.

Later, Christian sought to console him. She said that David had the best of it. He had gone to a better place, a better life. The sorrow was not for him, but for those left behind to mourn. But – no crusading for Patrick!

20

Edward Plantagenet, it was reported, was also at Acre where David had died, a port some hundred miles north of Jerusalem. From there, after a stay in Sicily, he was making raids inland, achieving some minor victories over the Muslims; but so far, it seemed, he had not ventured towards Jerusalem itself. He was, in typical fashion for that young man, calling himself the First Knight of Christendom. King Louis of France had died, otherwise there might have been some resentment at his voicing this style and title. No contributions were sent to him from Scotland, whatever the papal instructions.

Edward's feeble father remained more or less powerless in England, with the barons ruling all, although in no very effective fashion, Simon de Montford sorely missed. So at present there was no threat to the Scots from the Auld Enemy.

Despite this, Patrick himself did have some English concerns to deal with, little as he desired them. The trouble arose out of that visit to Hexham to meet the legate Othobon, although this had no connection with Church revenues. The Cospatricks had always retained an interest in their ancient earldom of Northumbria, and a number of their former vassal landowners there still held certain hereditary manorial and feudal privileges granted to their ancestors by the earls. Their use of these was apparently being objected to by some of the other present-day Northumbrian magnates; and in the present state of lack of central authority in England, these were taking matters into their own hands. It was felt by the holders of these rights and favours that the earl should come down to

Tynedale and vouch for and explain the situation to the complainers, and further friction be avoided. Patrick believed that he could not refuse.

So, with Cousin Will and Gifford of Yester, he rode for Northumberland, crossing Tweed as usual at Wark, and again persuading de Ros from there to accompany them, he always a helpful and useful go-between.

All hard riders, they reached Hexham well before darkening, where they were kindly welcomed by Abbot John, who agreed to send to inform Sir Thomas Devilstone, he who had sent the request to Dunbar, of their arrival, and urging him to summon representatives of the two parties of landholders to the abbey for a meeting the next afternoon. The abbot knew all about the disagreements, and was anxious to see it all settled.

They spent a comfortable night in his house, and this time met the bishop, who agreed to sit in on the discussions.

Devilstone, with the odd name – almost certainly it was a corruption of De Vilston – came in the forenoon, to thank Patrick for this answer to his plea and to discuss details, a forceful man of middle years whom de Ros knew slightly. He said that he thought that there would be a good attendance from both sides in the dispute, and gave some fuller indications anent the matters at issue. He told of some of the disturbances and actual conflicts, blows being struck among the tenants, cattlemen and hirelings, although so far none of the landed men themselves had done more than challenge and accuse, while verbally supporting their people.

In due course the contestants began to appear, from up and down Tyneside, not a few of them knights but none who could be called lords, not all of the names known to Patrick. They all eyed him questioningly, and remained very much in their two groups, the atmosphere verging on tense despite the efforts of Abbot John to dispel this, suitable for a meeting being held in a place of worship. With the bishop's approval, he called upon Devilstone to lead off.

That man declared that all knew of the disagreements and reservations that had arisen among them over certain age-old rights and customs, held by some of those present, and objected to by others, these mainly concerned with grazings, milling, the damming of streams, fishings, and the borderlines of common lands. So they had called upon the Earl of Dunbar and March, in Scotland, representative of the ancient Earls of Northumbria who had granted these rights and privileges, to come and explain, and confirm their continuing relevance. His lordship had been sufficiently concerned to come in person, for which they should all be duly grateful.

Then the opposition put forward one Sir Robert de Hepburn of Newton as spokesman, an elderly man of dignified bearing, who spoke more slowly but with sufficient emphasis. He said that not a few of them found it strange and unacceptable that they should be denied the right to graze their stock over certain lands on their own properties, have to send some of their grain to be ground at mills other than their own, have streams flowing through their ground diverted by damming, and stretches of rivers denied to them and their folk for fishing and netting. Also some barring from felling wood on open land close to their own properties. This was all unsuitable, and no longer to be tolerated.

He was applauded by some and glared at by others.

Patrick, at the abbot's invitation, stood to address them. He had thought long and carefully over it all. He had a certain sympathy for both sides. But there were centuries-old lordship rights and feudal duties to be maintained, and only he was in a position to see to it, if he could.

"My friends," he began, "I well understand the feelings and views of all here, and those whom you represent. I would wish to satisfy you, so far as I may, and to lessen controversy." He spoke as slowly as had de Hepburn, and sought to sound sympathetic, but also authoritative. "I come as an earl of Scotland, not of England. My line was never that, for when the Cospatricks became Earls of

Northumbria, this great area had been ceded to the Scots crown by King Stephen of England, along with Cumbria. We were given Northumbria by King Malcolm the Third, father of my ancestor. When these two counties, as they now are, were passed back to England, we were created Earls of Dunbar, and later the March, or Borderland, in Scotland. But the earldoms of Northumbria and Cumbria were not bestowed on others. This is at the heart of the matter. There is no English Earl of Northumbria or Northumberland. Yet the lordship rights were given to my forebears and have never been repealed nor allotted to others. It is a strange situation, I agree, but not one to be ignored. As the laws and customs of both England and Scotland stand, *I* still represent the Earls of Northumbria. Does any contest that?"

Silence.

"If the King of England chose to create a new earldom here, then my position could change, no doubt. But meantime certain overlordship rights remain with me. And with them the rights and permissions my ancestors gave to certain of your landholders here, their vassals, for service rendered. It is these that are now being contested. But in feudal law they still stand, until they may be rescinded, by agreement of the two monarchies concerned. I could insist that these rights stand unchallenged. But I recognise that conditions which applied two hundred years ago may no longer fully apply, and that later changes in landholding, manorial dues and privileges can change, *have* changed. So it is my desire that matters should be regulated and made more suitable to present times, that harmony may be maintained in Northumberland, as well as certain rights. I come with this intent."

There were murmurings now, men eyeing each other.

"I may not have full authority here, I admit, my friends – but no one else has! So, if a fair solution to the problems is to be found, my views can carry such weight as is available. Does any contest that?"

Still no contrary voice was raised, nor could be in the

circumstances, however questioning were the looks of Patrick's hearers.

"I say, then, that a conference should be held of all the landholders concerned. To discuss and come to terms. Awkward and difficult matters to be debated and improvements made, the holders of these ancient rights to yield in some measure, for the weal of all. Not every right, I say, but some. This of the mills, in especial. It was a recognised form of favour for feudal superiors to grant to those who had served them well the milling rights over certain lands and areas, with the milling charges thereof. This still applies in many properties in Scotland as a source of revenue. But where it has become manifestly inconvenient and is causing real problems, for tenants as well as landholders, I would advise a yielding on one side and a better arrangement. The same applies to fishings on rivers and streams which flow through lands belonging in themselves to others, on both banks. These barrings should not be insisted upon. It is not for me to go into details and cases. But a conference, with goodwill on both sides, should be able to resolve most of the troubles, with the objectors being moderate and not grasping in their requests. If I was still Earl of Northumbria, so I would direct. Now, I advise it. Is it agreed?" Patrick waved a hand for discussion. That was quite the longest speech that he had ever made, and one of the most difficult.

Abbot John raised voice. "I applaud the Lord Cospatrick's proposals," he said. "This would be wise and just. It could and should bring peace and well-being."

Men had their heads together among the hearers, with noddings and shakings, pointings and shruggings.

Patrick added one further point. "I would suggest that William de Ros, Lord of Wark, here present, one of your own barons, and a senior one, should preside over such a meeting, one of good judgment, much experience and knowing the area and what could be best decided."

De Ros nodded. And when the talk and argument continued, he presently held up his hand.

"*This* is not the said conference!" he declared. "What is required here is to agree to hold it, in due course. I would be very surprised and grieved if such is not held." He paused. "Sir Thomas Devilstone, how say you?"

That man, glancing at his colleagues, rose. "We would agree, my lords."

"And Sir Robert de Hepburn?"

"A conference, yes," Hepburn said. "With some hope of an improvement." He too paused. "And our thanks to my lord of Dunbar and March."

Patrick raised a hand in acknowledgment, and turned to the abbot.

Presently, with much talk filling the abbey, but none of it angry, he found Hepburn at his side.

"My lord, you have much heartened us," he said. "A deal more than we had looked for. I, for one, am grateful. We feared . . ." He left that unspecified. "When do you return to Scotland, may I ask? For, if you have a day or two before you do so, it would be my pleasure to offer you some small entertainment."

"That is kind of you, Sir Robert. I think that I might delay my going for a couple of days, if my friends agree. Abbot John, here, is a good host."

"Then, my lord, tomorrow I would welcome you to Newton. It lies down Tyne some eight miles. It is east of Corbridge, by north. Newton Hall, in Bywell. Do you care to hunt? We have deer in our low hills. Also boar, many boar – very many! Some sport, then some repast. That would be my pleasure to provide."

"Why, yes. I would esteem that. Tomorrow." He looked at his friends, who nodded.

"My lord of Wark. And those with you, also, to be sure."

"My thanks."

A comfortable night was spent at the abbot's house, all present declaring that the day had gone well.

*   *   *

In the morning, with a monk as guide, the Scots and de Ros rode downriver to Corbridge, four miles, quite a sizeable community, and there left the Tyne to proceed through pleasant country of gentle hills and open woodlands for another three miles. Newton of Bywell proved to be a large property with a fine manor-house, where the visitors were introduced to Lady Hepburn and her son Nicholas and a grandson Adam. They were told that all was ready for a hunt into the Newtonfell and Heathery Edge area to the north, wooded hillocks which stretched almost to the Roman Wall, and where they could be fairly sure of gaining some good sport, especially along the valley of the Brockhole Burn and its branch streams. It was their claim that this was some of the best hunting country in Tynedale.

Quite a large party, with their outriders to locate and herd the deer to suitable points for the chase, boar to be looked for anywhere, in breezy weather they set out northwards, the Hepburns friendly and informative. The countryside was none so different from much of the Merse, but held no major hills like the Lammermuirs.

It was not long before, in the marshy surroundings of a small burn, they saw a boar. But this, at the sight of so many horses, quickly turned and bolted away over the soft ground and scrub, where the horses could not follow for fear of being bogged down.

Presently they reached a junction of a larger burn with this Brockhole, creating two valleys, where one of the outriders was awaiting them, to say that there were deer up both of these. So the hunt split up, Patrick and his cousin going with Sir Robert and young Adam Hepburn, while de Ros and Gifford struck off with the son Nicholas.

Another outrider, awaiting them, led them into sloping woodland of birch and alder, where they soon saw deer ahead among the scattered trees. The hunters were equipped with spears and crossbows, and, as the deer sped off at sight of them, arrows were fitted to bows and heels kicked mounts' sides.

As the deer separated in their flight, so must men and horses. Patrick, chasing a buck, found himself accompanied by Adam the grandson, a young man in his early twenties.

Fallow deer, smaller than the red deer of the Scottish hills, can still run faster than can horses, and he saw that he was not going to get within range for an arrow-shot. But the doe which young Hepburn was aiming for suddenly changed the course of its flight, and raced slant-wise across in front of Patrick. That man hesitated, for it was the other's quarry; but clearly Adam would not be able to win it. So, despite the difficulty of hitting a crossing target, as distinct from an onwards-heading one, he took a chance and loosed an arrow, at some fifty yards. His aim was fair, and the bolt struck home, but not at the heart, penetrating the belly. The creature lurched, staggered on a few yards, and then collapsed, kicking. It sought to rise, and could not, remaining rolling and struggling.

It was one of the rules of this sport that wounded animals were not left to die a lingering death, if at all possible. So Patrick rode over to the doe, dismounted, discarding his spear and crossbow and drawing his dirk, he bent, to plunge the blade in, one hand's-breadth behind the animal's shoulder, where the heart was to be reached. The steel struck deep, and, with one or two convulsive jerks, the creature died.

Patrick, wiping his blade clean of blood, was straightening up when two sounds reached him, sufficiently urgent sounds, one a high yelling, the other a growling roar, one human the other otherwise. Jerking round, he saw Hepburn, still some seventy or so yards off, gesticulating and pointing to the right. And glancing in that direction, he perceived why. Out from a clump of bushes a boar was charging, head down, in snarling threat. And it was not at the shouting horseman that it was heading but at himself, standing beside the deer, a great tusker, heavy, massive, menacing.

There was little time for thought. The brute was barely

fifty yards away. Patrick's spear and bow lay on the ground, near his mount. But that horse was as aware of the danger as was its master. Rearing, it turned and bolted for the nearest trees.

In his alarm and dread, the man was scarcely aware of making a choice. That spear, and an effort at defence? Or flight, like his steed? There were only the briefest seconds to decide. Could he in fact reach the weapon, pick it up and level and couch it, lengthy as it was, in time? And to any effect? That question required little answering. Patrick turned and ran.

In long riding-boots, he was not clad for running. Those trees – could he reach one of them before the charging boar caught up with him? Get behind it, something between him and the brute. Dodge it, halt the rush? His only chance . . .

Horribly aware of the grunting, snarling creature so close behind, he raced unsteadily for the nearest tree large enough to offer momentary protection, an old, white-barked birch. He had his dirk in hand – but would that be of any use against a charging tusker? He knew that it would not.

Stumbling, he reached the tree, arms round its trunk, to throw himself behind it. And just in time. The boar, tusks gleaming, hurtled past him, only inches away, the stink of it strong. But despite its rush and weight, it was nimble on its small feet, and in only a few yards pivoted round and came back, its speed reduced but still at a run, its growling deeper than ever.

Patrick was reduced to circling round that tree-trunk, tripping in those heavy, long boots, breathless, clutching the wood. Again the boar all but scraped him as it hurtled past. And thereafter, once again, it wheeled round to come charging back.

Could this go on, the tree-trunk the only defence? As the return runs slowed down the animal, so it could aim itself more accurately. Patrick knew despair.

And then, barely escaping a third assault, he knew

something else. Adam Hepburn, on his horse, was there, close, spear levelled, seeking to gain a position to thrust. But his mount, like Patrick's own, was terrified of the boar, its snoring ferocity, its strong smell. It reared and plunged, despite all the rider's efforts to control it. It was for off.

Somehow the young man threw himself out of the saddle, that awkward long spear still clutched, as the horse dashed away.

The boar, in another of its rushes, came near enough to rip a tear in Patrick's breeches, knocking him against the tree and all but over-balancing him.

But now the creature saw another target, which did not demand turning around. Head down, it charged at the younger man.

Hepburn just had time to lower and point his spear. As the animal bore down on him, he stood his ground, and aimed. Steel tip did make contact. But the brute's hide was thick, and its rush carried it on, the spear only grazing down its side, and the shock of the clash sending the man reeling.

The boar, the more ferocious for the pain of that wound, performed its swift turning manoeuvre once more and came doubling back. Hepburn had only seconds. But he used them to extraordinary effect. He turned, sinking to his knees, and swung his long spear over from a pointing to a horizontal position held before him, gripped with hands widely apart, this at face level. And as the brute came up, jaws wide, he thrust that lance-shaft into the gaping, slobbering mouth.

That young man knew his boars. He knew that these great tusks, so menacing, would clamp up and down over the shaft, all but locking it in position. The force of the charge admittedly knocked him over, and he was trampled on by the creature, but it could not savage him. Indeed it was the butt of the lance that gave him the worst blow, striking his shoulder as it was carried forward.

Meantime, Patrick had not stood idle, clutching his tree. Seeing Hepburn fall, he hurried over to his aid. How long would it take that boar to get rid of the lance, to recognise that it must open its jaws, and therefore tusks, to free it? Until it did, it was vulnerable. Dirk clenched, he approached the animal as it turned this way and that, shaking head and heavy shoulders.

That shaft, being swung to and fro in fury, was the greater danger. Having to jump to avoid it, Patrick lunged in with his dagger. His first blow did not strike very deep, in that thick, bristly hide, and did not seem to do more than further enrage the brute, and the blade was almost wrenched from his hand as he dodged the swinging shaft, difficult to extract from the hide. But he managed to keep his feet, and got it out. The second stroke he drove in just behind the shoulder, for the heart. How deep it penetrated he could not tell, but it did not reach its target, for the animal continued to twist and turn crazily. He was still trying to get the dirk out, while avoiding the swinging lance, when he saw that Hepburn was on his feet again, his own dagger drawn, and seeking to strike also.

Even with the two of them stabbing and slashing as best they could, it seemed to take a long time for that boar to die. It was the younger man going over to pick up Patrick's lance and then using it to drive into the creature's rear, after three tries, that finally finished the battle, and their menacer pitched over and fell, the lance-shaft still between its tusks.

Panting, the two men eyed each other.

Patrick was first to speak. "God be praised!" he got out. "You, you saved me! Risked all, for me! This, this devil! I have never seen the like. So large, so fierce. But for you, it would have had me. You saved my life, man! I thank you, I thank you, with all my heart!"

"It took some slaying," the other said. "The worst I have known. You are not hurt, my lord?"

"A graze to my leg, that is all. That of using the spear-shaft to the mouth to hold its tusks. That was it, that served."

"I knew of that, yes. To use anything such. Long, held low. My father told me."

"And you did it, bless you. Here was the deed of a hero!"

"Not so, my lord." Hepburn gazed around. "The horses? Affrighted. They will not have gone far, I think. Into the woodland."

"Yes. We shall find them . . ."

Sheathing their dirks and collecting the spears and bows, they set off to seek for their mounts. The dead boar could be collected hereafter.

Sure enough, they found the two horses together, not far into the trees, the beasts tossing their heads at sight of their masters.

It was good to be in the saddle again. Patrick certainly did not feel like more of hunting, and Adam did not suggest it. So it was back to Newton Hall for them. The outriders could bring in the boar and deer.

Patrick's grazed leg required little treatment, and the younger man was only bruised. When the others returned from the hunt, it was all praise for Adam, Patrick declaring that he must be suitably rewarded. He had saved his life. The others made less of it, but he insisted on the need for some reward.

That night, back in the abbot's house, he thought much on this. Abbot John told him that Adam was the third son of Nicholas, his elder brother presently acting as esquire to the Percy lord of Alnwick, the other destined for the Church. So the young man was not heir to Newton of Bywell.

In the morning, on the way home to Scotland, they went by Newton Hall. And there, after a word with Sir Robert, Patrick approached Adam.

"My friend and, and saviour!" he said. "I have been considering. I owe my life to you, and am determined to show my gratitude. I have spoken with your grandsire. Here, as a third son, you will in time be given some small lands, two or three farms, perhaps. But, if you would come to Scotland, I would make you a laird of wide acres, with a hallhouse or manor of your own. You would be one of the vassals of my earldoms, a man of substance. How say you, Adam Hepburn?"

The other stared at him. "My lord Earl . . . !" he faltered. "I, I know not. I did little. Fought off a boar – that is all. To offer to give me this is, is . . . beyond belief!"

"Is saving my life so small a service?"

"The boar might not have killed you."

"I could not have kept that tree between it and me for long. I had only my dirk. It would have got me." He shook his head. "Would you not wish to come to Scotland? Dunbar and Lothian are none so far off. One day's ride."

"I had never thought of it, my lord. It, it is too much."

"For me, and from me, it is not. Think on it, Adam man. It would please me. And come to tell me, yea or nay. One day, before long."

They left it at that.

The Scots party took leave amid much goodwill on both sides, and wishing the conference, under de Ros, well when it came about.

They rode on, to cross Tweed at Berwick.

21

Christian, when she heard of it all, was greatly concerned, and full of praise for young Hepburn, agreeing that this of offering him lands in one of the earldoms was an excellent way of seeking to repay the debt. His rescuer would be foolish not to accept it. She would show him *her* gratitude also, to be sure. Had Patrick any notion of what property to offer him?

He said that he had thought of Hailes, a lairdship in the valley of the Lothian Tyne, so that he would come from one Tyne to another. A far-out cousin had died there recently, leaving no heir. It was only nine or ten miles from Dunbar. Or, if he would prefer a place in the Merse, there were one or two possibles. Cowdenknowes, for instance, near to Ercildoune, where the keeper was elderly, frail, and should be replaced. Others would come to mind . . .

They did not have to wait very long for a decision, for de Ros arrived three weeks later, with Adam Hepburn, to report the results of the Northumbrian conference, which had been a success apparently, with a fair exchange of views resulting in a reasonable agreement and not a little satisfaction expressed all round, with appreciation of the earl's efforts on their behalf. Patrick had made many new friends in Tynedale.

As for young Hepburn, he had come to say that, all unworthy as he was, he would be proud to accept his lordship's generous offer, his father and grandsire urging him to it. No large property was called for, they said; and Adam would prove a useful link between the North-umbrian landholders and the Scots, especially during this unsettled period in England, when there might well be support useful against possible grasping fellow-countrymen.

The young man brought that boar's head, cleaned and stuffed, as memento.

Christian made quite a fuss over Hepburn, Pate and his brothers finding him companionable, and their sisters still more so. Patrick had assured his sons that this gesture towards their visitor would nowise prejudice their own endowments in lands; there were plenty of lairdships in the two earldoms for all of them.

Their visitor was asked whether he would prefer to have his property in this Lothian, or in the Borderland, the Merse? He declared whichever best suited his lordship. So they all took him first to view Hailes, as nearest Dunbar.

This, a modest tower-house, but with fairly extensive land, lay directly beneath the north face of a highly dramatic and historic feature of the eastern Lothian landscape, indeed where the name Lothian had come from. For this isolated, lofty, whaleback ridge, called Traprain Law, had been where the ancient King Loth, of the Southern Picts, had placed his capital, he who had been the father of the blessed Thania, mother of St Kentigern or Mungo, who had founded Glasgow in the course of his missionary efforts. The abruptly rising hill, sometimes called Dunpender, forced the River Tyne to form quite a ravine to round it, the road from Haddington and the west having to thread this pass. And on a spur, dominating road and river, rose Hailes Castle, with one of the baronial rights accrueing to its occupier being the sanction to levy a toll on users of the road, part of which fell to be passed on to his superior, the Earl of Dunbar. Also there were the exclusive fishing-rights in almost a mile of the Tyne, which here, only six miles from salt water, was rich in salmon as well as trout. So it was quite a valuable as well as attractive and picturesque property, making a worthy reward for life-saving.

Young Hepburn was delighted with it all, although

protesting that it was far too much for the little that he had done. He was not concerned to go looking at other laird-ships, in the Merse or elsewhere. Here, near Dunbar, where he could perhaps serve his lordship and family, he would be happy to dwell.

So it was accepted and arranged. Adam would be Hepburn of Hailes, an adoptive Scot and a grateful one.

He remained with them at Dunbar for a few days, but saw something of the surrounding country, being especially impressed with the mighty cliff-girt coast to the south, between Dunbar and the mouth of the Eye Water, marvelling at the dizzy crags, precipices, caves and rock-stacks reaching to majestic St Ebba's Head, with its nunnery perched in unlikely site on the wind-blown summit. There the pious Northumbrian princess, Ebba, daughter of King Ethelfrid, in the mid-seventh century, had set up her religious community, known as Urbs Coludi – from which nearby Coldinghame took its name – this to escape the attentions of the pagan Viking raiders and ravishers. The still more famous St Cuthbert had come visiting a few years later, reputedly spending the best part of a night in the sea just below, in prayers and vigils, while the seals came nestling to his side. Adam was enthralled.

He returned to Northumberland, but said that it would not be long before he came back again, and for good, very good, a grateful young man.

This pleasant interlude was followed, only a day or two later, by a highly unusual, indeed scarcely believable, development for the Cospatrick family, the word of it brought by none other than King Alexander himself, come from Edinburgh Castle, and requiring action on Patrick's part. There had been a happening in the west, in Ayrshire, which all but defied acceptance as truth. The late Neil, Earl of Carrick, friend of Bruce and Patrick, had left only a daughter, Margaret, who thus succeeded him as countess in her own right. And she had wed one Adam de Kilcon-quhar, from Fife, who was granted the title of Earl of

Carrick, as her husband. But this Earl Adam had died on crusade, like so many another, of fever, about the same time as had David Lindsay. And now the widow had distinguished herself in a fashion which left all, including the monarch, in an odd mixture of astonishment, disapproval and amusement.

It seemed that the Countess Margaret had been out deer-hunting in the upland area of Loch Doon, where the Carrick lands met those of Bruce of Annandale, and there had met up with another much smaller hunt led by none other than Bruce's son, another Robert, Christian's brother. They had more or less joined forces, and after a successful day's sport, had gone to spend the night at the small Bruce castle on an islet in Loch Doon. What had transpired that night was unspecified but might be guessed at, Margaret being a lively and attractive woman. But after renewed hunting next day, the countess had insisted that Robert accompanied her to her own castle of Turnberry, some distance off. Whatever the reason for doing so, he had chosen otherwise, and the masterful lady, rejecting his refusal, had actually ordered her more numerous attendants to force Bruce to go westwards with her, all but a captive. Turnberry lay on the Carrick coast south of Ayr and north of Girvan, and there she had detained the young man. However unwilling he had been initially, he seemed to have become reconciled to the situation, for he remained with the countess for the best part of a week, before they both went to Crossraguel Abbey and were hurriedly married. Whereupon the countess announced that Robert Bruce was now Earl of Carrick, in her right, and as such lord of much of Ayrshire. The pair were still at Turnberry apparently. And all the vassals and landholders of the earldom were summoned to come and pay their homage and respects to their new superior.

This almost incredible story had them all bemused and head-shaking. For a woman to capture a man, not by her charms but by force, and take him to her home and bed, against his will, was something to be doubted indeed.

Christian was, for once, at a complete loss. She admitted that her brother was not the strongest character of their family; but to allow himself to be abducted by a female and forced into marriage was too much, just too much. Was it all some strange compact between them? Some elaborate playacting? But if so, why arrange it thus? If they wanted to have each other, what was to prevent them getting betrothed and wed in normal fashion? Was there some impediment to this? Were either, or both, committed in some other way? So far as her brother was concerned, Christian knew of nothing that could have prevented him from making such marriage. As for the countess, widowed and with no offspring, there seemed to be no call for any such dramatic and rather ridiculous performance, and one that made the man look distinctly feeble and spineless. Questions, questions.

What concerned the king, however, was not the oddity of it all but the fact that young Bruce was now to be called Earl of Carrick, and seemingly acting the earl towards the Ayrshire vassals.

No man could assume the style and title of earl, with its privileges, either by family succession, by conquest or by marriage, without the royal assent and authority; and in this case nothing such had been sought. Possibly the countess had not fully realised this; but certainly Robert Bruce should have known it. This must be emphasised and made evident to all. An offence had been committed against the crown, and must be rectified. And paid for.

The young man's father, Bruce of Annandale – had he any knowledge or hand in this? Alexander would have sent him to represent the royal displeasure, but it was just possible that he was involved in some way; and anyway he would seem to be an unsuitable representative of the monarch, as the father of the offender. So the Cospatrick was the obvious envoy, brother-in-law, and a senior earl as well as former regent. Patrick was to go to Turnberry and declare the assumption of the earldom by Bruce as invalid, until approval by the monarch, impose a requisite fine as penalty, and establish the crown's supreme authority. Nothing could be done about the marriage, however strangely brought about, nor about Countess Margaret's holding of the earldom, which had been granted some time before; but this of the young Bruce's position had to be rectified. Because of his father's long and loyal service, Alexander would almost certainly confirm the earldom to the son in due course, but only after the position was regularised and due atonement made.

Patrick did not relish this peculiar task; but the fact that the king had come in person to order it showed that he considered it of importance. There could be no refusal. He asked Alexander what sort of fine would be suitable.

Enough to make it clear that this misbehaviour was costly, he was told. That earldom, in mainly fertile Ayrshire, was probably a rich one, so more than any mere gesture was required. Patrick must use his own judgment.

Alexander was informed about the Northumbrian situation, the conference, and the links with the Cospatricks reestablished. He commended it all. He was also interested in young Hepburn's coming, and saw it all as a worthwhile exercise. Any friendly region between Scotland and the rest of England could be advantageous. It would be good to establish something similar at the Cumbrian side.

On the royal departure next day, Christian announced that she was going to accompany her husband on this difficult and strange errand; she thought that she might well be of use, another woman where one was the principal player in the drama, and sister of the alleged victim-accomplice. Patrick welcomed that.

They did not delay. They had a long ride to Lochmaben Castle, in mid Annandale, to see her father, before heading on westward for Turnberry, well over one hundred miles across the spine of Lowland Scotland, by the northern foothills of the Lammermuirs to where these all but joined the Morthwaites, then down the Gala Water to mid Tweed, on by Selkirk to the Ettrick and Yarrow rivers to Moffat in Annandale, hilly country all the way. They would hope to spend the night at Jedburgh Abbey, where Patrick knew the abbot.

On the way they discussed every aspect they could think of which might account for this most peculiar happening. Margaret of Carrick did not have the reputation of being a particularly dominant woman, and her previous marriage to de Kilconquhar had been apparently normal and produced no especial talk, as well as no offspring. Christian was fairly sure that there was more behind this incident than was being told. It would be interesting to hear her father's views.

Lochmaben Castle, the main Bruce stronghold, was unusual in its situation, and the most powerful fortress in the Borderland, which was saying something. It was built not on any cliff-top, but occupied a quite low peninsula jutting into the loch, this neck of land separated from the rest by a wide and deep ditch, the result forming an island of no less than some fifteen acres. Two additional ditches ran at right angles to the main one, all provided with drawbridges and portcullis defences. The walls within were high, and the keep massive. It made a commodious but grim-seeming hold; but Christian, born herein, loved it and its loch.

They found her father and her young half-brother, Bernard, as doubtful as was she over the entire situation, but little better informed as to the whys and wherefores apparently. Bruce declared that his elder son was perhaps not of heroic stature, but he could not see him as so weak and spineless a character as to let himself be the prisoner of any woman, and forced into marriage. They knew Margaret of Carrick, of course. One of her seats, Dalmellington Castle, was none so far off from their own boundary, and she visited Lochmaben on occasion, the last time only about a month ago. Some sort of compact might just possibly have been made between her and Robert then, although there had been no obvious close association. She was, admittedly, a spirited woman, and his son *could* have been smitten then, or previously, without revealing it.

Robert was not of the crafty or plotting type, so all this was seemingly very much out of character. But one detail of the affair struck him as perhaps significant. That evening, after the first day's hunting, they had gone to spend the night, and together, at Loch Doon, a Bruce place, and less than convenient, having to be rowed out in a small boat to the little castle on its islet, so precluding any sizeable number of their followers accompanying them, this while her large house of Dalmellington was none so far off. Why, if not to sleep together, and possibly hatch some plot?

Patrick asked whether Bruce senior would have withheld agreement for his son's marriage to Margaret? To be told that Robert was of full age, in his twenty-fourth year, and could wed whom he would. There had been some discussion months before of a suitable match for the heir to Annandale, the names of daughters of Randolph of Noddsdale and Carlyle of Torthorwald coming up – they would not have aspired to a countess in her own right – but nothing positive had been decided, nor any steps actually taken.

Christian declared that this might well be behind the odd development; that the pair had fallen for each other previously and were determined to make sure that no alternative marriage was arranged. But if so, why did Robert not just announce his desire to wed Margaret? Would there have been any real objection? It would have seemed a notable match, his son in line to become an earl. Was there possibly some other arrangement or understanding to counter this? She eyed her father with that direct gaze of hers.

Bruce smoothed his chin at that. Not really, he said. There *had* been talk that the lands of Hemplands and Branetrigg, belonging to Torthorwald, which jutted into the lordship of Annandale unsuitably, might possibly make a convenient dowery for one of Carlyle's daughters to bring with her; but that was only merest speculation.

Christian nodded. Perhaps enough, however, to alarm her brother. That could be the key to it all. She made that almost an accusation.

Patrick, anxious to avoid any family discomfort, asked Bruce what sort of a fine would be appropriate to meet the king's penalty for this of assuming the earldom without royal authority. His father-in-law, almost relievedly, declared that Carrick was a rich lordship. The countess would never miss, say, a thousand merks in silver, if it gained her and Robert what they had striven so oddly to attain. That is, if it was all indeed a device.

That seemed to be as far as they could take the matter meantime, and subsequent discussion spared them any discomfort.

In the morning, the pair were off westwards, by Moniave, the Glenkens, passing near both Loch Doon and Dalmellington, to Kirkmichael, Kirkoswald and Turnberry, over fifty miles. The seat of the Carrick earldom was a fine place, set above coastal cliffs, these with curious deep fissures which, bridged over, were incorporated in the fortalice, making it impossible to attack from the sea, and a sufficiency of defences from landward.

Their arrival coincided with the return from another hunt of the erring couple, and in the meeting and greetings and unloading of deer carcases, this did to some extent lessen the impact of what could not fail to be a difficult visitation, although Robert's embarrassment was not to be hidden, brother and sister eyeing each other doubtfully.

Margaret of Carrick proved to be a woman such as any susceptible man might fall for, in her late twenties, handsome rather than beautiful but with a sparkle about her dark eyes, proudly built and challenging in her femininity. She was the daughter of the late Walter, High Steward, and descendant of Earl Neil of ancient Celtic line, and this ancestry showed in her whole bearing and attitude. Certainly if any female might take a man captive by force, this one could. There was no doubt as to which was the more positive and assertive character here.

It was some little time, inevitably, before they could get down to the object of their visit, however much the others must suspect, hospitality being offered and accepted,

Robert keeping somewhat in the background, the countess seeming nowise put about. She even described some of the highlights of this latest hunt, clearly very keen on the chase.

When at length there was a pause and Patrick could declare, somewhat hesitantly, the object of his errand, he felt that it was unsuitable to remark, at least at first, on the strange way that Robert had come to Turnberry; and so he began by emphasising the king's objection to the assumption of the earldom without the royal approval and permission. This caused the younger man to bite his lip, but had his new wife shaking her dark head.

"The earldom of Carrick is mine, and has been since my father died," she said, although not aggressively. "My late husband held it, through me. Why not Robert Bruce?"

"It is not *who* holds it in your right, Lady Margaret," he told her. "It is the fact that you declared it abroad without the king's permission. That is required for all earldoms. His Grace would have expected you to know it, after your previous marriage."

"Adam went to see the king, yes. But he did not say that it was for permission, merely to render his loyal support, I understood. And Robert had no need to state that, his father's son."

"It was more than that, lady. The High King must give his royal authority before any man can be named earl. So here was error. He is . . . displeased."

"Then I regret displeasing him. That was not my intention."

"Did *you* not know of this?" Patrick looked at Robert.

"Not, not that it was so important, my lord. In due course I would have gone to the king. But . . ." His voice tailed away.

"Well, it is an offence against the crown, a denial of the royal right and rule. And, as such, must be paid for. It is my less than happy duty, coming from His Grace, to inform you that you must pay a fine, a substantial fine."

He had turned back to the countess. "I am sorry, but there it is."

"So! Ah, well — all satisfactions must be paid for, I suppose. And His Grace is ever said to be short of moneys!"

It was Patrick's turn to clear his throat. "It is not that, Countess. It is required, the penalty. The fine is . . . one thousand silver merks."

She raised her eyebrows. "Is that the price of the king's favour? A thousand merks? None so costly! We can spare that, I think! We must aid the king in his need. I shall send it where? To Roxburgh?"

That, at least, was easier than expected. "To Edinburgh, meantime. No doubt, in due course, His Grace will accept this of earl's rank for your husband," Patrick said.

"I should hope so. Whether the king accepts it or not, others do. Robert is now accepted as earl by all here in Carrick."

Christian spoke, looking at her brother. "Rob, was this of your being brought here against your will but a device? A play-acting, for some reason?"

He shook his head. "I came. Because it was . . . necessary," he jerked.

"Why necessary? When it makes you seem a weakling to have allowed it."

"Necessary, because I could have been with child." That was the countess spreading her hands. "Indeed, I think that I am so!"

"Ah! I see. And by Robert?"

"Who else? Sakes, think you that I am whore, some strumpet! I am Margaret of Carrick!"

"I beg your pardon," Christian said, but scarcely humbly. "So you two have been . . . friendly for some time past?"

Silence.

Patrick, ever the peacemaker, felt that enough had been said. They had done what they had come for and gained promise of payment of the fine. He was concerned about the hour. He, at least, did not want to spend the night here at Turnberry in this uncomfortable atmosphere. Crossraguel Abbey, where the pair had been wed, was none so far off. They could reach there well before dark. Indeed they might well go on further, so that on the morrow they could reach Edinburgh. There was a monastery that he knew of at Ochiltree, on the Lugar Water, which would bring them to within sixty miles of that city. Christian would be good for that amount of riding, he knew.

He looked at her. "We must be on our way," he said. "A long road for us. The king is at Edinburgh, and will expect me to report to him at the soonest."

"Then tell him that I will send my siller there. That he does not fret for it!" the countess said. "Tell him so, my lord. When he has gone to the trouble of sending you for it, with his empty coffers!"

"It is not so . . ." Patrick began, and then desisted. There was nothing to be gained by prolonging this awkward interview.

Christian inclined her head, so fair in contrast to the other woman's darkness. She probably was less concerned over this sparring, but she could recognise her husband's unease.

"We shall leave you, then, good-sister," she said, with a half-smile. "And wish this marriage a less difficult course than at its start! Rob?"

That man, who had remained very much in the background in it all, nodded, and with bows all round, led them out to their horses. Deliberately, in the courtyard, Patrick held back a little, to let the pair have a few words together, of whatever sort. With so much difference in age, these two had never been very close, but they were, after all, brother and sister.

The parting thereafter was restrained, but Christian did squeeze Robert's shoulder and kiss his cheek.

"The Lord be praised, that is over!" Patrick declared as they rode off. "I could do without such tasks in His Grace's service."

"My poor Patrick! You are not the one for disputes. But you played your hand well enough. And my new good-sister could not take the reins with you, as she clearly can with Robert."

"Yes, Robert. It is a strange match, that. I would not have seen these two as coming together of choice."

"Not so strange, perhaps. My brother has always been used to a strong hand to direct him. Our father has such. Robert seems to need it. And this Margaret requires to dominate, to act the strong woman, I could see. She would not be happy with an assertive man." She gave one of her little laughs. "I hope that *I* am not such? Am I? And you, a gentle man. But with your own strengths. Those two, I think, are well enough suited for each other. I think that they may well be happy. And if she has a child, then they could be the closer. I may be wrong, but this of her stated pregnancy may be her need. She bore no child to her former husband. If Robert can give her one, then they will both be fulfilled."

He shook his head at that. "It may be so, but it is all beyond me! I am glad that you came with me, my dear."

They found themselves able to get well beyond Cross-raguel and to this monastery at Ochiltree to spend the night, making it possible to reach Edinburgh the next day.

They found Alexander not in the great rock-top fortress but in the Abbey of the Holy Rude, a deal more comfortable, with its guest-house all but a monarchial retreat, and convenient for hunting in the royal forest around the towering Arthur's Seat, and for hawking at the reed-beds of Duddingston Loch. The king was interested to hear Patrick's report, well satisfied over the thousand merks fine, and agreed that if young Bruce and the countess came and made formal deference to his authority, he would be well enough pleased to confirm him as Earl of Carrick. He offered his thanks to the Cospatricks.

They stayed with the monarch and his queen overnight, well entertained.

In the morning, it was back to Dunbar.

22

They were surprised to find Adam Hepburn already back at Dunbar, and were not long in discerning what had brought him north again so soon. It was their eldest daughter, Beatrice who was the magnet, they perceived, and she not averse to his attentions, her sister Gelis all but jealous. This did not displeasure her father and mother, who saw the young man as a quite acceptable possible son-in-law. Beatrice was only of eighteen years, but fully woman. That Newton boar looked like being responsible for much.

Young Adam took up residence at Hailes quite promptly, roosting alone in the little castle, at least over-night, although the young people from Dunbar were much with him, and concerned that he made a worthy home of it. There was much to be done, for it had been neglected by its former occupant for years. As it happened, there were certain similarities in its setting and features to comparatively nearby Yester Castle, and Patrick suggested that a visit there might be helpful, to see Hugo de Gifford and his master-masons. Not that he was advocating any subterranean chambers, although it would be interesting to see how that odd enterprise was developing; but the Frenchman de Gobelin's ideas on other aspects of that castle could be of advantage for Hailes.

In the event, the entire family went to Yester to inspect this architectural wonder, of which de Gifford was now very proud, it all enhancing his reputation as a seer. And he had reason to be, for it proved a quite astonishing endeavour, spectacular as it was effective and ingenious. The enlarging of the cave, and the extension, had created a chamber of such dimensions as to outdo the great halls of any castle in Scotland, and not only in size. It was rib-vaulted, with the ribs splayed and reaching to a height of about twenty feet, this to a pointed arch. In the natural stone walls there were gaps for wooden joists at the splaying of the arch to enable an intervening floor to be inserted if required, an opening for this left as a doorway in the long straight flight of steps down from the main castle. Another doorway led into a passage of over thirty feet, cut through the solid rock to reach a postern about halfway down the steep descent, this provided with another three doors and sliding bars to prevent unwanted ingress. The hall itself was almost forty feet long by thirteen wide. A great fireplace, with a sloping flue to carry the smoke up to the open air, was in the north wall, with a stone hood above. There were, of course, no windows, so light had to be provided by lamps; and there were corbels or lamp-brackets projecting right down the hall. These stone walls were being painted in bright colours with elaborate de-signs, all a copy, it was declared, of French chateaux at Arques and Roch Guyon.

All expressed much wonder and admiration for this remarkable achievement, although young Hepburn was more interested in the upper works of this castle, which could be copied and adapted to improve Hailes. Patrick himself tended to wonder why all this ingenuity and labour had been expended, however admirable, its uses unex-plained in a comparatively small fortalice of no very important laird. What was the intention, save to enhance Gifford's already strange reputation, the master of Hob-goblin Hall!

The masons agreed to come and inspect Hailes, to see what improvement might be made in the cause of comfort and amenity rather than of defence, this especially con-cerning Beatrice, who obviously saw herself as becoming mistress there.

News of much importance reached Dunbar a few days later. Gamelyn had suddenly died, while on a visit to

Glasgow. This was bound to have major impact on the land, as well as the Church, for whatever else he had been, the Primate was a very able and effective administrator and latterly a valuable supporter of the crown. Also it would signal a further decline in the Comyn power.

Patrick was surprised soon thereafter to receive another summons from the king, to Edinburgh. This time the monarch did not come in person. He went, as ever, somewhat apprehensively.

However, it proved to be no very daunting demand on this occasion. It seemed that the College of Bishops had unanimously elected Bishop William Wishart, the Chancellor, to be the new Primate at St Andrews; he had been archdeacon there, and was indeed the obvious choice, a strong man and well thought of; he lived up to his name, which was only a corruption of Wise Heart.

One of the new Primate's first concerns, oddly enough, was to rectify a situation which had been an anomaly for over a century, comparatively minor as it might seem, but which had much preoccupied Wishart when archdeacon. It concerned the Cluniac priory on the Isle of May, none so far offshore from St Andrews. This represented one of the few errors of judgment of the excellent monarch, King David, he who had founded all the abbeys and ruled so very wisely. For some reason, he had given the Isle of May, at the mouth of the Firth of Forth, to his English brother-in-law, Henry Beauclerc, and with it the little Celtic Church monastery set up by St Ethernan, this mainly to tend and service the lighthouse, or beacon, he had established thereon, the first such in all Scotland. Beauclerc, on his deathbed, had donated the island to the Abbey of Reading, for prayers to be said for his soul's repose; and this establishment, Roman Catholic of course, had founded the Cluniac priory dedicated to St Adrian, the name David's mother, Queen Margaret, had changed from Ethernan in honour of the then pontiff, this although there was no real saint of the name. Now this strange situation of an English Church establishment on a Scots island, and only a few miles from the religious heart of Scotland, Wishart was eager to put right. He was prepared to purchase the island and its priory from Reading, out of Church revenues. But to avoid conflict with Canterbury, and possibly the Vatican, he judged that the initiative should seem to come from Alexander, who could claim that here was a Scottish island unsuitably in the hands of an English owner, and forming a source of contention. Payment for this would be made to Reading Abbey, or to the Archbishop of Canterbury, if so desired.

So the king desired Patrick to act as go-between in this matter. The Isle of May lay only a dozen miles off Dunbar, and he, with his ships, was in a good position to visit and inspect the priory situation, as a non-cleric, and to report, thus making it seem that it was an affair of the state, not of the Church.

Patrick was not averse to this errand, indeed seeing it as quite an interesting little trip, the isle in sight of his castle, and its gleaming beacon to be seen many a night. He had never actually landed there, although passing it frequently on various voyages. His father had visited it, he understood.

When, back home, he announced this latest royal requirement, Christian declared that she desired to accompany him. She had always had a notion to visit the May. And the rest of the family said likewise. It would make a pleasant outing for them all.

So the expedition was arranged, in one of the smaller Dunbar vessels, and they set sail in a holiday mood, Adam Hepburn coming with them, he now being accepted as all but one of the family, having sought Beatrice's hand in marriage and receiving her father's assent. The wedding would be celebrated before long.

The sail out, past the Craig of Bass, was of over an hour's duration, and enjoyable, although just off the Bass their craft did toss and heave notably, to squeals from the women, this caused by underwater cliffs at, as it were, the land's end.

When they reached the May, an island of more cliffs white with seabird droppings, a mile in length but less than half of that in breadth, they put into a small natural harbour at its southern end. Whether or not their approach had been observed from the priory, this on the higher ground, none came to meet the visitors.

They all climbed the quite steep and rocky slope, amid screaming, wheeling seafowl, Patrick explaining to Adam how one of St Columba's missionary disciples, allocated Fife to convert, with St Monan, had made this his *diseart*, or retreat for occasional solitary communion with his Maker, as was the custom in the old Celtic Church; and while so doing had recognised that, however excellent a spot it was for private devotions, the isle was also a menace for shipping in poor visibility or storm, with its rocks and reefs around, there in the entrance to the firth, and with wrecks frequent. So he had established his unique contribution, a beacon as warning of a night, for seafarers. It had to be fuelled with wood, and since no trees grew on the May's stony and exposed heights, the timber had to be ferried out from the Fife shore, to the north, in barges, all a most notable endeavour. This still had to continue these centuries later. Ethernan was a name that ought to be venerated by mariners and travellers; and to have it changed to the then Pope's name, Adrian, was as unsuitable as it was ridiculous.

They found a couple of distinctly glum-looking monks mending nets near the priory buildings, and were eyed curiously, especially the women – for it would be seldom indeed that such were to be seen on May – but they were not offered any actual greeting.

The priory itself was not extensive, and had a somewhat run-down appearance, with little sign of life about it. They discovered that it was run by a sub-prior, a character of unimpressive bearing and manner, and staffed by a mere half-dozen monks; indeed they gathered that it served as a sort of penal settlement for wayward or disgraced brethren, and as such was but ill-esteemed by all concerned.

Patrick could well see why Wishart wanted it brought back into Scots hands, renewed and improved. Also that it ought not to require any large sum to purchase; that is, if Reading was prepared to dispose of it.

They wasted little time over this sorry blemish on a quite attractive isle, otherwise unoccupied. All went on an exploration of the terrain, with its own fascination, however dangerous for shipping, barren as to growth, stunted wind-blown bushes, buckthorn and coarse grasses being its sole vegetation. But the scenery was eye-catching, even for viewers used to the cliff-bound coasts nearer home, and clamorous seabirds, the swimming seals and rafts of divers. It was a blessing that the weather was fine and with little wind, for the May would be no place to linger on in unfavourable conditions. St Ethernan must have been a tough individual.

A circuit of the isle and it was back to their vessel, to continue their little voyage, onward round the thrusting Fife Ness to St Andrews itself, that town, all but a city, of towers and spires and religious establishments by the score. Leaving his party to make so very different an exploration from that of the May, Patrick went in search of the Primate. He eventually found him in a new hospital and shelter he was establishing for the sick and needy. There he told Wishart of what he had found on the island, the poor state of the priory, and his impression that Reading Abbey might well be not displeased to get rid of it, so that the price could be none so high. The bishop thanked him warmly, but declared that he was willing to pay a quite substantial sum nevertheless, to bring it all back to Scots hands, and to right the wrong. He would not wish to offend the Cluniac Order, and would re-establish a better priory there of that community; also see that the lighthouse was well supplied with fuel. He would be prepared to pay as much as three thousand merks in silver, although the payment must seem to come from the king, to avoid archepiscopal objections from Canterbury and possible claims from York that this toehold in Scotland was valuable in his assertions that he was metropolitan superior over the Scots Church.

Patrick promised to do what he could in the matter, and would report to Alexander.

They sailed back to Dunbar, well pleased with their day, the ladies declaring that they found St Andrews very fine, only sadly lacking in womenfolk, although there were two or three nunneries, much enclosed. In the old Celtic Church this of priestly celibacy was not enforced. Christian thought it a pity that it could not be amended.

Two days later Patrick was off to Edinburgh, and there learned that his errand was only half fulfilled. He was to go on down to Reading, in the royal name, and seek to come to terms with the abbot, or bishop, or whoever ruled there. But he must make it clear that the proposal to purchase came from him, the king, not Wishart, for these churchmen could be difficult indeed and very jealous of their rights. Point out that he, Alexander, could take over the Isle of May by force, and expel the English monks; but he was prepared to do it thus to avoid controversy. Reading was on the Thames, near to Windsor, and Patrick, with trading-ships at his disposal, could make the journey by sea quickly and without having to gain any safe-conduct. He might be able to get his ship not much westwards past London itself, but could continue the journey by a smaller boat.

This all made sense, less than eager as Patrick was for this further duty as envoy. He judged that three thousand silver merks was a higher sum than ought to have to be paid for a lump of rock in the sea, with only a small and neglected religious house on it. Patrick should seek to scale down that price somewhat.

That man learned that Robert Bruce the younger was now indeed accepted as Earl of Carrick.

Enquiries at Dunbar harbour revealed that Dand Shaw and his *Meg* were due back from the Netherlands at any time. And since there was no desperate haste about this mission, Patrick decided to wait for his favourite skipper and vessel.

A week later, then, it was to sea again, and southwards. If Dand and his crew would have preferred a somewhat longer spell at home with their families, they did not say so to their lord.

Patrick quite enjoyed sailing, the enforced idleness on board being a welcome change from his busy life, and allowing him to dwell on matters that usually tended to get pushed to the back of his mind. Also he liked to talk with Dand in comradely fashion, a man he esteemed.

As ever, the prevailing south-westerly winds made it take longer to sail south than north, and with tacking, the three hundred miles became well over four hundred, so that they were three days and nights before they turned westwards into the Thames estuary, that busy waterway. Dand said that with the river narrowing and apt to be bridged after London, it would not be practical to take his ship much past the last dock area of the city. They could easily hire a small craft to take them the rest of the way, unsure as he was as to how far upriver was this Reading.

Past the teeming miles of London town, they docked at the westernmost end of the port area. They had no difficulty in bargaining with a boatman and his crew of four to take Patrick, Dand with him, upriver. It was forty miles to Reading, so represented another full day's journey.

Because of a great bend in the river, it was further past Windsor than Patrick had thought, so that it was evening before the spires of the town, in Berkshire, rose before them. There seemed to be many more churches here than the large abbey. Landing, they found a Greyfriars monastery to put them up for the night; and therein learned that there was a bishop over the diocese but he was usually in London, and Abbot William was very much in charge here. This was a relief, for if it had proved that the bishop was the one they had to deal with, they might have had to do more journeying to find him, and the links with Canterbury stronger.

So in the morning they went to the Benedictine abbey, this founded by Henry the First, who was indeed buried here, about one hundred and fifty years before, a handsome edifice not unlike their own Melrose. Needless to say, the proud-seeming Abbot William, who took some time before he received Patrick, was surprised to have a Scots earl visiting him, although the style of Dunbar and March clearly meant nothing to him. But when, in the circumstances, very quickly, the subject of the property on the distant Isle of May was introduced, he promptly showed interest.

"What have those wretched caitiffs been doing now, my lord, to bring you all the way here to protest?" he asked, frowning.

Noting that question with interest, Patrick chose his words carefully. "They do not do great credit to your abbacy here, my lord Abbot," he said. He did not know whether this cleric was entitled to be called lord abbot, as were only mitred abbots in Scotland, but thought it judicious to style him so. "And there is concern for the lighthouse, because it is not tended as well as it ought to be. That island is a very great danger to shipping entering the Firth of Forth, where much trade is carried on, many *English* ships come there, and the beacon should be kept burning brightly of a night. I can see it, when it is lit, from my castle of Dunbar." As an afterthought he added, "No doubt you have heard of this from your London shipmasters?"

"M'mm. No, I have not. I have no responsibility for that," he was told haughtily. "You should see the prior. Prior Edmond. He is at Henley, nearby, and appoints a sub-prior for that grievous place."

"But it is yourself, Abbot of Reading, who *owns* the island is it not?"

"It was ceded to the abbey, yes. Unfortunately. Many years past. To my little advantage."

The abbot's attitude struck Patrick as hopeful, and he went on, seeking to sound sympathetic as well as protesting; rather difficult.

"I came not in my own right, my lord Abbot, but as

representing the King of Scots, His Grace Alexander, married to your own monarch's daughter. He is concerned over the state of affairs at the May, and would have it improved."

"Then I regret His Majesty's concern. But, as I say, the responsibility is not mine but Prior Edmond's. You must go to Henley, my lord. It is but a few miles down Thames."

"Yet this prior does not own it, does he? Only administers it? And it is ownership that I am concerned with, or His Grace is. For he wishes to purchase the May, and improve matters."

"Purchase?" That was quick, and very positively interested.

"Purchase, yes. If a price can be agreed, a fair price for a small isle of perhaps one hundred and fifty acres."

"How much?"

"It is rocky and will grow nothing, as you will know. It is the beacon that is important."

"Yes, yes. But if His Majesty Alexander sends you, my lord, all this way, it must be of value to him. So he must be prepared to pay adequately for it."

"You will sell, then? Or must I approach your Archbishop of Canterbury?"

"No, no. The property is Reading's. One hundred and fifty acres, you say?"

"Rocky acres, yes."

"But important ones. Or you would not be here. And a priory thereon."

"A decaying priory. Your price?"

The other took a pace or two up and down. "Land can sell for two pounds for an acre."

"Good land, fertile land." Hastily Patrick was calculating, and could scarcely believe his summations. A silver Scots merk was, he understood, worth one-third of a pound Easterling, English money. That meant at, say, this acreage, three hundred pounds, or nine hundred silver merks, a third of what Wishart had been prepared to pay. Trying not to let his voice sound in any way elated, he pointed out that this value was for good, workable land, not naked rock and reef.

"But of value for its position," the abbot declared. "I would consider a little less. But only slightly so."

That had Patrick calculating again, this time all but confidently. "Shall we say eight hundred silver merks, then, my lord Abbot? That is about two hundred and fifty pounds of your money. I think that His Grace might be prepared to pay that."

"M'mm. Two hundred and *seventy*, say. Yes, I might consider that, my lord. Two hundred and seventy. Yes."

"For a complete handing over of the Isle of May to the Scottish crown. A written charter to that effect. And the removal of the present sub-prior and his monks from the island."

"That is understood. I will instruct Prior Edmond. And my clerk will give you my signed paper to that effect. You shall have it forthwith. And, the moneys?"

"I will give you my own signed paper in promise of it now. King Alexander will send on the silver."

"See my clerk, then, my lord. He will deal with that. And offer you some sustenance. I will inform him. Give him one hour."

That, apparently, was that, all but dismissal. Patrick did not take exception to the manner of it, its almost curt form, glad enough to be out of this proud but money-minded cleric's company and almost afraid that the man might yet change his mind and ask for more.

"Where do I find your clerk?" he asked.

"Wait in the refectory. I will send him to you. And I shall look for that silver before long, my lord."

"You shall have it so soon as it takes me to return to His Grace, and the moneys to be sent south. Perhaps two weeks?"

Without further delay Patrick, keeping a stiff face and bearing, left the abbatial presence, to make for the abbey's refectory, where he found Dand awaiting him, already sipping wine and eating pancakes.

They did not have to linger long there before a priest, presumably the abbot's clerk, and quite a young man, came with a signed paper, which passed the Isle of May to be the property of King Alexander of Scotland, this on reception of the sum of two hundred and seventy pounds Easterling. This with another paper to be signed by Patrick accepting the transfer and agreeing payment.

Normally they would have expected to pass the night in the abbey's guest house, but Patrick chose otherwise just in case its so haughty master thought better on the bargain. So they went not to the Greyfriars establishment but down to a riverside change-house where their hired boatmen had based themselves; and in these lowly quarters settled for the night. Almost certainly never before had an earl so graced the premises.

With an early start, they were off next morning, down-river; and with the current in their favour now, they made better time than on the journey up. They were back to the *Meg* by noon, and set sail with little delay, Patrick well pleased with himself. He quite probably had made a friend for life of Bishop Wishart. The Archbishop of York would be incensed over the deal, undoubtedly, but fortunately Reading came under his rival metropolitan, Canterbury. Ths Isle of May would be no outlier of England any longer.

23

Patrick reached home, with the king's thanks, to find his family planning an early wedding for Beatrice. He had no objection to this. And it occurred to him that instead of having the ceremony at Coldinghame Priory, which would be the normal choice for such, where he himself had been blessed after his wedding at Lochmaben rather than the Trinitarian monastery at Houston nearby, they could just as easily, indeed more conveniently, go by ship to St Andrews again, and there give an account of the Reading bargaining to the Primate, and have the marriage celebrated in notable fashion, perhaps by Bishop Wishart himself. So Dand was sent north to inform of this proposal, and, taking agreement for granted, messengers sent south, by land, to Northumberland, to invite such of the Hepburn family and friends as would care to come as wedding guests. A date one month hence was suggested.

Meantime, renewals and improvements were in progress at Hailes Castle, Beatrice much involved, and with her own ideas as to amenities.

They learned that Wishart would be glad to marry his benefactor's daughter in St Rule's Cathedral, actually the premier place of worship in all Scotland.

Three weeks later quite a party of Hepburns and their associates arrived at Dunbar, and Christian was kept busy entertaining them all, so many indeed that with the Cospatrick family's own friends and senior vassals, another ship as well as Dand's *Meg* was required to transport them all to St Andrews. The Tynesiders were well satisfied over what Patrick had been instrumental in achieving as to their problems, and this renewing of the ancient links with the

Cospatrick earls. King Alexander was pleased also, this Northumbrian goodwill forming, as it were, a useful moat between Scotland and England.

The notable day dawned, and bride, groom, family and guests set sail from Dunbar, a wedding progress never before experienced by any of them. As they passed the Isle of May, Patrick recounted to the visitors the saga of Reading Abbey and what it all implied, to much interest, amusement and congratulations. Christian declared that her husband was in danger of over-esteeming himself.

At St Andrews the ships were met at the quayside by a deputation of senior clergy, who conducted them up the hill to the town, to the accompaniment of a chanting choir. They reached the Primate's castle-palace, where Wishart awaited them, declaring that the situation gave him great joy. They would go in procession to the cathedral, and after the service he had arranged a banquet for all, and an outdoors feast down at the harbour for the ships' crews and the local folk there, this a thought which commended itself to Patrick. It came to him that here was a man with whom he could perhaps have closer dealings, involve him in his trading ventures, bringing in Holy Church's great productive capabilities, to the advantage of both, of all.

The procedure was well organised. Two separate processions would head for St Rule's Cathedral by different but parallel routes, the bride's and the groom's, both with music and singing, the latter to arrive first. He, the Primate, would lead Beatrice, with her father, mother and family; and the archdeacon would conduct the Hepburns and their friends. All the bells of all the city's churches and religious houses would ring out in salutation and goodwill.

So it all went, heedfully directed and planned, to the clamour of hundreds of the bells, the air all but quivering with it, so that the musicians and singers could scarcely be heard, the streets thronged with cheering crowds, the clergy, like their visitors, robed in their finest. Beatrice, who was a forthright and spirited young woman, taking after her mother, could scarcely believe that this was *her* wedding, more like some queen's.

The cathedral of St Regulus, or Rule, who was reputed to have brought a bone relic of St Andrew to Scotland, to Kilrymond, which became St Andrews, the ecclesiastical capital, was a magnificent building within a high-walled enclosure which also contained the priory. It had a central tower over one hundred feet high, a buttressed lofty vaulted ceiling and clerestory, three tiers of arched windows, the chancel, nave and transepts supported by decorated pillars, an Augustine fane built over a century before on the site of an ancient Celtic Church monastery of the Keledei, the Friends of God. In at the high-arched west door they paced, to find the Northumbrian group already there, Adam with his father and brother and grandsire waiting up at the chancel steps. The bishop led the bridal party up to join the groom, amid smiles and bows, and then left them to enter the sacristy, while the choir sang praise.

When Wishart emerged again, with the archdeacon and prior, he himself conducted the service, and most kindly, warmly, the solemnity and import of it all tempered with smiles and gestures. Beatrice looked radiant, her partner distinctly embarrassed, as young men can be on such occasions, and Christian, who had come to stand beside Patrick as he gave the bride away, squeezed his arm in memory of the day, almost thirty years before, when they had stood thus in the Lochmaben chapel, less grand than this but equally effective, and they were made one.

Adam's elder brother acted groomsman, and seemed to enjoy it all, handing over the ring without the usual fumbling, clearly amused at Adam's unease.

The ceremony was not lengthy, and when the couple were duly declared man and wife the choristers raised voice in ringing salutation, and the cathedral bell, high above them, marked the moment. The archdeacon and prior each presented a token gift posy of little flowers to Beatrice, and the bishop blessed the newly united and all present comprehensively but with evident sincerity.

It was a wedding none would forget.

Then, the two parties joined, they processed back to the castle, still to choral accompaniment, to prepare for the feasting.

Wishart's hospitality was on a par with all else, with entertainment rivalling the provender. Blessedly there was here none of the roistering which was so apt to develop at marriage banquets as the drink flowed. Wine there was, but in moderate quantities, and the ecclesiastical ambience restrained overmuch exuberance. There was no need for the bride and groom, nor the ladies, to retire early.

The married couple had been allotted an angle tower of the castle courtyard to themselves for this bridal night, and disappeared thereto in due course, led by the archdeacon, to smiles and wavings and wellwishings, but spared the so usual advice as to subsequent behaviour.

The entertainment went on for all the others.

Patrick was able to sit beside Wishart now, and told him of the proceedings and bargaining at Reading, the bishop as interested as he was grateful. He said that he would devote some of the moneys thus saved to some memorial feature at the priory of St Ethernan which he was going to re-establish on the May, still Cluniac but larger and greatly improved. He was in favour of the ancient Celtic Church custom of having *disearts* for clergy to retire to on occasion to be able to commune privately, as it were, with their Creator and Father; he thought that he might build a small chapel somewhere else on the island for this purpose, and encourage others, as well as himself, to use it in the timehonoured fashion. His lordship of Dunbar should have credit for this.

Patrick disclaimed anything such, but commended the project.

In the morning, before the wedding guests left for their

ships, he had another talk with the Primate, approaching his subject cautiously at first, but speaking more freely as he perceived interest in his hearer. He told of his trading efforts to the Netherlands and the Baltic and Norway, Wishart saying that he had heard something of this, and knew of the Cospatrick shipping which made it feasible. This enabled Patrick to declare that the said ships could, if so desired, carry others' goods and products. Holy Church was the principal source of such in the land, and no doubt had the use of merchants' vessels for foreign trade; but it had come to him that some sort of compact or alliance between his own endeavours and the Church's might well be of advantage to both. Was this of any interest to the lord Bishop?

Wishart slowly nodded. "You mean, for overseas trade? Using your ships for what we produce from our priories, monasteries and the like. Would there be a market for such, think you? After all, the Church in other lands produces its own commodities for use."

"Yes. But the Scots do make especial products: salted fish and meats. The monks at our Carmelite priory of Luffness do this, from their salt-pans for boiling the sea water. We have sent some of it overseas, and had it welcomed. Many other of your houses could do the like. Then there is spun wool, thread. I know that monks do much spinning and weaving. I sell some of my Lammermuir wool to Coldinghame, even to Melrose. Other lands are less rich in sheep than are we. I have heard that your people dye wool. Could that make some merchandise for others? You may think of more than these, from your busy clergy and lay brethren."

"Perhaps, yes. But how would this benefit you and yours, my lord? This aiding of Church revenues."

"Some small part of the Church's gain could be paid to my people, for the shipping and the selling? Some token moneys. If it grew to a worthy trade, as I judge that it could, then it would serve us both well, no?"

"It may well be so." The other plucked his lower lip.

"There is mead. The liquor we make from honey. I have not heard of it being made in other lands, and saw none of it when I was in France. Much mead is made here, but more could be, and traded overseas for wine. We have to spend much on wine from the warm countries. This would make a saving for us, possibly a large saving."

"To be sure. I have some small trade with France, through Normandy and Gascony, using the Flemish merchants. Mead might well aid in that. It is distilled from heather, is it not?"

"It can be, yes. But heather mead is inferior to that made from cowslip plants. That is best. Many of our monasteries grow beds of cowslips just for that. But such trade would require much cask-building."

"Could you use the casks that bring the French and other wines? Would these not serve?"

"That might be so, instead of burning them for fuel. I have often deemed that a waste."

"There might well be other goods, when you have time to think on it, my lord Bishop. Do that, and we shall speak more on it all. To the weal, I hope, of many."

"You, my lord Earl, are unlike any others of the nobility that I have known or heard of. Most have little interest in such matters as trade and commerce. Over-proud, indeed, for such. Yet *you* have wrought much in this. What made you turn to it?"

"That, I fear, I cannot tell you. But always I have seen the need and the worth of it. My father had some links with the Netherlands, and that started it. And having the ports of Dunbar and Eyemouth and Berwick in my earldoms showed me the way. Also there was all the Lammermuir wool."

"Then would that there were more like you! The realm would be the better for it, the people gaining. We, in the Church, always seek, or should seek, betterment for God's people, not just the lords and lairds. You are to be praised." Wishart held out his hand to shake. "I will think further on this. I will speak with Archdeacon Thomas. He it will be who will see to our working together. You have my thanks. For much."

That handshake signified much, and for many.

Then it was back to Dunbar.

24

Important news reached them all shortly after that wedding, indeed all but alarming news. Henry of England had died. This in itself did not so greatly concern the Scots, save in that he was the father of their queen; but it meant that his elder son, Edward, would now be King of England, and that could indeed be cause for concern. For Edward Plantagenet was so very different a man from his father: aggressive and proud, and his mounting of the throne could well have its repercussions on the northern kingdom, and the peace which had been maintained these last years, threatened. He might well have trouble with his barons, of course, when he got back from Gascony where he had been acting governor since getting back from his crusading, these lords having been more or less ruling the land during his somewhat weak father's later years. So that might hold Edward in check for some little time. But none knowledgeable doubted that he would prove an awkward brother-in-law and neighbour for Alexander of Scotland.

Adam Hepburn got word from his Northumbrian kin that they were not welcoming the accession of their new monarch. That at least indicated that Edward might well have his preoccupations at home, to keep his assertive gaze from turning northwards.

Nevertheless, an indication of his attitudes was not long in reaching Scotland, this in the form of a summons, for that is what it was rather than an invitation, for Alexander and his queen to attend the coronation ceremony at Westminster Abbey, the wording of the letter which came with the safe-conduct missive being all but peremptory, requiring not requesting.

Alexander disliked this sufficiently to call a meeting of his close councillors to advise him as to reaction, Patrick one of those to attend at Edinburgh.

All there deplored the tone of this demand. Yet it was felt that a refusal to go would be considered a challenge to the Plantagenet, and result in a spur to his aggressive tendencies. Whereas the visit might possibly tend to establish some sort of concordat between the two monarchs. And, of course, Queen Margaret was concerned to see her brother crowned. So it was decided that an attendance would be wise, although going with much care to avoid any situation that could be construed as according Edward any superior role in status or authority. A prestigious party would accompany Alexander and Margaret, of which Patrick, needless to say, must be one. It was a pity that they could not all sail south in one or more of his ships, but to travel in merchanters would not serve the dignity of a king and his senior nobility.

Before the due date for leaving, Patrick had a visit from Archdeacon Thomas of St Andrews, to announce that the Primate was in fullest agreement with the joint trading venture, and sent various suggestions as to other products than those mentioned previously which the churchmen could send overseas, these including goods and garb made of cowhide, carpeting and wall-hangings made from woven horse-hair, goat's-hair and the coarser wools. Admittedly France was famed for such, but Scots work, less costly, might well be welcomed in Norway, Denmark and the Baltic. Through the Cospatrick trade links already established, and the shipping to carry the exports, the Church would pay a proportion of the gains made. Also it would be grateful for advice on *imports*, carried on the returning vessels in exchange, as well as the silver payments.

All this suited Patrick well, and there was more hand-shaking over the terms.

The assembly at Roxburgh to commence the great journey down through England was ready to set off on the Eve of the Blessed Virgin Mary, 13th August, the coronation to be on the 19th. Patrick found much indignation and offence aroused there by the arrival, two days previously, of another messenger from Edward, bringing the sum of one hundred and sixty-five pounds Easterling, plus one hundred shillings for each day of travel to aid in the expenses of "his dearest brother and vassal, Alexander". This courier had been promptly sent back, with his moneys, and with instructions to inform his monarch that the King of Scots was well able to pay his own expenses, and that while he appreciated his good-brother's kindness, he would attend the coronation as no vassal but as an independent sovereign. Warned, therefore, of Edward's likely attitude and claims on reception, they crossed the border with no very celebratory anticipations.

It made an interesting journey, however, for the large and distinguished company, for they learned of other attitudes as they went, those of the lords and churchmen of England towards their new king. The Scots were less than surprised at the baronial feelings, for if these had been critical of the late Henry and the burdens he had sought to place upon them, they were anticipating still worse from his so assertive son. It was the clergy's views which more interested them, and they had ample opportunity to learn of these, for it was at the great abbeys and religious establishments that the travellers put up on the five nights of their journey. The bishops were already gone, to appear at the crowning ceremony; but the lesser clerics did not disguise their unease and fears. Edward was known to have designs on the Church revenues, as on the lords', for he had come back to an empty treasury, and his grand and ambitious plans he had not attempted to hide. The clerical approval he had gained by his crusading had faded and been replaced by fairly general apprehension and criticism.

None of this plunged the Scots into gloom.

When they reached London, however, it was to find such fears and grudgings scarcely evident in all the flourish of the holiday atmosphere which prevailed there, with

Edward, treasury empty or not, acting the generous host to all, rich and poor alike, feasting in the streets as well as in the palaces and halls, the carnival spirit fostered, with processions, music and entertainments.

The new king was basing himself at the mighty Norman Tower of London, above the Thames north bank, and there the Scots party presented itself. Alexander and Margaret were well received at least, the Plantagenet greeting them with every appearance of welcome whatever his feelings about the return of that one hundred and sixty-five pounds and the message therewith.

Edward, now in his thirty-fifth year, was a big man, powerfully built and good-looking in a masterful way. He was lavishing hospitality on all, although in lordly fashion, and making it very clear that this was monarchial benevolence. His wife, Eleanor of Castile, was a silent and reserved lady, as well she might be.

The banquet that evening was, as might have been expected, all but too much, even for ardent diners and drinkers and enjoyers of spectacle and revelry. There was a boxing-match between two performing bears, and a quarter-staff battle involving a full score of contestants, and more of the like. Edward, clearly, had a preoccupation with fighting. Alexander sat at his right hand at the dais table with Queen Eleanor on his left, Edmund, King of Sicily next with their sister Margaret, with the Archbishops of Canterbury and York. Patrick and the other Scots lords were placed well down the hall.

The ladies mainly followed the two queens' example and retired early. Not a few of the men would have done the like probably, had it not been customary never to go before the monarch. Next to Patrick, Malcolm, Earl of Fife, fell asleep at the table.

The procession to the abbey, in the forenoon, was so lengthy that the principals reached Westminster before the last of the guests left the Tower, all to an accompaniment of trumpets, drums and cymbals. Again the Scots were well to the rear.

When Patrick got to the abbey it was with difficulty that he and his colleagues managed to squeeze themselves inside, so packed was it, almost all having to stand. Many of the ladies went up into the clerestory galleries to watch from there. The chancel was full of mitred bishops and high officers of state. Alexander and his Margaret sat on chairs at one side, Edmund at the other.

When Edward and Eleanor were ushered in by heralds, to more trumpeting, he a pace or two ahead of her, the Archbishop of Canterbury, backed by York, stepped forward to lead them to their thrones, where they seated themselves, Edward's head held high, while his wife eyed the floor. A prayer was intoned by the celebrant, a hymn led by massed choirs was sung, and then the coronation ceremony began, a lengthy and involved procedure, with the officers of state as well as the clergy having their parts to play, presenting to the monarch the royal sceptre, the orb, the spurs, the sword of state and eventually the crown itself.

Finally Canterbury performed the crowning ceremony, to the rolling beat of drums at the heralds' signals. England had its ninth monarch since William the Conqueror.

Patrick, with the other Scots present, watched all with interest, comparing it with their own king's enthronement. There were many differences, the old Celtic traditions not applying here, such as the open-air celebration at the Moot Hill of Scone, the earth-scattering by the earls and nobles, the hand-taking and oath-swearing, and of course the monarch's sitting upon the Lia Fail, the ancient Stone of Destiny, with its volutes, decorative carving and mystic meaning. Most of them had seen the seven-year-old Alexander crowned all those years before, and judged it a more meaningful and significant rite – but they were prejudiced, of course.

Thereafter there was more procession, as the newly crowned monarch showed himself to the populace, a quite major traversing of the streets of London town, all these having been carefully swept of their filth and strewn with greenery and flowers for the occasion, the crowds cheering, even though the nobility and gentry were less enthusiastic. It all took a lot of time.

Then it was back to the Tower for more feasting and diversion, with some of the guests scarcely recovered from the previous night's excesses.

The following forenoon Edward summoned the Scots party to an especial meeting in a lesser hall, this to seek to establish and emphasise his monarchial superiority, his senior nobles present. It was, of course, the crucial point of the entire visit, as far as Alexander was concerned. It had been suggested to him by the chief herald that he carried in the sword of state at the coronation ceremony, and this he had declined to do, as seeming to rank him almost with the officers of state. Moreover he had sent, with the messenger who had brought that money, a letter to Edward declaring that his independent status must not be prejudiced by his attendance at Westminster. So Edward would know that this present occasion was going to be something of a confrontation.

"Husband of my good sister, and my friend," Edward said. "Now that I am crowned monarch and Lord Paramount, it is meet that the matter of homage be dealt with, no? This is the time."

"Homage, Edward? *Homage*? Let us not spoil this great occasion by such considerations. I am here to witness and acclaim your coronation. At your invitation and under your especial safe-conduct." Alexander spoke carefully; after all, he had well prepared this speech. "This is a time for more princely and fraternal talk, is it not?"

Edward frowned, opened mouth to speak, and then closed it again. He raise a hand, to point an imperious finger. "Homage is required," he said, voice grating. "You owe it to me, now that I am king."

"As am *I*, my friend. I shall indeed pay due homage hereafter for my lands in England. As I did to your father. And for my wife's lands here. But such homage should be paid on the lands held. That is our Scots custom, if not yours. Here and now is no place for the like."

"Homage for Scotland, man! For your kingdom, held of me!"

"Held of God, only! I am an independent monarch, as are you, Edward."

The other was having difficulty in containing himself, features working. "Not so. Ever since Canute's time, the kings of England have been Lords Paramount of Scotland. Your Malcolm the Second agreed it. And my own ancestor, William the First, the Conqueror, held the paramountcy over your ancestor Malcolm the Third, Malcolm Big Head!" He all but shouted that. "*I* now am Lord Paramount, by right, and will have it so!"

Alexander shook his head. "These yieldings, they were both gained by aggression, by armed invasion of our land. And both were renounced later by the said kings of Scots, as gained by force. No overlordship of our ancient nation, much more ancient than is this England, is acceptable. It is not to be considered."

"Fool!" Edward barked. "We shall see about that!" And, turning on his heel, he strode from that chamber.

His lords, looking uncertain, eyed each other, and then followed him out.

After that, there could be no question of remaining longer in London. The Scots went to pick up Queen Margaret, who was with Eleanor of Castile, Edward fortunately not present. Alexander took leave of Eleanor, declaring that he had already had word with her royal husband.

All were thankful indeed to set off on the way back to Scotland.

25

In the months that followed, Edward Plantagenet was much too involved with affairs nearer home to seek to demonstrate his enmity towards his brother-in-law and Scotland. He did not even send word demanding the offered fealty for the English lands inherited by Alexander from the marriage of King David and the heiress of Huntingdon, nor his own Margaret's dowery portion. Unpopularity with his lords grew, he making it worse by increasing levies upon them, announcing that each baron must supply him with the service of armed men for forty days, this at their own expense, for his campaigns against the Welsh; that or an equivalent in silver, with which he could hire the services of paid knights and men-at-arms. He announced new powers for his parliament anent taxation, which further offended the nobility. Also got royal authority to levy dues on both imports and exports; and these, being largely the products and requirements of the clergy and monks, resulted in the further disfavour of Holy Church. He had returned to England to find the crown heavily in debt, owing to his father's inadequacy. His methods of dealing with that were thus typically drastic. So the First Knight in Christendom, as he still called himself, grew in unpopularity. And his efforts to bring Wales under his sway demanded ever more moneys. Edward was making himself the least loved monarch since the hapless King John of the Magna Carta.

The Scots at least had reason to be thankful.

Alexander had his own worries. Ever since the birth of their second son, David, his wife Margaret had suffered from internal bleedings. Now these had become more frequent, and her general health in consequence suffered. With their elder son, another Alexander, sickly, the king had reason for concern. But at least the Highlands and Islands situation was now satisfactorily settled, the Comyn power was diminished, and the English threat hopefully postponed if not removed.

Patrick was not long in being given another royal mission. Alexander was anxious that, following the satisfactory matter of the Hebrides and Western Isles, those other offshore islands situated only ten miles from the northern coast of his kingdom, the Orkneys and Shetlands, should be likewise improved as to allegiance and authority. At present they were and had been long subject to Norway, hundreds of miles away, an irritating situation, especially with practically all their trade and relations being with Scotland. Patrick was to go over to see King Magnus Hakonsson, and try to come to some arrangement with him whereby this anomaly could be rectified, preferably by outright ceding of the isles, but if not, by lease or other practical transfer less than sovereignty. Magnus had inherited his father's debt to the Baltic Hansa merchant league, and was known to be chronically short of money. So a rental for the islands could be offered, if an actual purchase was refused. And as an added inducement, the possibility of a royal marriage link could be considered. Magnus had a sixteen-year-old son, Eric, his heir. A betrothal between these two might well seal the compact; after all, Princess Margaret presumably would have to wed *some* prince. Patrick, with all his trade associations with Norway, was the obvious envoy.

So Dand Shaw and his *Skateraw Meg* were once more readied, and the vessel loaded with hardwoods and wool. This time, Christian was going to accompany her husband. She had always wanted to visit other lands. Here was opportunity. Their family was now all of an age to be left on their own, Gelis able to act mistress of the house. And with this talk of Princess Margaret's possible betrothal, a woman's presence could be helpful. This well suited Patrick.

255

They made a pleasant voyage of it to Bergen.

King Magnus and Queen Astrid received them gladly, the Scottish trade being important to the King. He was an easy man to deal with; and Christian got on well with his Astrid. These Norse monarchs were much less princely and formal in their attitudes and behaviour than those of most nations, which was a help. And Prince Eric seemed a lively and friendly youth.

When they got down to discussions as to the Orkney and Shetland Isles, Magnus was interested. Although he made it clear from the first that he would not consider any actual ceding of the territories to Scotland, he was most evidently prepared to try to make some suitable arrangement. After all, now that the Norsemen had abandoned any claims to the Hebrides, these northern isles were of no great value to Norway, as stepping-stones as it were; and there was little trade and dealings with their earls. But they had been under Norwegian sovereignty for centuries, and *he* was not going to be the one to change that. But some sort of rent or lease . . . ?

Patrick had been given some figures to suggest. He hoped that he would not have to try to bargain with Magnus, as he had done with the Abbot of Reading: that would be unsuitable with a king. But when he made the first suggested sum that Alexander had given him, of one thousand silver merks down and one hundred annually thereafter, he had it accepted promptly and without debate. Magnus's need must be great.

Thereafter, with the matter of a possible marriage between his heir, Eric, and the Princess Margaret of Scotland tentatively raised, this was frankly welcomed, at least by the parents.

Patrick and Christian remained at Bergen for a full week, being kindly entertained, and taken to see something of the country. They were greatly impressed by the dramatic scenery of the fjords, so different from their own Highland sea lochs. They noted the absence of hardwoods, oak, elm, ash and the like, and that such birches as there were grew only in small and stunted fashion. There was much fir and pine. They wondered why this should be, with Scotland more or less in a similar position on the face of the earth, judging it to be something to do with the seas, the Western Ocean being warmer than the Norse Sea probably. But it was good for their timber trade, at any rate. And on the subject of trade, one of the features they were taken to see was a great establishment at Stavanger for the extraction of whale oil, whales apparently being very prevalent in these waters. And the oil, being gained from the blubber, it seemed, was a valuable product, being used for leather-dressing and the making of paints and soap. Patrick saw possibilities for this in Scotland, and decided to take a sample cargo of it back with him.

Christian was quite sorry to leave for home, in the end, she and Queen Astrid suiting each other.

Their return voyage, against westerly winds, was slower, but not in any way a trial.

They had been gone only three weeks, but in their absence there had been dire events. Queen Margaret had had her last bleeding, and had passed on to a better realm than Scotland. Alexander was devastated, left with three young people, one of them sickly. He had never been passionately in love with his Margaret – royal marriages being usually arranged, and seldom so blessed – but these two had been well matched, and she had proved a good wife and mother, despite her disagreeable brother. The elder son, Alexander also, was unwell, his mother's death grievously affecting him.

The news from Norway, then, received less attention and praise than it might have done.

Bishop Wishart, conducting the funeral rites at Roxburgh and Kelso Abbey, was thereafter interested to hear about trading matters, and especially of this of the whale oil. He thought that he might find worthy uses for this among the churchmen's various productions, the Abbot of Kelso agreeing.

The queen was not to be buried at Kelso but at the royal

mausoleum at Dunfermline Abbey in Fife. So thereafter a sad procession had to wend its way northwards, to halt at Edinburgh's Holyrood Abbey overnight, and then to cross Forth by St Margaret's Ferry to the old palace of Kings MacBeth and Malcolm Canmore, the abbey adjoining. There beside that other Margaret the late queen was laid to rest.

The next day, Alexander could turn his mind to other matters. While over Forth he decided to inspect the small royal castle of Kinghorn, some dozen miles to the east along the coast, which he had never actually visited. On the way there, he referred to the Orkney and Shetland situation with some satisfaction, and declared that to emphasise the new state of affairs for these islesmen, Patrick should sail up there and acquaint them that they were now more or less under the authority of the King of Scots. He was to tell the Earl of Orkney that he would now be accepted as an earl of Scotland, with its due privileges, whatever allegiance he might still pay to his royal namesake in Bergen. Bishop Wishart added that the Bishop of Orkney and Shetland should now be expected to come under *his* authority rather than that of the Archbishop of Trondheim.

The castle of Kinghorn proved to be no very princely establishment,but it was picturesquely situated on a spur of rock just east of the high cliffs of Kinghorn Ness. It seemed that MacBeth and Malcolm the Third and their sons had used it and its little haven of Pettycur for its convenient access to the holy shrine on the island of Inchcolm dedicated to St Columba who had established Christianity in Scotland; also to Inchkeith, another island with royal connections. Indeed the king's own father had all but drowned on one such venture from here as a young man. Alexander liked Kinghorn; its keeper told him that the name had nothing to do with kings nor horns, but referred to the minor headland of the beacon.

The castle was not large enough to put up the quite

numerous royal party, so they returned to Dunfermline Palace for the night.

Patrick left the king's company next morning, in a small local vessel from nearby Kirkcaldy, to sail down Forth to his Dunbar, and there change into a larger craft of his own to take him the three hundred miles up to Orkney. He asked Christian whether she would like to accompany him again, and she was happy to do so. She had become quite fond of voyaging.

Dand Shaw's *Meg* was away to the Low Countries but they found another ship available, and took Pate with them on this occasion. The journey took them three days and two nights, and was not the sort of voyage to take in rough weather, particularly once they reached the Pentland Firth, where the roosts were the dread of mariners, tidal races and all but whirlpools where the waters of the Western Ocean met the colder ones of the Norse Sea, and the Orkney Islands sent out underwater fangs to create overfalls. Here navigation had to be careful indeed.

Patrick would be interested to meet the present earl, or jarl, Magnus Magnusson, descendant of a long line, which included Thorfinn Raven-Feeder, MacBeth's half-brother, a mighty character, and the Magnus who had built the great cathedral at Kirkwall, an extraordinary edifice to be located up in these northern isles.

Their shipmaster managed to avoid the more dangerous roosts, although the vessel did heave and plunge alarmingly on three occasions. They skirted the islet of Copinsay and rounded the Skaill headland to enter the Wide Firth, as it was known, although that seemed to be an exaggeration, to reach the harbour of Kirkwall, the capital town of the Orkneys, on what was termed the Mainland, very much the largest of the literally hundreds of isles.

This was a new experience for Patrick as well as Christian and Pate. They found Kirkwall to be larger than they had expected, narrow climbing streets under the splendid red-stone cathedral and the nearby palaces of the earl and bishop.

The folk eyed the visitors interestedly but in no hostile fashion. Patrick had been prepared to hear them speak in the Norse tongue, but when he sought directions he was answered in a form of their own Doric. They learned that the Earl Magnus was not presently at Kirkwall but up at his favoured seat of Birsay on the west coast of the north tip of this Mainland, almost twenty miles off, which was unfortunate; but Bishop Kjer was in his palace. Thither they went.

However surprised he was to learn the identity of the newcomers, that elderly prelate received them civilly, although clearly wary as to their purposes, no Scots earl having set foot in the Orkneys in living memory. When he heard that he was now expected to place himself under the authority of St Andrews instead of Trondheim, he did not hide his astonishment. He asked what this implied, and had Patrick confessing that he did not really know, but assumed that it was almost certainly largely nominal, and probably meant that he had a seat in the Scots College of Bishops. But he would find Bishop Wishart an amiable and worthy Primate, anything but demanding. Had he, Bishop Kjer, had close links with the Archbishop of Trondheim? The other admitted that he had never actually visited the Metropolitan, save to be consecrated; and he hoped that he would not be expected to travel down to St Andrews any more frequently.

When he learned that they were on their way to visit Earl Magnus, he informed that although it was much longer to go by sea, that was much more convenient than travel over rough and fairly empty land. Most journeying was done by boat in the Orkneys, he said. This suited the Cospatricks very well, needless to say.

So it was back down to their ship, to set sail north-about, past the isles of Gairsay and Rousay, round the headlands of Costa and Brough of Birsay to Birsay itself, about thirty miles. Clearly these north and west coasts were less inhabited than the rest.

They found Earl Magnus and his family, large and

noisy, at the castle perched on a cliff-top, he proving less suspicious than the bishop had been, however unprepared for the visit. He did not seem to take it amiss that it appeared that he now had to pay nominal homage, only that, to be sure, to the King of Scots instead of the King of Norway, for his all but independent isles, declaring that he would be well pleased to be an earl of Scotland, in name at least, laughing loudly as he declared that he would point this out to the Earls of Caithness and Sutherland, across the firth, who were only *one* earl each, whereas he had seemingly become two!

Christian quickly made friends with the Countess Margrete; and they were invited to spend the night at the castle instead of down at their ship, amid distinctly boisterous company.

That evening Patrick took the opportunity to mention that he had seen little woodland in these Orkney Isles; and would the Earl Magnus be interested in importing timber, for shipbuilding and otherwise, from Scotland? He was told that they got their wood from Caithness and Sutherland, at a price. When he was promptly offered a better price from Dunbar, he accepted the suggestion with alacrity, and asked what Orkney products he might send in exchange. Patrick was doubtful that these islands could supply anything that they did not themselves produce in Scotland; but when he heard that whale-fishing was much pursued here, he saw that whale oil might come to them more cheaply than from Norway. Also apparently shellfish and lobsters abounded in much greater numbers than around at least the eastern Scottish coasts, so there were possibilities in that. And, for the first time, he learned of kelp, that is burned seaweed which could act as a great improver of soil for the growth of grain. Raw seaweed was sometimes used at home for this purpose, but it demanded much labour; this kelp was evidently many times more effective – as it ought to be since it seemed that it required twenty-four times as much seaweed to create one of the kelp. Here was something that might be home-made as well as imported. Bishop Wishart might well be interested in some of all this.

Such talk of commerce and industry rather embarrassed young Pate, who considered it as unbecoming, below lordly rank, even though he was glad enough to participate in the profits therefrom.

In the morning, they were for on their way southwards, Earl Magnus warning them not only of the whereabouts of roosts on this west side of the Mainland but of a particularly dangerous tidal bore and whirlpool known as the Swelkie, which lay off the north-west headland of the island of Stroma, which they would be apt to pass near on their way back across the Pentland Firth.

So one more mission was accomplished, and a highly satisfactory one in Patrick's estimation, new links forged.

26

Alexander was well enough pleased with the success of the
Orkneys visit – the Shetlands could be included in it all, as
under Earl Magnus – but his mind was presently concentrated on other matters. Edward had sent desiring him to
come south to pay the delayed homage for his English
lands. This was not to be refused, having been thus
postponed; the question was where was this to be done?
Alexander claimed that it should be at some place suitable
on the actual ground that he owned, preferably Huntingdon itself, the seat of the earldom to which he was heir; but
since Edward apparently had sent his envoy from Gloucester, he was prepared to go there, and take soil from
Tewkesbury or Cubberley in that county to stand on when
he took his oath of fealty. But the emissary said that his
monarch was going back to Westminster, and would have
the fealty-giving there, declaring that this would in no way
be prejudicial to the Scots' interests. And he sent friendly
greetings, enquiring for the health of his late sister's
children, and giving safe-conducts for the journey south.

Alexander felt that this homage must not be allowed to
become an issue that could endanger the prevailing fair
relationship with England. So he would go to Westminster. But he would hold to the Scots custom of the soil-
taking and standing upon. Which meant that his journey
must be diverted to reach some part of his property to
collect the said earth. Fortunately Huntingdon was none
so far off the normal route south, in Huntingdonshire. He
summoned a group of his senior nobles and churchmen,
therefore, to accompany him, Patrick inevitably included.

That man arrived at Roxburgh, in consequence, to find

that Bruce, his father-in-law, was sick, and had sent his son, now Earl of Carrick, in his stead. Also that Bishop Wishart was likewise less than well, but hoped to be able to follow on in a day or two, and catch up with them before they reached London. Sickness indeed appeared to be prevalent that autumn, for the young Prince David, always frail, was less than well.

So, with the Earls of Fife, Menteith and Carrick, and the new Chancellor who had taken over that office from Bishop Wishart, William Fraser, Dean of Glasgow, they set out, to get this annoying task over, Patrick again wishing that Alexander would get rid of these English lands, sell them, and avoid this homage-giving, however useful they were in providing revenues. He would surely get a handsome price for them. It was to be hoped that, on this occasion, Edward would not bring up his claim to paramountcy over Scotland, requiring their denials.

Their journey went well enough, the comparatively small company being able to pass the nights at lesser monastic establishments and so not have to turn off to reach larger abbeys and priories, their safe-conduct letters ensuring them due hospitality. By Wark, Wooler and Hexham, avoiding Durham as ever, they went, on to Northallerton and Darlington, Ripon and Leeds, to avoid York also, ever concerned over ecclesiastical claims. Then by Doncaster and Newark and Peterborough, to reach Huntingdon in five days' riding.

Huntingdon proved to be no very large town, but old, smaller than Peterborough none so far off, which was also in Huntingdonshire, and which had a cathedral and the seat of a bishop. But the little town was more ancient and characterful, sited on the River Ouse, over which there was a fine bridge to Godmanchester; also a hospice dedicated to John the Baptist, this with a school attached, something new for the Scots.

The prior in charge of the hospice was all but over-whelmed to be visited by a king, and declared that he must send for his bishop. But Alexander told him not to, and said that all that he wanted was to dig up a handful of earth from the graveyard; which, of course, had the cleric completely bewildered. That took only moments, and rather than becoming involved in any way, it was better to be on their road again, for they could cover another score of miles, at least, before dark, and they were told that there was a large nunnery at Bedford, famed for its hospitality, and thereafter they could be in London in a day.

They reached the Tower of London in due course, to find Edward newly back from Gloucester, and declaring himself glad to see Alexander. He was not long in declaring that he had good news for his brother-in-law. Concerned as he was at the latter's bereavement and wifeless state, he had found a new spouse for him, the beauteous Yolande de Dreux, daughter of the Gascon Count de Dreux. Half of the princes of Christendom were seeking her hand, for as well as her good looks she was a great heiress, her mother having left her much land in France. She would make an excellent wife for the royal widower.

To say that Alexander was astonished at this would be an understatement. Since Margaret had died he had consoled himself with two or three mistresses; but he had not begun to consider remarriage. What was this design of Edward's? Why was he concerning himself with the like? Some device, some scheme for his own advantage? Alexander had heard, of course, of the Count de Dreux, an important noble, with large lands not only in Gascony but in central France; indeed Dreux itself was part of the kingdom of France.

Edward was over-hearty in his well-wishing in this personal matter, despite the other's obvious doubts and reservations. *He* was the Duke of Gascony, of course, and so in some position to negotiate this, for whatever reason.

The subject changed to the homage-giving. It was declared that this should be performed next forenoon, in Westminster Abbey, as suitable for such an occasion, Alexander admitting that he cared not where it took place, since he had brought the necessary soil from Huntingdon; at which Edward raised his brows.

There had been no time to prepare an especial banquet for the visitors, but a very adequate repast was provided nevertheless. At it, Patrick found himself sitting next to Edward's brother Edmund, at the dais table. He had heard Edward's declaration about the Lady Yolande de Dreux, as surprised as had been the others; and now he sought to discover, if he could, what this peculiar proposal might signify.

"You, my lord King, will know Gascony well, I think," he began. "And probably this Count de Dreux and his daughter? We are, to be sure, interested in this proposal of King Edward's. What makes this important for King Alexander? Is it so worthy a match?"

"De Dreux is important," Edmund declared. "Not only in Gascony. In France also he carries much weight. His daughter, her mother's heiress, would make a notable queen for your Alexander. To his much advantage."

"Forgive me if I do not see why. She is no princess, to wed a king."

"She could have more of influence than many a princess, my lord. This of France, see you."

Patrick pondered. France was important to Scotland, yes: the Auld Alliance, that unwritten compact between the two realms to north and south of England, which could operate in unison to keep that aggressive kingdom in check from assault on either of them. Why was Edward so concerned, then? Then a thought occurred to him. Could it be . . . ? Was that it? The French connection working in the other direction? If this de Dreux was a close friend and supporter of Edward of England, and his daughter married to the King of Scots, might not this drive a wedge between Scotland and France? Make the Auld Alliance the less effective? Was that the assertive and ambitious Edward's aim? It would make some sense of this curious suggestion.

"Your royal brother seems to consider this match as . . . of advantage?" he said. "Not only to our own liege-lord."

"No doubt," Edmund said briefly.

"And de Dreux? The count?"

"To have his daughter Queen of Scotland would serve him well against the King of France."

"Against? They do not always agree?"

"No. And King Philip would be glad to have Gascony back in his realm."

"Ah!" Patrick had what he sought, the reason. Edward Plantagenet was cunning as well as warlike. He would have Alexander beholden to him in this, and France and the French threat lessened, parried.

He changed the subject. "You, my lord King, do you see much of your Sicily?"

"No. That was a papal appointment. Rome, the Vatican, used to rule Sicily. Now Naples does!" And he shrugged.

They left it at that.

Next forenoon the fealty-swearing ceremony took place before a large gathering in Westminster Abbey, Edward professing to be much amused by the pouchful of Huntingdon earth, and calling it all play-acting. But Alexander was not to be put off by all-but mockery. There was to be no kneeling and scraping in this homage, as appeared to be expected. Up at the chancel steps of a side chapel he faced Edward, inclined his head, and taking the pouch carefully, scattered the soil on the stone flooring, then standing straight, put foot on it, and raised his hand high.

"I, Alexander, King of Scots," he intoned strongly, "become your man, my lord Edward, for the lands held of you in the kingdom of England, and for which I owe you homage. Reserving my kingdom! I shall have good faith in this. So be it."

Edward eyed him levelly. "And my paramountcy?" he demanded.

"Your paramountcy is over your own kingdom, not mine, Edward Plantagenet. The homage for my kingdom of Scotland none has right to save God alone. *I* hold it, of

Almighty God." And he lowered his arm and hand, and stepped back.

The three Scots earls, and Chancellor Fraser, promptly raised voice together. "We witness and confirm this homage for English lands, and that alone," they announced in unison.

There were murmurings and shifting of feet among the English magnates and clerics, while their monarch stood grim-faced. Then Edward shrugged.

"We shall see!" he said, and turned away.

Patrick, for one, felt like cheering.

Thereafter the two parties did not mingle. But an entertainment was laid on at the Tower's tourney-ground, which they were loth to attend, all only anxious to be gone, but with Queen Eleanor showing herself they could hardly refuse. There were the usual armed contests, duelling, single and joint combat such as Edward revelled in, that monarch himself demonstrating his knightly prowess by unseating from the saddle Richard de Clare, Earl of Gloucester and Hertford, possibly facilitated by that earl himself, this to loud cheering.

There were no royal protests when, after a midday repast, Alexander announced that he had been absent from his kingdom for long enough, two weeks by the time they won back to Scotland – this Edward would understand. The parting was less than fraternal for brothers-in-law, even though a reminder of the Dreux marriage proposal was the last farewell on Edward's part. Thankfully, the Scots headed northwards. At least the homage problem was dealt with; and without actual warfare they did not see how the Plantagenet could further seek to claim that he was Lord Paramount.

Needless to say, this strange marriage suggestion for Alexander was much discussed on their way home.

All had wondered at the non-arrival of Bishop Wishart at London. They did learn why, from de Ros at Wark, when they crossed the borderline. The Primate should not have attempted to make the journey south, so taxing to an unwell man. His sickness had proved fatal, and he had died at Morebattle, nearby, on his way.

Sorrowfully was the news received. William Wishart would be sorely missed by all, in especial by Patrick of Dunbar and March.

27

It took only two weeks for the king to summon his envoy extraordinary to Edinburgh, where he was now spending most of his time, and for a notable errand. Alexander wanted to be better informed as to this marriage proposal which Edward had put forward, whatever his reasons. Was he to reject it, and further incur the Plantagenet's offence? Or might it be none so ill a move, if it could be used to strengthen Scots ties with France, not weaken them? Was this Yolande as estimable a prize as Edward had asserted, in wealth and influence? And, ever a man for the other sex, was she indeed as good-looking as reported? He was not going to wed any ugly, graceless female, however rich and useful.

Patrick was the obvious enquirer to send. He could sail in one of his ships to Bordeaux, on the edge of Gascony, an English-held port, where he could use King Edward's name to gain access to the Count de Dreux's whereabouts. Any other emissary would have to make the so-lengthy journey by land, through England, across the Channel and then on down the length of France. And Patrick had proved himself a tactful and reliable ambassador, who would know how best to conduct himself and make the visit seem unexceptional and without any commitment.

Here was a highly unusual task, even for that man. It occurred to him that there could be little doubt that Christian would be a valuable aide in this, as well as a welcome companion, with another woman to assess.

His wife made no bones about it, even though it would mean quite a lengthy absence from home.

Fortunately this time Dand Shaw and his *Meg* were

available. That experienced shipman had never been so far south as Bordeaux, but expressed no doubts that he would find his way there, of nearly one thousand miles, he calculated. As well that it was still only October.

They were off without delay, concerned to get there and back before the winter storms set in. With south-west winds prevailing, Dand reckoned that they ought to take about ten days for the voyage.

Patrick was quite used, by now, to sailing down the English coastline as far as the Thames estuary, and crossing over to the Low Countries. But rounding the North Foreland and avoiding the Goodwin Sands, to head westwards down the Channel for the Atlantic, was new to him. They saw the white cliffs of Dover, passed Beachy Head and identified the Isle of Wight, to pass close to Guernsey, by which time they were ploughing into the long Atlantic swell, and more than halfway to their destination, according to Dand.

Christian enjoyed it all.

Turning south at the great headland of Cape Ushant, they commenced to roll continuously in the ocean's westerly tides, which took some getting used to. None was actually sick, but tended to feel no eagerness for their food. And there was much of this, four hundred miles, Dand said, down the French coast; but this was largely guesswork.

Three days of it and Dand was searching bays and estuaries, of which there were not a few, seeking that of the Garonne River, said to be wide indeed, opening into a firth as long as that of the Forth. Bordeaux, he had heard, lay over fifty miles up this, sheltered waters, deep into Gascony.

There was no mistaking the mouth of the Garonne, however, when eventually they reached that far, with poles and cairns on both banks, these two miles apart, to mark it for shipping. Indeed they entered the estuary with two other vessels, for this was one of the great trading ports of France, odd indeed to be under English rule. It was understandable why King Philip was anxious to get rid of this Plantagenet foothold on his domains.

They reached the city just eleven days after setting out, to find a very large harbour, covering miles of riverside, with quays by the score, and all under the command of an English harbour-master. They docked beside a large vessel from London. Using King Edward's name, they learned from the harbour-master that the Count de Dreux dwelled normally at the town of Bergerac, where he had one of his many castles. This, it seemed, was about fifty miles to the south-east of this Bordeaux, on the River Dordogne, a tributary of the Garonne. They could hire a boat to take them there, better than using horses.

They found Bordeaux a fine city, capital of the duchy of Aquitaine, which had come to the Plantagenets through the marriage of Eleanor thereof to Henry the Second a century before. They noted that the fine cathedral there was dedicated to St Andrew, their own patron saint. The ruins of the ancient Roman amphitheatre were a notable feature. This was clearly a thriving mercantile community, which interested Patrick, its trade in wines renowned.

They found no difficulty in arranging their onward journey, not having to hire a boat for themselves, the harbour-master, Dixon by name, now recommending that they travel in one of the frequent wine barges which sailed the Dordogne deep into Gascony. This was how many of the merchants journeyed into the wine country, these apt to have sleeping accommodation for passengers. Dixon went so far as to find them a suitable barge, so useful was King Edward's authority. Dand Shaw accompanying them, they set sail in mid-afternoon, and soon left the Garonne to enter the lesser but still broad river, to sail past the towns of Libourne and Castillon. Night fell thereafter, and the barge drew in, to moor at the riverside. There was only the one cabin for passengers. Dand would have bedded down on the deck, but Christian insisted that he shared the simple accommodation with them, to his protests.

In the morning, past St Foy, they came to Bergerac,

finding it a quite large town with many important-seeming buildings, including one pointed out as a former famous monastic establishment called the Recollets Cloister, its cellarage the greatest in the area.

There was no problem in finding the de Dreux chateau, for it stood out on the highest point of the riverside. Making their way there and climbing up to it, they saw it as more commodious and decorative than their own Scots, or indeed English, fortalices, if less defensive; but then, situated thus almost in a town, defence would not be a priority.

No guards barred the entrance to the inner courtyard, but their arrival had been observed and they were met by a quite richly clad steward at the great doorway, who demanded, in French of course, the identity of visitors, at this hour of the day, to His Excellency the Count Robert.

Patrick's French was fair enough, and he answered that he was the Count of Dunbar and March, from Scotland. This had their questioner staring, before collecting himself and bowing. He conducted them upstairs, Dand remaining below, to a splendid chamber, not a hall, all fine hangings, tapestries and ornaments, to leave them, declaring that he would fetch His Excellency.

Patrick and Christian eyed each other eloquently.

Presently a handsome man of middle years, less notably clad than the steward, arrived to greet them enquiringly, to ask if he had heard aright, and his humble house was being honoured by a count and countess from faraway Scotland? And if so, was he to assume that they had come as representing the king of that land, who had been wed to King Edward of England's late sister?

Patrick admitted as much, and repeated his name and style, declaring that he and his wife came on the orders of King Alexander of Scots on a mission of goodwill and enquiry. He presumed that he was speaking to the Count Robert de Dreux. Christian dipped a half-curtsey.

De Dreux bowed and repeated that he was honoured by this company, and would aid in the said enquiries in any way that he could. Meantime he would have some travel-cheer brought to comfort them. He went to ring a bell, for servitors, and drew out a seat for Christian.

It was, as Patrick had anticipated, a rather difficult task to introduce the object of this visit, especially with Alexander's reluctance to commit himself in any way to this proposed marriage. He had thought frequently on this, of course, and more or less compiled an opening gambit, and in French.

"My lord Count," he began, "King Alexander has been advised by King Edward that there is a possibility, merely a possibility, that you might consider the matter of a marriage between himself and your daughter. Is this indeed so?"

The other inclined his head. "It has been suggested, yes. By his Majesty of England, Duke of Aquitaine."

"His Majesty is concerned, yes, for his late sister's husband and for her children. But His Grace Alexander has not considered remarriage as yet. And has some . . . some doubts as to its need and advantage."

"Ah, so? Doubts? He is a young man yet, is he not? At least, of no great years, such as am I!"

"You, my lord Count, appear to be in the flower of life! His Grace Alexander is of thirty-five years now, and is in good heart and health. But he has a kingdom to rule, and his mind is fully occupied with this."

"His Majesty Edward, who is overlord of this Gascony, sees him as requiring a wife. But who am I to speak on that?"

At this rather awkward stage, Patrick was thankful for the arrival of servants with wines and cakes, which allowed Christian to come to his aid.

"His Grace made a good husband for Queen Margaret," she observed. "He is kindly towards women! But a second marriage is a large step." Her French was not as good as Patrick's, but her smile made up for that.

Pouring her wine, de Dreux nodded. "I understand, Countess," he said. "I have been without a wife for some years, and have not sought a new one. It was but King Edward's suggestion."

"King Edward will have his reasons, no doubt. But . . ." She paused, as two other people entered the chamber, otherwise than as servants, a young man and woman; and although the former was like his sire, good-looking, it was the other who all but caught Christian's breath.

Yolande de Dreux was quite the most beautiful female that she had ever set eyes upon, tall, dark, splendidly formed, with features lovely as they were delicate, eyes sparkling. Seeking not to stare, Christian turned to look at her husband.

Patrick *was* staring, frankly, all but devouring this creature with his eyes, sufficiently so for his wife to feel just a pang of envy, fair in looks as she herself was.

"Ha – my daughter, Yolande, and my son Jean," de Dreux introduced. "Here is a count and countess from Scotland, come from King Alexander. We welcome them."

Patrick sought for words. "My . . . our greetings, lady. And sir. I am Patrick of Dunbar and March. And there is Christian, my wife. We, we salute you!"

It was the young man who answered. "You have come far. And to see this sister of mine!" he said, grinning.

His father frowned at that. "The count and countess are here on the King of Scotland's royal behalf," he said. "To make . . . enquiries."

"And to consider Lande, no?" Clearly this son was of a spirited disposition.

His sister eyed him, cheeks dimpling. "Jean has a readier tongue than have I," she observed. "But I, at least, greet you more . . . correctly! You have come all the way from Scotland. For, for this!"

The way that was said gave Christian the thought that this one had her own noteworthy spirits to match her brother's.

"You are kind," she said. "We wish you well."

"My daughter understands the situation," the count told them.

"King Alexander has his questions," Patrick said. "A king must consider heedfully in all matters."

"Indeed, yes," the young man Jean agreed.

"Who am I to see it otherwise," Yolande added, again with her half-smile.

"But not here, not now," her father declared. "Our guests deserve comfort and hospitality, after long travel. Take them to the West Tower, Yolande. And have them kindly served. We shall talk more later." He bowed.

His daughter came and gestured to them to follow her.

As they went, Christian nudged her husband. "Do not admire so openly!" she murmured, in English. "Lest you commit Alexander beforehand!"

They were led, by corridors and stairs amany, to a couple of rooms in a tower, the young woman turning laughingly to tell them that they must not get lost hereafter. They would have a maid to guide them back.

In a well-furnished room overlooking the wide river, they heard that fires would be lit for them, and hot water brought for their washing, maids to attend them. Christian mentioned Dand Shaw, left behind, and Yolande assured that he would be looked after.

She left them, with smiles.

"So, what think you?" Christian asked. "Not as to her looks and person – that is sufficiently evident, my dear Patrick! Our Alexander would be likewise smitten, I have no doubt. But otherwise? Would she make a queen of Scotland? Or just a honey-platter, to draw you men and make their women jealous?"

"We shall have to see. It is not all this of the young woman. There is the wealth to be won. And the relations with France. And with Edward. A royal marriage has other concerns than with good looks and graces."

"To be sure. But . . ."

Two maids came to attend to them, and very heedfully; and presently another came to lead them back, through all those passageways and stairs, to a different but equally handsome chamber, set for a meal. Count Robert awaited them, and then his son and daughter arrived, and they sat, all seeming remarkably at ease considering the situation which brought the visitors. Yolande and Jean were lively company, their father quietly amiable.

When they were finished eating, and sipping wine from notably fine carved glasses, which the count explained were Venetian, he added that if his son and the ladies would leave them for a while, he could perhaps assist Count Patrick with his enquiries.

Patrick would have wished Christian to remain with him in this important discussion, but could hardly insist, the count presumably deeming it not a matter for women. She uttered no objection, and the three departed.

"First this of the *dot*," the count began. "Dowery, you name it, no? This would be in two parts. My daughter has inherited much property of her own, from her mother, the Countess Hélène de Limoges. This is not mine, and would go with her. The other *I* would give, as her marriage-portion. A considerable *dot*. Fit for a queen."

Patrick inclined his head. Expert at trading as he was, he was somewhat embarrassed at this sort of negotiation, too like bargaining with their host.

"I will inform King Alexander," he said. "For his part, should this marriage proceed, it is ever the custom and right for a new queen in our land to receive the palace and lands of Linlithgow, in Lothian, as her own. And other good properties."

"No doubt. The estates Yolande owns of her own right are large. They lie to the north of Gascony, in the Haute Vienne and Bourgenouf areas, as well as Limoges itself. Also at Clermont-Ferrand, to the west. Much rich land, wine country, and some olives. Also cattle. Your king would find it . . . of profit."

"It sounds very adequate."

"For my part, I would give with her the lands of St Amand and Miramont. Also the vineyards of La Rosse. How say you, Count? I shall take you to see these on the morrow, that you may judge for yourself."

"You are generous, it would seem."

"I would have reason to be so." He raised eyebrows. "Although there are many, of lofty rank and name, who would marry my daughter."

"That I can believe. And will tell His Grace so. And not only for her dowery!"

"Tomorrow, then, we shall visit the chateaux of St Amand and Miramont. No great distance. Now, shall we rejoin the others?"

Thereafter, they spent a quite pleasant evening, Yolande proving a good hostess to add to her other qualifications, which included singing with a harp's accompaniment. The visitors were becoming quite in favour of the thought of her becoming their queen, ere they slept that night.

Next day, riding to inspect the two properties with their castles, with vineyards and olive groves and parkland, they were the more impressed. But there was still the question to which they must try to obtain at least some indication of an answer: that of Edward Plantagenet's benefit in all this, why he was so advocating this match? He was not the man to be doing it out of affection for his brother-in-law, nieces and nephews. Patrick sought some guidance as they returned to Bergerac.

"The King of England, Count," he mentioned, as opportunity arose when they were riding side by side. "He is your Duke of Aquitaine. And your friend?"

"Friend? That is perhaps over-close a term. But I am one of his larger vassals here, and we are on fair terms, yes."

"And would you say that he has much to gain by proposing this marriage?"

"Gain? Think you that it is for *his* gain?"

"That I do not know. But he is strong for it. And, and Edward is not usually so . . . concerned."

"He can wish his fellow-monarch well, can he not?"

"The King of France is also his fellow-monarch, to be sure. And *he* has sons of marriageable age."

"But Edward and Philip have their disagreements."

278

"And would this marriage help Edward in that? These lands in France coming to Alexander?"

"I do not see that it should. Edward already has Aquitaine and Gascony. Should these others, going to Scotland, make any difference? Not as I see it."

"Perhaps not. But . . ."

"You and your king are suspicious of King Edward, my friend?"

"Not *suspicious*, Count. But this is a new side of the Plantagenet, who seeks to be Lord Paramount of Scotland."

"My daughter, as queen there, would not aid him in that."

"If you think not . . ." Patrick had to leave it at that.

The visitors left next day, for Bordeaux and home, after quite warm leave-taking, in fairly optimistic mood as to their mission. They believed that Count Robert was in no way party to any plan to effect disharmony between Scotland and France, and saw Edward's proposal as only that of a well-wisher. And what he had to offer Alexander was sufficiently attractive. It was not for them to decide, of course, only to inform; but their advice could probably influence the king's decision. But what would be the effect on Philip of France? De Dreux had indicated no hostility in that direction.

They faced the Bay of Biscay's tides and swells with the wind now in their favour.

After an uneventful voyage, Patrick asked Dand to take his *Meg* on past Dunbar and up Forth to Leith, the port of Edinburgh, so that he could deliver his report to Alexander forthwith, and get this important matter off his mind. But on arrival at the Abbey of the Holy Rood, they found that other issues had developed in the interim, to concern the monarch greatly. They had been gone barely one month, but in that time there had been a sufficiency of events, two in especial, to distract the king. The young Prince David had died suddenly, second in line for the throne, to his father's shock and grief – that was the worst of it. But his little family was affected otherwise also. For messengers had come from Norway, to announce that King Magnus was gravely ill, and was not being given long to live. He desired to see his son and heir, Eric, married to the Princess Margaret of Scotland before he departed, which, it was emphasised, could be very soon. This just before David's death. So Margaret had been sent off to Bergen, at only some ten days' notice, in the care of a delegation which included the Earl and Countess of Menteith, Sir Bernard de Mowat and the Abbot of Balmerino, with seven thousand merks, as advance on a dowery of seventeen thousand. Undoubtedly, if Patrick had been in Scotland then, with the closest ties with Norway, he would have led the party.

Alexander thus was scarcely in a state for dwelling on the subject of remarriage at this juncture, anxious as he was about his family, for the older son, Prince Alexander, ever frail, was ill, although newly betrothed to one more Margaret, daughter of Guy, Count of Flanders.

Patrick returned to Dunbar, then, wondering whether their journey to Gascony had been worth while, although Christian declared that, given time to get over these upsets, the remarriage situation would surface again, and the report on Yolande and her dowery become important.

They were glad to be home, and thankful that they had escaped the winter gales, for these grew fierce indeed thereafter, so that for weeks on end Dunbar Castle, on its stacks in the sea, was all but enveloped in spray and spume, no weather for sea travel. And that fact was all too grimly emphasised soon after the New Year, when the ship bringing the company which had escorted Princess Margaret, was wrecked on reefs on the way home, none so far from Dunbar, with the loss of all aboard. If Patrick had been one of that party . . . !

28

In the spring, Scotland was faced with another demand from the Vatican, indeed much of Christendom also. A new Pope, Martin, had been appointed, and he was a still more enthusiastic crusader, at second hand, as it were, and was requiring enormous levies of men and moneys to assail the Saracens again. He sent a legate, one Boinamunde de Vitia, to Scotland – his odd name was quickly converted into Bagimond – to impose and collect tithes on all landed properties, not only of Holy Church, a grievous burden, under threat of excommunication if it was not forthcoming. This Bagimond was a dedicated, determined and efficient character, enrolling a tribe of assistants, who inspected and valued all the properties, compiling lists known as Bagimond's Roll, lords and lairds as well as bishops, abbots and priors highly resentful. And what made it worse, from the Scots point of view, was the word that if Edward of England would agree, as the First Knight of Christendom, to lead this new crusade, all the moneys collected from Ireland, Wales and Scotland, as well as England, would be put at his disposal, to hire, equip and transport a great army to the Holy Land. Seldom had the Vatican been so unpopular.

The levy bore heavily, of course, on King Alexander himself and the royal lands. Whether or not it was on this account, he began to turn his mind to a remarriage and the substantial dowery which could accompany a new queen. So Patrick's information anent the de Dreux proposal, and the scale of Yolande's *dot*, was very relevant, and details sought. Descriptions of the young woman herself were received with interest, but it was the financial aspect of it all which took priority. The fact that de Dreux indicated no enmity towards the King of France also carried weight.

Patrick imagined that it would not be long before he was sent south again to fetch a new bride for his liege-lord. Presumably this would please Edward Plantagenet, who apparently was still debating whether or not to lead this new crusade.

The Cospatricks had their own nuptial preoccupations that year, for John, their second son, had met and fallen for Anna Kerr, the daughter of Kerr of Sprouston and Auldtounburn, the laird of properties near Kelso, on the south side of Tweed only that river's breadth from their own Merse lands. These Kerrs were an ancient family of Norman descent, but proud to claim that they were of Norse or Viking blood, as indeed were many Normans, not French at all, the very name of Normandy referring to Norsemen's land, a belt of northern France settled on by the Norsemen, the first duke thereof being Rolf the Ganger, sufficiently Viking. The Kerrs had sprung from one of his captains. They explained that their name, having originally been Kjarr, was pronounced Kyar or Carr. Nevertheless, despite all this early eminence, they were now no great nobles; and for the son of the Cospatricks represented no very lofty match. But John was entitled to choose his own wife, and his parents voiced no objections.

So in due course a family journey was made southwards to Kelso, in the abbey of which the wedding was to be celebrated, Adam Hepburn and his wife accompanying them. Patrick had met Kerr of Sprouston on more than one occasion, but never the daughter of the house, and was interested to see his second son's choice, John asserting that she was quite the most delightful female he had ever encountered, although his younger brother, with his own preferences, pooh-poohed that. But when, in the abbey, her father led her up to join the groom at the chancel steps, Patrick was suitably impressed and well pleased, for this Anna was eye-catching indeed, clearly of much character, not actually beautiful but of sparkling good looks, all smiles and confidence without being in any way self-assertive, well-built and notably feminine. John was going to have a full life with this one.

Her father was a tall, heavy man of distinguished appearance, long flaxen hair only beginning to show strands of grey, suitably Norse-looking.

The ceremony went without a hitch, the bride considerably more assured-seeming than was the groom, as was often the case, and when the abbot declared them to be man and wife, squeezing John's arm, she turned to beam all round, whereas John merely looked at his brother Alexander, acting groomsman, eyebrows raised as though scarcely believing that this was all that would alter his whole life.

Thereafter all went to cross Tweed by the Hendersyde ford, Anna now in the saddle within John's arms, to reach Sprouston Castle, beside its own village not far from the river, between the other hamlets of Kerchester and Kersquarter, where, while feasting was being readied, Kerr took his new son-in-law and his father to see the dowery he was providing for his daughter, the farm of Lempitlaw four miles to the south, no very great property to come to an earl's son but quite adequate in the circumstances. Patrick, acknowledging this, announced that he would settle the couple in his little-used house of Earlstoun of Ercildoune, none so far away up Tweed and Leader, near to Dryburgh Abbey. Kerr, in his unusual position of being no lord's vassal but holding his land directly of the crown, the family having held this status for generations, just why not specified, expressed his gratification.

Well content with this development of the family, the bride and groom were escorted the fifteen or so miles north-westwards, by Smailholm and Redpath, to their new home, the castle under the Black Hill thereof, and near the small Learmonth tower of Ercildoune itself. The rest of the party went on to Dryburgh Abbey's guest-house for the night.

Now they had only Alexander, Gelis and Elizabeth, or Bethoc as she was usually called, to have married off.

When next Patrick was in touch with his monarch, at Edinburgh for a council meeting, he found Alexander with an unusual sort of worry on his mind, nothing to do with state troubles this time, which would have come out at the meeting. Privately thereafter, the king declared that he was worried about his son, now his only son, Alexander's wits, his health not only of the body but of the mind. However weakly in person he had always been, he had seemed to be normal enough in the head, indeed quite bright, acute. But now he had started to claim to be seeing visions, making efforts to foretell the future. This was upsetting his father, who was beginning to fear for his heir's sanity.

Patrick advised him not to worry unduly. One of his own vassals, he whom the king had knighted, along with others, after the Battle of Largs, Learmonth of Ercildoune, was similarly affected, or indeed talented, and it did not prevent him from being otherwise normal and effective, as he had proved in battle.

The king said that might be so. But his son was allowing these seeings and forebodings to affect his daily life and judgment. He was being directed, as he put it, to visit other localities, some quite distant, there to commune with spirits and dark forces, surely a sign of mental decline? He was foretelling, for instance, that his sister was not far off death. That Edward Plantagenet would enter into three battles, in two of which he would conquer but in the third would be subdued. That a King of Man would be born with three legs, of all things! And that the beginning of this world dated from 6,470 years before. He was even prophesying his own death, but giving no date; and after all, we all died at some time. Something would have to be done about his son. Perhaps one of the churchmen could drive the evil spirits out of him?

Patrick thought that, to ease his sovereign's mind, it

might be worthwhile to bring Thomas the Rhymer, as he was called locally, to see him, *he* believed to be no madcap, no charlatan or pretender, earning his other nickname of True Thomas. He would be seeing much of John and Anna these days, from his nearby little Tower of Ercildoune.

Some ten days later, then, Patrick picked up Learmonth to take him to Roxburgh where the king was back in residence, somewhat to the younger man's alarm over being expected to inform and reassure the monarch. But he could not refuse his lord.

They found Alexander more worried about his son than ever, who had just gone off on some strange mission of his own to Falkland, in Fife, the royal hunting-palace, declaring that he had to meet a little mannie there, who would tell him of things to come, great and terrible events. His father, unable to dissuade him, had sent his personal chaplain with him to seek to guide him out of the worst follies. It was all most perturbing.

Patrick pointed out that there had been seers and prophets since man was, and they had frequently been proved worthy and responsible characters, as well as giving warnings and guidance to nations. He glanced over at Learmonth.

That man was a little hesitant in raising voice. But when he did, and found royal attention given, he spoke more confidently.

"Sire, most soothsayers and predictors deem their abilities as gifts from God, no virtues or wisdoms of their own, but lent them by the Almighty. And so are honest in their foretellings and warnings, believing that they would be judged if they fail in this, or bear false witness for their own or others' benefit. I would think that your royal son, himself heir to this nation's throne, is surely unlikely to be otherwise. He could be mistaken, yes, misjudging his own insights; but that would be but error of judgment, not disorder of the mind. To go to these lengths, he must *believe* in what he sees. And if so, he may be gifted so, with worth in what he is shown. They need not be follies, Your Grace."

"No-o-o-o."

Learmonth paused. "Highness," he said, "my lord here told me of one strange sight the prince had. This of a King of Man who might have three legs. It comes to me, Sire, that this is the symbol of the kingdom of Sicily. Three legs joined together at the centre, like a starfish. Edmund Plantagenet!"

Alexander stared, taking a deep breath. "Edmund! Edward! And Man! Lord, could this be? The Plantagenet, aiming at Man. That kingdom is now mine, although I pay a yearly tribute to Norway for it. But it is none so far from the English coasts, Lancaster. The Isle of Man – is this Edward's next move?"

"It could be," Patrick said. "He has lain quiet for some time. Which is not like that man. This could be a warning indeed."

"A warning, yes. From my son!" The king turned on Learmonth. "*You* – you are a seer also. Do you see this as a warning? From, from wherever such comes?"

"It was the prince's seeing, Sire. I but deem it thus."

"And, and he foretold more. His own death. And my daughter's!"

"But not when," Patrick put in. "We all will die, one day."

"Yes. But . . ." Alexander frowned. "This of Man. I must act. If it is a warning. Take some measures. I will make a move. Will tell Devorgilla of Galloway and her Baliol husband, and Bruce, to assemble a force, make a sally down towards Man using Galloway vessels. Edward will hear of it. Cause him to consider, take heed. If indeed it is so. A warning. No harm if it is not. No harm done."

Patrick nodded "That would be wise, I think." He paused. "And you did tell me that Prince Alexander had claimed to have forseen something of Edward himself? Two victories, was it, and then a defeat?"

"Ah, yes. Two battles won and then he was to be

subdued. What this might mean I know not. Whether it has anything to do with Man. I think that I must appoint a strong governor there, not just the bailiffs who act for me meantime." Most evidently Alexander was taking this of a threat and warning very seriously.

"The people of that isle would not wish to have the Plantagenet tyrant ruling over them, I judge. So they will be the readier to rally to your banner, Sire."

"It may be so. But, my friend, be ready with your men and ships to aid in this of Man, if required."

Learmonth and his lord returned to Ercildoune and Dunbar.

Patrick had been home only a few days when another summons arrived for him: not to raise men and available shipping; one vessel was all that was required of him. The Prince Alexander had suddenly died, at Lindores Abbey in Fife. The king, stricken, would go there, to his son, and conduct his funeral to the royal burial-place at Dunfermline Abbey, also in Fife. A ship to pick up the monarch at Leith. That was the urgent message.

Late January was not the best time for sea travel, even short coastal sailing, but Patrick, sympathetic for his liegelord, recognised why this was being chosen. Lindores lay at the north of the great earldom of Fife, only a short distance from the Tay estuary. So to reach it by sea would be infinitely easier than the eighty-mile journey by land, with the Forth to cross at Queen Margaret's Ferry. It would be equally far by ship, but much more speedy, with no need for an overnight stop. And the body could be brought back, round Fife Ness and up Forth to Dunfermline, again in half the time.

Scotland was now without an heir to the throne.

In January the *Skateraw Meg* was apt to be moored in Dunbar harbour because of frequently dire sea conditions. But Dand Shaw did not fail to round up his crew. This time, Christian felt that it was not for her to accompany her husband, however much she commiserated. After only a day's delay they sailed for Leith, in sleety rain but the seas not particularly rough.

Patrick hired a horse to take him from the docks of the port up to Edinburgh Castle.

He found the king in a state of deep depression and anxiety. He had lost his wife, both his sons, and now he was fearing for his daughter. That prophecy . . . !

Alexander took no large company with him down to the ship, all gloom and disquiet. Dand was duly concerned with having his sovereign as passenger. He said that he ought to have them in the Tay at Lindores by nightfall.

They sailed north by east to the mouth of the Firth of Forth, passing the May Island and keeping well clear of its reefs and skerries, and thereafter giving a wide berth to the thrusting cape of Fife Ness. Then due north the score of miles of open water to the mouth of Tay, passing well seawards of St Andrews and the lesser estuary of the River Eden. The wind was in their favour, and they made good time of it, however much the *Meg* rolled and pitched, nothing so bad as the roosts of Orkney.

Having carefully to skirt the dangerous shallows of the Abertay Sands, they turned into the wide firth. They still had over a score of miles to go to their destination, but at least they were in sheltered waters now.

They passed within a mile or so of Dundee, on the north shore, a large and important town and trading centre, and still closer, later, to the notable abbey of Balmerino, whose abbot had been one of those drowned in the shipwreck coming back from taking Princess Margaret to Norway. That princess, now a queen, was very much on all minds on this voyage.

It was dusk before they reached Crombie Point, and Dand had to steer carefully a course between more sandy shallows, or banks as they were called here, and for which the Tay was notorious. Fortunately they were nearly all marked with tripod-markers of poles, to aid the local fishermen. Lindores Hill was just still visible, to beckon them on.

This Lindores was an area unvisited by Patrick, unknown save by repute, although Malcolm MacDuff of Fife had a castle here, to which he had been invited, this near the loch, a quite large sheet of water a couple of miles inland, on the far side of its hill. The repute did not refer to the castle however, but to an abbey, founded by King David and dedicated to both the Virgin Mary and St Andrew, much to the north of his other famed foundations. This was a fine place, notable as a seat of learning. It lay quite close to the shore, and had its own haven, for the *Meg* to tie up.

It made a sad introduction to the renowned establishment for most of them its abbot much distressed to be hosting the monarch in these circumstances. They found Malcolm of Fife present, and likewise grieving over the situation however welcoming towards his old friend.

The dead prince lay before the altar in the abbey chancel, with candles lit around the bier, looking more at peace than Patrick had ever seen that strange young man. Alexander knelt, weeping, beside his son, while the abbot intoned a prayer, and his monks sang in solemn chant. The onlooker could only shake their heads and murmur.

When the king had mastered himself sufficiently to withdraw to the sacristy, his chaplain, who had been with the prince throughout, informed as to the sorrowful events. They had been at Falkland, to the west, up Stratheden when the prince, less than well, had felt called upon to go to Cupar, the capital of the Stewardry of Fife. Something important would happen there, he had insisted, although the chaplain had advised against the journey on horseback. They did reach the town, but at the Dominican priory of St Mary the prince had fallen unconscious and scarcely breathing. They had tried to revive him, had prayed for him, as he seemed to hover between life and death. But with no change in the curious state, the prior had advised that he be taken to the abbey of Lindores, a dozen miles to the north-west, famed for its experts in all matters of learning, including the arts of healing, of the physicians' powers. So they had contrived a litter, slung between two horses, to carry the prince. Presumably he had breathed his last on the journey there, for the monks pronounced him dead on arrival, although he had been watched closely all the way and no change noted.

The king heard all this set-faced, wordless.

Night was upon them, and no feasting sought nor provided on this occasion. Indeed there was to be a vigil maintained, watchers kneeling beside the bier throughout the hours of darkness, and praying for the soul of the heir to the throne, the father himself taking the first watch, until midnight, Patrick to take the second and Malcolm MacDuff the third.

It made a grievous night.

In the morning the prince, wrapped in grave-clothes, was cermoniously carried down to the ship, to more chanting of monks, Dand and his crew, who had never had the like on their *Meg*, much put about. It was Dunfermline for them now, right round Fife.

It was not long before the king drew Patrick aside, a man in turmoil of mind.

"My friend, I have had a word with the sub-prior, there at Lindores, Peter by name," he began. "He it is who is most knowledgeable as to sickness and healing. This of the warnings that my son sought to give me. As of Man. And, and his own death. Which I failed to heed sufficiently, God forgive me! But, there is this of my daughter Margaret. In Norway. He warned as to her possible death, also. This I *must* heed!"

"It may not be so, Your Grace. Not, not nigh. Death could be at any time, for us all. Years hence."

"His own was not! Foretold at the same time, the seeing, the warning. I want you, Cospatrick, to go to Norway. You who know them well there. And take this Prior Peter with you, he who is wise to the body's ills. See Margaret. With child as she is. She may indeed be delivered by now. It could be that state which threatens her. *He* may save her . . ."

"Sire, I will do that, if you wish. But need you deem this so, so sorely? Prince Alexander may have seen only a distant death. All could be well with the princess. Or queen, I should say. The prince was a sick man anyway. His own death, so sorrowful as it was – at least for you, for the realm, although perhaps not for him. For he looked at peace, indeed; his own death could have been foreseen. But your daughter is different. She is not sickly. And having a child comes to most women. Without more pain than the birth-pangs."

"That may be so. But the warning was given. I must heed it. You will go, my friend?" He gestured. "With this Peter. Else my mind will not rest."

"As you will, Sire."

It was some eighty miles round to Dunfermline, and it took the *Meg* most of the day to reach the haven of Inverkeithing, the nearest to the abbey. There they collected horses to carry them all, and the body, up the four miles to the higher ground where stood Queen Margaret's shrine and her husband's palace side by side, the royal burial-place, where she herself was interred.

Unwarned, the abbot and his people were quite unprepared to have the monarch himself descend upon them, and his dead son to be buried. So the procedure was more hurried and less ceremonious than might have been, however taxing on Alexander. The prince was lowered into the crypt beside his younger brother David, and all the other royal departed. A lead coffin would be made to hold him.

They did not linger thereafter. And on the sail back to Leith, the king had another word with Patrick.

"This of the woman de Dreux," he said. "Without a son and heir, I must now consider marriage again. The dowery lands there sound rich indeed. And there appears to be no enmity towards Philip of France, you say, whatever Edward's reason for proposing the match. And you report

291

that she, Joleta is it? Ah – Yolande. She is a woman of looks and character? Who would make a queen?"

"She is very fair, Highness. Perhaps the fairest I have ever set eyes on. And . . . of spirit."

"Ah, well. It may be for the best. I will think more on this. No other has been put forward for me."

At Leith, when the monarch and his party disembarked, Patrick reverted to the subject of the Norway visit.

"When do you wish me to sail, Sire? With this Prior Peter."

"Just so soon as may be, my friend. And I will sleep the easier of a night."

"That I do hope. I shall not delay . . ."

He told Dand thereafter that there was another voyage ahead of him, winter conditions be what they were.

29

They made a stormy voyage of it across the Norse Sea, the Prior Peter being seasick despite his reputation as a master of ailments. Christian, who accompanied them on this visit, since a woman's presence might well be advantageous, looked on the discomforts and dangers as a challenge, and voiced no complaints. For his part, Patrick wished that the king had been less urgent about his daughter's health and well-being.

The Norwegian coast, in these weather conditions, was one to navigate cautiously indeed, with all its rocky headlands, fjords and reefs, the seas shrouding it all in a permanent mist of spray. The travellers were thankful to win into the comparative shelter of Bergen's own fjord safely, despite snow beginning to fall.

But at the city this thankfulness ended abruptly, met as they were with gloom other than that of the weather. Queen Margaret was dead.

Appalled, the visitors could only exclaim, and stare at each other. They were told that she had died in childbirth, or immediately afterwards, having had a long and bloody labour. The child, a girl, was apparently delicate as to her present state, but expected to survive. The young King Eric, devastated, had taken the babe up to Trondheim, St Olaf's town and seat of the archbishop metropolitan, for blessing and care, with two wet-nurses to suckle her.

What now, then? Patrick had no doubt, Christian supporting him, that they must go north to see this child; after all, she was their liege-lord's only living descendant, granddaughter and presumably heir. And Prior Peter might well have a role to play with his medical skills.

Prince Alexander had proved himself a notable seer, however melancholy.

So Dand was faced with more difficult sailing. Trondheim lay over three hundred miles north of Bergen, up that dangerous coastline in these grim conditions. They were, however, able to gain a Norwegian pilot from the royal authorities, but even so it was likely to be a hazardous journey. But Eric himself had covered it recently, with the infant, so they could not fail in the endeavour.

Their pilot chose to keep far offshore for most of the way, although they would have to move in landwards every so often to check on their position against the headlands, fjord mouths and mountainous background.

With these necessary inspections it took them four quite alarming and uncomfortable days and nights thankfully to reach the long, narrow and winding fjord of Trondheim and its calmer waters. The visitors gazed somewhat askance at the harsh, steep and rocky mountainsides that flanked them for miles on both sides, bare, craggy heights incapable of supporting life save for seafowl and perhaps the odd mountain goat. Small wonder that these Norsemen and Vikings were a tough race, and that they so frequently sought to win over kinder lands to the west.

It was a surprise, then, to come to Trondheim itself, anciently called Nidaros, on its inlet in a major lowering of the southern shore of the fjord and to find quite a large town, or city, since it had a great cathedral dominating all from high ground behind, along with both an archepiscopal and royal palace. Presumably there must be more level and kindly terrain beyond to support the population, as was so often the case in their own western Highlands.

Landing, the pilot conducted them up the climbing streets, telling them of King Olaf the First, who had been converted to Christianity three centuries before, and built this cathedral, a wonderful edifice indeed to find in such a location; and, some said, the model for St Magnus's Cathedral at Kirkwall in the Orkneys. Also of his son Olaf the Saint, who had made it a place of pilgrimage.

At the royal palace they found the young King Eric, clearly greatly surprised to see them. He was, as evidently, anguished over his wife's death and deeply worried for his infant's well-being, no very lusty child. They learned that she had little appetite for nourishment. She was to be called after her mother, another Margaret – or Margrete as they pronounced it – and weighing now less than when she was born.

Prior Peter asked questions of the wet-nurses and the physicians here, and examined the baby thoroughly. He came to the conclusion that she suffered from a form of stomach convulsions which brought up the milk she had swallowed within only an hour or so of suckling, this inevitably preventing growth and development. He prescribed certain herbs which, ground up and mixed with the milk, ought to help in some measure; but he feared that it might well be four or five months before these spasms died away and normal digestive processes took over. With God's blessing she should survive until then, after which there ought to be good progress.

Eric was grateful for this informed judgment, and said that prayers for the child were being offered daily in the cathedral.

Patrick and his wife were much moved and concerned. After all, this scrap of humanity was heir, at present, to the thrones of both Norway and Scotland, and precious indeed. Christian, cradling the infant in her arms, wondered whether the herbs advised by the prior were available in this rocky terrain, to be assured that they were, inland.

They remained three days at Trondheim, meeting the archbishop and other notables, and admiring the cathedral, with St Olaf's tomb and the fortress of Monkholm.

They set sail again. They would have voyaged due westwards, for home, but they had to return the pilot to Bergen, so the journey took three extra days. Perhaps this was proved none so ill, for the weather did improve, and a light easterly air, very cold, prevailed thereafter, to help them on their way, much to Prior Peter's relief.

Patrick was not looking forward to telling King Alexander of the death of his daughter.

The prior had to be taken to Lindores before they could go to dock at Leith; and there they learned that Alexander had returned to Roxburgh. Also of a surprising move. In their absence the king had sent a delegation to Gascony, to confirm the marriage compact and to bring back the beauteous Yolande. They had gone, not by sea but overland, with a safe-conduct from Edward to travel through England and be given ship over the Channel, this arrangement hopefully pleasing that awkward monarch, and possibly restraining him from any immediate assault on Man.

So, back at Dunbar, Patrick had to leave Christian and take to horse for Tweedside, on the way turning over in his mind how best to inform his monarch of the fourth death in his family, and with only a sickly babe left in consolation.

He found the king angling in Teviot from the wall-walk of Roxburgh Castle, a favourite pastime.

"Sire," he began carefully, "I am come in some fear, in some disquiet. I . . ." He started again. "I bring you ill tidings, to my sorrow. But also some good. Some, some solace."

Alexander turned, to search the speaker's face. "Ill?" he said. "Ill? Margaret?"

"Yes. She died. Before we won to Norway. After the birth of her child. A, a difficult birth."

The king turned away, to gaze up the river. For long moments there was silence.

Patrick had to break it. "The baby survives, Sire. A girl. Another Margaret. Your Grace has a granddaughter. And . . . heir."

"Margaret . . . dead!" That came choking-voiced.

"She will have joined Alexander and David, Your Grace. And her mother. In, in bliss." This had been Christian's suggested offering of the dire news.

Almost angrily the king turned on him. "Is that . . . do you . . . ? I am left alone, man! God help me! Alone! And you talk of a babe a thousand miles away! These are your tidings! Some good, you said!"

Patrick inclined his head, wordless.

"What have I done to deserve this? I have sought to be a good husband, a good father, a good king! I . . ." He turned away again.

Patrick decided that he should leave the monarch to cope with his own distress. He bowed to the other's back.

"I shall be . . . available, Sire. To inform you further," he said. "When required. Have I your royal permission to retire?"

Getting no answer, he backed away.

He was talking with the Chamberlain in the courtyard when Alexander came up to them, and with a flick of the hand dismissed that dignitary, still set-faced.

"I crave your forbearance, my lord Cospatrick," he got out stiffly. "I was . . . overcome. By your tidings. This of the child? Tell me of her."

Patrick related the circumstances, the visit to Trondheim, King Eric's distress, the infant's stomach problems, Prior Peter's advised treatment, and his belief that she would gain normal health in a few months. Then, choosing his words carefully, he gave some further information as to Queen Margaret's death and burial, which was received this time without comment. Then he was thanked, very formally, for his services, and his liege-lord left him, saying that he would speak with him again later.

Alexander did not dine with the others that night, but after the meal sent for Patrick to come to his personal chambers. There he asked about Eric Magnusson and his attitudes, and what might be his reaction to a request that his child be brought to Scotland, at least for some of the time. Patrick had to admit that this possibility had not been discussed. The king said that it might be necessary for him to make another visit to Norway hereafter, to seek an answer to this question. If the infant was to be accepted as heir to the Scottish throne, then some arrangement must be come to. It was a difficult situation admittedly, since she presumably would also be heir to her father's throne. Although Eric might well remarry and produce a son.

Patrick, in the circumstances, did not like to introduce the subject of Alexander's own remarriage, and the de Dreux proposal. But after some other talk about this strange situation of a possible queen-regnant, as distinct from a queen-consort, something which Scotland had never had to consider, the monarch brought up the matter of Yolande himself. He declared that it would seem more than ever advisable that he should find a new wife. He had sent envoys to Gascony under the new Chancellor – he would of course have sent the Cospatrick himself had he been available – to discover if the project was still agreed there, and the terms as formerly stated? And if so, to bring back this Lady Yolande for himself to meet and consider. He had emphasised to his representatives that this was not to be an actual commitment to wed, for since it was a queen for Scotland that was involved, it could not be taken for granted, if the lady did not prove to be fully acceptable; although he, Alexander, recognised that it would be difficult and cause some upset, not only with her and her father but with English Edward also, if she had to be rejected.

Patrick well appreciated the delicacy of that situation, if it occurred. Without seeming to overdo his advocacy of Yolande as bride and queen, he did indicate that he and his wife had both judged her as a worthy match.

His Grace might decide otherwise . . .

They left it all thus.

Next day it was back to Dunbar for Patrick, thankful to have got his mission over. His closeness to his sovereign did involve him in some taxing activities.

30

At home, it was to learn that while he and Christian had been away in Norway, their daughter Bethoc had frequently been at the Earlstoun of Ercildoune visiting her brother John and his wife, and while there had being seeing much of Sir Thomas Learmonth. This had her parents asking each other whether, if this was more than a mere passing fancy, True Thomas would make a suitable husband for their Bethoc? As an earl's daughter she could be married to someone more lofty than a vassal laird, although a notable and rather remarkable one. Patrick had gained a good impression of the man, and of his behaviour in the king's presence, and his sense of responsibility regarding his visions and prophecies. And he was a poet of some worth. Not that these qualities would raise him higher in status, but they might well help to make him an interesting and satisfactory partner. Christian thought that Bethoc probably needed someone of this unusual sort, and if she remained attached to him, and he to her, they ought not to stand in her way.

Questions of marital suitability were not confined to royalty.

It was not Alexander's problems in this respect which demanded Patrick's presence at Edinburgh before long, for the Gascony party was much delayed in reaching Scotland, as was inevitable on an overland journey of over fifteen hundred miles. It was the more immediate matter of the succession. A council meeting was called to consider this.

Held in the Abbey of the Holy Rood, it was a vital and

difficult decision to be made, indeed a unique one. At all times, the reversion to the throne had to be established, in case of the sudden death of the reigning monarch. And now Scotland was faced with the only close heir being an infant in a foreign land, and this infant a female. Yet there was no other to be considered, save for far-out possible claimants, including, to be sure, the Cospatrick. The king's grand-daughter was the obvious successor. Yet this faced them all with a hitherto unknown situation: a queen who would reign, not just the wife of a king. The ancient Scottish succession had been matrilineal, yes, the High King having to be the son of a royal princess. But never had the princess herself, or a daughter, been monarch. Could a woman sovereign rule the land? Kings had to wield the sword of state. Could any woman do so? Admittedly, on this occa-sion, the child-queen, if Alexander should die untimely, would have to have a regent, or regency council, who or which would be the actual ruler until the monarch's coming of age. But, then? Great was the debate. Alexander himself was in an equivocal position in this, for all knew that he was at least contemplating remarriage and could well produce a son, so that this strange female-succession situation might never arise. But meantime, he had to support his grand-daughter's prior claim.

In the end, the decision was unanimous. This Maid Margaret of Norway was to be declared heir to the throne of Scotland. Whether she would also be declared that of Norway remained to be seen.

It all made a highly unusual council meeting.

Patrick, throughout, was concerned that he might be called upon to make yet another voyage to Norway to discover King Eric's attitudes to his small daughter's coming to Scotland frequently, if not permanently, as would surely be desirable, possibly essential, as Alexander had mentioned previously. He was thankful that this matter was not raised there and then. He could do without that, meantime.

* * *

The next development in this involved situation was the arrival of an emissary from Edward Plantagenet, seeking to turn it all to England's advantage. The suggestion was that the infant Margaret should be betrothed to one of his younger sons – he had four already. This would depend on the Vatican giving release from the bonds of consanguinity, she being, of course, Edward's own great-niece; but, because of the Pope's concern that he should lead the next crusade, this was not likely to be withheld. Allegedly this match would be for the better harmony between the kingdoms, although most saw it as one more project to obtain a grip on Scotland. The Plantagenet was not the man to miss any of his opportunities.

Alexander, in the circumstances, did not commit himself.

That summer, at Dunbar and in the Merse, daughter Bethoc's liking for Thomas Learmonth became an accepted fact, although so far he had not actually committed himself to asking for her hand in marriage, he no doubt well aware that his lord might have considerably more ambitious ideas for his daughter's future. Patrick and Christian let the matter take it own course.

They were, to be sure, much concerned with the situation regarding Yolande de Dreux during these months, whose coming to Scotland would surely not be long delayed now. Admittedly she would almost certainly be entertained at Edward's court for some time, on arrival in England. Christian was in fact thankful that they had been away in Norway when Alexander had sent his alternative envoys to fetch her, otherwise she would probably have been parted from her beloved for long months.

At last the news did reach them. The Gascony party – apparently including Yolande's brother Jean – was in London, being royally received and feted. This, of course, would make it all more difficult for Alexander to reject the union, as Edward would calculate.

The expected summons came, presently, from Roxburgh. The Earl and Countess of Dunbar and March were to come to join the monarch in a welcome to the Lady Yolande and her entourage across the borderline, this in one week's time.

Christian said not to worry about the king's reaction when he met his potential bride. If he was anything like her husband, and any other men she knew, he would promptly succumb to that female's charms, whatever her dowery and the Plantagenet's plottings.

The fateful day arrived. The company from Roxburgh would meet the long-travelled party across Tweed from Wark, dramatically to mark its arrival in Scotland by this splashing across the wide river, however many lesser fords they had had to negotiate on their so lengthy journey. De Ros would escort them over, with a suitable flourish.

It was a large and distinguished array which eventually set out, downriver, Alexander in a strange state of mixed anticipation and doubts, to meet a possible but unseen bride. Kings were used to marrying princesses whom they had never met; but not at his age, as a second wife, and no princess.

Actually they reached the Wark ford before the Gascony party arrived, and Patrick was sent across to discover the situation. De Ros there told him that the word was that, coming from Norham, the visitors ought to arrive soon after midday. So rather than wait on the riverbank, the king's group rode across for some refreshment at the castle, while watchers were sent out to give them warning of the other approach – for Alexander was determined that this of splashing over Tweed should be his would-be bride's introduction to Scotland and himself, its monarch, a sufficient and memorable occasion, to indicate that she was entering an especial kingdom, one of the most ancient in Christendom, and no sort of appendage of the English Edward, as that man would undoubtedly have sought to have her think.

It was not long before they had to go hurrying back to the river.

When, presently, waiting on the north bank, they saw quite a procession coming down from the castle, Alexander, waving back the others, himself rode back into the water, to midstream, there to draw rein and remain, alone, a telling measure and gesture.

Chancellor Charteris and de Ros led their company into the Tweed. No doubt the king scanned them keenly, searchingly, for there were four women among them; but when one of them, and a young man, splashed ahead of the others, he would have no doubts.

The watchers witnessed the meeting, but could not see reactions at that distance, there in the swiftly running water. That was no place to linger long, of course, and as Alexander turned to conduct the newcomers into Scotland, Patrick and Christian rode down to meet them, as arranged, they having been the original go-betweens.

Yolande, clad for travel as she was, remained eye-catching indeed, and at sight of the Cospatricks, exclaimed aloud, smiling and waving, a pleasing acknowledgment. Alexander rode on one side of her, brother Jean on the other, the rest of her escort falling back a little.

"My friends!" she called out, in French. "At last, I see you. Good! Good!" She turned to the monarch. "Majesty, these please me much."

"They are my good friends also, lady," Alexander said. "And have told me very well of you."

That was a good start, at any rate.

They rode up on to Scottish soil. "Welcome to my kingdom," he went on. "When France was still Gaul and there was no England, nor Normandy, Scotland was an ancient realm. Welcome to it!"

She turned to her brother. "Aid me down, Jean. I would pay my respects."

Helped from her saddle, Yolande, with a little laugh, knelt down on the grass to kiss the ground, to the wonder of all – and to Alexander's obvious gratification. He too, promptly dismounted in order to assist her back on to her horse in gallant fashion, this to some confusion around them, for when the monarch was afoot none should remain seated, mounted.

The laughter was general then, and there was much exclamation and controlling of horses. No element of stiffness and formality remained.

Chancellor Thomas and the other envoys had their say, loud in their praise of the visitors, and the excellent travelling companions they made.

They all rode back westwards for Roxburgh.

Patrick and Christian were directly behind Alexander and the de Dreux pair. She nudged her husband's arm at one stage.

"Methinks our liege is no stronger than were you!" she murmured. "Or other poor men! See his closeness. Hear his talk! How he shows her the land. We shall have a new queen before long, I judge. And I shall have to watch *you* when at court!"

Patrick pulled a face at that.

Passing Kelso Abbey, all had to draw rein to admire its splendours. And again Patrick was nudged.

"An excellent place for a wedding?" it was suggested.

Yolande and her brother exclaimed over Roxburgh Castle, wedged between two great rivers, with its succession of towers. They waved towards the high Cheviot Hills to the south and the three outstanding, isolated, peaks of the Eildons to the north, much impressed. They were conducted to the easternmost tower, above where Tweed and Teviot actually joined, and were left in the care of the Chamberlain and no lack of servitors.

That evening there was great feasting and conviviality. Yolande was now dressed strikingly and looking stunningly beautiful, vivacious and enchanting, obviously enjoying everything, her enjoyment infectious. When it came to the entertainment, with dancing, she was clearly in her element, gracefully active. Alexander, normally no keen dancer, partnered her with alacrity, and when she offered her arms to others, including Patrick and Bruce of Carrick, waited for her to return to him with signs of impatience.

When the ladies retired that night, the king was not long in doing the same.

Patrick, on retiring to Christian's side, in another tower, could not but agree with her that it looked as though they were indeed shortly going to have a new queen in Scotland.

31

They got back to Dunbar to find an unexpected nuptial problem of their own family's, a complication. Patrick's old friend Malcolm of Fife had died some time before, leaving two sons, Colban and Duff MacDuff, Colban married. He succeeded to the earldom, held it for only a very brief period, and also died, his infant son Duncan becoming earl, but in the guardianship of his uncle, Duff, who would, to all intents, be the earl for years. And now this Duff MacDuff presented himself at Dunbar Castle, from Tantallon, to ask for the hand of the Lady Bethoc in marriage.

Here was a difficult situation. Thomas Learmonth had not come forward to make a similar request as yet, however fond he and Bethoc might be of each other. And the earldom of Fife was one of the most ancient and prestigious in the kingdom, offering the sort of match their daughter *ought* to be making, probably. Suppose Learmonth had no intention of marrying her? Believed it beyond him? They could not tell MacDuff that she was already betrothed.

So Patrick had to temporise. He had known the Mac-Duff brothers all their lives, as had Bethoc. He liked Duff. In the circumstances he could only say that he would consider the matter, that Bethoc was young yet and that there were other possible contenders in the matter.

Thereafter they had to put the issue to their daughter. Bethoc was much upset. She said that she was quite fond of Duff, but not in the least in love with him, and certainly did not want to marry him. She was sure that Thomas wished to wed her, and was probably only afraid about asking permission. And she would wish it. If Duff wanted a Cospatrick wife, could he not ask for Gelis?

It was all very difficult. Christian told her husband that if *she* was in Bethoc's position, she would elope with True Thomas.

They decided to let their temporising continue for a while, in the hope that between them the three young people would solve the issue.

The news from Roxburgh was what they had come to expect. Alexander was continually in the company of Yolande, she and her brother still in their own tower of the castle there, and none doubting that a royal wedding would be forthcoming. But when the king sent for Patrick again, it was not to announce his betrothal but, as had been more or less anticipated, to have him go to Eric of Norway again, tell him of the Maid Margaret's adoption as heir to the throne of Scotland, and seek his agreement for her, in due course, to come, or be brought, over to the land of which she might well become the monarch, at least for visits. Eric would be well aware of the situation, of course, and hardly be surprised at the request.

So it was for Bergen again, Christian glad to accompany her husband on one more mission.

In the event, it proved to be demanding of less persuasion than Patrick had expected, although of longer duration. They learned that they had to travel some distance south and east of Bergen, to Oslo, to find Eric, which took some time, this up a still longer but less narrow fjord than that of Trondheim. But once there, they discovered that these Norsemen did not consider females to be possible occupants of their throne, warlike folk as they were; and Eric was already on the lookout for a new wife to produce the hoped-for son, fond as he had been of his Margaret. He, in fact, was surprised that his little daughter could be considered as possible Queen of Scots, and saw no difficulty in allowing her to visit Scotland when she was old enough to do so with any point in it. He did ask, was King Alexander not thinking of marrying again, as seemed the obvious course – as he himself was doing?

When Patrick indicated that this was indeed a possibility, the other announced that he had a new queen in mind, the Princess Karin of Sweden, which was why he was at this Oslo, more convenient for an approach to Sweden, the border not far off.

The Cospatricks, therefore, were able to return home with satisfactory tidings for Alexander.

It was strange tidings for themselves which awaited them at Dunbar. Daughter Gelis told them that Bethoc had disappeared. Spending much of her time these days over at the Earlstoun, her sister had not been concerned for her absence for a while. But when her birthday passed and still she did not come home, Gelis had gone to her brother John's house to enquire. And he and his wife knew nothing to effect. Bethoc had been there, yes, a few days back, and had gone, as so often, to see Learmonth. But she had not come back, and they assumed that she had returned to Dunbar. John and Gelis had then gone themselves down to Ercildoune Tower, to find that neither True Thomas nor Bethoc were there. Presumably they had gone off together. But where?

Patrick was concerned. But Christian, raising her brows, reminded him that she had said that if *she* had been in Bethoc's position she would have eloped. It looked as though the pair might have done just that.

Husband and wife eyed each other.

Patrick, of course, had to go to Roxburgh to give the king the Norwegian information. There he was interested to find Yolande and her brother very much at home now, her betrothal being more or less taken for granted.

Presently Alexander spoke to Patrick privately, and in a somewhat hesitant, almost embarrassed fashion.

"This of Sir Thomas Learmonth and your daughter," he began. "They came to see me soon after you left for Norway. They said . . . said that they had secretly wed! Secretly, so as not to cause you trouble with MacDuff of

Fife. That he was giving you concern over her. So while you were away, they had done this. It seemed a strange measure to me, but both were clearly much moved. They had come to me for help. This Learmonth said that he had been given to understand that I would aid them. By whoever or what or why I know not. Whether vision or none. But that it would help *you*."

Patrick smoothed his chin, looking doubtful. "It, it clears my way, certainly, Sire."

"I took it to do so. I did what I could for them. And for yourself. I have sent them up north, to the borders of Moray, Mar and Buchan, where there is disagreement since Dorward of Atholl died, and the Comyns grasping. Dispute over lands. The crown has lands and superiorities there. I would see this matter settled. So I have appointed Learmonth to be my steward or baillie thereabouts meantime. Based on the Priory of Monymusk, on the edge of Mar. This is crown property held of me by the Church. So he will have the help of the churchmen in the area. He may achieve something of use, with his seeings and visions, who knows? And can do no harm, I judge. How say you?"

It all made a surprising situation for Patrick. But True Thomas was now his goodson, it appeared, and Bethoc had gained what she sought for. He at least could tell Duff MacDuff that she had made a better match than had seemed likely, with the king advancing Learmonth in position thus. He nodded.

"Your Grace is kind. I trust that your kindness is . . . repaid."

Alexander sounded all but relieved. "You have served me passing well over the years, my friend. And — and I have another task for you now. I have decided to wed the Lady Yolande. As you and your wife have judged that I should, have you not? So now, before we can wed, she has to go back to Gascony to her father. To settle all, before she becomes my queen here. I have to state to the Count de Dreux her marriage-portion here. You will inform him of this. He will be satisfied, I think. Then bring his daughter back to me. Take her in one of your ships. A deal swifter than to travel overland as she came. You have it?"

One more long journey and mission for Patrick. But no unpleasant one this, nor difficult, he judged. And Christian would wish to come with him, of that he was sure.

"Very well, Sire. As you will. When do you wish this to be?"

"So soon as may be. The sooner you go, the sooner you will be back. To my . . . satisfaction."

"Then I must go and arrange for the ship to take us. I think that it will be possible to use the same vessel, and the same shipmaster, as before. He is an excellent and experienced navigator, and knows this journey, Andrew Shaw by name. He has just brought me back from Norway."

"Very good. I will have to reward him, in some fashion, who has served my causes well."

"That would be kind. I shall go and have him and the ship prepared. Then come back for the Lady Yolande and her brother."

"No need. I will bring her to Dunbar, to see her on her way. How long? In two days, three?" Clearly Alexander was in something of a hurry to get this matter over, and have his bride-to-be back.

"Shaw will not have departed again on one of his trading voyages, Highness. So there should be little delay, I think."

"Good. So be it."

With much to tell Christian, her husband rode home.

Three days later the king duly arrived at Dunbar with Yolande and Jean, to find Dand Shaw and his *Meg* and crew all ready and waiting, that man much embarrassed to have the monarch actually congratulating, praising and thanking him, and promising reward. Christian was ready also, and glad to be, she and Yolande now close friends. All boarded the *Meg*, the king with them, to inspect the accommodation prepared for the Gascony party, scarcely palatial but the best that could be done at short notice.

Alexander kissed his smiling lady-love, telling her to come back to him with not a day's delay, repeating this to Patrick. He went ashore, to wave them farewell as the *Meg* cast off.

They made a reasonably swift and quite enjoyable voyage of it, Yolande and Jean excellent company, and her ladies easy to deal with although two did suffer from seasickness. Because of the south-west winds again it did take them some sixteen days, but there were no grumbles, even at the turbulence and discomforts of the Bay of Biscay. Dand took them into the Gironde and then the Dordogne, with praise for all his nautical skills.

At Bergerac the visitors found the count warm in welcome, and happy, it seemed, to hear of his daughter's success with King Alexander. When Patrick informed him that, as well as the queens' traditional dower-house of Linlithgow Palace, Yolande's portion in Scotland would include the lands of Craigalmond in Lothian, Denny in Stirlingshire and the castle of Kinghorn in Fife, he expressed himself as well pleased. For his part, he declared that his daughter was much taken with her royal suitor, and had no reservations about her marriage.

Patrick felt in duty bound to emphasise his liege-lord's desire for haste, the which Yolande in no way sought to play down. But a more or less immediate return was not possible, for Count Robert said that he would, to be sure, come to Scotland with her, to give his daughter away; and he had of course various matters to see to in his properties before he could leave for a quite extended period, even though leaving his son Jean in charge there.

So they had a stay of some ten days at Bergerac, very pleasantly passed, before the return voyage could be commenced, a somewhat smaller party this time. The count was much interested in all that went on. At least it ought to be somewhat speedier sailing back northwards, with the winds now in their favour.

It proved so to be, all going well and the company good, Yolande ensuring that. When they finally passed the mouth of Tweed, she was eager and knowledgeable in pointing out to her father sundry features of this land which was now to be her new home, the Cheviot and Lammermuir Hills, the towering cliffs of St Ebba's Head and the Merse coast, the astonishing rock-isle of the Craig of Bass ahead, and the green pyramid of North Berwick Law, all so different from where she and he came from.

When they landed at Dunbar, the castle there itself sufficiently dramatic even for Scotland, on its bridged stacks in the sea, Patrick and Christian were surprised to find Bethoc there. With their guests to install temporarily, and arrangements for riding on to Roxburgh to make, it was some little time before they could learn what had brought their daughter down from the north, where they understood that she and her husband were now based by royal command.

She explained that Thomas had been summoned south by the king, and was presently at Roxburgh. It seemed that he had fallen out with Sir Reginald de Chien of Inverugie, the Sheriff of Banff, who was controlling the large royal estate of Fyvie, but sending only a small fraction of its revenues due to Alexander. Protesting at this, which was his duty surely, there had been trouble with the sheriff, who had in fact gone down to the king to complain, and Thomas had been summoned thither to give his explanation. So he was now at Roxburgh, defending his stewardship, and she had come home for a brief visit.

When, after a day's rest, they all set out for Roxburgh, Bethoc accompanied them. She was able to give her parents details of the new life she led at the Priory of Monymusk. She quite enjoyed it there, but was worried about Thomas. It was all proving to be a difficult appointment for him. The Moray earldom was in abeyance meantime, the earldom of Mar in the hands of a juvenile, and the Comyn Earl of Buchan gone on crusade. And in these circumstances, lesser men were taking the opportunity to help themselves to lands and revenues. This de Chien, the sheriff, was wed to the Lady Mary Comyn, and in a position to take full advantage of the situation, and was certainly doing so. Thomas had had to act, even against a sheriff, but that man made a powerful opponent.

As well as all this, she was concerned over her husband's state of mind. She tended to be unhappy, admittedly, when he was having his visions and foretellings, for they seemed always to be gloomy and grievous, seldom joyful. And recently he had been much troubled by the like, particularly the apparition of a large black bird hovering over the land, more vulture than eagle, which he saw as an ominous evil. This depressed him, and worried her, for his sake. Not all seeings and omens came to pass, of course, but . . .

When they reached Roxburgh gloomy forebodings promptly evaporated, with Alexander's joyful reception of his bride-to-be, and her evident pleasure in the situation. Her father was well received, and seemed to approve of the man who was to be his son-in-law. He was of course much exercised over the royal romance, and in the wedding plans and festivities. Patrick and Christian were inevitably caught up in it all.

Bethoc found her Thomas very quiet and anything but festive. Not that he had been reproved by the monarch over his behaviour in the north, the reverse indeed. Sheriff le Chien had been sent back to Inverugie with a flea in his ear, and orders to account for the Fyvie revenues and remit the dues a deal more favourably.

The wedding preparations were well advanced. The Primate himself would officiate, supported by other bishops and prelates, and a major representation of the nobility would be present. Kelso's Abbot Richard was much involved necessarily, and proud that this should be so. The ceremony was to take place four days hence, on 27th October, the Eve of Saints Simon and Jude.

Bethoc came to her father that night, in some agitation, to announce that Thomas had had another of his visions, and a dire and urgent one. Three times he had seen this calamity, the roof of Kelso Abbey falling in, and killing much of the congregation worshipping there. He was greatly alarmed and fearful over this, and asserted that the king must be warned. Would her father tell their liege-lord?

Patrick's reaction was to shake his head in utter disbelief, all but scorn. How could such a thing be? That man was letting his imaginings run away with him, becoming obsessed with disasters and predictions. Kelso Abbey was a great and well-built edifice, one of the finest in the land, the chances of its roof collapsing beyond all belief. Bethoc would have to be chiding her husband as being in danger of becoming out of his wits.

Almost in tears, she said that Thomas was sane and responsible; but when he had a specific and repeated seeing like this, felt bound to inform of it. His gift of the sight, if that is what it could be called, had been proved accurate in the past, in some events at least. Her father must at least inform the king.

Reluctantly Patrick did so, and was surprised to find that Alexander took it all much more seriously than had he, accepting it as a warning. That young man had foretold the deaths of his son and daughter. Admittedly for Kelso's roof to fall in seemed highly improbable, but it was not impossible. He dare not ignore this warning.

Patrick suggested that men, experienced stonemasons and master-builders, should be sent to inspect the abbey and its roofing. But the monarch said that would be unsuitable, would get noised abroad and all would learn of it, with the wedding ceremony becoming something between a dread and a laughing-stock. No, he would change to Jedburgh Abbey, none so far off, up Teviot. Just as fine a shrine and only a little further to reach. He would give orders to that effect. Announce that it was his royal decision, no reasons given, no need to announce why he had changed the venue.

Great was the upset for Abbot Richard over this change of plans, and much the surprise and to-do for the Abbot of Jedburgh, who had suddenly to make the necessary pre-

parations and arrangements, however grateful and gratified he might be over his establishment being thus honoured. The visiting prelates and guests did not greatly
concern themselves. One abbey was as good as another.
Bethoc reported that Thomas was much relieved.

32

The great day arrived, amid much excitement and anticipation, the bride's personality and looks ensuring that. It
was seldom that a royal wedding was conducted for a
couple obviously in love, however important the arranged
match. The evening before, Yolande and her father and
party, including Christian, were taken to Jedburgh by
Alexander, to spend the night in the small royal castle
high above both town and abbey, while the king returned
to Roxburgh, as was suitable.

So a splendid procession set out next forenoon – with no
word of the Kelso roof having fallen – up Teviot the nine
miles, to where that river was joined by the Jed Water.
Nearby, Jedburgh Abbey's spires and buttresses rose on
the hill above the town, somewhat smaller than Kelso but
almost more handsome, and quite different as to archi-
tecture. Patrick and Bruce rode behind the king, all clad in
their finest. Patrick had never seen Alexander so joyful and
worked up. He was glad for him, deserving of this elation
after all the sadnesses and bereavement he had had to bear
of recent years.

They entered the abbey church to the sound of trumpets, music and singing. The building was graceful rather
than massive, remarkable for the three tiers of arcading
above clustered pillars on both sides of the long and lofty
nave, no fewer than thirty-six arched windows lighting the
clerestory gallery, today filled with onlookers.

Yolande and her father were already standing at the
chancel steps, contrary to the usual custom of the bride
coming slightly later to the nuptials, this because it was not
considered suitable for a monarch to seem to wait for

anyone when in his own kingdom. She was, needless to say, looking radiant, and gowned with appropriate splendour. She turned to welcome the advancing groom, curtseying, while the music reached a crescendo, Alexander bowing to her, something he seldom had to do.

Bishop Fraser and his fellow-prelates were also already waiting, to be assisted by the two abbots, for Richard of Kelso was being compensated, in some degree, for the change of location by taking prominent part here. There was no groomsman, but Patrick and Bruce stood behind the king.

The service was conducted with an appropriate sort of flourish, without sacrificing dignity, and was not lengthy, certain normal pronouncements and invocations being dispensed with in the circumstances. Bride and groom made their responses in happy and confident fashion, Count Robert playing his part approvingly. When declared man and wife, the couple embraced each other there before all, in frank satisfaction, while choristers and musicians all but lifted the roof off *this* abbey.

Thereafter, although the royal procession was on its way up to the castle, it actually moved downhill first, in order to parade through the crowded and decorated streets of the town, to the delight of the populace, musicians and singers still accompanying them, and even dancers and performers capering alongside, however dignified was the royal pacing and waved greetings. Again Patrick, with Christian now, walked just behind the newly-weds. Somewhere, considerably further back, came Thomas Learmonth and his Bethoc.

Up at the castle, eventually, there followed lavish feasting, that comparatively small establishment all but crowded out. This presented problems, for, after the banquet an entertainment of an unusual sort was to be presented, this requiring space and a cleared area in the great hall. Alexander was anxious that there should be none of the noisy and undignified revelry and excess which so often followed wedding feasts, with the abundance of wines and ales available. There was to be something of a pageant, in the form of a four-part masque; and this, appropriately, was to be a condensation of the lengthy poem of *Tristram and Isolde*, the Cornish-Irish Celtic romance translated by their own poet Thomas Learmonth, in his capacity as Thomas the Rhymer, Alexander much approving of this. Bethoc had expressed herself as distinctly doubtful about it now, not the masque itself but her husband having to direct it in his present state of apprehension, all but depression; but the king ordered it all to go ahead under the poet's control. Between the episodes, while the scenery was being changed, there would be dancing, for guests and performers, in the limited space left in the hall.

Patrick and Christian were very much interested in this entertainment, for Bethoc had persuaded two of her brothers to take prominent parts in the masques, John being Sir Tristram himself, and Alexander as King Mark of Cornwall. She and Thomas, in due course, took a place at one end of the dais platform, on which the principal guests sat watching, with the king and the new queen.

Thomas, rather tense, introduced the first scene, at Tintagel in Cornwall, where King Mark ordered Tristram to go over to Ireland to fetch his chosen bride to him, she Isolde, the daughter of the High King of Ireland, all very apt for the occasion. This went well enough, even if the players, unused to acting, were somewhat stiff about it, the audience laughingly cheering them on.

There followed dancing, Patrick and Christian participating.

The second scene was at the Irish High King's court at Tara, with Tristram meeting Isolde, and being much impressed by her looks. The young woman, Eala, who played this part, was more confident, and this had the effect of encouraging the others, although the High King did lack grandeur.

At the second interval, the royal couple joined the dancers on the floor, this at Yolande's urging.

It was when Thomas was proposing to introduce the third episode that he suddenly went through an extraordinary change. Not entirely at ease as he had been, now he became transfixed, staring, pointing down at the dancers, gasping for words. Beside himself, he all but collapsed on to his chair, from standing, still peering, gesticulating.

Much perturbed, Bethoc at his side sought to calm him, gripping his shoulder, questioning, urging heed, control, explanation, lowering of voice.

He rounded on her. "Death!" he panted. "There! Death dancing there! With the others. God help us – death!"

She gazed from him to the dancers, and back. "Thomas, I see nothing. Nothing, my dear."

"It is there; I saw it, I tell you." He had covered his eyes. Now he freed them, to peer again, and groaned. "Saints of Mercy, he is still there! See, in the midst. A skeleton! A white skeleton. Grinning, a grinning skull!" He hid his face again.

"But there is nothing there, my heart! Naught but the dancers, the king and the others. As before."

He rounded on her. "Then you are blind! Look, there he has come to the front. He stares at us. Through empty eyes. Grinning. Horrible! Horrible!"

Others on the dais had heard Thomas's voice and were gazing, exclaiming, questioning each other. Clearly none saw anything unusual. But Thomas's reputation was sufficient to ensure that what was being seen by him was not to be laughed off, ignored.

Gradually the dancers grew aware of a different sort of drama being enacted, and faltered to a halt, the king and queen included, as the musicians also faltered in their playing. Frowning, Alexander left Yolande, to come striding up to the dais platform, to demand what folly was this. What was this interruption of the entertainment? Had Thomas taken all leave of his wits? This was disgraceful, spoiling the festive occasion.

Thomas shook his head, wordless, not even looking up.

"Save us, man, take hold on yourself. What is to do?"

"Death!" The younger man clenched his fists so that the knuckles showed white. He straightened up, peering towards the now almost empty space of the dance-floor, then rose to his feet beside the monarch.

"I saw it, Sire. An evil sight. Dancing among you all. A gleaming skeleton. White. Capering, vile."

"I saw nothing, man. Save our people. Nor did any. You dream, Thomas. You are overwrought." He raised a hand. "And spoiling all!"

The other shook his head over the royal rebuke, but was not to be silenced. "I *saw* it, Your Grace. As clear as I see you. It was a sight most terrible." He all but pleaded. "Saw it, again and again."

The king stared at him, biting his lip. "If you did, what does it mean, then? What does this mean?"

"It cannot mean . . . anything but ill." Yolande had come up to stand beside them, lovely features drawn with concern. Seeing her, Thomas shook his head. "The ill — it may not be for you, Sire. You and the queen. It could be anyone."

"It is *my* wedding, my banquet. Spoiled!"

"I am sorry, Sire, sorry."

"Too late to be sorry! What to do, now? We cannot continue with this."

"No, Sire, I could not do it."

"The rest of it. The masque. The poem. The reciting . . ."

"I could not do it now. Not after . . . the warning. Death itself, I say. Warning!"

Bethoc was seeking to calm her husband, desperately upset.

Alexander, despite his wrath at this so untimely interruption of his wedding-day's enjoyment, could not but be somewhat otherwise affected. Probably it was the word *warning* which reached a corner of his mind. He bit his lip, turning to look at Yolande and Patrick, who had joined him.

"A, a vision!" he said. "Another warning, he says!"

The new queen was looking bewildered.

"Be not over-concerned, Sire," Patrick advised. "It may be none so ill. Do not let this spoil this night. It could be but a delusion. He has been distraught of late, my daughter tells me. And even if it does mean someone's death, sooner or later, there are scores of us here. It could be anyone."

"Why here? Why now?"

Yolande laid a hand on his arm. "Let us not worry over this meantime, Alexander. Lest it ruins this great, this so good day. Have the play-acting another evening, perhaps? And I would . . . retire early, moreover!"

"Ah, yes; yes, to be sure."

Bethoc at least was thankful for that.

"And Sir Thomas should retire also, I think," the queen went on. "He is not . . . himself. Do you not agree, Lady Elizabeth?"

Alexander sent word for the remainder of the pageant to be concluded.

That evening's events had their repercussions far beyond those who had partaken of it all. The land soon echoed with various versions of it. There was scoffing and mockery, but also anxiety and fears, Patrick himself not entirely free from these. Alexander, however concerned he had been over previous visions, did not take this one very seriously. He was too happy and preoccupied with his new wife, and she not one to cherish gloomy forebodings.

Their bliss, evident to all, soon dispelled anxieties from the court, whatever the talk throughout the land.

The storms commenced soon thereafter, such storms of wind and rain, hail and thunder, as none could remember before, and continued day after day, week after week. In consequence, the rivers overflowed, all the low ground became flooded, roads were impassable, cattle and sheep drowned, battered land cowering. Many declared that this was what True Thomas had foreseen: death, for men and women, as well as animals, drowned in crossing rushing river-fords, thatched roofs fell in or were blown off. The seas at least did not cower under it all, but rose in wild fury, hammering at the coasts, smashing boats even in harbours, drowning fishermen foolish enough to venture out. No trading vessels dared set sail from Dunbar, Eyemouth, Berwick nor other ports, as weeks developed into months.

Dunbar Castle became all but untenable so high the waves, its towers hidden in more than spray, actual seas crashing up to them, all but shaking them in the constant assault. Patrick and Christian soon decided that they would be better elsewhere, however grim were conditions for travelling.

They made a difficult and dangerous journey, by circuitous routes, to the Earlstoun of Ercildoune, choosing high ground as far as possible, avoiding river-crossings. Although the normal distance was only thirty-five miles, it took them two days, passing the night at the priory at Duns, and thankful indeed when they reached John and his wife.

Ercildoune was on the Leader, a little way before it joined Tweed, and the river had risen so high that Thomas's tower, on the lower ground, was islanded in the water, its vaults flooded. So he and Bethoc were also up at the Earlstoun castle; indeed quite a few others had taken refuge there on the hill.

There was much talk, of course, of chaos, ruin, doom and death, with Thomas somehow considered almost to blame with his prophecies, his great evil bird and his grinning skeleton. Was the dreaded Day of Judgment coming upon them, as certain churchmen were wondering?

On St Donan's Eve, of all days, a courier arrived, drenched by more than rain, and afoot, for his horse had been carried away in the swollen Leader, he only escaping by what he declared was a miracle, a tree-trunk brought down by the gales floating past near him as he tried to swim, enabling him to cling to it until it grounded at a bend, and he had managed to clamber to safety. He had come from Edinburgh, by Dunbar, to summon Earl Patrick to a council meeting called for this very day.

It was impossible to attend, needless to say, but Christian would not have let Patrick go anyway, had it been later, so hazardous were the conditions. The courier himself remained at Earlstoun.

The next day, oddly indeed, the weather quite abruptly changed, temporarily probably, the wind dropped and skies cleared for the first time in weeks, although no doubt the seas would continue to toss high and rivers showed no sign of receding.

And that evening, at table, Thomas had another of his visions, starting up, to the astonishment of all, and pointing high.

"A storm!" he cried. "A great and terrible storm. It shall smite the land. Smite! Carry much away. That bird hovers, to strike, hovers over all! I see it. A great and dire storm."

Patrick, shaking his head, told his son-in-law to control himself, to sit down, to spare them this. No call to upset the company with the like. Sit!

"My lord, this is . . . otherwise," he was informed. "This storm is not just of winds and rain and lightning. This is a storm of dreadful might and blight. Striking not just the land but the nation. That bird has talons out! To stoop and drop and slay. Can you not see it?" He pointed up again. "There, hovering, ready."

"Beth, I think that you should take Thomas to his room," Christian suggested. "Until he recovers himself. He is sore troubled."

Her daughter nodded, and taking Thomas's arm, led him away.

The repast continued, but the diners ill at ease and fairly silent. There was no harp and lute-playing that night, nor ballad-reciting.

In bed, later, Christian said that she was beginning to fear for their son-in-law's sanity. These visions and illusions were becoming ever more wild, distressing and frequent, and must impose a great toll on his mind. Perhaps they should seek the help of some wise and able cleric, to see him, pray for him, possibly offer some remedy. That Prior Peter, at Lindores?

Patrick said that he would consider it.

In the morning, the weather was still quiet, and Thomas's forebodings the more discounted. The royal courier, given one of the castle's horses, decided that he would attempt a return to Edinburgh, although Patrick feared that the conditions would deteriorate again. Thomas lay low.

The Cospatricks decided that they might risk going back to Dunbar.

They had been home three days, with the seas beginning to sink, winds blowing but comparatively moderately, when the same courier reached them, from Edinburgh again, but not from the king, from Chancellor Charteris, although it was to summon another council meeting, and this urgently.

The king was dead.

Appalled, all but struck dumb, Patrick could only gasp.

Christian did find voice. "Dead! Dead, you say? Slain? How, how can this be? The king . . . ?"

"Not slain, lady, but dead, yes. Fallen from his horse, over a cliff. Two nights back."

Scarcely able to take it in, his hearers stared at him.

The courier, himself head ashake, sought to inform them in some lucidity and order. After the council meeting which Patrick had been unable to attend at Edinburgh, the king, having left the queen at Kinghorn Castle to be present, declared that he was going back to her there, this as night was beginning to fall. Charteris, Fraser and the others attempted to dissuade him. Darkness, flooding, the windy weather, and an inevitably rough crossing of Forth at Queen Margaret's Ferry, all made the journey, of some twenty miles, highly inadvisable. But Alexander was not to be prevented from getting back to spend the night with his Yolande. With three companions as escort, he set off without delay. At the ferry, only a royal command persuaded the ferry-master to risk taking the four, and their horses, across the mile of heaving waters. But, landing safely, they had headed off eastwards along the Fife coast, round Inverkeithing and Dalgety Bays. Despite the conditions and darkness, they had got as far as Aberdour before there was serious difficulty. There they had to cross the Dour Burn, and it was running high, its ford impassable. The four had temporarily split up, all seeking to find a possible crossing. When one was located, only three of them were able to win over, for they could not find the king. Presumably he had won across further down, and had not waited for them. At the other side, there was still no sign of him, so they pressed on, as he must have done, for Kinghorn, another six miles. Reaching the castle there they found that Alexander had not yet arrived. When still he did not appear, in much agitation they and the queen had waited for him, eventually deciding that he must have taken refuge in some house or cottage on the way east. But in the morning, in search of him, they had found the king and his horse dead, on the rocks at the foot of the cliffs of the Ness, at Pettycur, where they had fallen in the windy dark.

His hearers listened with head-shaking distress.

When they were alone and could think more clearly, and visualise the resulting situation and contemplate the future, for the nation and for themselves, at length Patrick came out with his conclusions.

"Here is the end of a journey, a course, for me also, my dear," he said. "No more errands as envoy extraordinary. No more royal missions. There will be no royalty to send me on such. Alexander was my friend as well as my liege-lord. I am going to miss him, as well as mourn him. But I will now be my *own* man! And yours, my Christian!"

"I shall see the more of you, then. My regrets will be tempered by having some respite from being a neglected wife, all too often! Although the council may still wish you to keep in touch with Norway, in especial, and the child there."

"I will leave that to others. It need not be me. I was Alexander's man, not a foreign bairn's!"

"And Yolande's?"

"Yolande I liked and admired, yes. But only that."

"Ah! Perhaps I misjudged you! But it was not your admiration for her that I meant now. But her state. She could be pregnant, see you."

"Pregnant! Lord, I had not thought of that."

"It might well be so. And if she is, and bears Alexander's child, if a boy, he would be at once King of Scots, no? If a girl, second to the Maid of Norway, and possibly to be preferred. Think on that. You may not be a free man yet, my Lord Cospatrick!"

He stared at her. "Here's a thought indeed! A realm awaiting on a woman's fertility! To know if it has a monarch! Scotland, the most ancient royal line, in such state. What a coil!"

What a coil indeed, for any realm.

EPILOGUE

Scotland waited those so vital months, but in the end, Yolande de Dreux proved not to be with child. Sadly, the lovely widow returned to her own Gascony. And when, five years later, at the age of seven, the Maid of Norway, in theory Queen of Scots, set sail to take over her throne, she fell ill on shipboard, and died at Orkney. Scotland was without a monarch for the first time in history.

The realm had to have a king. There arose many competitors for the throne, far-out descendants of David's son, the Earl of Huntingdon, who had died before his father. Over a score of them put forward their claims, including Robert Bruce, Earl of Carrick, Christian's brother. How to choose between all these? Who could make the decision? Unfortunately for Scotland, the Competitors for the Crown, as they were called, asked Edward Plantagenet of England to decide who had the best right to it. And Edward, perceiving his chance, agreed, and chose John Baliol, son of Devorgilla of Galloway, a weak character known as the Toom Tabard, the empty coat, while Edward himself adopted the style of Lord Paramount of Scotland, and sought to direct all in his own and England's favour. And when even King John Baliol eventually could stand no more of this dominance, and asserted himself, his divided and scornful nobility did not support him, and the ancient kingdom was plunged into anarchy. Baliol was banished to France, and Edward invaded Scotland and sought to take it over by force of arms. William Wallace arose, and endeavoured to rouse the divided nation to fight for its freedom, in time persuading Bruce of Carrick's son, another Robert, to join him. Wallace died horribly at

Edward's hands, but Bruce went on with the dire struggle, and eventually, at Bannockburn, there was victory, freedom gained.

Kelso Abbey's roof did indeed fall in, during worship, but this was not until 1771.